A sickly child at birth, at the age of eight Dexter Hand was diagnosed with TB. This required a lengthy stay in a sanitorium, which saved his life. But the ravages of the complaint did not go away. They remained to haunt his life. He participated in all the sports and although he had the instincts for the games, he did not have the capacity.

He lived normally when he could and adopted excuses when he couldn't. He worked as a technical author for a good part of his adult life. So elaborate was his world of deception, excusing himself over his lung condition, that a deflection to romantic writing was an obvious recourse. He could be someone else if needs be. The characters he portrays here are all him. The covert world of secret illness, and its unsuspected torments, has its day here too.

Ingrid (1949–2013), generous in all things

The many minds I have plundered and who have shown me great generosity and patience, Paul, Tony, Abd El Taji, Don and Sylvia, Jack and Henry, my boy.

My respects to Stan Kenton, Joni Mitchell, Puccini, and Dowland for providing the voice that, for years, I did not think I was allowed or capable of rendering myself.

Dexter Hand

A Small Tale of the Great Circle

Austin Macauley Publishers

LONDON * CAMBRIDGE * NEW YORK * SHARJAH

Copyright © Dexter Hand 2023

The right of Dexter Hand to be identified as author of this work has been asserted by the author in accordance with sections 77 and 78 of the Copyright, Designs and Patents Act 1988.

All rights reserved. No part of this publication may be reproduced, stored in a retrieval system or transmitted in any form or by any means, electronic, mechanical, photocopying, recording or otherwise, without the prior permission of the publishers.

Any person who commits any unauthorised act in relation to this publication may be liable to criminal prosecution and civil claims for damages.

This is a work of fiction. Names, characters, businesses, places, events, locales, and incidents are either the products of the author's imagination or used in a fictitious manner. Any resemblance to actual persons, living or dead, or actual events is purely coincidental.

A CIP catalogue record for this title is available from the British Library.

ISBN.9781398465626 (Paperback)
ISBN 9781398465633 (ePub e-book)

www.austinmacauley.com

First Published 2023
Austin Macauley Publishers Ltd®
1 Canada Square
Canary Wharf
London
E14 5AA

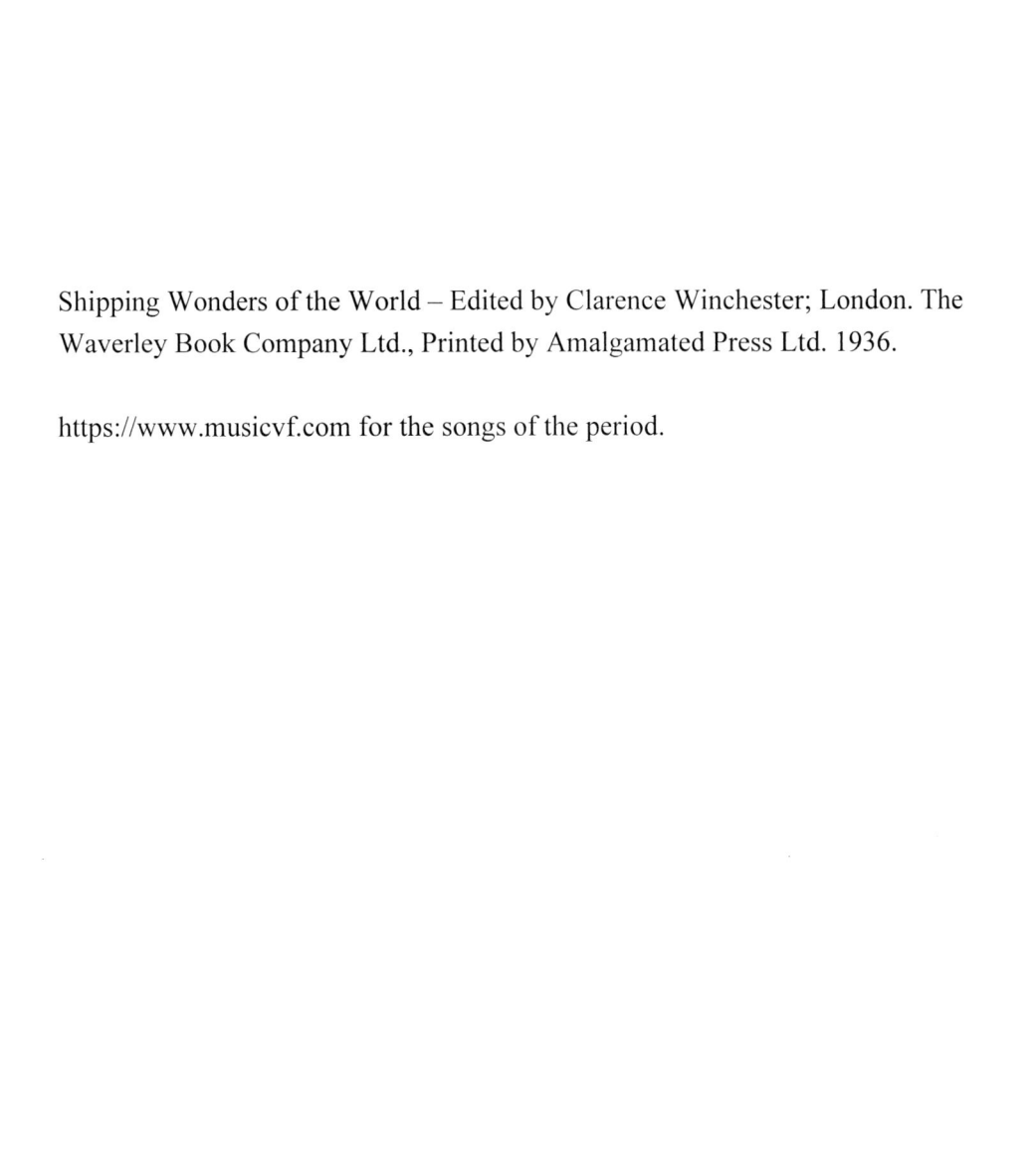

Shipping Wonders of the World – Edited by Clarence Winchester; London. The Waverley Book Company Ltd., Printed by Amalgamated Press Ltd. 1936.

https://www.musicvf.com for the songs of the period.

Chapter 1

*"Destiny urges me to a goal of which I am ignorant.
Until that goal I am invulnerable". Napoleon Bonaparte*

Someone far wiser than me commented, "Each day has its own destiny. Yesterday is history, today is opportunity while tomorrow is a mystery." If you have reached today, just be grateful, seems to be the message supplied by fate. You have little or no control of what is to come while having had some success in negotiating the past, to your credit. The 'tomorrow' conundrum happens to us all; it was to happen to Jimmy Wilde. Yes, that Jimmy Wilde, the 'Mighty Atom', world champion boxer, seemingly super-human pugilist. In 1923, at the end of his career, the five feet two inches of indestructability accepted the purse of $65,000 to fight Pancho Villa, a man whose name sounded like that of a matinee idol or a bold mountebank, but who was, actually, a fighter of Philippine extraction. Obviously, Jimmy was hopeful for tomorrow, especially with that purse; oh Jimmy, count your blessings. At thirty-one years of age, he should really have had more regard for the moment and lived it more fully, rather than taking on this gamble. Subsequently, he was pummelled for seven rounds and then knocked out. He came too three weeks later in a bungalow on the east coast of the United States without any recollection of the intervening time. Does tomorrow exist if you're in a coma? Life is a mystery indeed.

Today is a gift from all that went before without having any inkling of 'tomorrow'. Yet hope lends a warm glow to its possessor, like the innocent man-child here, Able Seaman Plum. For some, it's all they've got. We are leant the encouragement we need to bother to go on, especially with our not knowing the time or place. But tomorrow is a lie, a false hope, the semantics of which can be complex. Best that we give that point in time a date. When defined, it ceases to be tomorrow and takes on a more substantial reality. Ceases to be a nebulous miasma out of which a life experience might form. Yesterday, today, tomorrow, three sides that do a prison make, from which the spectrum of our lives emits. Hopefully, the trick that such physics can conjure with the sun will throw some light and colour on our tale. But don't let us wallow in tomorrow's 'might be', there is so much to be accomplished today and it should not be put off.

Plum was a man without qualification who had grown up in a world where there was little expectation of children being 'something'. He had no conceit. No view of 'the self'. He just *was*. He grew-up in a comfortable world of well-ordered life, the son of an artisan. There's the house, a yard (where the khazi was, situated by the back gate) in a terrace of workers cottages that were indistinguishable individually but which harboured a diverse and pleasant, ordered, satisfied society. His family were the top end of the 'scraping by' and as such had a prominent role in that street's affairs. Prior to leaving school, Plum had accomplished some writing skills, could add and subtract a bit; had a modicum of skill in spelling. His headmaster, he recalled, had written on one report that Plum was 'erratic'. The word sounded sort of exceptional, positive. It transpired that erratic was not to be considered an accomplishment. For him, erratic was not settled, always searching, an adventurer in the making, undaunted by method or possibility, feasibility. Was it his fault that he always had his focus out of the class window? He was quickly bored? He demanded activity not the detail, could 'not be doing with that'. Boxing was the real world. How come that, because he was so much better in the ring than anyone else of his age, that the ones who could not spar decried his command of the ring, the art? Could ignore his natural grace, his superb balance, his springing mousetrap reactions, his courage, as being nothing; just because they followed, did as they were told and, even at that age, came over as dull and biddable without any sign of exception.

Plum's dad was a wag. His cosseted boxer son was his audience, a ready sponge for the collective detritus of sayings and allusions that his dad had attached to, just as his dad before him, with memories in family lore that went back to the assassination of Spenser Perceval, at least. They had all 'served' in that family. Dad could picture his son in uniform doing his patriotic duty as the men in the family had always done. Although 'invited' to serve in the navy, Plum had considered the air force without thinking too deeply on it (not knowing anything about engines or aeroplanes for that matter). The fact that aircraft were a new invention and Plum was really excited by all that was new, could, should have tempted him. But no. The army was a non-starter. That force seemed to be a lost cause, a ticket for the mortuary. The attrition in the trenches filled the newspapers and commanded the gossip in 1916. He, sort of, came to attach to himself a degree of self-importance. Well, there were so many vying for his signature, even though he was no one in particular. But he could see how a uniform transformed the shabbiest individual to a new level. You could see the ladies were impressed (while he himself was not being particularly interested in them). Yes, they had thrilled at his fighting skills. But he knew if he lost, should such an unlikely thing occur, that tomorrow would never come, they would desert him just like that. He'd seen it happen. Girls were fickle and had a corrosive influence. Lads went flabby, seemed to lose courage after messing about with girls. Just when they were at their strongest there seemed to be a demand of nature to give it all away, drink too much or go out with girls. Down at the docks there was opium, heard tell, all was dissipation. If they only knew. A world of distractions designed to curb your strength, knock the froth off your energies. All concocted to debilitate, weaken, spoil. To anybody that would listen, he would state categorically that he wasn't interested in what happened in the cemetery after dark. Whatever it was, seemed to him that it bred guilty looks, crying and rows. No joy emanated from liaisons, just grief. Anyway, he took care of his body. No drinking, no smoking, exercise was the thing.

No, the navy had made such a polite request for his participation, he would choose the navy, they seemed quite keen. There was a romantic attachment to the sea for him. A couple of years before the war, a day at the seaside and a short trip on a paddle steamer, only around the headland, had instilled such an immense sense of excitement in him as to have occupied his mind ever since. The power of those enormous paddles, the thrusting persistence of the hull laying aside a squally sea, carving it up with ease. Such an otherwise solid looking wall of water, cliffs and valleys. Set free from parental observation, walking the decks and braving the spray, he recalled such a spiritual transcendence which he could not put into words, while the 'oldies' just sat around on their benches on the upper deck, unmoved, unmoving, bored even, pulling down their headscarves, holding onto their hats. Had a shaft of light beamed down from the heavens that moment and taken him for a sunbeam, life would have been complete. So what? Forget tomorrow.

The navy was not so exciting. He soon found, that while they seemed to be greeting him at the induction, it took no time to forget his name, make him anonymous. But boring inactivity had its place when, in the background, torrid tales of hundreds, thousands, dying in terrestrial theatres of war, all around the globe, were endemic. Basic training was a breeze, he was fit and strong, unlike so many of the others. They attempted to furnish him with a skill, which he had not contemplated, the ship of his recollection seemed to progress without the assistance of men apart from the casting off and tying up part. He found out abruptly that he had a sketchy understanding of what sailors actually did; it certainly was not just swanning up and down an unsteady deck admiring the sights. Sad to say; yeah, it was a bit of a disappointment. It was while on the rounds of the various training camps and temporary assignments that he made the acquaintance of another boy who, by comparison, was so…so worldly. The boy's vocabulary was astonishing, very…colourful you might say. Everything that passed his lips was smutty, basic and unexpected, accompanied by lots of spitting and crotch scratching. One of the lad's main topics was girls, their seduction; the moving from 'first base', by degree to the unmentionables, as Plum would have it. Not so much a thrill or excitement but more a victory over an adversary. A battle and a conquest. A sort of confidence trick, it seemed. The association of guile and pretence that led to 'move three', the girl's capitulation and his victory over her, his mastery.

"I've chalked-up a few," he would say, triumphantly, about having reached some 'tart's' their 'bits'. He had fooled her in some way, with guile but where was the pleasure? Won some sort of scheming campaign victory, gulled another one. Plum feigned interest. Absent-mindedly, he sang that song, *They'd never believe me*, trying to impose what he perceived as femininity and its associations, softness and sweet talk, a world away from Matey's callousness. Yes, Matey caught onto that one and its delicate and loveable lyrics soon became corrupted to, 'your eyes, your nose, your facial hair'. And that, such a lovely song about romance and soft, fragrant girls. It was like being tied to a crocodile, get me a Matey and make him snappy, when instinct told you it would be best to stay away from such animals altogether. He did not like his new mate and some of the talk seemed disrespectful, at the very least. If he had had a sister, in the company of this 'Matey', then Plum would have been concerned for her and may have been induced to use his fists to put him right, warn him off; a fanciful aside.

All these thoughts went through Plum's mind as they wandered, sometimes aimlessly around, off-duty, but always looking for tarts. Could any self-respecting girl fall for such an obviously arch adventurer? Not understand how she was being duped? What do their mothers tell them? The lad knew every nook and cranny in this port town, the streets and dingy alleyways. This was his hometown. He was known. Some people greeted him warmly, others seemed to display the same sort of circumspection that Plum himself harboured. He thought he recognised, in some of their faces, a disgust. The quick turning away of the head; sometimes an almost frightened looking countenance. Not that 'Matey' saw anything of the sort, too tide-up in himself.

Plum would sometimes get an uneasy feeling that he was abetting his mate in his grim campaign. Acting as a sort of authentication for his character. More often than not there would be two girls, the one that 'Matey' fancied and her mate, who was less desirable; which normally meant she was a bit on the plump side, smelly or spotty. "She's pox ridden. You can have her. But mind you wash after." Matey intoned disgracefully. She was someone's daughter. The apple of someone's eye, they would have hopes for her. After the fatuous attempts at humour or derring-do, like climbing lampposts, knocking on doors and running off, 'Matey's' demeanour would change (usually when he'd got them laughing or taking part in pretend wrestling). If the one Plum was destined to be with tried to join in with the couple, Matey could be really nasty. Refer to her as 'your fat friend'. "Ain't you got some tripe waiting for you at home? Cold tripe and vinegar, a big bit, and half a loaf!" He lost a few with that sort of assault. The 'don't you talk to my mate like that, she can't help it if she's not skinny like your mate' thing. They would make to go and then he would let them have it with both barrels. They would be left in no doubt what he really thought of them. "Go on, bugger-off back to the slums. I bet you're poxed-up anyway. I bet you've been out with a Frenchie. I bet you've got crabs. I can smell your armpits from here." Plum would try and pull him away at this point but having been near a victory perhaps his blood was up. But he knew better than try and hit out, although he drew back a couple of times, as if he was going to try and belt Plum. *Yeah, just try it*, Plum was thinking. Just give me an excuse.

So, Plum would wait by the entry with the other one (who always wanted to go home, would keep on calling down the entry that she was tired or something, wanted a pee. Anything to get away). He wasn't offended. Plum stood there like chips, not knowing what to say. What do girls talk about? It was the same mystery as what do adults talk about? Everybody has a lot to say but about what? These girls were of a different race. Some were like, throwing themselves on the fire. They were like Lemmings and ready to jump as if it could not be avoided. They seemed particularly interested in his 'size'. Curiosity, well you see what it does to cats. After, when they'd gone (no suggestion of walking them home because of the dark or safety) he would tell me in minute detail what he'd done or even what she'd done! It was like he was pressing flowers or pinning butterflies.

It came about, one particularly boring weekend out of the many, that they were let-out as a sort of reward for a particularly arduous week of exercising and trying to learn stuff (half garbled, partly understood). Perhaps in a circle of recruits gathered around a Petty Officer and Plum, being a bit on the short side, in a crowd, only seeing half the knot making or a bit of the ensign folding or whatever. If the accent was difficult, then some of the terms the man used made the topic really obscure and made you doubt your sanity. The boy could have cried when the questions were asked afterwards; if he was asked, Plum would mispronounce some of the garbled stuff and get laughed at, the P.O. threatening to put him on a fizzer, 'jankers' (saying that the boy was having a laugh at his expense), what! The worst aspect of that was when your error was the Watch's punishment, not just yours; punish them all for my error? That's not Plum's way. You could quite easily assume yourself 'thick' after an hour or two of that. You quickly learned to copy what your pals were doing, that way you learned, a bit, anyway.

Anyway, the weekend was interrupted by – what was his name, 'Matey'? Anyway, he said that he had got this 'bloody relative' who he'd never liked but he had been told by his 'f-ing mother to f-ing go and see 'im because he was ill' and, what was his name, could perhaps help, give him a hand. How far did they tramp? How many turns down alleys and across thoroughfares, passed little parks and sandstone monuments and buildings with entrances supported by huge stone columns? Saw whole streets of Cardinal Red doorsteps. It was like those stories where someone had to pay-out a length of line or trickle some salt on the ground so that they could find their way back out. If 'what's his name' ran off, he, Plum, would be right in it. That would be a power greater, more effective in controlling, than Plum's puny threat of a punch in the gob should he think things had gone too far.

Eventually, they came to a house as common in design and ordinary in context as the house that Plum had been born into. The windows were filthy and the curtains, such as they were, were drawn. Inside, his mate greeted the infirm man. No, greeting is the wrong word, that makes it sound warm and friendly, it was nothing like that. Just the sort of on-sufferance familiarity that goes on. Desultory conversation ensued. He had good as said that he didn't want to be with the old man, he was there because the 'old girl' had insisted. When the old guy wasn't looking, he would put his fingers over his nose, like a peg, and pointed at the reclining figure, jab his finger in the man's direction. The old chap was really poorly. Plum's uncle had gone like that, in pain, grey complexion, far away eyes, not enough money for a doctor, no relief; it's a universal look it seems. Like he'd ascended into Heaven already and just his body had been left behind, neglected, ashen, while God made room for another spirit.

It was all very awkward. Nobody addressed Plum directly so he found himself half smiling at the bloke in a sort of 'idiot nods and grins' kind of way. The man kept on closing his watery eyes like he was looking at the world to come in his mind's eye. Does that sound fanciful? The old man motioned to 'thingy' over and in a croaky, parched-lipped voice, asked him to go and get a milk stout from the 'offy', the money was on the mantlepiece. Matey was irked. He was nobody's servant. "You coming?" he asked Plum sullenly.

Plum thought he'd hang about in case the old guy needed help. Grudgingly, 'Matey', what was his bloody name, gathered the money from the mantlepiece in a sweeping gesture and flounced out of the room dramatically.

He had not been gone long before the old chap suddenly seemed to come-to. "See that box," he said, gesticulating towards a sort of bookcase-come-ornament stand, while simultaneously tugging at Plum's shirt with those spidery hands with the yellow nails. "See the box, the wooden box," he rasped urgently. There was only one box. "Bring it 'ere. Quick. We don't want him in on our business." Plum did as he was told. The olden was surprisingly deft at opening the catch on the box, focused and urgent. Looking into that jumbled interior, it was a bit like his mum's sewing box. There were all sorts of bits and pieces salvaged from things that had once had purpose. From this box, the man fished-out a piece of stiff paper, a bit like a more supple form of velum but similar, weighty. He told his story while brandishing the scrap. The paper had a map drawn on it, quite ornately pictured really; it had an air of authenticity about it. "I want you to have this," he imparted slowly but with force, pushing the scrap of paper forward briskly. "I was once a medical orderly in London and he gave me this, one of the patients, gave it to me, Mr Johnson. See here, it's a map of the Cocos Islands, somewhere off South America it is. It's a treasure map that is." A soft romantic look in the rheumy eyes. "I want you to have it", he insisted, looking up puppy-like, soulful. Johnson was gifted it by Thompson, he had it off of Keating and Keating had, took it, from the dead body of 'Benito' the pirate, master of the

'*Relampago*' what was sunk by the navy ship, '*Mary Dier*'; right back to the start of the last century, a heavy sigh and a reflective silence ensued. But this survived. "Johnson should have gone back but…" The old man paused painfully as though having been prodded forcefully, oh, took a breath, held his finger to the corner of his mouth as if clearing a crumb. "If you show this to that ingrate" – waving a hand airily – "I'll see you in hell. Tell me I picked the right one? You're an honest cove, you is, ain't you?" Plum assured him he was while caught up in the emotion of the man's obvious suffering. The man settled back like a small ebbing wavelet leaving the shore. With a stretched spittle mouth and those red eyes, which Plum would never forget. A promise had to be solemnly made to the old guy, that he would not divulge this secret to anyone; it was a precious gift; it was the making of a fortune. Above all, it was to be Plum's secret. "Promise me, promise?"

The rest of the day panned-out as expected. A few choice words about the 'smelly old guy', once we were clear of the house and off we went down the tortuous route we had taken inbound. How odd, it seemed to Plum, actually remembering some of the sights on their way, having only glimpsed them in passing earlier. How much you take in when you're not trying. Perhaps that's why he couldn't learn so readily, he had been trying too hard. To him, it seemed that some of the people he had seen earlier had barely moved despite the passing of time. The idle poor. What's-his-face took Plum to a pub; grim, filthy windows, of course, and nicotine-stained walls, smoke, golden cupids, a picture of a reclining nude behind the bar and loud banter, which got louder, as people had to talk louder to make themselves heard over the hubbub, who were having the same problem shouting over the others.

"Your shout," says what-his-face.

"I don't drink," says Plum.

"That's all right," he says, "you can still get them in or have you got short arms as well as a short arse. Can't reach your pockets, eh?"

All the time, Plum had this stiff paper in his pocket that he was careful not to crease if he could at all avoid it. Having only glimpsed it briefly he could hardly wait to spend a few moments pondering the illustration more closely. When the chance eventually came, all the thoughts of the paddle steamer and the freedom of the sea which this bounty promised, almost made him swoon, like hearing the finale of Respighi's *'Pines of Rome'*, that we might know, not him in his head, a translation of emotion; soaring, exhilarating. People get over-excited and their breathing becomes shallower, they can soon become wobbly and their minds race ahead, knees go weak. Plum suffered all that. The, it's just there for the taking, soon passed when, after the initial flush, he started to think about all of the impossible things that first had to be surmounted. For a man that could barely swim, the sudden realisation that this island might be thousands of miles away hit home, all those oceans. As quickly as the excitement had come upon him, equally rapidly, the parlous state of his position turned the venture into a great dollop of impossibility and mental torture. The man who had bought a winning lottery ticket but misplaced it! The conversation went on around him and he had to nod or give a timid laugh depending on what the barely heard background noise seemed to demand. Matey even had the temerity to say meanly that he thought Plum a barrel of laughs, sarcastic like.

He went through the rest of the training comprehending even less. He had entered the service knowing little, thought he had grasped some skills, only to find that not only had his new knowledge evaporated but there was a great big map draped over his head now obscuring all that which he had been taught, depriving him of anything else, bar none, that he should be absorbing. Things, matters, which had suddenly turned to mouths moving but no sound coming out; being continually asked to repeat actions and drills having made a 'balls-up', again. He was shouted at during drill, let the side down in team exercises, he was cursed during general duties and seamanship, well that was in another language, for all he knew.

He grew apart from his fellow student but was grateful for that. 'Matey' had gone off with another one, equally famed for his spirited attentiveness to the ladies. Plum did not miss him one iota and although it meant he spent an inordinate amount of time by himself, the time was not wasted. Given enough leeway, peace and quiet and, most importantly, seclusion, out would come the map and the great dream machine would come into operation. Never did an abbreviated piece of geography hold so much wonder and convey so much excitement. He knew everything but nothing. Constant reinforcement replaced doubt. The first thing to be done was to post the map home. If the paper was lost or, God forbid, nicked, that would be worse than death itself. The paper was posted home. It was a family rule that the letters for others would not be opened. They were private. Whereas, everything else in the house was everybody's in the house. But a letter, one of those infrequent and novel missives, was absolutely private. The last letter he could remember was one sent from a relative where the envelope was edged in black and when opened it had touched his mother so deeply that she had to leave the room in floods of tears. His letter would be waiting on his return untouched. Sat there on the mantelpiece. On that mantlepiece, next to the Doulton pottery figurine with the chip taken out of its nose, damage that he himself had inflicted when a child and which was now part of family history and inevitably referred to when illustrating Plum 'growing up'; never to be jettisoned, even though imperfect. The place where a relative would leave a Florin. "For the little man." By the photograph of a 'Crazy Day' in the street, one of the few pictures of his gorgeous mum and her sweet smile, sitting on a cart with musicians he didn't recognise, with their painted-on moustaches and clown outfits. She was a beauty. *'Hush little baby don't you cry; you know your mother was born to die'.*

After the letter had gone off, time hung *really* heavily. But a firm resolve was coalescing around the expectations of adventure and riches, the glorious tomorrow. The most important thing was to start paying attention again. It was paramount, obvious, that some sea skills had to be learned. The whole issue of navigation and seamanship was crushing. How was he going to get to the island, wherever it was? There was so much to learn that the issue of where to start was almost disabling. Being around the junior officers, some of them no more than children, made him feel profoundly inadequate. They told each other technical jokes and treated everything so matter of fact, so easy. They all had accents that you immediately associated with posh people, that universal intonation attached to breeding. That put you on your back foot straight away because of the prejudice pumped into him about the 'posh'. Even when you had been listening and felt brave enough to withstand the ribaldry if you asked something stupid that you should have known from last week, it wasn't personal, was it? Get it wrong and your Watch would mock you in a way that was manic, grotesque at times. Is that human nature? You would pipe-up with a half reasonable enquiry only to be met with a quizzical expression and a request that you repeat what you had said as your voice was accented the wrong way. Sometimes, a chum butted-in on your behalf, like an interpreter, interlocutor, to ask your question for you. Yet you had no problem making yourself understood at home.

But all of that was so quickly behind him and the great rush of events was in-train. He reflected that he was incapable of conventional learning as he was too scared of the teaching environment, constant judgement, that and the map sliding in and out of his consciousness, drawing curtains around a subject's accessibility.

Chapter 2

When Plum first got to his posting, it was like no other feeling he had felt before. Everybody around him was so purposeful. No matter what he turned his hand to, the inevitability of getting it wrong grew more and more apparent, certain. No matter which P.O. he was placed with, even the mildest of them, would soon become exasperated with Plum's ineffectuality, not dumb Plum but traumatised Plum. Their resolve would gradually decay into a request that Plum should, what, get the tea, yes, go and get the tea, cocoa, Horlicks and a left-handed screwdriver, some skyhooks. We'll try again some other time, eh? It wasn't that Plum was stupid he was a round peg, a bit…'erratic'. Most of the time he was just flustered.

    The ship he was on was massive; a fighting ship, it had a brilliant history of successes right up to the recent Falklands campaign against the German's Pacific Fleet, which had ended-up with them all being sunk and *'Coronel'* avenged, here tell. Everything on the ship had to reflect that heritage; there was a lot to live up to. The more frightened and apprehensive he became the worse his blunders. He had not even got his map with him to provide an element of support, comfort, somewhere to run to. Some sort of consolation to tell him that this was just a temporary glitch and, once this show was over, he would be reunited with his true fate and off (the war might have furnished his hope originally but now it was just in the way). But those thoughts, usually in the waking hours of the early mornings, he would usually supplant them, his parlous situation, drive them out by dwelling on the sadness of his mum's death, the usual go-to sadness that he often re-visited when down in his boots needing 'a dose of broken bottles'. That place where his mother had smilingly met his minor infractions with "I'll swing for you laddie!" jokingly. The thought that he would never have enough skill to enable him to fulfil his scheme's ambitions and he would let her down again, errors contended in his mind for prominence. That was truly chilling. Many a fevered, sweaty night ensued.

So, it was, quite out of the blue, when, one day, the P.O. did the rounds of 'Not bloody likely', 'Eh, Chief, I was a delicate child', etcetera, and so on, when the Watch was asked for volunteers to fight, box, another ship's boxing team in a sort of local tournament. But it was like manna from heaven to Plum. Inside his mounting darkness the Eddystone Light beamed out. Him, a really nimble ten stoner that was startlingly impressive against people of any size in catch weight competitions. Never floored. No scar tissue and the sweetest and most unexpected jab, especially for such a fairly small chap. He was the embodiment of the 'Mighty Atom', Jimmy Wilde. Five foot two of coiled viper, who went on too long and got beaten by someone not fit to lick his boots, too much tomorrow and tomorrow. The word tomorrow should be abandoned; it's just bad shorthand for naming a day. The conundrum of tomorrow never coming would be solved if the term was ignored, after all tomorrow led to his mother's demise, led to all sorts of endings and unexpected, black bordered letters. She'd still be here if not for 'tomorrow'.

Jimmy Wild, the champion of champions and the patron saint of all small men. The change was remarkable. Plum virtually won the first tournament single-handed. So impressive was his display, and so unexpected his prowess, that some of the sailors gave him gifts and thanked him for holding up the name of *'HMS Invincible'*. Some wanted to kiss him, but that was another story, it happens, in the navy, 'rum, bum and concertina'.

Plum found that, over time, he was doing more boxing and getting better duties; it soon became common knowledge that Admiral Beatty was taking a special interest in him, fancy that. These Admirals and their ships. They treated their boxers in the way that gamblers use fighting cocks, pigeon fanciers and their lofts, it was as impersonal really and as careless as that. Beatty liked a winner it was *his* prestige. Only Plum was special and he was starting to transcend from music hall straight man to a much higher status. He was so good that other officers around Rosyth baulked, would not put up a challenger for fear of the ship becoming a laughing stock after a visit from Plum. Former heroes and the favoured, suddenly found themselves shunned. The sheer inadequacy of their former fame as nothing against Plum who was magnificent, in an understated and artless manner that no one could take exception too. No one could find a nasty thing to say about him. He did not induce envy. No, he conjured pride and brought people together. If there was only less jealousy and more ambition in the world. His watchword was not envy it was ambition. You could not say anything against Plum without being subjected to derision or worse.

Plum had a code. He recognised that some of the men put against him were brawlers or had been coaxed to the ring or bullied there. He would never hurt anyone more than sufficient to deter them. Some would instantly realise what they were up against and after a spirited start, when met by the implacable Plum (who dodged and feinted them into confused dispiritedness) would feign insensibility and fall down like mown wheat. After one such palaver, Admiral Beatty asked to meet the 'that little squirt'. Beatty had an unconventional manner, his cap worn at a jaunty angle, yawn. He approached Plum with a sort of super abundance of swagger and self-assurance, the fingers of his hands in his jacket pocket but with the thumbs left on the outside. "You're good, sailor. Keep it up. It's the pride of the fleet, you know."

This was the penultimate step in the story of Plum's deification. A match between Rosyth and Scapa Flow, the Battle Cruisers versus the Dreadnaughts, came out as a win for Beatty and Rosyth. Plum had crafted, side-stepped, glid, dodged and whacked a few on that day and you could not perceive from his look, his breathing or his face, that he had been in the ring at all. The final bout was the great test and the hoi polloi and the great and good all showed-up such was the advanced billing.

When a fireman called Logan, from one of the destroyer Dreadnaught escorts, entered the ring, it seemed to Plum that the lights had dimmed. A big, burly man, Logan was well known around about, the fleet, the 'Arbroath behemoth'. If he breathed fire according to his billing, you would not be surprised. Oh yes, he was feared. Previous competitions had shown Logan to be the entire opposite of Plum. Plum, all delicacy and slightness and Logan just plain big, the thud of a stamp on a death certificate. Prone to making those he fought suffer from 'stoker's arm'. Plum just wanted his opponents to know that they were in the wrong league and sort of give up; it wasn't as though they were capitulating. They preferred to watch him and his craft rather than stand with him, 'the wraith', 'son of a sea fret'. But Logan would get his satisfaction from nothing short of knocking a man's eye out. His sneer alone could induce a blackout, memory loss.

He had this manoeuvre called the 'Highland Charge'. From the get-go, once the instruction to box had escaped the ref's lips, Logan would just virtually run-over his opponent. Some, who had watched rugby league, likened his manner to what was euphemistically called the 'St Helens sidestep', harking back to the days of Winstanley (of whom, it was said that, at the end of the game, he would spend a reflective ten minutes or so in the pavilion picking opposition players out from between the studs in his boots. People he had just unwittingly 'runover', not side-stepped at all). But Plum thought little of reputations. Nothing he had seen to this point spoke of being trained, being fit even and was certainly devoid of art. Even when, true to form, Logan came at him, Plum just danced away from the oncoming steamroller. Logan stood this sort of tactic for a little while with steam venting out his ears. He reset and then advanced menacingly trying to trap Plum in a corner with all the wiles of a sheep dog, or so he thought. He just didn't see it coming. In the first few seconds of the bout, he had convinced himself that his opponent was a snivelling little cowardly runt, adept at running away, or perhaps trying to take a rise out of him, but, obviously, just petrified, as all his opponents should be. So, as he advanced only to find his head jolted back; it was done in such a dramatic and emphatic way, that it made the monster raise a bemused smile. He had pause for reflection. He advanced again and did not see the uppercut emerging from outside the scope of his squint. Round one had been a salutary affair. The crowd that formed the ring were ecstatic. They could hide their inherent fear of Logan behind Plum's right jab.

Round two and three were dispiriting for Logan, but he had a plan. It was only a matter of time. Plum wasn't going anywhere, other than down. If he ever caught this imp, he was going to spoil him; enough was enough. Logan resolved to back Plum into a corner, as he had tried before, but this time there would be no mistake. He would then proceed to batter him. He vaguely remembered, afterwards, getting out of his seat in the corner and then had a Jimmy Wilde moment. Later, Plum went to the man and actually apologised. Hoped he wasn't hurt. He had not meant to knock the fellow over like that it was just that Logan had walked on to the punch so briskly that he had contributed to his own downfall. Logan saw another red mist while contemplating what sort of story he would have to concoct to explain his failure, such an ignominious loss to such a squirt. He touched gloves and nodded but all the time thinking malevolent thoughts.

Beatty let it be known that Plum was a 'treasure'. The Captain of *HMS Leopard* arranged a bit of a soiree and Plum was invited along, much to the glee of his watch-mates who saw Plum as their hero getting to officer class through the hawser pipe, the equivalent of starting in a factory as a menial and eventually becoming the boss. Elevated in their status in one of those, I'm Spartacus', moments, they were all now Spartacus. Mention your ship and straight away came the retort, Plum! Quietly, behind the back of authority, they were busy trying to come up with ideas as to how they could make some fast money on the back of Plum's prowess. Too good an opportunity all around. Good job they didn't tell Plum, he would have scotched that right away. There were bouts against the army and the air force, money to be made. In the midst of all the plans, someone mentioned that there was a war on somewhere.

The little party that was thrown was an eye opener. What with being used to food shortages and now, all the plates of sandwiches and pickles and fruit laid on, it was a feast to behold; he had the key to the castle. They did their best but could not avoid making him feel awkward. He was straight away handed a drink, what could he do with it? He didn't drink. He suffered horribly at the thought that he might squirt some sauce down his uniform or commit some other sort of social indiscretion, a gaff. After all, he was, underneath it all, the kid from the back streets introduced to dominance having its privileges. He now had a drink in one hand and a plate with cheese and pickle on it in the other. None of his deftness in the ring would help him here. The fact was that he was now actually the king amongst these luminaries, sought out and tolerated. I bet if Plum, through pure ignorance, affected some sort of pose, or accidentally committed some social faux pas, the others would copy him so as to ingratiate themselves, imitation, flattery. There was enough gold braid at this gathering to put the coronation jewels in the shade. You needed shaded glasses really to deflect the light's intensity, sun blindness, from the glint reflecting off the officer's insignias. Beatty hung back. When he eventually rolled-up, swaggered-up royally, he was in the company of an equally grand individual, Rear-Admiral, the Honourable Horace Lambert Alexander Hood, K.C.B., M.V.O., D.S.O, whose full entitlement was whispered to Plum after a firm handshake and a swift departure; they're building a battle cruiser in his name, '*Hood*', scuttlebutt has it. The biggest ever, said my mentor of the moment. Not a name meant for the back of a football or rugby shirt. Fancy trying to fit that moniker on a strip, the honourable…

But nothing lasts for ever and it wasn't long before that was all behind them. Steam was up, signals hoisted, 'junk' tied down or netted. The fantastic rumble in the belly of that huge ship. The whole thing coming-to like a 'trotter' under the whip. Plum was at his new post in the 'Control Top' looking down on his own ship and out to the fleet beyond manoeuvring to their positions in the tight waters of the Forth; like being in the quid seats at the 'Gaiety'. The fabulous sight of the destroyers their glowing red-hot funnels, plunging bows breasting the waves in the way that they do, like steeple chasers. Dull of mind you would need to have been if not stirred by this powerful evocation of man and machine, this expression of firm resolution and calm self-assurance, invincibility. British history laid-out before you carrying that expectation of duty, firmness, stoutness, victory. Plum took some time to adjust to being at such a height above the deck. Every pitch and roll at that sort of elevation in the 'tops' was exaggerated. The infrequent excursions out of the Firth of Forth on exercises made a new experience imprint itself in a way that few other adventures do.

As an observer, Plum kept watch and reported to the officers in attendance matters of significance, so that the information could be fed into the 'Firing Table' in the bowels of the beast. Like the sighting of the German High Seas Fleet. As soon as action was in-train that vast expanse of sea off Jutland gradually became crowded and a blur. Mere glimpses of ghostly, vague shapes, covered and then uncovered by swirls of smoke. *'Invincible'* strode in amongst it but, in short order, hardly in the fight, took a hit, several hits in succession, and shockingly, and inexplicably, the ship just blew-up. Plum's next recollections were of seawater enveloping him and him finding it difficult to catch breath, so cold were those waters. He managed to haul-out onto a library table that was floating past. It was then that the fearful percussion he had experienced started to take hold and he began to care less whether he hung on to the flotsam or just gave up. He cried, screamed and screeched and the heaving, ranting and bellowing acted to warm him up enough to ward off the despair laden frigidity. The rest was history. Whatever the time scale was, *HMS Badger* picked him limp from the water. He was wrapped in a blanket, tried to drink some cocoa and then, thankfully, slept.

By degrees, Plum came too. Of the transfers and the transportation, he knew little. So, this was tomorrow, not much cop, nothing to write home about. Vaguely recalling rough old tars and nurses alike assuring him that he would be alright, that he'd done his bit. It was here that his mail caught up with him, one package with individual letters, all but one from his dad. Part of the content was the letter he had posted to himself and which had been placed on the mantelpiece, he envisioned, next to the shoddy Doulton porcelain, the source of another petty guilt. Pardon me for living.

This was a sort of rest home, somewhere in the country. Plain walls and a strong smell of carbolic. A great house given over to war. There were traces of its former grandeur but, institutionalised, now it was just bleach and beds. There were other patients and the occasional nurse. Plum was out on an extensive veranda sitting in a wheel chair, bandaged profusely. In some former time, people of great standing would have lounged here and exchanged talk of the country set, had servants trying to tempt them with a sandwich which, because of their meagreness, was obviously not intended as food. The equivalent of a bowl of pork scratchings to go with your Daiquiri. He had the impression at times that people were speaking without sound, like having him on, what do they call it…miming. A nurse says something to him which he doesn't quite catch but he smiles pleasantly to her anyway. Not that he wants to engage with her as the map is here and he needs its reassurance, a fix, now. The nurse, who he estimates must be in her early forties, has a little moustache of light-coloured hair which catches Plum's attention when she is close-up. She has bent over him and embraces him, her breast touches upon his shoulder lightly and he is embarrassed and he stiffens. Such a warm gesture and the smell of a woman not too different from the cologne smell of his mother back then and the goodnight kiss.

Love is a binding thing.
Love is a chiding thing.
Love has its duties as well as its joys;
It comes all too easily,
Unexpected, unbidden,
And when it leaves little lives it destroys.

'Love is the sweetest thing'
The completest and fleetest thing.
Love is with bustle and passion replete.
With Mother love, no reward
Asked for or needed.
Natural, factual and without conceit.

Love is a given thing.
Love is the warmest thing.
Love from the heart for children well meant.

Now her removal
Gives anguish in hours
And reflections eternal on how lives are spent.

Love is a crying thing.
Love is a dying thing.
Love, more than anything, defines who we are.
With its sad passing,
While awaiting renewal,
Direction and guidance seep in from afar.

Love indefinable, unceasing, undeniable,
Prayed for and raged for and dreamt as our own.
All praise that we've known it,
Perhaps, only in passing,
Only seeing its completeness when we are alone.

She moves away, resuming her stern business-like look. Plum looks about himself cagily and then produces the map from the envelope half hidden under the blanket on his lap. It is the map of the *Cocos Islands*. There is a legend on the map which reads 5° 3' South, 87° 2' West. *'Chatham Bay'*, *'Wafer Bay'* are also signified. An arrow points eastward which has the words *Costa Rica, 300 miles*, at its point. All the time, he is looking at the map he is looking about himself furtively. Instantly, his spirit starts to stir and he ponders it exclusively until people start to edge closer to him. Other people in other wheelchairs, on crutches, who just want to share their load, their uncertainty and fears, their awful memories. To try and cast them off from their terrors by being calmed and understood by others, pitied or reassured, just bloody listened to. Heh! You bastards, there's a man inside these pyjamas! Searching for some other who knows, who has the time and can understand their desperation, anxiety and their crushing sense of failure. The shared incomprehension: we would be better off dead. The map is put away and one of the other letters retrieved. Yes, that's his dad's writing, it certainly isn't scribble and so unique to his father. He writes about politics and shortages of virtually everything and hardly touches on the war. Almost as if there is a transparent gauzy sheet with the map under it, the letter is viewed as secondary to the obsession. The map appears to intercede between himself and all other matters, a net of a moderator. He gathers that the drift of his father's opinion is that we are not so much fighting the Germans as fighting our own government!

Came the day when that nurse came to him and proffered a new uniform; it is time to go. He wants to hug her. Inevitably institutionalised, there is an attachment formed. But he can't quite get over the impropriety, the woman's breast, that feeling. So, he offers her a hand shake which she takes, but she kisses him anyway. What terrific medicine. Plum can't understand such selflessness. Two people, unacquainted, sharing a moment of such inexplicable intimacy; no such thing happens in the animal world. Such things mark us out as different and yet we fight each other too! Sort that one out!

Chapter 3

At the tribunal building, he is accompanied by a Petty Officer to the interview room. They want him to give his recollection of that awful event when, it transpires, only those in the 'Tops', out of the whole ship's complement, survived. You start to play a game, Plum calls it flags of all the nations, in memory of a magician he once saw doing a trick whereby, out of a shallow vessel, the prestidigitator produced a whole line of flags of every nation from around the world, on a string. Only, instead of flags, each pendent has a picture of someone from the doomed ship he recalls. In those too early mornings, in his cot, that image would play and would, in future, vie with the memories of his mum and treasure, he knew it. Plum walks smartly into the designated room in his new uniform. He follows the ritual of presentation. The people at the long table have a strong sun at their backs obscuring their faces. They 'kibbutz' some pieces of paper, talk amongst themselves in low sonorous tones, like the imagined chatter of whales. They are mouth to ear, reminiscent of that ubiquitous ivory carving, a line of elephants, trunk to tail. By gesture and negative responses, they are in the process of kicking Plum out of the service. He has, 'done his bit and they are grateful', intimating their admiration for his sturdy attitude, his stoicism during his tribulations. Suddenly, inside, everything turns to water. He sways momentarily and checks himself in case he faints-over. A sweat breaks-out at his forehead but, at attention, he can't dampen the obvious, the irritating trail meandering down his face.

    The Petty Officer marches him out of the room when he is dismissed. His face is very glum. He is close to tears. Once out of the room, the Petty Officer makes it known that the officers don't know what they are doing. There is such a shortage of trained men too. Calling the officers 'dilatants', or some such things. He pats Plum on the shoulder to demonstrate his sympathy with his situation. Plum is distraught and complains to the non-com his urgent need to stay in the service, almost shouting at the poor man, all the time fighting a tear, his voice becoming hoarser. But the P.O. understands, he knows what service people are like. They don't like to be thought of as having run away. Plum is now outside the building and sits on a bench under a tree which is dropping autumn leaves on to him but he doesn't move, he can't. Those leaves, the awful loss of men seemingly being wept-over by the world through nature. The thought that the dropping leaves, each one a life, not lost to him. In the intervening period, the Petty Officer has returned to the offices. There is a notice on the board which propels him into action. He rips away the pinned paper and runs outside after Plum, waving the scrap, but in hope and not surrender. The paper he is brandishing is a request asking for volunteers for a hazardous mission. Plum pushes his hat to the back of his head and stares rigidly at the paper, almost forgets to thank, to acknowledge the Petty Officer for the information. "This is you," says the P.O., "just your ticket. They can't stop you sodding-well volunteering."

Plum's sunken body seems to fill up again, like the Dragonfly in its becoming. The two men shake hands. They stare at each other and a stream of energy seems to pass between them as the P.O. reinvigorates the once depleted frame of the other.

-oo0oo-

This is tomorrow? So, this is what it looks like. Plum is running, wearing shorts and shirt. He has a broad smile on his face as he passes-by. He looks in great physical shape with just a small area of scarring on his forehead still a bit livid. He is running seriously, quickly, along a country lane, passing the sign that says Queenstown (a line of black paint has been painted on through the 'Queens' portion). He does not lessen his pace, uphill and down again. The same rhythmic flow. Eventually, he comes to an old crone standing on the doorstep of a meagre cottage. He pauses and offers a cheery greeting. She turns without acknowledging him and calls indoors. A little boy appears. She tells the lad, "Brick him!" The lad reaches for some pebbles off the path and is about to throw them at Plum. But Plum quickly speeds up and runs out of reach, hearing the clatter of small missiles behind him skittering on the road's surface, a sound like a sudden burst of heavy rain against a window.

He enters the camp ignored by the guards. The gym is empty. Plum uses a skipping rope cleverly, manoeuvring the rope in patterns as he dances in time with it. He puts down the rope and turns to the punch bag which he hammers around, throwing the odd round-arm punch, uppercuts, jabs, crosses. His body feels so robust. Do all men feel this? Is there nothing in the world they cannot do when so strong and purposeful? Later he is showered and dressed, Macassar oil on his hair. He smiles broadly at his reflection in the tarnished mirror. He seems to have grown. He grins at himself and thinks himself quite the masher.

-oo0oo-

Fifty or so men are unloading from trucks amongst a rural scene, a church in the offing. They assemble into disorderly ranks before a memorial. Captain Cathcart addresses them. He has that look of a belted earl about him. Tweedy and roundly comfortable, probably, normally, a man who, in manorial surroundings, would command respect just because he looks the part. A man that would have a wife that dresses in twin set with pearls (that look that every doorman in the capital knows, 'quality'). The voice so posh. A voice that encourages a belief that the speaker is honest and educated, and that many a rogue endeavours to emulate. The men are a raggedy bunch. No uniforms except for the three officers and very little discipline. They do not take kindly to being told what to do evidently. They are not overtly military men apart from the two young Royal Navy Sub-lieutenants; Captain Cathcart is Merchant Marine reserve. As to the men, Royal Navy, perhaps one or two escapees from the formal ranks, while of the others, a real rag-bag of merchant men, trawler men, at least one lighterman and rather exotically, a chap of Indian extraction.

Cathcart struggles momentarily to gather attention to himself; the Sub-lieutenant insist, vie with the crowd in heavy whispers. When the captain speaks, it is with an unnatural, theatrical sort of gravity. More the voice of what someone might think the occasion demands, rather than a natural, fluid sort of approach; perhaps the voice of that Lord he resembles? Perhaps the Lord he would wish to be right now. This is a sombre place currently being enfiladed by a mounting wind that rises and ebbs in staccato bursts, sending the Whins into bouts of violent fits of tribalistic swirling Dervish dancing. Cathcart finally has the right moment to proceed: "This commemoration…of the poor souls, civilians…that met their doom in an incident…so dastardly that it…beggars-belief. Sailing from America…a passenger list which counted in its number a host of women and babes in arms, young people, no experience of the world. They were all savagely slaughtered." A jut of the jaw, like someone easing a stiff collar that is pinching, for emphasis and then a lingering glance. "Can you imagine the terror that those souls endured in the moments between the U-Boat's strike, that brief, fleeting time that the *Lusitania*, mortally holed, stayed afloat before being enveloped by the cold, dark depths…off Kinsale?"

The men shuffle about and there is some murmuring of oaths.

"It is a horror story." A searching look down the ranks. "No opportunity for heroism or honour to be displayed by the crew. Women and children, mark you, swallowed grimly by the spume. What did those women go through in that awful moment? Their lives snatched away. The unknowingness, bewilderment, disorientation, their children right there before them in difficulties, drowning. The terror followed by the…horror." It starts to rain. Cathcart looks at the skies momentarily. Men pull their jacket collars up, none of them is really dressed for such weather. Cathcart tries in vain to position an arm over his script to ward off the downpour, turns his back on the wind which has the effect of making him virtually unintelligible to his audience. "If any of you had any doubt about your mission, capture this moment in your mind's eye. Think on the loss of all that innocence, prettiness. Is there any man here who cannot harbour anything but thoughts of revenge in their bosom?" The wind carries away his sentiments. The script is now wet and the hand holding it sags down to his sides, in a gesture of discard. "Soon we will be…out there, that dastardly U-Boat skulking who knows where, who knows where?" The captain's beautifully tailored Masters' uniform is now wet at the shoulders. He does not cringe, his head erect. "We have a weapon that those fiends do not possess. We have the armour of our right and just cause about us. We are weapons honed by our faith, our country. Our mission is to inflict the same terror on the Hun's sailors as they so…". The men are becoming agitated due to the rain which is sweeping across the ranks in glistening curtains of flushes. The occasion is turning to farce as the disorderly lines break even more as men try and seek shelter behind their neighbour. "…indiscriminately, discharged against our people, our…loved ones, our brothers, sisters…babies, I ask you."

Vaughan lowers his head to one side and whispers exaggeratedly to the man next to him, who he nudges. "Come on you old duffer. Pack-it in. We're taking-on water. Oh no, he's carrying on."

Cathcart feels that he is getting into his stride and beginning to conjure ever more passionately… "Babies, gentlemen, babies…Just think, little babies…Before we go, I would have you witness this stone, this commemoration and the names it bears. Take an individual's name to your keeping, to your heart and act to so as to avenge that Christian soul. Is there anyone here with a voice?" His eyes, now squinting against the squall scans the men before him. "I would like someone to lead us in. *For those in Peril on the Sea.*"

Someone starts feebly on the verse; Vaughan is almost beside himself, apoplectic. "Shut up, you mugs! I'm wet through!" he hisses

They all eventually join-in in a desultory manner. The song is cut short and the men are directed by the Subs, Senior and Hodge to file past the memorial, some paying more attention to it than others.

The men clamber back into their lorries. Soon the atmosphere under the truck's cover is a warm fug of wet dog and kitchen waste bin surmounted by a hint of sewage. They sit in two rows opposite each other in the back of the vehicles. The trucks start-up and move away. The men sit in silence until someone starts to sing.

I didn't raise my boy to be a soldier,
I brought him up to be my pride and joy,
Who dares to put a musket on his shoulder,
To shoot some other mother's darling boy?
Let nations arbitrate their future troubles,
It's time to lay the sword and gun away,
There'd be no war today,
If mothers all would say,
I didn't raise my boy to be a soldier.

As normally happens on this sort of occasion, as soon as the solemn proceedings are over, the rain stops and the weak November sun break through. Vaughan continues his moan. "Look at me, wet through. I can't swim! Who did you pick, what name? I had Pappadopoulos, good old English name that." Another had picked Mary Lambie; she was only two. There'll be no little lamb for poor Mary, Mary. Miffed by the weather and being dragged-out here, Vaughan seeks to vent his spite on someone within easy reach, an easy target. Heh, Plummy, you went down on the North Sea, didn't you? How romantic was that? He smirks casting his eyes around the others for appreciation of his quip.

Plum can think of a list of sharp retorts he thinks he should make but settles for. "It wasn't the slightest bit romantic, as you put it. The Huns blew up my bloody ship!"

Vaughan is peeved at the imposition of the morning wasted. "You was Daddy's boy, on a cushy number, I hear tell. Stories get around. Excused duties they say. In the *Control Top* wasn't you, Plummy? Well out of the way of the muck and bullets."

Plum strains to be civil. "I *was* in the *Control Top*. Bloody good job too. There were six of us all told. We all survived. *Kismet*, eh?" Then suddenly taken over by the passion of the thing, he barks, "It was no cushy job! You had to be there. Where were you on the day Vaughan-ie? Not within a million miles of Jutland, I'll bet. Warming some poor dead matelots bed, eh?"

Plum turns to the others, checks himself, resumes the quiet voice. "Lucky shot…'Flash Doors' not closed properly, they reckon. There was a bit of ordinance on deck. You know, gun cotton." He acts it out. "A hit, a spark and the whole bloody issue went up in the air. She split in two, you wouldn't believe it. The old *'Invincible'*, star of Admiral Sturdee's Falklands exploits and all. I still can't believe to this day that something of that size could just, like, melt away. Go up like that. I still have trouble with my ears, even now. Bump!" He gesticulates an upward motion with both hands: "The next thing I know, I'm in the water with all sorts of unmentionables drifting past." The truck sways and jolts down the road while gradually also filling with exhaust fumes under the canvas. The men hold on to the benches they're sharing. He passes into a sort of revery. "All sorts, bodies. I was on a table, clinging to a table. Bits of uniforms, a mess tin. Yes, I'd made a grab and hooked onto some flotsam, the table from the purser's cabin I think it was. *'Badger'*, from the first flotilla, almost ran me down. But I was spotted. They took me in." He pauses as the emotion builds in him, remembering his utter desolation at that time. He catches a sob. Then continues to speak at the same level. "It wasn't cushy!" He has almost lost his self-control, the enforced recollection and that snide sniggering bastard taking a rise, he shouts to Vaughan. "It wasn't cushy, Vaughan! Show some bloody respect." Vaughan shows him two fingers. "Typical. Anyway…that was in another life." Plum goes into a sulk. A small silence.

At the tail end of the lorry, someone pipes up, "They're going to drop us in town on the way back. Day off. Weather's bound to pick up, look." He has raised the canvas flap and yes, the sky looks more hopeful. Some of the fumes dissipate.

They return to silence. The trucks are in open country with Queenstown beyond. More jostling and banging into potholes; smarting eyes from exhaust gas. Eventually, they pull-up by the quay in Queenstown and the men start to get out of the transport.

A shipmate turns to those still unloading. "I'm going sight-seeing. Five minutes should do it, if that long."

Vaughan has his plans. "Totty, that's what we want. Totty-totty-totty. I wonder if we'll see Captain Cathcart in the 'Dog and Typhoid'? A pint of cholera, barman! See, if we were in Russia now, we could get rid of brass like Cathcart, old fart. This country is ruled by stuff shirts, a circle of them, in the know." His shipmates are walking away from him but he carries on with his diatribe. "When this lots over, I'm taking myself off to London and I won't be sober for a year. I'm going to give it to every girl I meet. I'll dine-out on being a 'hero'; girls love that hero stuff, uniforms…Kitchener gone, just Dougie Haig to go, oh and the Old Goat, Lloyd-George. Then, perhaps, we'll get leaders that aren't murderous no nothings. Haig, what's that, Scottish? An Englishman, a Welshman and a Scottish man walk into a war, there's a joke in there somewhere." He sings, *"They're no bloody use to anyone, they're no bloody use at all."*

As Plum entered the mess hall, he is conscious of that indiscernible smell associated with mass catering, a slightly off-colour, brown sort of scent. The emanations from a decade of bain-marie's, steam, waste food products and a lack of any conflict with polish to scent the air. Dressed in his training gear, a towel around his neck, the meal he contemplates will be stodge, just something warm, vaguely animal and vegetable that has been sapped of its will by over-cooking. The focus on quantity, overriding any other factor. He is known to the people he passes as he walks to the serving hatch. There is no shortage of those who pretend to spar with him in recollection of his reputation. He throws in the odd pretend lead. "Watch it, mate, I've got the reactions of a Cobra, you might catch one accidentally."

They all smile; it's the joke that keeps on giving. At the serving line, he picks up a plate and an operative shovels food onto it. He asked for the Irish Stew; he'll be thankful for whatever he gets. All that training, takes it out of a man and even though naturally slender, he can demolish the plateful of a much bigger man (as long as that chap isn't looking). Looking around, he sees a trestle table that has free places. He sits next to a dark man who is staring quizzically at his plate, ignoring all else. He addresses some men that are sitting on the other side of the table, who are about to leave. He speaks to them casually as he places his plate and cutlery. "What was the big shemozzle again last night then…? All that shooting, again; how many nights is that? Don't them guards sleep? They should put something in their tea. Is that their revenge for them doing nights? Keep us all up?"

It's all sort of routine chat that is half expected. The shooting has gone on forever. Now is not the time to be asking about esoteric matters. Once their conversation would have been easy to negotiate with the usual give and take over sports that men have. Just like animals bum sniffing, you get to know quickly the demeanour of a man over a dose of who scored what when. Who are you for, is the question? The men opposite give disparate answers to a casual interaction. 'It's been going on for weeks. There are these dogs gathering at the fence, some say. Near to where the slop bins are'.

One of the sailors offers an opinion, "They get in among 'em, that collection of bins. Knock the lids off. Tip the bins and spread all the scraps everywhere. The guards then have to clean it all up. Must be starving, poor sods, and the dogs. The plodders shoot 'em-up for a bit of something to do, bit of fun."

Plum turns to the brooding man already at the table when he sat down. He has deliberately flopped into his seat to attract the stranger's attention. The man doesn't budge. This bloke at the table is odd. He looks neither right nor left. He seems bulky. But, strangest of all, he seems to have a sort of force field around him that emanates a quiet, low, hum; a trick of the light, water from the showers in your ears. There must be something in that. Plum is still struggling with his hearing anyway and for him to sense sound is different, quirky.

He's a gregarious type, Plum, these days. Building on his experiences as a successful boxer he's cultivated a persona. He casually nudges the dark man next to him and even the brief contact does much to confirm an impression of stolidity. Plum addresses him while organising his eating posture and the eating irons, a cautionary look into the depths of the stew just to check that there is nothing there obvious that he shouldn't eat, nothing moving, it's been known for a sticking plaster or some such thing to be in the mix before now. Nothing new under the sun. "Did you hear it? Last night?" He strives for eye contact but the man ignores him. Perhaps he's deep in thought. "What am I saying? You would 'ave needed cloth ears not to hear it."

The other men are about to leave. One points at the dark man and laughs. "You'll get no sense out of him" he mouths. "Foreign. See yer!"

Plum's eyes bore into the big presence sitting next to him, not intimidated by size. The others walk off. "Is that right chum? Foreign, is it? We've got all sorts in the service. We've got a mulatto with us. Exotic, eh? What language are you in then?" The lump doesn't answer. Plum looks at the man's plate forensically, colcannon and champ, a knock-off of a local dish. Close-up he thinks he feels heat issuing from the interloper. Plum tries to draw the man, does an inventory of positive things that he can think of on the spur of the moment. "Don't take on, it gets better." *What do they do?* he thinks. "We do er, football, basketball, there's always a game of cards goin' on somewhere. Proper holiday camp this." Plum points at the man's plate, not having been able to put a name to the dish for sure following his investigations but thinking it is Colcannon, vaguely. "What have you had? Mm, don't recognise that; looks like an experiment gone wrong. I think it started out life as Colcannon but took a wrong turn somewhere. Lucky dip? Sweepings?" He points to the plate but his invention fails him. He motions towards the collation on the plate before the interloper. "That used to be food once, until those chefs got their hands on it. A bit over the left, you might say, not a sincere attempt at cooking." Plum dips the lump of bread he brought into the viscous part of his own dish he's thinking of starting on. "The officers don't show their faces here. I bet it's because they're eating too well. You can only imagine what it is they're noshing. Who'd ask for seconds here? Nobody. Good for the figure. Very slimming. I had a buffet with the officers in Scotland." He confides. "That was a lot better than this. As a rule, I'd say, if you do manage to find something you like here, have it every day, it will be on every day, they serve it up until it's all gone, waste not want not. You're lucky, that what you've got looks like something almost recognisable. I could put a name to it if I wasn't so hungry, but it would only be a guess. Don't experiment; it won't get any better. Doesn't matter if it's a reheat job. If it comes away from the plate without too much pulling, or as long as it doesn't fight back, you are in luck. I've found its no-good experimenting; all the stuff is made from the same recipe book, same recipe even, maybe, just different amounts of gravy browning. Only some is cooked longer than others or plied with a different grease, sorry, gravy; probably the same cheap ingredients. Look here, take my plate. This is Irish Stew. No, honest, it is, honest. Look at it, what a gloomy painting that would make. Grey-gravy skies with cumulus cloud mash. There's a storm brewing. A solid sea set about horse meat rocks. Mark my words." He continues to eat. This monologue is just becoming more of a challenge and Plum is going to stick to it until he solicits a response.

"Here." He ribs the big man with his elbow, you've seen less of an issue start a fight in a pub. "You one of our French friends then? Sorry I can't speak-er the lingo. You will be the boss, be in charge, when you get back home, if they carry on dying at Verdun like they are. All the girls to yourself. What do you think of the place, eh? Not as bad as the old hulk on the island where we were supposed to billet. Leaky old crate that is. All Sir Garnet this is. Well run. No gripes. Which language are you?"

Still staring at his plate, the man speaks. A guttural tone, low down, suitable for talking to whales. *"Waar zijn we*, where are we?" he asks.

Plum is eating ravenously now. The tension is eased. Taking mouthfuls of bread as he scoops up the stew. But the question stops him in his tracks. "Now, there's an odd question. How come you got here when you don't know where *here* is?"

"Eish!" Erupts the man. "How do I know what people are saying? They talk about me not to me." He pokes at the food on his plate. "There is a chance that I am not in England?"

Plum's fight with his dinner is well under way. "Too right you're not. Blimey! This is Ireland friend. Yeah, Ireland. Heard of it have you? The less you say about England here the better, here in the south anyway. The northern part, is friendly to us English, I'm told. The rumour is that the north, it was won from the south. They call it Ulster up there. But the name was mixed around to disguise the snide bit of victoriousness, they did not want to provoke anybody too much so they changed their original name, but used the same letters. So, they got Ulster from the word 'result', victory like. They'd won it, see. Here, the kids chuck stones at you, chase you off and the grown-ups cheer them on. Believe me, I've been on the receiving end of it." He continues to attack his food. He explains with the addition of body English and gestures with his cutlery. "This here is Great Island next to *the* Ireland, which is bigger, greater, larger. Do you savvy? Not far off is Little Island. Keep up! I'll only say this once. Over there is Scotland, they're nice, well, Edinburgh is. I've not seen much else. I was stationed there once you know. Then you have Wales, good singers, reputed to be. Eat up! *Taffy was a Welshman; taffy was a thief. Taffy came to my house and stole a leg of beef.* That's how my dad talks about them. But that's another story, that's Wales, not here. Go on, eat it, it's not going to kill you." Scraping his plate with his bread, his taste buds are numb, Plum is seeing his neighbour as a challenge and persists out of kindness, him being so artless, friendly. "I exercise a lot" – he beams – "gives you an appetite, exercise. Then I get so hungry, if this was cardboard, I'd eat it, hang on, what am I saying, it might *be* cardboard. The magic ingredient; just having a laugh, ignore me. What's your ship, your posting, then? And where *do* you come from? I don't think you are French, are you? You don't grunt like a Frenchy."

"I'm, er, Dutch," says the man as though his origins had escaped him for a moment.

"That would give my dad a laugh, *Hogan-Mogan* as my dad use to say, 'cus of the way they talk, see. You sure you're Dutch? You don't sound too convinced yourself? Still, if you're new here I suppose…it's easy to get confused. The accents don't help, I can see that." Plum reflects on his situation never having met a real foreigner before. But he knows from his own experience how British accents can throw a bloke who has lived somewhere else, brought up without English as a first language, maybe. He addresses the man speaking very deliberately. "My name is Plum." He points to himself just to remove any doubt. He pats the brooder on the back and originates the clincher that will calm matters for once and all. "We could be maties. I'll see you right. So, what is your posting? What ship?"

The huge presence bridles a little. He produces a typed piece of paper from his shirt pocket. "S. S. Horton Lodge. Do you know it?" he asks.

Plum jumps on the announcement immediately, all tension released. "I'd say! That's my ship! Well, I never. What a small world." He starts about burnishing his plate with the bread. Someone passing acknowledges him.

"That's 'Butty'. Name speaks for itself; you'll meet him later no doubt. Nice people, well, most of them." There is a brief silence. "Again, last night, rat-ta-ta-tat! Them soldiers letting off. You must have heard it?"

For the first time, the man looks directly at Plum. "I wasn't here last night. I was travelling out of England, from London."

"London, that's nice, a good billet. I've passed through a couple of times. Big, isn't it?"

Plum has hit a nerve; the man turns back to his plate. "Eish! No. Not if you are in prison!"

Plum pretends not to have heard him. "No peace for the wicked, eh. Them poor army lads letting fly in the dead of night on the perimeter fence." Plum studies his plate running the word *prison* through his head. "Still, it's better than some places they could be, I suppose, France for one. This is a little refuge for them, army. Fattening them up before they go for slaughter down in Picardy. We're better off here, not so many guns…well, enough." An orderly walking past quickly takes his plate away. "Oi! That isn't a crack on that plate, it's what's left of my gravy!"

He turns to Wauters, nudges him with his elbow. "I was just lining that up." He considers eating what little is left of the bread but throws it onto the table instead. He calls after the orderly. "Oi! You missed a bit! You know, I should have gone into the air force. In the air force, the squaddies stay at home and the officers go off to do the fighting. All the blokes taking care of the aeroplanes stay down here, all the clever bastards are…up there, flying. Cushty. I always knew there was something dangerous about learning, all them Grammar school lads, pilots; a little learning, as they say, is a dangerous thing; me, school, books, cane. You could be bunking with me, on the ship. There's a novelty." A small silence. "I thought Holland was neutral?" says Plum.

The man looks away. "Yes, well."

Plum is undaunted and is determined to try and get the man talking. "Yes, there are a lot worse places, like those soldiers could be in, well, you name it. Turkey, Palestine; do you know Tanganyika, Afrika? Now, the Western Front, that's a good one, a short life and a muddy one."

"I was offered the Western Front," says the man.

"Nice one," Plum retorts. "You did well to turn it down."

The man fixes Plum with a marksman's eye. "I had no soldier experience. But boats, I know."

"Boats, eh! What sort?" enquires Plum.

The man changes his posture to be more face on to Plum. "My Pops had a *coper*, a *grog boat*. We would go onto the North Sea and take schnaps, beer and tobacco, to the herring fleets. That's how I came here. Picked-up by the coastguard, you know? *Swak*."

It must be what a dog hears, blah-blah-blah-sailing. "Ah, a sailor, eh? That's good, I mean that sounds a bit rough. You were doing a good thing, bringing comfort, like." Suddenly, Plum is being swamped at the thought of knowing someone who can sail.

The man continues. "The coastguard did not see it that way. The fishermen, they cannot take drink or tobacco to the fleet, it is illegal. Perhaps the herring have the better part of the deal. These little men on the boats do the netting and then feed like, factory ships? Back and forth, as they say."

Plum's mind is way ahead. "Oh, I see, I think. So, what happened like? It all sounds a bit *like Fred Karno's Army*, as my dad would say." Plum smiles broadly and vacantly.

"Never saw them coming," says the man. "Like low visibility."

"So, you and your dad were put in prison? That's a bit off," Plum opines.

"No, not my Pops. He says that he is ill and that *I* threatened *him*. I *made* him sail! He was thinking well on his feet that day, was *umlungu*. So, they let *him* go and called *me* cruel. He sailed off winking at me, bastard! *Eish!* They took all the stock and cash though. He didn't get away with anything 'cept his liberty." The man emphasises his point by thumping the table as if he was playing Skat.

The gesture feels a little bit threatening and makes Plum start a little. "He sounds like a man you could warm to. Dropped you right in it." Plum sloughs off his surprise with guile.

The other continues in a reflective vain. "The *Coper* was a miserable life anyway. I got to prison without any papers and then I was told I was South African, despite all else. They got their languages confused. I was made South African for their purposes, like as it came later, that as a South African I can fight on their side, a Dutch person, no," the man scoffs.

"You'd do well in the music hall," says Plum. "What a palaver. Do you have any other disguises? You could dress-up and imitate people. I bet you could be *'Tommy in the trench'*, double-up with our Gertie."

"Could I? I'll take your word for that," he says. "I have no appetite for this." He shoves the plate away.

Plum smiles a little. "Well, you'd better get one. That's all there is until we get on ship and even then, I've no idea who our cook will be and what his speciality turn is. Pot-luck. Might be good, you know, but knowing our luck…Perhaps you need a bit of exercise? Work up an appetite. You could come running with me, if you don't mind being 'bricked' by the locals, that is." He looks the man up and down; there is obviously no appeal in running. "Have you got any money? You could do with some warmer clothes by the looks of you. Wouldn't fancy being on the North Sea dressed like that. What say me and you go to town, tomorrow, eh? Get some clobber? Eh? Duds, clothes. There are some good second-hand shops."

The man feels the threadbare material of the thin jacket he is wearing. "I have some pounds. But not riches *mompie*."

-ooOoo-

In town, in the morning, they walk out under dull skies. There is a poster on a wall, asking the men of Munster to join up, to avenge the *Lusitania*. Wauters and Plum walk around together. They find a second-hand clothes store and the Dutchman tries some clothes on. Plum toys with some hats for fun. The stranger shows Plum the price tags and grimaces. Later, leaving the store. Wauters has a brown paper parcel.

"You've got some nerve, Dutchy," says Plum. "There can't be any profit in old rags."

"I have been in all sorts of markets" He checks himself. "Here and there. They expect you to argue the price. It's part of the game." Wauters holds the parcel up.

Plum nudges him. "The shop keeper did a double take when you spoke to him. What did he say, *Menheer* or something? He thought you were German, I'm sure. He looked at me in that way that people have. You know, 'do you know who you are with here, seriously? Should I call for the Bill, coppers?' Come on then, job done. My turn now. Let's find somewhere for a cup of tea."

"We could go for a proper drink, you know, schnapps," retorts the big man quickly.

"Sorry to disappoint you, mate," says Plum. "I don't drink or smoke."

"*Eish!*" exclaims the man. "Are you religious or summat? I can pick 'em."

"No. Boxing," Plum qualifies. "I have to keep in shape. Nothing like drinking to do for your breathing. Muscle cramps are what you get from boozing."

"Boozing?" asks the man quizzically. Plum motions to drink. "O.K. then. Can you get coffee here?" asks the man.

"I'm sure you can," answers Plum.

In the side streets of Queenstown, the two incongruous men walk on vigorously. Dull skies persist and the breeze from the sea is chilled and damp. They walk on together exchanging the odd word. At one point, Plum sees

Vaughan talking to a girl. Plum points to the couple. "What do you reckon to Vaughan? All mouth and no trousers, eh? The man I waved to back there."

"Him with the *kreef*? I should know him from where?" enquires the man. "*Die wêreld is vol vreemde mense.*"

Plums face creases up in puzzlement. "Yes, I couldn't agree more. Perhaps, one day, we can go back on some of what you just said, just then. Was it clean?"

"Nothing of importance. Just words," qualifies the man, waving it aside with a hand wafted across his face, forget it.

They come to a café and find a table. The menu is consulted. The coffee and tea arrive. Plum has a teacake with his order. "It seems about right for us to introduce ourselves. I'm Plum, no fruit jokes; and you are?"

"*Jah*. I'm Wauters."

"Wauters, that's a name and a half. Proper *Hogan-Mogan* name that is." Plum conjures with the name.

"What's that you have there a cake?" Wauters jabs the confectionary with his finger. Can I try a bit? Mm, that's not half bad. What do you call that? He calls the old lady over. "Mrs, I would like one of these." She signals that she has the order. Wauters is now visibly more relaxed, less on his guard to all intents. "It looks good, that cake." He sips his coffee and winces a little at the taste. "What is it with the food here?" he asks looking sideways at the cup.

"It's the war, that's what's wrong with the food here, everything's gone ersatz," Plum muses. "What were you before this? Will you stay in sailing if this war ever ends?" enquires Wauters.

"More or less straight out of school, me, into the navy. After this, I've got fish to fry," Plum says enigmatically. "Look at that sky, suddenly come over as black as club ten."

"You want to be a chef?" suggests Wauters.

"Sorry?" says Plum.

Wauters reflects on what was said. "Oh yes, selective hearing, an accident no doubt. I suppose loud explosions…frying, you said."

Plum tunes in to the error. "Oh! I see. No, not frying *cooking*. I mean to say I have other plans, other things, other things to do, cook-up."

Wauters comes over almost warm. "Hey, *chommie*, we have no secrets, eh?"

"What's that? *Chommie*?" Plum asks. "Yes, '*chommie*' has to have secrets. You must have secrets. That fishing and your dad. I bet it doesn't end there?"

"I have a boring life," says Wauters. "It's you that has the adventures, I think by the sound of it."

Plum is on the defensive a bit. "Getting killed nearly, like what I did, is no adventure, it's a pain, well, can be, I didn't mean to be funny." He collects himself. "I got blown up at the *Battle of Jutland*; Jutland, heard of it? Near to Denmark" The teacake is placed on the table and Wauters looks at it searchingly. "You're funny with your food," Plum whispers. "I'd a thought that being in prison would have cured you of that?"

"All the food here has its own surprise, eh? Best to be cautious. My little *paw-paw*. There is a lot of odd food around, especially in wartime, especially in a foreign country. I cannot take to whale steaks, they come back at you when you have the, er, wind, like acid, a nasty taste in the mouth. Your soldiers were practising quite a lot last night? What was it?" Wauters tries his coffee again. It has not improved. He puts two more spoons of sugar into the cup, imitates a machine gun firing.

Plum leans in confidentially. "It's their own sodding fault. A mangled fence and the pig bins, where they are. Them soldiers must be very, very bored. They don't mix, you know. They are a race apart. They only go with their own. Talk a different language…worse than you. They're very disciplined though. Poor blighters."

Wauters had circled the bun but when he eventually pounces, he finishes eating it quickly. With a mouthful, he says, "No one mentions of the ship. Is there one?"

"Yes, there is a ship." Plum points over his shoulder as if the ship could be in the kitchens in this restaurant. "They're fitting it out. Everyone tries not to mention it in the hope it will go away, the war I mean. That's what I think anyway. Being here sometimes you forget. You can get used to being a masher, like Vaughan."

"Well, *masher*, where is this ship? There are no big ships on these quays." Wauters observes.

"No, it's not here," counters Plum. "It's over on *Haulbowline Island*, next to *Spike Island*. Out there, Royal Navy docks. You might think that Ireland is famous for its islands, like where it sounds it got its name from. They have a lot of them here, islands. Great Island, Little Island. Altogether, this, here is one of biggest natural harbours in the world, it's said. Titanic came here back in, that would be 1912, yes. We've been lucky really. If we were billeted over there, on the island, we'd be stuck over there, on *Haulbowline*. Fortunately, some yanks brought a couple of old destroyers over for us to use. I might have mentioned it. They lent them to us. They took all the beds on the hulk moored by the island. Here we have the town and a bit of freedom. Over there, it's a bit desperate. You'll see it soon enough. The scuttlebutt is that sea trials are not far off; there's a lot to do changing over nearly four thousand tons of merchant vessel to be a warship."

"I can't wait," says Wauters ruefully. "I enjoyed that. What do you call them? Tea Cakes, *teekoeken*?"

"Yes," agrees Plum. "That's right. You've got good English for a foreigner. What am I saying? it's probably better than mine!"

"Perhaps I have gone native. *Sharp*, man. Everything is good, yes?" says Wauters through a meagre sort of smile.

Chapter 4

There's the ship, at last. The cargo vessel seems nowhere near readiness. A great black hull surmounted by white superstructure. Dock workers are welding and fashioning wood, drilling, banging and clattering. Everyone has their purpose. Wauters is greasing machinery, splicing ropes, sewing and replenishing canvas. Every day, at the moment, a selected few go over to the dock on *Haulbowline Island* and work alongside the local men fashioning a weapon of war within the benign environment of a trading vessel. When in the canteen Wauters now tends to sit with Vaughan, they talk conspiratorially. Plum continues to go for long runs in the countryside around Queenstown, thinks nothing of eight, ten miles in a session. The exercise takes is mind from the separation from Wauters. They were getting on. Why has Dutchy suddenly attached to that slob Vaughan? Mile after mile he lopes. He inevitably comes across the same child who threw stones who now, without the old woman's bidding, lies in wait and throws stones at him which are more difficult to dodge.

It's the fag-end of November. This particular day is dry but there is a keen wind out of the northeast. Yellow-black smoke trails from the deck office's chimneys. There seems to be no pattern to it all yet. If you had the time, you might perceive some order gradually imposing itself. On the quay, the whole crew are assembled in work gear. They stand around in their preferred societies. The two trawler men are quietly rubbing shoulders away from the body of the crowd. Plum has the ear of another gunner. There has been very little gunnery practice, insufficient in Plum's mind for his own peace of mind. He seeks clarification urgently, away from the main body of gun crews. He has that old fear that during instruction he missed some sort of vital manoeuvre that could put the whole issue into jeopardy. His mate is self-assured, he had been to *HMS Excellent*, the gunnery school. The gunner is attentive and calming, after all, it's his life on the line if this little bloke he's talking to gets it wrong. Best to spend some time on this. Apparently, there are no concerns. The gun is, notionally at least, being served properly. Sub-lieutenant Senior steps in front of the men. He is wearing smart slacks and a heavy jacket having ditched his uniform to comply with the ruse they are trying to perpetrate, but he still looks…tailored. He opens-up. "If I could have your attention," and then more curtly, "…when you've finished there." He gives the accompanying standard stare. He's young, but he's learning. The men go quiet. The 'Sub' is hardly recognisable out of uniform, no one has a uniform anymore. The difficulty is that uniforms confer power, authority. It's difficult to be subservient to someone dressed not that much different to you. This man, Senior, looks so much younger now. Only the silk neckerchief he has adopted marks him out in any way, that and his decent clothes. "Come in closer," he says. In these new conditions, you almost expect him to say please and thank you. The men shuffle closer. "Today is the day that you have all been looking forward to," Senior intones unsmilingly. "This great iron beast behind me…" He points vaguely in the direct of the '*S.S. Horton Lodge*' tied up at the quayside. Squat it sits behind its towering bow, rhythmically squeezing against its buffers, tightening and slackening its tethers. "It has two gangways attached to it." A crane chuffs away with its own boiler issuing forth a smear of smoke. At the end of its boom and jib swings a stout net filled with a load of kit, articles being heaved onto the ship's deck, steel cables hanging taught. The whole contraption handled deftly by civilians in overalls shouting their commands and instructions noisily, repeatedly. The bumpers make a squeaking sound as the vessel presses, compresses against the quayside, onto them, squeeze, squeak, then releases. Sometimes Senior's voice gets lost in the screech and thump of dozens of tools and the insistent chug-chug of the crane. "…is a hungry creature. It lives on coal, lots of it and the government have been very generous with its supply. Over there, next to the dock office, is a bunker. It's filled with coal you will be pleased to hear, no shortages here. But it's no use over there is it!" He pauses tilting his head waiting for corroboration of his rhetorical question which comes but in a sort of desultory fashion not as a blast but as a cascade of tenors, subdued. "Well, is it?" he asks sharply. Some men say 'no'. "This is like a bad night at the Glasgow Empire," the officer offers, rocking on his heels, his hands clamped on his hips. This is his little joke. It gets the same treatment as would an actual English comedian at that aforementioned renowned amphitheatre. It's of no consequence. The line amused him, he thought of it on the spur of the moment. He continues, "No, it's no use whatsoever; it needs to be over here, doesn't it? Well?" The 'Sub' in his civvies looks to be about seventeen years old. He's addressing a lot of middle-aged experienced, grizzled matelots. To some of them, it's like witnessing their own sons coming the high and mighty. Some of these men have witnessed the actions of bully mates come within inches of a criminal 'bat', its menacing nail driven into it, being swung at them. Well known, real hard case officers, like the one that shot a sailor who had severe frostbite in his feet, for not following an order, the story goes. Problem is, such is the reality of those times, that the story is quite believable. This boy, they feel, they can safely play-up to. The men reply 'yes, sir', as though they are clearing their throats, a troop of children in class, good morning Mr Senior, that drawl. Senior starts to stroll up and down the line, speaking as he goes. "The objective today, is to move the coal from over there to the bunker on the ship, here. We have thought hard and long about the task"

Well, that's encouraging.

"It is our intention to make it as easy for you as we can."

Well, that's new.

"To this end, over here, there are a pile of hessian sacks. The idea is that *you* will form a long line, like a conga at a New Year's party, remember New Year, parties…"

Do we laugh? Not at our Christmas parties, not on your life. Auntie Flo' after her annual sweet sherry, always good for a laugh.

"…and, systematically, one at a time, present a sack at the bunker over there, where an operative will pull a handle that will shoot a measured amount of coal into your sack." The fact dawns that this is going to be hard and messy. The men look at each other warily. Some venture to joke about it. Someone asks if the 'Sub' is going to demonstrate the procedure. Senior likes his own jokes, but attempts at humour coming from the ranks, no. He puts on his stern look. "Stow it there!" He slowly removes the scowl and looks like a child again. "Then comes the jolly bit. Having had your sack filled you will progress, in turn, to the ship, up the gangway provided" – he indicates the gangway nearest to them – "left-hand side gangway up, right-hand gangway down; left-hand side gangway in, right-hand side gangway out! Clear? You will then re-join the 'fill' queue in your position and so on and so on, until you are told to stop." To the crowd of men, the officers voice sounds fluty, perhaps he's had his 'tackle' removed. Is that a requirement to become an officer, castration? "Here, sack, bunker, fill. Gangway left-hand side, in, right-hand side, out. If you think that this is a bit of a crippler, bear in mind the two trimmers inside the ship's bunker who have the onerous task of ensuring that when you have shot your load…" – a ripple of titters which distracts the instructor, not understanding what's the point of this unintentional crudity, but only momentarily – "…is distributed nice and even inside the bunker, inside that hole into which you are shooting the contents of those sacks."

He doesn't give up this one, more tittering.

"If anybody wants to change places, you only have to ask. Anyone for the bunker? No? No, I don't blame you. At the end of this exercise, when, in the future, the fireman calls for fuel, a 'trimmer' with a wheel barrow goes to the bunker we are filling. A lever is depressed and the issue falls nicely into the barrow for its distribution to the furnace plates; whereupon, the fireman, stoker, will shovel the appropriate amount of fuel required into the furnace. Is that clear? Are there any questions?" Someone asks if the Sub-lieutenant will provide refreshments, the crowd laughs. We get the 'we are not amused look'. "There's always one. I ask again. Are there any *serious* questions?" There is a pause of quietness only intruded upon by a distant clank-clank of a large hammer hitting a metallic surface. "That man there. You at the end of the row. You have the honour." Senior walks briskly towards the designated leader of the troupe. "As you move to the sacks, the next man will follow and so on." He points to the next men in the line. "The sooner this is done the sooner you have your shower and something to eat. It's up to you. Go!" The 'Sub' pushes the first man forward, gently in the right direction.

The grudging chain gang starts the process. Soon the process is working smoothly. The men may have even been listening after all, which is a bit of a triumph for a young officer. The process, in-train, is near faultless. Sometimes the bag loading is disrupted by the mechanism jamming, sacks burst, men fall down. One man on the down side stumbles which propels him into those disembarking in front of him causing them to all go down, one on top of the other. A few expletives. One man brushes himself down as if he's fallen wearing his Sunday best; old habits. Coughing becomes endemic as a result of the coal dust. Spitting starts sporadically and in no time develops into background music. The light starts to fade noticeably. Some men have finished and stand about, some are smoking. Odd refrains of *'keep the home fires burning'* accompany the late finishers. The quay is swept. They are all blackened from head to foot and weary. Wauters and Plum have managed to stay together and stand at the quay. As the last sailors come down the gangway, a man approaches Plum. Logan fronts-up Plum. "I thought it was you. It's Plum, isn't it? Rosyth? You bastard."

"Aye, aye. Fireman Logan?" replies Plum, meekly, taken aback.

Logan lifts his cap gratuitously and tries a smile that looks to all intents and purposes changes his look to that of a Hyena. "The very same. I'm glad to see you are being kept entertained. Not been too strenuous, I hope, has it? We don't want any sweating, do we? Unsightly, sweat. Who's this?"

"It's Wauters. He's an…engineer, electrician, sort of thing."

Plum is still adjusting to this unexpected interloper.

"Well, Mr Wauters," one big man addressing another big man on equal terms. "If you want a peaceful life, you've struck lucky. This man, Plum, knows all the wheezes. If you ever miss him, try 'the heads'; 'admiral of the heads', he had it conferred on him by Beatty. Well, I never. I cannot believe it. I thought this would be the last place I'd find you." Logan looks Plum up and down much in the way that a lion might look at a wildebeest. "Too much like work I would have thought for the likes of you. The svelte Sassenach! Well, I can't waste my valuable time idling about here. I have a boiler room to inspect." He turns to Wauters. "A greaser? Em? Amongst other things, you say? No doubt, we will be seeing a lot of you down in the inferno, the underworld, hell's kitchen. Plum here, can't stand the heat, so he'll not be enjoying our hospitality. Go and have a rest, *wains*." Hoisting his Donkey Bag onto his shoulder, Logan goes on board. Plum looks after him.

Turning to Wauters he jerks a thumb in the direction of the jauntily departing stoker and exclaims incredulously, "See what we're up against? I wonder how long it will be before he gets onto *your* case. What would it take for him to be pleasant? Not much."

"I'm glad I heard that," says Wauters. "I was beginning to think this place was too good to be true. It's just like anywhere, *Eish!* same things, different duds," he says with a sort of a sigh. "I'll see you later. I have some business to do." Wauters moves away and catches up with Vaughan.

Plum is a bit miffed. Am I not enough friend for Wauters? I'm trying my best? How could Wauters get on with both of us when I'm nothing like Vaughan? What's Vaughan done for you? He endeavours to turn the issue to one of his being a Samaritan, helping another, yet, at the back of his mind he churns the words that Wauters' spoke about sailing a *Coper* on the North Sea. Was this not the answer to so much that plagued his own mind since he had started to assemble the nuts and bolts of his adventure? The realisation of where the *Cocos Islands* were, off the *Isthmus of Panama*, out there, had been a stunning blow. He could not imagine being in the service long enough to learn enough that would enable him to travel so far to find the place. Back at the billet the crowd are still discussing the 'Sub's' naivety, not understanding his unintentional euphemism. They have all showered and dressed.

His mind racing, the killing parlousness of his situation demanded quiet and reflection. Having had an upbringing of embeddedness and reliance on the family he was left ill-suited to creating friendships, being expansive, having a ready wit. His problems as a child really only lent him to meeting other lads of his own age in the ring and trying to hit them. Hardly a good basis on which to find a chum, making those you meet cry. He could not avoid the inevitable. He was going to have to court Wauters, no matter what. Him getting on with others, well that was no cause to be miffed, especially when he wasn't actually that relaxed in his company anyway and certainly didn't seem to share any of the of the other man's interests. In the half-light, with the yard lights already on, there was an aridity about the place. In the cold light of day, he had to be a bit more resolved, steely. Any way you looked at things, at this moment, he had total reliance on Wauters and has to take it on the chin, these minor irritations. Wauters *has* to be his friend although, from a lifetime of solitariness, he was not entirely sure what being a friend was, what it could entail. By now, the tide was out and the ship lay lower to the quay. A quiet had descended and the place was deserted and unlovely. Only the smoke issuing from the deck office chimney spoke of life, so eery after all that bustle and noise.

-oo0oo-

In the yard outside their billet, Plum is doing his washing when he is joined by Wauters who has his washing too. Funny how Plum could sense Wauters' immanent arrival before he showed. Odd how a space that was all his, seemed quite roomy, quite exposing, suddenly, with Wauters in it, the space became constricted and uncomfortable. All the hardware is there for the washing. There is a corrugated aluminium dolly-tub filled with boiling water and a hand-cranked mangle, a washboard litters the floor adjacent to some large tongues. There are copious amounts of *Puritan* soap powder. Wauters gazes at the collection of devices at Plum's disposal. "How does this work? I use your tub?"

"No," Plum replies disbelievingly and a touch peevish perhaps. In truth, despite his fresh reasoning, he is still a bit miffed from the thought of Vaughan and Dutchy consorting. Why? "In the shed just behind you, it's got all the kit in it." He wrestles mentally over the question; is afraid he'll suddenly blurt it out. "You'll need a large tub, a dolly peg, a pair of tongues." He holds-up his tongues. "A washboard. Hot water, in the boiler in there too; buckets. We can share this mangle." Wauters scratches his head looks askance, then enters the shed.

Amid cursing and banging about all the stuff is assembled and Wauters starts to wash his clothes. Not sensing how hot the water might be Wauters scalds himself. "*Mein Gott!* that water's hot."

Plum is on to him quickly. "My Gott the water's hot, my Gott the water's hot. My Gott the water's hot." He starts to drum on the various bits of equipment in time with his made-up tune. That soon wears thin and didn't amuse Wauters anyway; the big man is still wringing his hand shaking-off the effects of the scold. Plum starts to sing. Suddenly, the thought comes over him that his companion might take offence at being mocked in such a silly way. Already the thought of what this association is going to cost him reveals itself and, no doubt, more is to follow. He literally changes his tune. *"You made me love you, I didn't want to do it, I didn't want to do it"*, his disbelief, his niggle, gets the better of him.

"What's with your romance with Vaughan, then?" He tries vainly to make light of it. It's no matter. He picks-up his tune again. *"I didn't want to do it. I didn't want to do it."*

"Romance!" Wauters bridles.

Plum points his tongues at the man. "Well, you know. You two seem to be hitting it off. Can't say you're suited, *a love that true. Yes, I do, indeed I do.* I couldn't imagine you and Vaughan having much in common". God, I hope I don't sound jealous. His internal monologue intervenes and the whole problem he faces takes on even more definition. *"You made me happy sometimes…* Is he scrounging? What does he want from you?"

Wauters shrugs. Any insinuation that Plum could imagine is lost on the other. "*Eish!* He's just a little boy wanting help from an older man, *Praatsiek!* He is so childlike. All that brag, brag, just a front, you know?" His eye suddenly catches the soldier's gun emplacement. He points over his shoulder with a thumb in the direction of the Khaki clad group standing by their sandbagged emplacement. "Is that the gun that's making all that racket?" In the half-light, the small huddle is enveloped in mysterious magical smoke from a round of 'ciggies' passed round, all it was needing, a Genie. Lost in their own world and their own immediacy.

"Yes, that will be the one," affirms Plum, glad of the change of tack.

Wauters weighs it up. "That's a lot of gun there to shoot a dog. Or are they just bad shots? Need all the help they can get? From there to that fence." He weighs it momentarily in his head… "Why, a Mauser 93/95 would be enough. More than enough."

Wauters pushes the dolly peg up and down in the large tub of boiling water with more vigour than is necessary, he is miffed for some reason too. Het-up about something. He looks hard at the contents of the tub. "Perhaps I need more soap? What a boring sort of place life can be."

Plum looks at him disbelievingly. All sorts of things contend for attention in his mind and the more they pile up the less lucid he becomes. Amidst all these present thoughts, their intransigence, up pops his dad with one of his daft asides, he splurts it out, "*I am his Majesty's dog at Kew. Pray tell, whose dog are you?*" Think, think, man, he quickly chides himself internally.

Wauters eyes all the devices he is surrounded by and curses the mechanics and the ways of modern life. Plum pounces; always in at the deep-end. Where's this one going. "How can you say that? I know we're in a war now but the possibilities for us all have just, well…opened up, 'beyond the dreams of avarice', as Dad would say." Plum lays off working and starts in on his pet topic. "Ten, fifteen years ago, we lived in a different place. Suddenly, out of nowhere, radio communication, aeroplanes, gas turbine propelled ships, motor cars, have you ever seen a Rolls-Royce car? Well, I've seen pictures, they're unbelievable, amazing? The Suez Canal, Panama Canal, cinema. The women are bolder, all that suffragette stuff. Perhaps the best inventions of all cylinder and disc recordings, music from America, negro jazz, wow, amazing. We are in a world of wonders. You can go to a cinema; it leaves you gasping, the extent of man's ingenuity? Poor old Rolls, he was killed last year in a plane crash."

Wauters barely looks up from his task. "All those things. Eish! They eat their inventor. Mr Rolls, took his own life. What if I tell you we have gained nothing? They are turning the world upside down, for what? Nothing we could not do without. Trinkets, playthings, nothing. I have never been to a cinema; I have no intention to go either. I find no attraction in that sort of thing, play acting. And the ships. What art is there in shoving coal into a boiler and pointing a ship in some direction and then hanging onto a wheel? Just ploughing ahead with no thought for the sea beneath your feet, tide and wind, the nature of things, the art, yes, the art. We lose the family of sailors, the shanties, all pulling together, *'Rolling Home* or *'Hanging Johnny'*, *'Goodbye, fair thee well'*. Them shanties may never be heard again, bar as a comedy turn at the Burlesque. We will lose complete attachment to nature and then we will all be dead. Yes, nature can do just fine without us. We are just inventing more ways to kill one another, as if we had not got enough already."

Plum smirks. "You're showing your age," he expresses this more timidly and less self-assuredly than his natural inclination would have him do.

Wauters puts a shirt through the mangle. "*Loskop*, you have your head in the clouds, up your arse. You are in the world but will never understand it."

There is now a perilous road to travel. Even the expression of an opinion to this stranger becomes dangerous territory and the reaction far from assured. "I could, if I had an aeroplane. I might learn to fly one day," Plum insinuates. How could you live in a world that could incite anger if you spoke what you believed. No, England, the home of free speech, till now. What words could be inflammatory? What thoughts, expressed?

Wauters leans on his tub. "Have you ever sailed, really?" he starts. "*Eish!* It's the most exhilarating experience you can have. The wind and spray in your face; the snap of the canvas; squeezing out an extra couple of knots; sending-up sail. We have 'all set' with studding sails, almost emptied the locker of the *Storm Suit* and he's calling for *'Sky Sails'*, *'Pocket Handkerchiefs'*! The smaller the sail the bigger the name, like tyranny the smaller the man." Is this a reference to Plum? "Off you go to the sail locker. We're a team. He, the Master, over-steps the mark. That tell-tale judder when he over-loads the canvas. What is the *verdommet* use of studding sails? But he insists and you do it. Can you imagine the wealth of knowledge that is going down the drain because of steam ships?" He pretends to spit to one side. "Just when they have it absolutely right, in sail, thrown out the studding sails, know about the way the bow 'gripes', its due to pressure on the leeward bow you know, it brings her head up to the wind naturally. They know that now. Put the *'lady's pocket handkerchiefs'* where they belong, in the locker. Along comes steam and all that knowledge goes down the scuppers, just when we were getting to grips. You cannot make a judgement about things because you want everything, what do you say, on a plate. You have no idea of what true values are until you lose them. Free clean wind. Why coal, quicker, well maybe, yes. Predictable, I can see that. All these new routes where sail wouldn't work. Are they necessary.? Then you have to have coaling stations and you fight to make some other *paw-paw* give up his land and resources to get you around."

Plum holds his own but more timidly than his leanings call for. "For the majority, like, who have little or nothing, there's new work; better pay now with all this inventing. We all need something to make our lives worthwhile. A good bit of harmless fun, just the ticket. It isn't as though there is just one lot pushing for change. Look, how would we be now if only the Germans had planes? There's no *Dukes or Darlings* in this, no toss of the coin. Can't you see? It's all meant. Like me, I intend to follow my dream and then marry, a girl called Thalia. When I can afford to keep her well, that is. That's me."

"Thalia, you say?" grimaces Wauters. "*Eish!* That's a new one."

Plum plunges the dolly peg into the tub with just a little more vigour to slough-off the obvious jibe. They're hammering their washtubs unmercifully, an improvement on actually hitting one another. A proxy war. Normally, he would stand his ground but things are different now. They both punish the clothes in their tubs for different reason jabbing at them ferociously in turn. But better that than fighting. "Thalia means 'blooming' and not as bloomin'-heck either; 'bloomin' as in flower. I mean to take advantage of it all and England is the place to do it. We invent everything." Plum takes clothes from the dolly tub with the tongues and puts them through the mangle, one by one, catching them in the bucket after they have been through the rollers, alternating with Wauters in the mangle's use. "What have the *Hogen-Mogen* invented apart from the tulip? We, my friend, excel. Even now, we have ships as big as some island countries, *Berengaria*, *Aquitania*, they must be like, what, 90,000 tons? I bet you'd need a scout to take you around them, in case you get lost. I bet they find lost tribes in some of them big ship, they're so big"

Wauters leans into Plum. "I can see where it comes from. It's like people want distraction from their conditions. I have seen a bit of England and it was not nice."

"What, prison!?" Plum spouts incautiously. "Prison isn't meant to be luxurious."

"I could see it from my cell." Wauters relates his imaginings looking distantly, pointing at the unseeable with the tongues he is wielding. "Smoke. Row after row of the same house; filth, noise. I hear there is a lot of poverty, I dare bet. It's good then that you have a war. Despite all your inventions, you cannot feed your people or keep 'em proper. Those poor soldiers that you speak of would be glad to get away from England so they get fed, find a warm climate, out of the rain, if nothing else. Even the threat of death does not put them off, *eish*! Better that than those smokie rows of little houses around Wormwood. No wonder you have armies all over the world. People getting away from that awful place."

Plum is pricked by this assault on his country, he can be provoked. Plum walks over and stands looking into Wauters' face. "Automobiles, trains, trams, ships." Each item a separate jab for emphasis with his tongues. They are starting to look like two crabs with make-do pincers challenging each other. "We sell to the whole world. The whole world looks at my country and wishes they could be us. Our soldiers have had some set-backs, like in the Dardanelles, South Africa before. But look at them now. We cannot be put down by anyone. We stand-up to Fritz because we can. You can't sum the whole of England through one small window. Anyway, it's the people, the people. Perhaps them people like those neighbourhoods what you see. *You* can't imagine it, but perhaps *they* actually like where they live; don't want to eat cream teas in Devon or live on a mountain in Wales. People who come to my country and criticise, well, what do they want? It's all there; it depends on what they want and what they want to see, like, you, now." He returns to his washing. Injudiciously, he can't shut up now and knowing so little about his grouchy mate might be sailing into a storm. Shut up, Plum says he to himself within! "We have now invented the 'war of movement', that's what they are talking about now, not playing the German's game. We invent you see, adapt. We've got the most terrifying weapon ever dreamed, they call it the tank. They brush aside the enemy like, like. That's not the German's game because they are dull and boring. Where in the world is there a nation that could stand up to Kaiser Bill? Look at Vimy Ridge…well, it was the Canadians what did that; but they couldn't have had their moment of glory without us. Before they fought there, they were just a country, they're a nation now." Wauters actually smiles wryly and goes about his work. "Did you know that, at this moment, we are building a massive battleship, biggest in the world, named after my old commander, Hood. That vessel is so big; some say it's going to be 100,000 tonnes, more! Its guns will be able to knock out a flea's eye at a range of 25 miles. The way things are going, these ships are getting so big. In the future they'll be able to manoeuvre some of these leviathans in such a way that you'll step onto them at Dover, walk down the vessel and get to step off at the other end, onto French soil. You couldn't make it up."

Wauters chuckles. He lays a heavy but gentle hand on the little man. "It's like somebody talking loud 'cus they're scared, all this big talk. But America, they are bailing you out, right now. That's what they think of you. Poor neighbours. You said it yourself; they have sent you some old destroyers. Crumbs from the table."

Plum hesitates. There is a washing line to hand and he starts to peg up the post-mangle clothes. He addresses the clothes. "The Yanks couldn't think it through at first. It was a mental thing. While we were fighting and dying, they were all, 'Oh no, it's too dangerous we might get hurt'. Suddenly, they realise that they are in as much of a threat than, well as much of a threat as us. Pershing? Perishing, you mean. They want us to die for their country rather than them dying for theirs."

"But they still give away their ships," tauntingly Wauters adds.

Plum recomposes himself. "What they lack is…ingenuity, yes, ingenuity. Listen to this." He walks up to Wauters and talks to him confidentially. "There is a run-in with a U-Boat, just off the Isle of Wight, Solent, down south you know, Isle of Wight, hear tell? The Q-Ship, like ours, only called the *'Penshurst'*, I believe, takes a torpedo. Is that the end? Is it over? No, the ship pluckily fights back. *'Penshurst'* is now listing in a swell. The U-Boat takes off thinking 'Mein Gott, Englander, the war for you is over'. Job done. But it has also been damaged by the 'Penshurst's' guns as well, can't submerge. Clever sods. What happens? The holed ship, *'Penshurst'*, radios, radios mark you, the position of the U-Boat. Another ship nearby, wait for it, has an aeroplane, on board! Now, this is English ingenuity; the plane takes off, finds the U-Boat and bombs it, sinks it. Ingenuity you see. Clever thinking."

Wauters waits expectantly. "And that is that?"

"Well, no." Plum backs off. "The plane had to ditch into the sea. The pilot was killed, sad to say."

Wauters throws his arms wide. "So that's your marvellous English invention, is it? The plane drops into the sea? Is a mankiller? Was it made by Mr Rolls the suicide?"

Plum absentmindedly gathers more washing to peg on the line. "Perhaps that plane was built in Scotland. Wales, probably. Not in England, I bet. *We* are going to save the world's bacon."

Wauters surveys the washing area. "Now you are making me feel hungry."

They both go back to their own thoughts. Plum looks-on at Wauters and tries to make out what he is. What's a foreigner doing here? Was he, like, sent? Some sort of Biblical story made real? Behold a pale rider? King Arthur? Plum wonders if he is any further forward. The soldiers are settling down in the sand pit as he pours away his filthy water down the drain. Replaces the washing kit in the shed and by now feeling utterly shattered physically, leaves the scene, his washing flapping idly in a breeze. He needs to do more work on his stamina. Needs to find a library, they will have stuff about the *Cocos Islands*. Wauters lags behind.

Chapter 5

Captain Cathcart had to run a little bit to catch up with Plum on the dockside. He had leapt out of the dock office having seen the sailors leave their ship. He could have shouted but he deemed that a bit common, unworthy. So, a little out of breath, he managed an interception. He asked the young man to accompany him back to the office. As the captain had never addressed him directly before, Plum was a little concerned as to why this meeting had been ordained, now. Outside, the wind was steely, face chapping. Entering the office, a warm cosy atmosphere was maintained by a raging coal fire. Intermittently, the flue would spit back a puff of smoke into the room, like there was a little dragon stuck up the stack occasionally coughing out smoky grot. Captain Cathcart was sweaty despite the outside temperature. There was little space in the room. The high wooden racks ranged around the walls were laden with rolls of paper, plans you would have to suppose, technical drawings. There is a dress hanging behind the entrance door that swung in a feminine sort of way at the hip as the door opens and closes. Cathcart ushered his young crewman in. What little space there was became even more cramped by the large desk behind which Cathcart now sat. The wonder was that the desk was not smouldering, such was the intensity of the fire, or the captain choking from those occasional gusts of grey clouds blown back into the room from the grate-dragon. On the desk were various sporting magazines and a book about dry fly fishing. Cathcart removed some papers from a chair and piled them onto the table. He gesticulates around the room.

"I'm not in control here and I hate it. I share this space with the chief surveyor, scruffy cove, I say. Take a seat, here." He motions to the seat that has just been cleared. "How are you doing, young man? I'm afraid the ship is still being…made ready and, talking to the local authorities, well." He raises his arms, shrugs. "I'm quite exhausted." He flops back heavily on his chair whose upholstery meets the copious bottom with a sigh of squeezed-out air. He has a flustered almost embarrassed demeanour, or is it the heat? "A man of my age. I expected to be well away from all this stuff, down in my bolt hole on the *Beaulieu River*. The *Buccleuch* estate, do you know it? Fine country. It was all planned and then…well country comes first, you know? I get letters from Mrs 'Captain', but it's a poor substitute. You spend your whole life striving. You make Master. You do the cruises. All the time you have your eye on that cottage that the Montague's promised you for services rendered", a faraway look in his eye. "Then what happens? War happens! There she sits, my queen, looking out down the river towards *'Buckler's Hard'* with only the dogs for company. It's almost as though there was no mention of retirement and she is now a victim of events beyond her, beyond us both."

Plum could feel the side of his face nearest the fire starting to smart. The fire was making less smoke now as the heat mounted and the coals turned to red briquettes.

Cathcart was still trying to find the right tone. He was still in uniform and the blue cloth and the gold braid enhancing his presence, sort of regal. He could have been a Lord, reminiscent of the gold mine that those officers represented in the good old days of boxing and fame the young man had experienced before Jutland. Plum had not spoken to him before, all the information being relayed under the old uniformed command structure, through one of the two RN Sub-lieutenants that the ship boasted. "Quarters all right? Do you fish? What's the time? Odd place Queenstown?" He points out the window. He fidgets for his watch. "Weathers not been too bad. I would have expected the work to have progressed at a rate of knots." Yes, relationships are changing. The steady erosion of formality with the insignia disappearing leant for a strange atmosphere. You could almost feel matey with your officers, a thing which they found awkward and always represented a trip-wire for relationships.

Plum sees the man's dilemma and strives to interject. "I'm finding…"

Cathcart cuts across him. "Look we don't think much of people who 'snitch', do we? But it's, look, that man you're associating with, the foreign chap? A *downy bird* I think, up for a dodge, d'you think? Know what I mean? I don't want to be…I don't want…I hate it when someone pre-judges. Not good, is it? But this chap? You have to take who you are given."

"Do you mean Wauters, sir?" Plum intervenes.

It is as though the waters have broken. Cathcart can now proceed. "That's him. Yes, that's the one, Wauters. What is he about?" Pause for reflection. "Do you know, I'm damned if I do? I've had all sorts of crew around the world but he stands out, oddly. You know, the Chinese were the best." Fiddles with the watch. "I mean…if it wasn't, *isn't,* difficult enough." He reorders the papers he took from the chair. "To have to take on a person who is…doubtful, a, can I use the term, rotten apple?" Ponder, squirm. "What's to be done with him?" Plum has no idea. Cathcart has got to the nub of his enquiry. "I think that all I can say is that you should keep an eye on him. The records are scant, to say the least. Bits of it are redacted you know, crossed out. Looks shady to me." He leaves his seat and looks out of the window. Consults his watch again. "In my off-moments, I get this image of me driving the dog cart in some pleasant country setting, it makes me sad. Buccleuch was in commerce you know, in the West Indies. Then the settlement with the French, we gave his Island away, his living. Can't keep a good man down. He went into ship building, ships, warships eventually."

There is a silent moment of reflection which lingers, seemingly, amongst the smoke hanging, writhing beneath the ceiling. "Yes, well, I'm glad I've spoken to you. A bit smoky in here." He cranes to look at the sky. "Bit of a low-pressure area by the looks of it." He turns to Plum. "A lot might rest on your shoulders and then again, not. Who knows? Quarters all right, are they? Well, that's all for now. I'll see you '*in camera*', a tap on the side of his nose. Keep me posted, eh?" He taps the side of his nose again. "Between you and me. No one else need be troubled; occasionally, now and then, we'll have a chinwag, eh? Thank you for being so decent about the whole thing." A pointy finger. "Watch him!" Cathcart goes to the door. As it is opened, Plum motions to salute. "Oh no, young man. None of that navy malarky. No saluting. What a give-away. We're supposed to be *'wavy navy'*, I think that's the term. Casual, nothing military. Anyway, I'm not wearing my cap. Even those Sub-lieutenants have stowed their uniforms; clever men, good boys, so young; sharp as tacks. Should be on a proper ship. We don't want to, what do they say in modern parlance b-b 'blow our cover', yes,' blow our cover', is that right? Something of the *Father Brown* about that. Saluting no. It's an absolute bugger without uniforms, rank, eh. Grave times and much subterfuge. That's what we're all about here."

Plum refrains from saluting, regards the dress hanging behind the door. A nice floral pattern which swings in rhythm with the door's opening and shutting. A dress? No problems there.

-oo0oo-

It is night-time in the billet. Now is the time for letters home, talk of future intentions or reminiscences of what this time of the evening would occasion in the previous existence. Many a finger ink stained and many a nose, cheek and shirt too. Gas lamps cast a dingy, sepulchral light. The men are milling about. Some are chatting, others engaged in token physical exercises or making beds, coming back from the washroom. A letter is read for the umpteenth time, that strange passage, what did it mean. *"He said that in your absence he would come along occasionally to see the garden was right."* The spelling, blots and smudges, priceless. That innocent reflection on temptation turned to torture in this reality. Some are sullen. Some are single without connection and burdened about how much of themselves they can tell without giving advantage or saying something that was only ever meant to be said to someone that cares for you, if only a little bit. A Petty Officer appears at the door, commands the room.

"All right, you lot, get that gas switched off and get bunked down. Testicles, spectacles, wallet and watch. Lights out. Look sharp there!"

One by one, the lights are dimmed. There is a little bit of chat between the men. One of them leaves his bed and runs to the washroom, that sound of bare feet slapping on tiles, the ubiquitous human signatures, returning after a minute or so. Somewhere in the near distance, a dog whines. Around the room, one by one, the settling down ceases and soon there is a warm, snug silence only intruded upon by mumbling, a cough here, someone jumps up with a cramped leg, curses broadly, but soon settles back. A leg lolls from under its covers. Someone groans unintelligibly. Sleep ensues for all. But not Wauters. He is alert. Time passes. Suddenly from the velvet snoring, wool blanket and dark dreams darkness, Vaughan approaches him quietly. Whispers in Wauters' ear. "Ready?" Vaughan motions away. Wauters hands him a small bag which he has fished-out from under the bed. Wauters unwinds his ungainly frame, quietly leaves his bed and stealthily makes away. Plum makes out the shadowy figures in the scant light of a lamppost outside their building whose beams only illuminate standing figures over a certain height, the window ledges making for a sharp delineation between golden outside light and inner impenetrability. The two figures are anonymous at first then the light catches one and then the other as the two steal forward synchronised in the shadows padding towards the washroom. Wauters feels at home without shoes and the cold floor against his feet calms his verruca somewhat. Concealed from view, Wauters points to one of the windows to the right of the washbasins and proceeds to give Vaughan a leg-up to the half open window. Vaughan manoeuvres, ready to slip through the framework. Wauters hands the bag up to him.

Vaughan drops to the floor outside, stands motionless in the shadows his heart racing. Then, stealthily, in quick darting runs with intermittent stops, makes his way to the perimeter fence a hundred yards or so from where the soldiers have their post. He feels blindly around the fence, finds a gap and crawls through it. No wonder foxes find chicken coops so easy. His blood is up and it drives him on, the pumping of his heart resounding in his ears. He eases through, snagging his jacket briefly on one of the wire fence's broken loops that caused the hole. A quick tug on the coat frees him. Once through, lying in a tangle of furze and tall grasses, he pauses, the light catches his eyes, wary, alert, animal like. He knows fear. His heart is racing faster. Is this what the fox feels or the wary hen on her roost, head tilted, beady glistening eye unwavering; still, listening. Yeah, but that might equally be excitement. He has thought the whole thing through meticulously right down to the nitty-gritty of…congress. A dog approaches him cautiously, appears out of nothing. Sniffs him like an untouching handshake before loping off into the undergrowth from where it came. The camp seems so odd in this light and this quietness equally odd, without purpose. Vaughan slithers on his belly further into the banks of dried winter grasses into which he has landed beyond the fence, their feel made waxen against his skin by cold and drying. Eventually, he feels safe enough to stand up and takes his bearings. The moon appears from behind thin cloud. It is all so easy, so perfect, so…intended…even down to the moon lighting his way. This was meant to be? He walks along confidently swinging the bag that Wauters had handed to him. He can hear the cans in the bag rubbing together dully. His progress is good. The uneven ground is a bit of a challenge and he stumbles on tussocks of grass or the ground in places hollowed-out naturally falls away beneath his feet, unexpected. He has a misstep which jars a little. It is cold, bright, sharp. The air is like spring water at the back of his throat. There is the Lee River beyond. In the patches of silvery light reflected on by the moon; he can see birds flying in the bright pools, spotlights furnished by the great orb; flat calm, glassy; flying and then touching down leaving a trail of disturbed glinting water like a knife slash in the liquid flesh with blood easing through. Liquid flesh, that will be her. All that pent-up emotion of the two. Occasionally, a bird calls-out shrilly which attracts his attention. There is a tussle between unseen adversaries witnessed only by the commotion on the river's surface and the splashing. Somewhere to his right a horse, maybe two, give-out a little shivering huff and appear to be approaching him but still at a distance, the padding of their hooves dampened by the sandy loam. He walks on. He knows the feeling, the feeling that the searching fingers know, the triggers to the inevitable. Eventually, he comes to a stile, the stile standing-out tinselled by the tracery of silver moonlight streaming from the pellucid skies. He's a bit breathless, some from effort and a little from anticipation and takes a second to get on an even keel. He listens intently. "Are you there?" He hisses. Nothing. "Are you there? It's me Vaughan. Hello!" And then says, in a tempting come hither voice, "It's peaches time." There is a rustling sound. The dog appears first. Recoils a little on seeing the man, then moves forward again cautiously. Carmen appears washed of colour by the lunar palette as an outline against the high drab colourless winter-dried weeds and grasses leading up to the woodwork of the fence and style... "It's me, Vaughan."

Carmen stands off him. "So, it is. This is Rollo. Rollo, this..."

Vaughan interjects, "Vaughan, obviously."

She nods in the direction of the dog who is scenting his way towards this stranger. "Good boy, Rollo," she says. "Of course, you two have met already."

Vaughan ignores all of her introductory chat, holds up the bag, swings it towards the woman so it touches her, just in case she can't see it.

Vaughan can't help looking about him, animalistic. The place has to be free of interlopers to make what is to come perfect. The whole thing is a pulse raiser. The walk along the river, the smuggler's moon, the attention-grabbing antics of river poultry. The subject doesn't need broaching. The horses, perhaps disturbed, still grunting in small voices back down the trail. She's a slut and he's a handsome sort that she definitely does not deserve. In normal circumstances, would she get a look in? Not on your life. He's doing her a bit of an honour, a favour. She must be right up for it, can't get too many offers, her being like that, if any. When she eventually meets the tramp in her life, she'll look back on this little bit of romance fondly and castigate herself for being so plain and without appeal. "Here, look, I've kept my promise. See, tinned peaches. They were a bugger to get. Bit of a risk I can tell you. Good job I've got some pull. The stores, they're like the Bank of England, guarded that closely. You can get all sorts there, some other time, eh? He smiles at her keenly, invitingly, lecherously. What do you think?"

There is a quiet pause, she makes conversation. "There's not much you can say about two tins of peaches until they're out of the can. They're very welcome, I'm sure. Sorry I'm a bit late, you know it's late."

"Well, what do you think, then?" urges Vaughan, feeling the great urge mounting inside him, the anxiety of anticipated pleasure.

"What would you have me think?" she asks. "It's late." Rollo was glad to come out. "He's on a mission." She speaks with a little laugh in her voice "He's peed-up everything that's standing up. I had to go back for my shawl. Do *you* know Rollo, what the man is thinking? Why is he doing this? He's not very nice normally, yet he'd do this for me as an act of friendship?"

Vaughan is getting heatedly excited, stirred. A woman coming those feminine wiles, making herself out to be unlike a man, coyly incapable of intense urges, only serves to excite this man. This is the high point of the game; the consummation is extra.

"I can't stay long. They have inspections and stuff, back at the camp. Sorry it's a bit of a rush." He looks at that the dog a bit nervously. "It doesn't bite, does it? You know. I don't want him biting my bare arse, do I?"

She pats Rollo who fauns on her hand rolling his head in her fingers, licking the fingers slimily, the lolling ears warm and velvet comfortable to cold hands in a clinging cold night. Rubbing her hands together she has an insight of understanding at his words. "Only now and then. He's a bit unpredictable…but he can give you a nasty suck."

He points at the dog repeatedly. "I'll give it a kicking if it comes near. They carry rabies dogs do!"

"Don't be horrible to poor Rollo. He may have the odd tick now and then but…" She puts on a hurt look not that he can see.

Vaughan ignites with a sense of urgency. "I haven't got long. Got to get back before they miss me." His voice softens. "I bet you've missed me, eh? Been looking forward to seeing me? It's nice along there by the river. I bet it's very pretty in the grass down there in the daylight, good place for a romance, eh? The birds are still flying even in the dark." Apropos nothing. He jabs his thumb in the direction from which she came and he almost starts to hop from foot to foot. "Is this where you live then? Somewhere over there, perhaps. I thought I saw some horses, you've got horses, right?"

She nods. "Horses, dogs, chickens, we've got a goat or two." She does not want to believe the worst but she is increasingly cautious. All men are a threat but in town, in the press. Ah, but then your brother across the street keeping watch. He has a knuckleduster; he has a knife. She wants to get away. She has the fruit and she wants to get to her bed. "Perhaps you should start back then?" she suggests. "A very good thing you've done. We'll enjoy these." She holds up the bag. "I appreciate your effort. A good weight."

"Well," says Vaughan thinking her timid, "is there something *you* want to do for *me*? You know? As a sort of thank you. I bet you like me a bit, don't you?" he says lamely. He motions to the bag she is holding. "That's me, see, true to my word. The sort of bloke a girl can trust, to do the right thing. I've done as I said." He moves towards her but she tries to maintain the distance, steps a pace back. She glimpses behind her to judge the distance, there's only so much room between herself and the stile at her back and him moving forward. He could press her against the woodwork and she would be trapped.

"A sailor, far from home." He moves to touch her hair. "No, you know, home comforts." She moves her head away. That sort of threatening voice he addresses her with, menacing even. "Gets tedious, lonely. I bet I'm the sort of man you could go for, am I right? It brings a lump to your trousers. I could tell the moment we met you thought I was a 'looker'. I bet you could make me feel a whole lot more…at ease."

"Oh, yes? How?" she says mockingly, deridingly cautiously. "Home is best isn't it now? The old fire and slippers. Get your clogs off and wiggle your toes. Best that you be going back perhaps, you know the camp, time? I'll see you in town. And thank you for these" – she holds up the bag – "it was good of you. You were true to your word, that's worth a lot these days." She's buying time working out how she will slip away from him. "I'll see you around, eh? Best you go back, it's late. Good luck."

Vaughan tenses, this is not what he planned. "Go back?" It is a bolt passing through his heart, his guts shrivel. "I was hoping. Look, we get on all right. I thought we had an understanding, that we'd get something going here." Even he can sense that this might turn a bit violent, he's feeling denied as well as sensing that he's a bit of a chump. "I sort of hoped you'd like to give me some loving. Women say I'm good at it. I always take my socks off in bed." He laughs coldly. Moving forward towards her. Takes hold of her by her shoulders. "I bet you have a good imagination. I bet you could make me really comfy, bring some…warmth into my life."

She does not like his hand there, menacing, controlling, stifling. You got yourself into this now what you going to do you feckin' eediot girl!

"Oh, I see. Call me slow. There's nothing I have in mind at this moment except for getting me some sleep. The fruit is great, I have to say. But I'll be missed. They'll come looking. Best that I go back now. If you would just take your mitts off me. You're getting a bit scary," she rasps as she squirms to avoid his touch.

Vaughan moves his hands down her arms and, pointedly, a trailing thumb down her breast. "I want to be gentle with you, show you the stuff; I'm 200% man, a real man. I'm very experienced. I come with recommendations." He sniggers. "I'll be careful. Come on."

She struggles in his grip as he tries to shove her over to the floor. He begins to sound more assertive. "I've gone to a lot of trouble for you. Now it's your turn to show some gratitude," he says gruffly.

They tussle and he, intent on touching her breast, has left her arms free to swing. She punches him square in the face, swings the cans at him striking him on the cheek. He lets go, springs back a little expecting another blow. Hurt in so many ways, his cheek stinging; his looks, his looks!

She reels away. Rollo barks assuming a squat position as if ready to pounce but she and the dog run off into the dark. She has disappeared just like that; like an apparition and he is left in the moonlight looking about him his mind grasping at air. He feels his face where she hit him, there is a trace of blood, the flesh is tender. He licks his lip, gets a hint of salt; mumbles something under his breath and kicks the stile. He mounts the step. Standing there, he strains to look into the grey dead landscape, a more meaningless gesture you could not imagine, thumps the woodwork and then subsides almost in tears, sits on the stile's foot plank, looking over his shoulder occasionally. But all is still and deathly silent.

"Tart! Bitch!" He spits-out venomously. He starts to walk back along the path by which he came, kicking out at anything that represents in his path, mumbling crudities under his breath, sobbing with the frustration of his failure and the crushing of his expectation, his certainty, his face throbbing. The breeze starts to get up after a while and cloud increasingly, hastily, scuds across the face of the moon. He sees the rainbow colours that the moon discovers in the highest of the clouds. The cloud intensifies. Soon the darkness is almost complete, impenetrable and the wind is getting really strong, forces him to push against it to make progress. The uneven ground is even more difficult to traverse and he falls frustratingly, often. Suddenly, the rain starts to lash down, icily, cuttingly cold. He stumbles along, his sobs louder and louder. Eventually, cold to the marrow attired in what is now like sleet clinging to him, invading that skin at his neck below his chin, which was his last refuge of warmth; lashing his ears. Sleet, sneaking in, turns to cold water and trickles down his chest. He can see the dim lights of the camp and moves towards them with new found resolution, the new imagining of warm bedding and a release from the stinging wound and the vengeful weather. Approaching the camp's fence, he finds himself in with a pack of dogs snapping and growling at each other. He is by the fence, on his knees, Vaughan moves along the line of it, feeling with his hands for the hole that he accessed earlier. He thinks he has found it and moves towards it precipitously. But a bloody dog gets in front of him and, in throwing it out of the way with the collected venom of one so deflated, scorned and mocked, propelling it to one side, it yelps. At that moment, the soldiers beyond, in their rudimentary, windswept, comfortless bivouac emplacement, cursing the duty and fighting the tiredness which, in the early hours, seems almost unopposable. Cold and tetchy, they open-up with their machine gun in Vaughan's general direction. He is shot and agonises, his mind instantly resets, rationalised, emptied of thoughts, before rolling over, his face looks surprised, questioning, not hurt. Part of his head is missing and his neck is covered in blood which mingles now with the unthreatening melt. He has fallen, leaden. The dog returns momentarily, sniffs his body before moving away.

-oo0oo-

Later that morning at the billet, who has known the night and its rain and sleet, who was conscious of the cold? Who dreamed and thought themselves at home, snug by a woman, alert to the whimpering of a child nearby in its cot, or vaguely conscious of the milk delivery or some other early morning cart down the street? Early morning, in the dull light and thin airs, gaslights lit. The smell of effluvia leaking from the showers, a gaseous effusion and its time-honoured verbal reactions solicited. The men are already advanced in their ablutions and dressing. Vaughan's bed is empty. The Petty Officer bustles in, falls in, covered in the fresh scent of the new day, neat, groomed, stolid. So hastily is the door swung violently against the hut wall it springs back shut, but not before allowing some of the chilly airs that will inform the day to seep passed him. He calls the men to listen. He has an announcement.

"At last, we're all going home, the war's over," some wag suggests.

The Petty Officer is not impressed. "Quiet there! This is serious. There has been an incident, over-night, Vaughan" – he points to Vaughan's bed – "the bed wetter…well, Vaughan, mustn't speak ill, he's dead. He was shot dead by the camp guards last night, accidently, I hasten to add. He was on the outside of the fence for some reason, coming, going, who knows. There's not much to tell, there's nothing to tell. He was found this morning on the other side of the perimeter fence, which is a bit of a facer. He was in a state. They did a job on him, the khaki cult. He couldn't have suffered, that's one consolation at least. It's a mystery, lads. No rhyme nor reason. We will have a service for him of course. His body is going to be taken back home, Norwich, I think; we'll do the decent thing."

"I said that gun was far too big," Wauters whispers while looking sternly straight ahead.

"Suffice to say," continues the Petty Officer, "if any of you have anything that might cast light on this…he was on the outside. He was here at lights-out; I saw him myself. Sometime between lights out and the early hours of this morning, for some unfathomable reason, he must have took-off, was he deserting? Did he say anything to any of you?"

Silence. The P.O. looks slowly around the room. After scanning those present, he rolls back Vaughan's bedding, gives the mattress a cursory look over. Opens the man's locker and removes its contents, little there to say much about a life. Hands cradling the kit removed, another look about the room. "In the meantime, business as usual. That's all. Carry on." He's almost out the door when he pirouettes to face the men again. "And clean the 'shitters' after you've used them. Don't make me appoint somebody Captain of the Heads!" He goes. There is a general hubbub.

Plum edges up to Wauters. "Norwich, eh. 'Knickers off ready when I come home'. That could be his epitaph!" he suggests. "Every bullet has a billet, they say."

Wauters nods solemnly. "Oh, yes?"

"Wauters, it's nothing to do with that woman, you don't suppose? That one we saw him with in town?" Plum whispers urgently.

"The *kreef*?" Wauters reflects. "What makes you think that, *Crunchie*? Who's to say?"

Plum closes on Wauters confidentially. "You and him went to the wash room after lights out. Was that something to do with it?"

Wauters looks away. "It could have been. It all depends on what sort of mind you've got. You could make something of it if you had that sort of turn of mind, I suppose." Wauters looks about him then leads Plum off to a quiet corner. He addresses Plum confidentially, "We couldn't talk out there, like last night, we would have been real popular waking them all up, eh? *Eish!* Vaughan was a very troubled sort. Odd, insistent. All that braggadocio, swagger, front, all front. He wanted home. Said he couldn't stand it here, the prospect of dying and all, and him so bluff. Wanted to live it up but, er, that girl, wanted nothing to do with him. I knew that, not even her. His age, you know? Him being a charmer. I spoke to him briefly and then he broke down. Just like that. Tension can do that to a man, I've seen it come on. They put on a face for so long and then. I can't stand to see a man cry. I left him to it. There's only so much you can do. '*Totsiens*', says I. Went back to my bunk. He was dead set. Made his mind up, I think. I'm not one to stand in another's way. I did my bit."

Plum is thinking whatever the truth is what can he do? He has to act mollified. What's Vaughan to him? Do you think you should tell *them*, help clear things up? Tell *them* what? Drop the whole issue into the pan for what, a ha'p'orth of tar. What do I know? He could not make himself see a connection; he was too invested in Wauters to cause him any trouble. There were too many unknowns already to throw things up in the air. He was Wauters' man, come what may and did not choose to ponder the moral issue. Friendship had jumped the gap to complicity. Wauters didn't kill Vaughan, the soldiers killed Vaughan. They could have had a grudge, a score, dealings with Vaughan. They were the instruments of his death not Wauters. Wauters' story was plausible, yes eminently plausible. Plum himself had had dealings with Vaughan; he was so unkindly, rough, snide. That man could have invited trouble from so many quarters and Wauters, new to the place, might have been a reformer, might have found some good in a bloke who seemed irredeemable; perhaps it was with Wauters being foreign that he could find something of worth in Vaughan. He hadn't known him long enough to form an opinion. They were never seen falling out. No, stow it. Wauters will be back in Plum's company again now.

Wauters looks Plum in the eye. "I think that would be right weak. We've got enough on our plate. No. *Eish!* The *Loskop* was a pain in the in the backside. He would have been trouble like being *'iron sick'*, held together with loose rivets, know what I mean? Things start breaking apart inside him. Unsafe, you know how the temperamental ones can do for a crew. You would never trust them. Up in the yards with a *Packet Rat, a Paddy Wester?* You've got to be sure of the man you work with when things are on an edge. No ifs, buts or maybes. Him, very odd, unreliable, trouble." Wauters makes to walk off. "Listen, it's up to you. The truth is we don't know. Perhaps he was just feeding me lies. He was obviously not quite right." He points a finger to his head. "He cried. I had to leave him. There was no getting any sense into that one."

Chapter 6

On a day gilded with bright sunshine, the deck of the *Horton Lodge* was being tidied by degrees. There was definitely less hammering, less swarf, less new kit being dumped on the deck by the large cranes on the dock. There were less plans being queried and far fewer civvy dock workers. The seagulls were venturing closer and receiving the odd crust for their boldness. The great ingenuity of the guns hidden about the deck was in the testing phase, a novelty. One gun, secreted below deck, would pop-up when the lever was pulled and be available for immediate action. Another was concealed in a false deckhouse. Plum's cannon was, to all intents and purposes, just a lifebelt cupboard, stowage under a lifeboat on its davit; kick away a panel and the gun was ready to blaze in what, a minute? Less, with training, practice. The important factor was those that manned the guns had to have faith in the strategy. So, they had not been able to rehearse the procedures up to now, but the ingenuity of the concealment and the anticipation of the surprise they were going to spring was all very re-assuring, even if the fine detail was wanting. It was good to know that the process had been used elsewhere to deadly effect. Not so entertaining that the Germans had had their successes too and now, with talk of Total War and the adoption of the convoy system, the single ship alone on the sea was the target of choice. But heh, why be glum? What an adventure, eh?

Wauters has been given a 'shit' job. Something that you could load onto a foreigner, being the end of the food chain. Clearing junk from the deck without sturdy gloves had its problems. Left-overs, inevitably, had jagged edges, protruding nails unspotted, swarf as deadly as shrapnel. He was coiling some rope when Plum emerges from under a lifeboat. He catches a glimpse of the man uncoiling out of the corner of his eye. "Hello, *crunchie*, what's this? A Hermit Crab? Nice shell you've got there, *paw-paw.*" Wauters points to the davit and its lifeboat.

Hidden behind his foreign tongue he felt at liberty to pour scorn on his mates, delighted in it. Whatever he said, no matter how cruel, would inevitably be met with a smile. How good is it to call someone an idiot to their faces and not illicit any rancour? Plum was inevitably cheery. Like everyone else, he had his moments but he sublimated his fears and doubts for the sake of the other person, especially Wauters, yes, especially him. His pact with the Dutchman was Faustian. Wauters actually put the fear of God up him. Wauters would do nothing overt, there was never a confrontation or anything like that; it was just that Wauters had an aura about him, a force field, some sort of extra sense that invaded your head and disorientated you. Was it his fierce stare that did not shift, bored into you if you held a conversation? Wauters was a moving shoal, a shifting sand bank that you could fetch you-up without warning.

Plum regarded Wauters. The man seemed more beastly today. He had a beard now where formerly he had an emery cloth chin of short stubble. Yes, Plum was beset by Wauters but held his own council as much as he dared without alienating one who might be his mentor. The man could sail! What worth could you place on that? In the world of tomorrow, it was priceless and Plum was wedded to tomorrow, fool. Tomorrow is a mystery, marsh gas, unicorn droppings.

"Best that we are doing something busy, eh? Take our minds off things, Vaughan and all," Plum offered as he straightened-up after the confinement of his hideaway.

Wauters dropped the rope he had been coiling. Looking over Plum's shoulder. "What you at under there? Sloping off!"

Plum was, of course, cheery. Looking back at the lifeboat davit, both arms in a 'walk this way' manner. "Welcome to the church of *St Barbara*. See this, my gun. A twelve pounder." He reveals the weapon to Wauters by completely removing a wooden panel, like a mother pulling the coverlet back on a bassinet to reveal her pride and joy.

Wauters' curiosity was tickled. His eyes wandered around the structure. Looking up at the lifeboat and the davit assemblage. "Not much good under that lifeboat, *crab meat*. Still, it keeps the rain off, I suppose. Stops rust." He grinned that grin, the assassin's grin.

Have you ever had one of those conversations when the other person says something and then smiles? A job interview, perhaps? If you stay unmoved perhaps you missed the point being expressed, showing how slow you are, or, if you smile, they immediately qualify that with an expostulation, saying something that obviously reflects on matters not being humorous at all, or just merely frown out you, a querying look?

Plum knows something, now that's not happened often. He can explain to Wauters what it's all about. "How do you suppose this all works, eh?" he asks.

Wauters throws his arms wide. "*Eish!* Who's to say. I'm only the fish bait here. They may confide in you but I am the outsider, not trusted, eh. Why should I be in on the plans, I'm only here to make up the numbers."

Plum giggles. Well, it was meant to be humorous, wasn't it? He recovers from his doubt, smiles flatly; Plum has something to say, he's been tutored. Where did he get all this from? He sidles up to his shipmate. "We're not going around showing the guns, are we? What would be the surprise in that? Who would be that foolish, attack a ship showing its ordnance? Look down the deck. How many guns can you see?" Wauters looks about him cursorily and shrugs. Plum is on his own territory and playful now.

"None you think? Except this one of course. We've got six guns, six of the buggers! We've got two twelve pounders, two six pounders and two three pounders, bit of over-kill really. Bit of a *'Dreadnought'*, eh?" Wauters gives another swift look about him. Look around and a small shrug. "Has it never occurred to you why the crew is so big?" Wauters raises an eyebrow. Let's the boy ramble on. Make him think we are 'besties' and that we are, like, joined at the hip. He needs to have confidence in me, I'll stick this out. Well, at least, it beats having your hands torn to shreds by scrap iron. "Most of us are for the guns, see. You don't need this many people to run a ship this size." There, he does know something. Wauters gives a 'yes, I see your point' sort of look. Plum is now in full flow. "Come the time and we just flip the lid off the housings and 'Bob's your uncle'. Bang! Job done. The gun at the bow is on springs would you believe, pull a lever and it pops-up, that's clever, isn't it? It can serve either port or starboard."

Wauters homes in. "Sounds a bit rich. You don't see any practice going on, how can you…you flip the canopy and…"

Plum is almost guilty of being dismissive, he may know this subject but how far do you go before you come-over as a smart arse know nothing? "What job in war doesn't carry a risk?"

He wants to put a fist in his mouth. A slight 'tell'. A pause. A split-second. He tries to right himself but only seems, in his own mind, to dig himself deeper. "We've got guns galore; what has the U Boat got? A peashooter by the con?

Even if we load a *stumer*, like a dud, we've got all the advantage." Wauters raises a finger, the finger of reason. Plum is not brainless, well, not completely, he mulls. He may not have knowledge, but in his own mind, he sees dangers. This know-nothing with just a sprinkling of intelligence, he's bound to try and make things palatable all round, something they can all swallow, make things into a normality that they all can share. "Play fair! What!" Plum heaves a sigh, "Yes, I'll be out here many a dark night going through the drill. We'll be in ace condition when we're called."

Wauters looks about him. "That's perhaps OK for you. What about others? There's nowhere to hide. So, what happens to the rest of us while you're playing shoot 'em-up?"

"You're not here," says Plum simplistically, enigmatically.

"OK, I'm not here. That feels better already." Wauters brings his arm up in front of his face and peers over the horizontal limb.

Plum suddenly remembers the captain's reservations about Wauters. What if he is a spy or whatever? But he can't stop himself. He can't believe that people could be so duplicitous. He is so nonchalant. "The gunners don't disembark, unless we have to abandon ship for real. You and the rest, you, are gone over the side in the boats, this boat for one. A ruse. You'd be way off, over the side by the time we open-up. At the signal 'abandon ship' and them that is not gunners take to the boats it's the *'Panic Party'*, that's everybody except guns. Lower the boats and you all get off, the ship's cleared for action, we're left on board, out of sight. Then, next, the *Battle Ensign* goes up when you're 'away' and the conditions are right. Old *pointy-head* is gobsmacked, his *hauber* well and truly pickled. We smack his arse!"

Wauters has lowered his arm. "Right, forgive me for being sceptical. But it seems to me a bit, how can I say, a bit less than perfect. How do you know this will work, this play acting?"

Plum's quickly retorts, "It's been done before. Like the *Penshurst*, remember?"

Wauters gives a knowing look. *"Penshurst?* Oh yes, 'plucky' *Penshurst*, a collection of disasters. The Welsh people or the Scotsmen, their bad workmanship. I remember. *Baas* Rolls' aeroplane." He mimics a plane crashing. "So, *they* know all about your ruse? It's been done before, like you say…so *everybody* knows? I bet when they see your…'party' leaving the ship they'll be in fits, they'll drop their sausages nearly. It's enough to make you spill your lager. Once they have the order to stop laughing, they have suffered enough of your play-acting, they sink you anyway."

The wind is a bit out of Plum's sails. "It's a risk…Fritz will not be in fits."

Wauters senses a win. "How do you work that out?"

"Because he has a tiny-tiny problem," says Plum, moving even closer to Wauters and taken to speaking in a near whisper. "He travels all this way to the South of Ireland, salutes '*Fastnet Light*'. His fuel is OK, his food, plenty of sausage for all. Some say that there are them, down there abouts, that victual them, from fishing boats, scuttlebutt. I bet it's been done, no proof mind you, scuttlebutt. Anyway, so food no problem."

Apart from a slight look of incomprehension Wauters is not involved with this claptrap, his mind wanders. Wauters looks in the general direction of Queenstown. "I don't feel any lack of friendship there. Apart from your experience, the old girl and her pebble throwing child, I'm amongst friends, I'm not British. So, what, you could get any of that stuff anywhere? I get the feeling I'm not liked. They think I'm German, your mates."

Plum dives in without his oxygen apparatus. "Yeah, but you're one of them, as good as. A foreigner, how could you understand?" Oh dear, and things had been going so well. Well, not so bad. Not so bad? Why couldn't matters done be positively 'so good'?

Wauters catches sight of his face framed in the confines of a windowpane. Having no narcissistic tendencies, the occasional glimpse of himself seems to deny his sensibilities and his disposition. That hairy apparition looks almost avuncular. A rubicund face interlaced with wiry black hair, large lips framing perfect white teeth, the deep green eyes viewed through a sun-glint squint. He looks away. He would prefer to be anonymous to work his disappointment and intolerance in his own way. He reflects on starting this episode of his life with a clean slate. But now, he has announced his Graymalkin, a killer, nagging malignity is becoming exposed and he finds himself slipping into the lives of others and haunted by what their understanding might be. This character here, Plum, he could make things hard for me. If I had been him, I would not have swallowed a hastily assembled tale concerning the fate of Vaughan. That *Kreef*, she has to know me. Vaughan was not so ignorant as to associate Wauters with his doings, but Wauters' presence was in the periphery. Even the tinned fruit could sink him. Even if the fact that Wauters took it from stores for the sheer pleasure of putting Vaughan in the Guardhouse, a dodge worth a snigger. Being sunk by tinned fruit. You could not make it up and all these years on the lookout for guns and machetes and the real threat to life was in the stores, in a tin! Wauters is in front of Plum. The man's jaws are very animated but against a background of the dogs, death and the *Kreef* he tunes-in and out of what is being said. The end game is less apparent now. What does that woman know? Plum, I'll play up to you. I'll maybe get an opportunity, you know? It is war and things happen in wars that you would not believe. Where are we up to Plum? Can't you just shut up?

"As I was saying, it's his ammunition that's the problem. He wants to stay on-station as long as he can. If he fires all his torpedoes-off, what then? Back to Bremen or Ostend or some such to re-arm. Torpedoes are big things, room for but a few? Away for his patrol for weeks, re-arming? No, he wants to put a slug in us. He wants to get really close and hammer us with his deck gun. It's like this, the birds." Plum flies off into some home spun philosophy. "Birds are a terrific design. Fly around the sky, like they do, marvellous, the envy of us all. But, where do they nest? Where do they feed? Down here. The cats know this, no wonder cats appear so idle they're used to waiting, it'll come, I don't have to go after it." He is short of a simile and is in danger of falling down a metaphoric hole. Give up Plum! Give up! He'll want away. He won't want to associate with you if, out of your nervousness and discomfort; you blabbering-on every time you meet. But no, he can't stop. A lifetime of being his own company tends towards the occupying of anyone that might chance to talk to him, seek his company, it's a disease of the lonely. He can't let them go when the alternative is to be condemned to solitary. "It's like women and their choice of blokes; they have to come down into our territory, our rules in the end. Brought down to earth by necessity. Bugger all that ribbon and lace palaver."

Wauters pretends a slight amusement just to simulate some sort of focus. "Well, I'll tell you what, *Piet Pompies* if *I* was paying for *this* message your advertisement would not encourage me to pay-up."

They walk the deck and Plum describes his ignorance about ordnance and other things. After gassing for so long, Plum, the affable and easy going Plum is running out of script. There are long silences. Wauters is eyeing the job he has to do that this interlude interrupted. "You know, there is as much canvas on this ship as there was on a barque. When the sailing ships ended, I think they transferred all the canvas here. Hatch covers, lifeboat covers, canvas buckets, awnings. The best tools on a steamship like this, 'needle and palm', like a throwback. By the time that you've put right all the slack rope work and the sparks from the funnel have done their damage, there'll be enough work for an army of shell-backs." Wauters, in his own mind thinks the needfulness of his employment will even be apparent to Plum and this is a good point of departure.

But Plum touches him on the arm, mindful that he might get a shock. "Wauters, I've got something to ask of you? You've sailed a lot, with your dad?"

No shock, it's just a jacket he was touching. In that laconic way he has, Wauters gives him his attention. "Sure, me and the Pops, yes, sure," Wauters drawls.

"You can say no if it doesn't appeal," says Plum.

"No!" comes the retort, quick as a flash from the other.

Plum is turned into a puppy. "I want you to teach me to sail."

Wauters looks at his shipmate askance. "No boat. Mine is in Holland, remember."

Plum signals no problem. "That's all right, I've looked into it. I can hire a little boat in town. Just a few hours. Out and about. The basics."

Wauters puts a heavy hand on Plum's shoulder. "A man, facing his end, suddenly decides he would like to sail? Curious, how odd. Not the first odd thing that's happened here, you'll understand. But odd in its own way. *Eish!* Perhaps you ought to be practicing first aid or swimming? Two skills of great importance *chommie*; things that might save your life or some other poor bastard's." In the brief second, he had to decide his action, the big man sees that there is a distraction value in agreeing to such a scheme.

"Never mind that." Plum is in danger of deep water. Why can't he be a bit more casual. "Sailing would be far better than sitting around playing *Derby Nine* or *cribbage*. Cricket in this weather is plain daft and besides I reckon you have no taste for the game anyway and you're certainly not one to play football, rugby, maybe. Besides, sailing, it's something you're good at."

Wauters removes his heavy hand. "And, you know this because?"

Plum suddenly feels a bit chilled and sticks his hands deep into his pockets. "You've been on the North Sea. I've been on the North Sea as well and I know that a shallow sea is a difficult sea. Lots of currents, tides, choppy. If you can handle that, well, you must have some skill."

Wauters ponders for a moment. "I'll think on it."

-oo0oo-

Daytime today in Queenstown is a quiet day. Collars-up on his jacket, Wauters wanders the streets, ostensibly looking at restaurants but it's that girl he seeks, what was her name, Carmen, the *Kreef*? After a while, he sees her. She's very shoddily dressed but her face is animated. A dog, which he assumes is hers, is sniffing at the crotch of a middle-aged woman that Carmen yes, it is Carmen, is talking to. He approaches her. Carmen is negotiating telling a lady's fortune. Wauters, unsubtly, buts in, he's not one to take turns. "Carmen? Is that your name?" Carmen is dressed in shapeless oddments, has a woollen shawl crossing her chest clasped together with a safety pin, looks unkempt, unwashed. "I want to speak with you."

The middle-aged woman talking to Carmen tries to elbow the interloper away. "Heh! Wait your turn you rude devil! Good Lord, the men today, what are they like?"

Carmen doesn't want trouble she places her hand gently on the irate woman's arm. "What, me?" she says, addressing Wauters. "Can't you see I'm kind of busy here." She is about to attempt reading the woman's palm. Carmen wants the money and the woman is in a rush. The older woman is not giving way.

"Hey, you! Shoo, you feckin' arse, yes, you! You don't frighten me you black devil." She pushes at him. "Don't come the ignorant with me I'll let you have it with my umbrella, yer big lug, I'm not afraid of you." She shakes the umbrella in his direction.

Carmen cautions her, "Madam, stop, this man could pull your skull out through your mouth by the looks of him".

Wauters looks at the woman earnestly. Anyone else talking to him like that is about that far from landing on their back, bruised. "Yes, I will go, straight. I'm sorry about that, butting-in. It's important." He dissembles gathering all his strength just to keep himself in check.

At a short distance away from this fractious group, there is a young man in working clothes who is caressing a short-bladed knife he has in his jacket pocket. He motions to Carmen, wordlessly asking if she needs help. She mimes no, a hand across her throat in a lateral motion and then carries the gesture on to push her hair back. "Sorry dear," she says to the woman and then addresses Wauters. "Important, you say? To who?"

"It's about the man, Vaughan." Does she know?

"Heh, yer big lump," says the woman. "Will you not take bugger-off as a hint?" Carmen hardly misses a beat. The middle-aged woman pushes her hand forward. Addresses the pair curtly. "I'm away from St Colman's." Turns back to Carmen and speaks in an altogether gentler tone. "We're paying an ecumenical visit, from Cork. After all that hell fire and damnation, I'm due a bit of light relief. I have to meet the girls in the café." then, more pointedly, looking at Wauters occasionally. "They'll be waiting for me. Do you want the business?" Again, but pleasantly. "I've heard it said that you give a good reading? They were here last year. What you said helped out, it did so."

Carmen is split between demands. "That's nice. Yes, of course. That's why I'm here. If you'll just let me finish with this feller. God is good but His purpose for us is not always that clear, don't you think?" She turns to Wauters. "*Finny's Bar* by Roche's Terrace. I don't know when I'll get there, but if you've a mind to wait. Now scoot, will yer!"

Wauters asks for the place name to be repeated. Carmen turns back to the woman. "Now dear, what is it? Would it be your health, the husband?"

The woman flaps a hand. "No. No, I want to know, should I keep off the g-gees? I have word of a good nag at Fairyhouse. Church says it might be the devil whispering in my ear. I need a bit of…confirmation, listen to me would you, and me confirmed."

Carmen turns to Wauters. "Yes, Mr, I'll see you with my brother at *Finny's*, later. Ask anybody, they'll tell you where *Finny's* is. Go on! Go on!"

Wauters turns away after giving a small nod to the woman. Carmen deals with her client. He sets off. Now he is conflicted as to why she agreed to see him. A stranger making such a request? Eventually, he comes to the bar. It looks unpromising, unkempt, dark. Perhaps it's a trap. A set-up. Her and her brother? He sits at a table a bit out of the way from the others, his back to the wall. Time passes slowly. He has toyed with the idea of going; another day perhaps? A dog barks and Carmen walks into the room, walks up to Wauters. Meanwhile the girl's brother has peeled-off, hangs about at a distance. Yes, she knows Wauters by sight and by reputation. She is of the street and alert to any interlopers. He is a friend of Vaughan. Vaughan who having been given his just desserts has stayed away, and good riddance too. Just another one of those chancers wanting favours. There's no love lost.

"Can I buy you a drink? The dog?" asks Wauters.

Carmen is a bit discommoded. "Yes, you bloody can and you can get the *phral*" – She gestures to the man at the back of the room about him having a drink – "one for him as well, while you're up there. He'll have a pint of best or whatever's in the pump. Cider, a half of cider for me. I think the dog'll pass, heh Rollo?" Rollo looks at her with the dog smile, mouth a little open, the pink gums shading to brown, nose burrowing, wide-eyed searching, following his nose; evidently unsure as to what is being asked of him. He follows his mistresses' eyes waiting for a clue, nose still scanning in small sweeps. Wauters goes to the bar and orders the drinks. He gets jostled a bit with no apology but refrains from saying anything, this is like a dock front dive, there'll be a shot gun behind the bar or a baseball bat, maybe a wooden stake with a nail in the end like the Bully Mates used to have for their 'bats'. Especially a few of them on the Tea Clippers, where time was serious money and ten shillings a chest bonus on the first cargo to dock, worth an effort. The questionable character, the brother, approaches him and takes his drink. Nods cheekily and walks off. The other drinks are placed on the table, his tot and her cider. The girl pays him little attention, is patting the dog. "What do you want, mush? There's a bit of a crowd today for St Colman's, it's always good for business. I need to be back."

"It's about Vaughan." Wauters leans over the table, whispers. "I take it that as you've bothered to come you have what, some curiosity?"

Her eyes go up to heaven, she screws her face up, as in, 'not that one again'. I gathered that. "What's your pitch? What's he said, the lying bugger. He didn't get anywhere and neither will you. Whatever he said is all lies. I can only think he's learned his lesson. He's keeping a low profile, not seen him around for days."

"I don't know how to put this," Wauters continues quietly, reverently.

Carmen lifts her glass. "Spit it out, man, me drinks evaporating." She motions to the glass.

He puts on a face. "He's dead. He was shot, the other night, at the camp. Killed. I thought you would need to know."

She reacts but barely perceptibly, you would have to know her to have seen it. She looks out the corner of her eye, head tilted to one side. "And? Are, you what? Taking the hat 'round? Well, there you go." Wauters continues to look at her expectantly. She looks back at him defensively. "You're not saying me and Rollo had a hand in it are you?" She sits back, a look of exasperation on her face. She has good features, he thinks, as an unwanted intrusion in his processing. She has an air. She's not grimed but she certainly isn't clean and she has a whiff with her too. But there was that story that Napoleon asked his misses to promise not to wash before he came home from campaigning. Wauters wants to think the worst of her but she has a power now and there is no telling how she would use it. She could drop him right in the 'cack' should she have a mind. Apart from mentioning that she would quite like some tinned peaches if they could be got, she has no mark against her. "We barely knew him." She addresses the dog. "What you been up to Rollo behind me back? Mullering folks, is it?"

Wauters comes too, picks up his shot glass, thinks and then sets it down again. This is not what he expected but then again. He failed to read her not being staggered by the news and him so perceptive by trade. Her wondering if this lump next to her is going to put the arm on her, if not the law. She had led an…odd sort of life but despite the rumours attached to her tribe, she is a good Catholic girl and had never stolen anything. She's mullered the odd chicken for the table, but chickens, do they really expect anything better? They never have a food worry that would attach to many another sort of bird for a start and they are too stupid not to live away from our protection. Some life instead of no life. How did that man die? Could she have been in the vicinity? She takes a good swig of her drink. Is he going to use this to try and squeeze me arse, filthy beggar, like all his lot, men!

"I seem to have…got it wrong. I thought you were sweet on him, perhaps. Have I misjudged something?"

She needs to buy time. What do the cops say, anything that you say may be used ag'in yer? In that first flush of being found out, the reaction is to gush. Nobody likes being found out. She is mindful of how it happens and is not about to cough-up to something that's nothing of her. "Yes, my foreign friend. I have no responsibility for him or his fancies. I'll be honest with you…" A quick aside. "You're not the police!" Wauters shakes his head. "All he was to me was…" She turns aside. She has to say this unequivocally and minutely, not too much to remember afterwards that might not tally. She approaches it like somebody on a tight rope. "…that he offered, promised, me some tinned peaches. I didn't ask why, why would I? He offered. It was his bidding. A nice gesture, you would think. Anything else?"

Rollo walks around the table and inspects Wauters, staring into the man's eyes, examining his inner consciousness. Wauters does not like animals, especially dogs. They carry rabies, don't they? You see rabies abroad and what it can do to a man, never mind malaria, whooping cough, pox. The dog seems to sense the antipathy and backs away before wandering off around the bar and reacquainting himself with the bar's regulars who, for some odd reason, like dogs in any bar, bistro or pub, always illicit the soppiest talk and a good stroke from even the toughest of toughs. "So, who *are* you anyway? You're definitely not from around here. Let me guess. From the Continent?"

"Between ourselves" – he looks around the room and then whispers to her – "I'm from elsewhere." She gives him a look that says what is that supposed to mean, which prompts him to say more. "I'm Dutch. I'm not British. I'm not one of them, do you understand."

She claps her hands on her thighs. "Oh, look at you, so you've told me now and spoiled it all. I was going to read your palm and tell you who you are. You've spoiled the game. There you go. Many more like you and I'll be broke."

"Palm reading?" he suggests disparagingly. "Is that what you do? That's junk, isn't it?"

She pushes at him. "Mind yourself. How rude." She is acting deeply offended, pulls her shawl more tightly around herself. If ever you could be placed in the company of someone and be seeking a way to have a rapport, watch here. Wauters sees the signs of her relaxing and finding amusement in his talk not threat. Her body is no longer rigid and she has an inclination to smile, riley. She has never come across anyone as practised or restrained as Wauters before. She has no idea what she's up against. A lifetime of reading what people want to hear, in their manner, is good business. "Who are you? You push yourself on me, tell me your precious little secret, for what it's worth, and then call me skill shit! That's not a bad record for half an hour or so. I wonder where else this is going to go?" She claps her hands on her thighs and gives a small squeak, the tail end of a shriek.

"You should be telling me shouldn't you," says Wauters confidentially, recovering quickly from his initial timidity but reading her signs.

She looks at him sternly, long and hard. "Ha-bloody-ha! That Vaughan." She gathers herself. "He said he would get me some bloody peaches, God knows why, forgive me Father for blaspheming. I think it was him getting his foot in the door, and I was foolish enough to say yes." She crosses herself. "I just wanted rid of him. But fruit is in short supply; it never goes amiss. Yes, I met him I shouldn't a done really. I met him to get the peaches, they're like gold. Nothing else." She points a stern finger at the big man, assertively. "The thought of them peaches burnt into my soul like original sin. I hated myself for me guilt. We met out by our camp; he tried stuff, so, I punched him in the kisser. Floored him." She is suddenly afraid that that was the cause of his dying. "I can't believe that would have killed him though, I'm hardly a slugger. Then we ran off, me and Rollo. That's all I had to do with him. I punched him; I didn't shoot the bugger; he was still crawling when I left him." She knocks her drink back in one big gulp. "What are you men like? You see how I am? Do you see how I am dressed? Those bastards. I swear if I wore a turd on a string around my neck, they'd still try it on. I've tried dirty clothes, that just made them come on stronger, a bit of rough. Oh yes, it's written all over their faces. I am on my pipe smoking, in me dirty routine, picking-up the dog's doings, now, does that put 'em off? Not them and not even the flies." She looks away from Wauters' seeking a distraction. The brother, that Wauters bought the drink for, is waving an empty glass. "The *phral*, you bought that the drink for?" She points her glass at the brother. "He has to stand guard on me to stop the buggers from pawing me in the bloody street. He's an idle sod, thankfully so, it suits us both. He's got the time. By the way, I think his glass is empty. Now there's a thing, mine is too."

Wauters gets the drinks. He returns to Carmen. She picks her theme up again. And she was the one that was going to be cautious, but she doesn't normally drink that fast and the effect is to make her loquacious. "That Vaughan; he thought he was a *masher*. What did he take me for? I'm certainly not about selling me'self for a couple of tins of fruit, government rations at that, courtesy of his friend, *you*. Yes, I know *your* part. I'm worth more than that. My poor dead husband would turn in his grave if he could see me here as I am." She sighs and crosses herself in the Christian way again. "Holy Mary mother of God. How did you get here, what's your name?" He holds his palm towards her as if offering it for a reading and she pushes it away as if disgusted with his joke.

"Wauters," he announces.

"That's it. I remember now! Wauters. I knew it was a stupid name. So that's what people are called in Dutch land? Oh well, it takes all sorts. OK. So, Mr…Wauters? What brings you here?"

"*Eish!* Working for the British. Our people, we've come to help, to fight the common foe, it's said. My country is neutral but the British, they must be running short of people, they, like, 'pressed me'. I'm a sailor by trade."

"The hell you are," she shouts to her brother. "He's a sailor!" The brother holds his glass in recognition. "He likes to be kept informed. Here's me, one of 'the walking people' and there's you, a sailor. A man of the world? We both ply a lonely trade. You wouldn't want some lucky heather, would you?" She 'pats' herself down. "Shit, I've not got any on me. Travelling the world, eh?"

"Not all the world," he qualifies, "but the Indian Ocean, South China Sea, yes. In big sailing ships. Many, big, sailing ships."

She picks-up the theme. "In all sorts of weather, I bet; by the way, this is me making conversation, if I had known you, I would never have liked you, but I'll make an effort. Seas as high as mountains." She throws her arms up. "Fabulous sea monsters." She turns the hand of a sinuous arm into a snapping animal. "I can give an account on any subject. You just make it up, a good game, eh?"

Wauters sort of smiles. "You're taking the piss?" He looks to his feet.

Carmen is unrelenting. "Putting a port and lemon into every girl?" She's jolly with the company. "Sorry, I'm getting carried away. I don't usually drink cider. I don't know why…"

He leads her on. "*Eish!* Yes! Monsoons, storms. Waves tall as a house, not quite mountain high. Water spouts, like wet tornadoes…"

She takes up his drift. "Sea monsters?"

Wauters takes a sip of his drink. "Not so much." She's showing curiosity now. "That's the western Pacific or Greenland I hear tell, *Kraken*."

"That's a pity," says Carmen. "I thought those exotic places were filled with natural wonders, like in the funny papers."

He looks into his glass. "Some, yes. Huge birds, Albatrosses. You see whales, out and about. Whale Sharks, but they're big harmless fish. Back in the eighties there was a big volcano exploded by Sumatra and some of the dead drifted right across the Indian Ocean to S.A. Came over on great rafts of pumice, volcano spit. There's a lot of volcanos out there, perhaps they make the place so hot, as hot as it is. There was some talk, the pearl divers, spoke of giant squids and octopus…"

"Rollo would chase octo-pussies" she teases.

The last comment passes-over Wauters' head. "But we…always thought that they told such tales to keep people away from certain 'beds' they were keeping for themselves. There were sea-going crocs, big as a teak tree. They have big birds in South Africa, stand as tall as a man. Have you ever seen an ostrich?"

Carmen is taking an interest. "Give over. What sort of egg would a bird that size lay? You'd need an egg bucket not a cup." She sips her cider. "So, don't tell me *you* dipped for pearls, *you*, dived for pearls! That's exotic." He nods in the affirmative. "Why don't we find pearls in oysters around here? I feel sure we've got oysters here abouts, I know we have." She points towards the great bay, out there.

Wauters holds his hands twelve inches apart or so. "These are a special type of oyster, the *Gold Lipped* sort. They grow to the size of dinner plates."

"To think, the amount of flesh in one of them! Must be the size of beefsteaks! They could feed a number I bet, be more valuable than the jewels." She marvels.

"The flesh is not for eating; it was thrown over the side." They're not good eating at all. Then there's the nacre, the mother of pearl, the shells, that's worth a bit if you get to them before the file fish and the star fish have had at them." He looks reflective for a moment. "But, like all things, you think you've got something good and then."

"Uh huh, how's that then?" she enquires. She's hooked on his tales and his lucid communication.

"The Orientals came in, dredging. *Shark Bay* to start. Covered the grounds in silt, interrupted the oysters spawning. Killed-off a lot of coral. Why can't people be satisfied? Let things be?"

She says with a smile, "Where was it that you did all this, you sodding little liar?"

He holds his hands up to his chest palms outwards. "True. North Australia, off Queensland. Well, all along that coast, across to *Broome*. But best by *Thursday Island*. But all along that coast by *Milingimbi, Darwin*…the *Gulf of Carpentaria,* around there."

"How long would it take me to travel there, Wauters?" She looks into the middle distance trying to picture what the place might be like. "Like Paradise. I can picture it. I bet the water is blue and warm and the sun shines every day. Apart from that, apart from being beautiful and warm, I bet it's a bit like here, on a dull day could be anywhere." She wants to know more. He has triggered-off her age-old thing about lack, ignorance and not knowing how to go about redressing it.

"No joking," he submits. "It's glorious every day, yeah. You could get to *Thursday Island,* from here, in a clipper in about, what, eighty days, ninety. It's a long way."

"All that talk of sun and sea water has made me quite parched." She smiles. "Shall we have the same again? *Kushti*!"

Wauters digs into his pockets. "I'm running out of money," he opines.

"Just one more, then we'll all have to be going soon anyway. There's Colman's and all that lovely Cork money floating around."

She beckons to her brother. "I've got to get back to *Colman's* with me sympathy bait, me starving dog. He'll have a pint, the brother, not the dog!"

As soon as she makes eye contact with the dog, the animal stands up with his forefeet on her thigh and wags its tail. Wauters goes to the bar and gets the drinks in. Carmen looks at him and taps her fingers on the table looking pensive. Wauters comes to the table with drinks, returns to the bar and comes back with an ashtray of water for Rollo which the dog laps-up. My goodness she thinks, that was a crafty gesture getting to me by way of the dog. I wouldn't say no to seeing you again. Shut up girl and make do. As he sits after fetching the drinks, she asks coyly, "I don't suppose you've any pearls left over?"

He claps a hand on the table. "Not so much as a blister pearl, a skimmer or a baroque. You have to know that these places are more remote than you can imagine, nothing to do but work and drink. You couldn't save if you wanted to, unless you're Japanese, they know how. You work and get drunk. They even check you all over before you leave the dive, and I mean all over, all. Even if you did manage to secrete some, the market is all sewn-up. You would have to go to Paris to sell them, that's where the market is, and they only deal with agents. They want verification on any sale."

Chapter 7

Always cold these days. The brisk wind shaves your cheeks like nature's depilatory. The harbour waters are choppy and the seagulls seem ill-disposed to be taking to the waters. The water by the quay is a miscellany of flotsam both natural and domestic. It is a testy Wauters with Plum, together by the quay. It is cold enough for little tears to form in the corner of the eye. Plum checks a piece of paper and looks about him. They stroll on looking at the boats. Plum checks the paper again. Wauters hopes that the craft's is not here. What would it take for a rogue to promise something like a boat that did not exist? "That's it, there!" Plum shouts excitedly. This is the real start of the adventure for Plum, it is no longer tomorrow, nebulous, purely imagined, the time and place have a date. A mystery is being solved. This is where the dream begins, where all that imagination coalesces. They stand by the boat as it bobs quickly at its mooring, the tide, the wind, first pulling the painter tight and then relaxing it. Plum casts an eye over it. He looks glum, disappointed. "It's a bit small," he observes upon scrutinising the craft.

Wauters' face says, so what. "Same difference. Are you sure you want to go through with this?"

No turning back now. The boat looks barely sea worthy but to Plum it is like a first-born covered in caseosa, unappealing at first sight, but. The craft is of a caravel construction. There is a single spanker bound poorly to a boom, not the neat harbour furl that Wauters knew of old. But if you can sail Jury Rig then you have mastered your art. Inside the craft, fish scales strewn like confetti. In summer, this vessel would have stunk to high heaven more like 'rubby-dubby', shark bait, but in this freeze the smell is suppressed. Perhaps, once upon a time, the skiff would have had a foresail but no elements of its employment are visible now. Plum surveyed his first command with the quiet pleasure, the inner glow of a new parent. "I'm keen, yes. I've paid-up now."

Nothing is easy for Plum. Right from the bit about casting off. Everything he attempts is cack-handed. Wauters climbed aboard and asks Plum to release the painter, which he does, throwing the rope aboard. In the intervening period between untying and boarding, the boat swings out a little from its mooring leaving a gap of nearly two yards of water. Urgently, Plum makes a leap for it but falls slightly short. His legs are in the water and his arms draped over the gunwales. Wauters make no move to right the man's dilemma and Plum has to wrestle with limbs made heavy by the drenching to heave himself aboard. "Wow!" says Plum at his most diplomatic. "I almost didn't make it."

Wauters gives a small shrug. "You would have us both in the drink. Hang on to the painter next time." Wauters is miserable and doubtful about the whole exercise. But despite his need to grumble and throw his weight about he thinks that he must not give Plum cause to dislike him, cause unnecessary friction. A man too derided might give him up. They get under way and spend some time with the wind from aft so that Plum can get the feeling of it all. But eventually, they have to tack back. Wauters explains the rhythm of the manoeuvre, tries to emphasise the flow of actions that will bring the boat around and hopefully, prevent it from stalling. "Imagine a bar of soap on the bathroom floor," he tells Plum, you stand on it and it shoots off along the line of least resistance. Yes. Plum is teeth-chatteringly with him. This is a how the boat moves against the wind, this is how it tacks. The whole thing sounds like patting your head while rubbing your tummy at the same time. Everything is about synchronisation. Plum is not a natural. From getting his foot caught up in the main sheet and being taken from his feet, to being pulled around by the boom as he attempts a tack, to taking a smack around the head from the boom itself as they go about. Plum has a torrid time, constantly assured by Wauters on the tiller that it is all good practice and will make the actions sink in. The lesson is a necessarily short one. Apart from being wet through from the dousing he took at the start Plum has been clouted by the boom on a couple of occasions causing more harm to his head than the dozens of boxing bouts he has participated in. "I forgot to ask you, can swim, can't you?" Wauters asks, suppressing a smile.

Plum is concentrating really intensely. "A bit. Don't worry about me" Plum occasionally breaks into song. He sings snatches of *'You made me love you'*, *'When Irish eyes are smiling'*, *'I'm on my way to Mandalay'*, although on the sustained notes he finds it hard not to put in a little bit of uncontrolled vibrato brought about by the fact that his core temperature being down is inducing him to shiver.

> *"All night long, by the sea, by the sea, by the sea,*
> *her love song Rings for me, rings for me, rings for me,*
> *All the world will seem just a lovely dream,*
> *And I'll never stray far from Mandalay,*
> *I'll live for one who lives alone for me in days to be."*

Eventually, the light starts to fade and they take the boat back to the mooring with Wauters manoeuvring it. They get out of the boat. Plum is blue and convulsing. His voice trembles as he speaks, "That was really exciting. I think I've got the hang of it. I think I've got sailing in my blood."

"After that? You've certainly got a lot of sea in your stomach. But you have to start somewhere," says Wauters.

He has little control over his whole body by now. But he is elated. "I think next time I'll be up to the mark. That was worth a *Bradbury* of anybody's money. I'm clemmed-deeth. I'll wear something warmer next time. You forget how cold it can be in the waves." They stand by the boat and Plum, though dead cold to the core, feels a sense of accomplishment. "You did very well, my old mate," Plum tells Wauters. "You never forget, eh? According to cocker, we go on sea trial next week. We'll have to cram as much practice in as we can."

Wauters looks ahead. "I might have my own plans, *crunchie.*"

"No," replies Plum. "You have to get your priorities right."

"Sharp!" retorts Wauters, the balance in his head tipping this way, then that.

"I think I've had this dream, *this* very thing. I've done all this, just like this, before," says Plum.

Wauters frowns. "What did I tell you? Keep off the cheese," he drawls.

Plum squeezes some water out of his jacket. "It's frightening what your mind can do to you. What it gets up to without any reference to you."

"Perhaps you're *Bosbefok*, like shell shocked? That sinking you suffered?"

Plum concurs as if that is a new perception. "That's it. I think you've got it! The explosions have reset my brain and what were straight thoughts once are all thrown up in the air, have come down and reconnected to the wrong things. You hear about people taking a knock, waking up and they can talk foreign, like from nowhere."

Wauters is getting a bit tetchy. A wasted afternoon for him and this man and his endless wittering. "It doesn't do to have a fuddled head when you're sailing, you could put yourself on a shoal that way, put yourself aground, get the sails flapping in a big sea, nice start to a sinking. Get you your head straight. Enough of dreams *Jou blikseme*!" he says vehemently. Wauters had so much fun putting Plum through it in the name of friendship. He could have done so much more to make the sail more comfortable and instructive but the punishment that Plum took was hidden behind good intentions, or so it looked. You have to get your fun where you can and your revenge when the opportunity arises.

-oo0oo-

In town, the drizzle has emptied the streets. The pavements shine like shellac and the empty space of road, cobbles and pavements are filled with reflected lights from a myriad sources. Wauters has his reefer jacket pulled up tight. He is watching Carmen from a distance. But she has seen him. Being on the streets anything different stands-out immediately. After a while, she turns and walks towards him. Rollo recognises him and after a nose tap on the man's leg, the dog steps aside, sits down to lick his bits, sniff the wall and shake the wet from his coat. Wauters moves on slowly. She catches up with him. Carmen is dressed noticeably more tidily. Whisps of hair protrude from under her headscarf. She even looks cleaner. The cold in the air lends tone to her skin and the mist of rain in the locks straggling out from under the scarf are garlanded with tiny globular decoration, lending her face a soft focus. She smiles at him, a gesture that had escaped her after the tragedy that she had endured, the loss of her partner and the reality of street trading with its coarse people and its demands for value for money. "Hey, you, sailor. Wauters, where are you off?" Rollo seems to be sanctioned by the greeting and, reinvigorated, sniffs about Wauters' legs again just to catalogue the scent; the hound looks up at him with that dog smile and lolling tongue. "Where are you running off too? I've been watching you. Well, you're a bit obvious, stick out like a sore thumb in this neighbourhood, yer big lump. I wonder that the carts don't reroute to get around yer, like road closed."

Wauters pushes his wet hair back and the wipes his wet hand on his jacket. "I just had an hour. I thought I'd take in the scene. Go for a stroll. Well, now you're here…would you like a coffee or something?" he suggests, pointing the way onwards. He urges her to follow as he takes off down the street.

Occasionally, he turns to ensure she is keeping up, but she is almost on his elbow, smiling broadly now at the incongruity of her situation, feeling part of something. A little…excited at something stimulating, different.

Wauters talks of himself, "I think I'm a novelty. I get a better response than them from over the waters. They seem to think I'm German or summat. They seem to like my voice. Keep on asking me to repeat stuff."

"Sorry, what did you say?" She smiles at her little joke, laughs in a way that was of her girl time, unheard in recent years. She wants to link his arm but refrains, that's for him to start that sort of stuff. "Welcome to civilisation. Yes, well, I'm freezing me bum off out here. There's hardly any bugger about," she chides lightly.

Wauters catches the mood but must be objective he is not in the first bloom of romance or even trying to cement a relationship. If he reassures her and cosies-up she will find that she can't shop him, cause him problems. With Plum mollified and her tended there is the question of his losing control. He'll figure it. He always does. "There's a café just along the way that my mate and me went to. What would you think of a hot cup of tea, would you like a hot cup or something?"

She pulls at him causing him to come to a halt. "Is that wise? I am a gypsy, remember. Would they let the dog in? Come to think of it, they might let the dog in and not me. You don't think we should go to the bar because we like it, do you? It's the only one that lets us in."

"The *Brown Café*?" queries Wauters. "I've been in worse, a lot worse. No, we are going to this café down here. I like it." She adjusts her scarf and takes a quick look at herself in a shop window. "There we are then. Tea cake and a cup of hot coffee."

"Not if it's like the coffee at home," she says, adding, "tea, if you don't mind! Are you sure?"

He grabs her by the elbow and pulls her along.

"I'm coming! Leave go!" she yelps excitedly. Rollo barks repeatedly and his tail thrashes about. He dances with both front legs raised like those old pictures of horses before it was found how they really moved. The scene is one of controlled, measured joy teetering on a thrill.

Inside the café, it is warm, thankfully. There is a quiet thrum of conversation. She has looked sheepish as they entered. Even the dog was reluctant to enter. She is nervous when the old lady comes to offer them a table to sit. She might be about to ask her to leave so she looks away. The old lady ignores her, pays her no special attention. Wauters chatters with the woman about being there before, goes on about the teacakes. They are led to a table; Rollo sits under it. Even he is a bit sheepish, 'doggish'. In the bar, he would do the rounds and let the crowd love him, 'Yes, it's me Rollo, sea king, loved by all his subjects. Here, no. They place their order. The old girl asks about the dog's name and everybody, even the dog, relaxes.'

Carmen looks after the retreating waitress. "Now, isn't this nice. All the time I've been around this place and I've never stepped across the threshold here. Table cloth. Nice and clean. This must be like all the other folk must feel. I've been through me tugs" She pulls at her clothes. "This is the only thing that wasn't 'off'. She stops and ponders looking unfocused to the near distance. My brother would think me a right divvy doing this." She leans over confidentially. "We've never been...encouraged to mix with this lot. They make it known they're not too happy with us *knackers,* at the drop of a hat. That's what they call us, *knackers*, that's nice, isn't it?"

"You're as good as any other," he confides, ingratiating himself artfully.

The food and drink are brought to the table and the old girl gives Carmen a little, but genuine, smile. Carmen is thrilled by the gesture. "Did you see that, for goodness' sake? The owd girl? Must be blind or daft. She smiled at me...Nice looking teacake". She looks at him urgently, insistently. "I suppose it's different for men, you can get things done with your snarling." She puts three teaspoons of sugar in her tea. Wrinkles her nose at Wauters. "Well, it's paid for, isn't it?"

The old girl comes back with a bowl of water for Rollo. And so, they sit there having little regard for the big steamed-up window at the front of the café, they are encapsulated; not heeding the quiet chatter from humble folk around them. Carmen's feet snug under Rollo's coat, him sprawled luxuriously only minding to open an eye when someone passes or a morsal of teacake comes down from the table.

Early evening and the shop lights are glowing in the dusky light, waste paper trying to lift its sodden limpness from the ground when worried by the gusts of wind, like, in another horrid way, a creature with its legs mown down trying to rise. Lifting and flopping back, as the waves in the bay and the solitary flag on the town hall. The anthropomorphised detritus of a newly activated mind, like the sun switching on for the first time out of the once impenetrable useless dark. Everything seems to have submitted to the cold wet and its mean dispiritedness.

Wauters and Carmen walk along side by side. She feels warm enough to remove her scarf, would do except that her hair will frizz-up if she does in this damp. Why does she care about such things now? She stops occasionally to look into shop windows. She has a great new sense of freedom, of herself. Wauters has the dog by a string lead now as they have grown tired of fetching him from side streets which he has a needful desire to investigate…

"*Dat was lekker?*" he says in a growl of a voice.

She imitates his gruff voice. "Dat vas lacquer, whatever that is, he-he. If I'm being truthful, the cake was a bit on the small side. I didn't like to say."

"You could have had another," says Wauters defensively.

"No, that was nice." She is not criticising such a wonderful gift but you can so easily adjust to the new reality, apparently. There was no criticism. "Just to say if I was running the place, I would make the portions bigger."

Wauters is content. They walk on. Apropos nothing, he floats a thought. "I tell you, a woman's company makes all the difference; it civilises you. Everything tastes different even. You want to be correct, use the right manners. Poncing about has a lot going for it."

She looks up to him. "And I'm on my best behaviour. It cuts both ways."

"No problems," he says. He pauses, stops.

"Did I do wrong?" She ventures. "I found myself copying them others". She nods her head towards the hinterland. "Back home if the food gets as far as the table there's a fight. It's all fists and elbows."

He is trying to not be drawn-in. Doesn't want to know. You can know too much, it's happened. One minute you're an observer and the next you're in the picture. They walk on a way. She continues occasionally looking into shop windows. She takes her scarf off and starts messing with her hair which then blows about by the wind. It seems an unequal battle. She puts her scarf on again. "There's not much in the shops," she says.

He turns to her as they are walking. "So, has anybody asked you about Vaughan?"

She screws her face up. "For goodness's sake, stop going on! Let it go, will yer! Look, I'm sorry for him and I'm not. But give it a rest." They walk on again when, suddenly, she stands away from him. "Now look, well, here's a thing. I have a confession. Ronan and me, the *phral*? We played you, at *Finny's*, the bar? It's a habit like, street nous and habit, a mix. I owe you. I know exactly how much you spent on us to the farthing. I'm in the chair next time. My treat."

He pats her on the head. "I don't think that keeping an account is the way that friendship works. You don't count cost. I spend like a sailor, when it's gone, I get some more. Anyway, my shipmates put up the cash. A good lesson for you. Don't steal a lot from one, take a bit from the many. It's a bit time consuming but they don't miss the change."

"I don't know when you're joking," she says warily. "A charity case. They must have taken to you."

He smiles thinly. He has stolen the money. He stole the peaches. There is nothing he would not lift given an opportunity and a requirement. He has no qualms, which makes him a brilliant thief. The more looking around you do when lifting stuff, the more noticeable you become. Being purposeful and quick is the way and that is Wauters to a tee.

She carries on. "Anyway, not in my Vardo you don't. I'll keep my own end up, if you don't mind, without any bloody reference to yous." She smiles and they walk on. Some people that pass nod to them and she takes to smiling back, that's new. A mother and child approach and the child goes to pat Rollo, the dog growls. The two walk away briskly. "Rollo! Bad dog! That's not like you. Rollo was a sea king, you know. He was full of grace, you can't just walk up to him and pat him, you have to be introduced," she says loudly for the benefit of the other people. Rollo wags his tail. She wracks her brain for something to say wanting to contribute to the conversation. "What a dreadful dog you turned out to be." She looks to Wauters. "And you. Dat vas lacquer, ha-ha!"

"Keep trying. You'll get it right one day," he chides.

They continue their walk largely in silence. "Why do you call me Carmen? That's not my name."

"Isn't it! I don't know. I was led to believe, I suppose, all gypsy girls are called Carmen. A bit of *skinner*, gossip, I guess. I just inherited it somehow. O.K., so, put me right. What is your name?"

"I'll tell you if you promise not to laugh" She waits for qualification which does not come. "I was christened Brianna, 'honourable and noble'. Don't you dare feckin' laugh. I shouldn't have told you." She looks away, then casts her eyes down "They might as well have called me carthorse; it would be more fitting, especially from what is expected of me in life. But if you call me by that name, I'll cut yer bits off!"

He weighs it. "But it's such a romantic sounding name."

"Oh, yes?" she scoffs. "Is that what you think? The threat stands. You knew me as Carmen and Carmen it shall be. Brianna indeed. If I was Brianna, I would be some bugger else, wouldn't I now? Probably have a moustache and bowed legs, or a squint; wear frilly collars and prefer wearing brown. It could have been worse. I only just escaped being called Brighid, rhymes with idjut. A good name for a nun. Sister Brighid, maybe. I'm no nun. You haven't asked, and I don't know why I'm considering it even. Let's sit down over here."

"Aren't you cold?" he asks more matter-of-fact than solicitous. He feels the chill for sure.

The evening has closed in around them. "Cold, me? I was born to the streets. Here, sit yourself. Lie Rollo, down! My name is Carmen and I'm one of the *walking people*, a traveller. I'm twenty-nine, she lied easily, going on forty and feel a hundred and two. I was married to a man called Cornelius, Corny, a lovely man" – she speaks behind her hand – "a lot of the time." Resumes speaking directly. "I was a good girl before when I met him, and had to be, it's our way. And after he went. It's very hard in our lives for a widow, you…lose your…attraction. He was good worker, strong, with just a little temper. He died, poor chap, in his thirty-eighth year, kicked in the head by his favourite stallion, would you credit that? Two strong characters coming together. There's something quite poetic about that. I'm as rough as a bear's arse. The most unloyal person you could ever wish to meet. I'm crafty see. If you saw me fishing off the quay, you'd want to disown me; it's not a thing lady's do, so they say. Me and me pipe, smoking. But it suits me. I'm a little liar and he that believes me deserves to be done. My mammy says I'll come to no good. But mammy's all say that don't they, to shut yers up. *Dukkerin*" – she picks his hand up and drops it again – "and the heather in me *skip,*" she picks up her basket and drops it – "is the only thing I'm good for. And now, you. I don't believe in messing about; you are an old man. You must be forty-odd at least. I bet you've seen it all in them far-away places with their water spouts and crocodiles. I'll tell you, no word of a lie, you got me thinking. I like the way you handle yourself. You are generous, to a fault; you hold yourself well, for an olden and I think there is a bit of the *knacker* in you. But you kid me something rotten; you've got me down as a *divvy.*" She looks away wistfully, closes her hand until the nails dig in. "I want to know stuff like you know, for myself. I want to be my own person and hold me head up, not live like a mouse. Just to walk around the town and not be looked down on, it's a lovely feeling. You can be drugged into thinking this is all there is, the tealeaves and all. I find it sits well when people treat you like some bugger. You seem to like me." She quickly follows up. "As long as we can be friends, we'll be good company. No funny stuff. Make a play for me and I'll kick your bollocks-in and set the family on yer. But I can, well, at this moment, I can tolerate you." She lies at every turn. Her feelings run deep and already she thinks, not in Gypsy terms, but of a soulmate, provider, helpmate and protector, lover, father?

He nods. "They say that like-sorts don't attract, us two, outsiders. I would hate to think that's the case here."

She grizzles at him but not understanding the onionskin nature of Wauters she is bound to betray herself, her excitement and nascent contentment configuration, at every turn. She should put a gag in her mouth. She is not used to love games; she has never been involved in them. She is always leading and not qualifying his approaches. She forces the pace, which with anyone other than this man, could lead to thoughts of her being 'easy' rather than proper, straight, as she is. He is consumed with putting her at her ease. Not giving her any cause to ponder on Vaughan's fate and him. He is on a narrow course and mindful of rip tides and shoals. Wauters can wait you out. She mistakes his lack of warmth or encouragement, for gentlemanly behaviour. Is reassured by his disinclination to clinch or grope. He stands off and gives her space, He stands away and feeds her a rope which she could be in danger of hanging herself on; it all speaks to her of an equality she has not known. She has a feeling for how she could be equal if life was only truth, conversation and opinion that meets with respect. There is no tomorrow here and no wish for it; it's all about the day. She luxuriates in her new attractiveness and the encouragement it invokes. He waits to find what she knows and cannot precipitate her into initiatives which might end up examining his absurd corruption. "The best you can say for me is that I put on a good show." She adds, "I'll take your terms now and you can walk me back to me pitch and then go your way." They stand up and she measures her height against his. She jumps up to make up the difference which causes Rollo to be disturbed, wondering what's going on. "You are a big lump aren't yer." They walk on. "I bet you're as tall as *Big Frank*. Big Frank, seven foot eight, he was. How tall is that? They say he used to have to duck through doors, was in danger of snapping like celery in a wind."

-ooOoo-

The sailing boat is in its usual place. A sort of normality that provokes contentment in Plum but which miffs Wauters. Poor Wauters, he did have a passion but spent it all on one throw. He shakes his mind and moves on. One thing less to worry about. In a world that's raging, and in raging young bodies, this is something to hold onto. A bit of flotsam amongst the swift moving tide. Just a few bits of wood, rope and canvas become sanctuary and hope for one while undefinable bitterness for t'other. Yet, for another, an irksome, uncalled for trial that he has put himself in for with no quid pro quo. What a price to pay. Perhaps he should take the ultimate play, he muses grotesquely, and do for Plum and Carmen. Pandering to others does not sit well and nothing to lose. To sit in a confined space and to be subjected to that constant stream of the little guy's jabber. Like being constrained in a mad house. Wauters looked over the vessel with growing anger and distaste. The old predator in him was smooching around. Hyper sensitive, a constant play of percentages, odds. If something as much as touched its tail, in no more time that it takes to fall from the yards, less, there would be trouble. He could turn like a reptile, a 'King Brown', with all the venom that such a creature can muster. Wauters was straining to sublimate his natural feelings, his inherited rage primed. He adopted a quiet demeanour, not even an expletive. "More of the same? You catch on good. Try and make your tacking smoother. Ease it over, going about. You've got to be into the wind. More than forty-five degrees off point you'll lose way. I'll try and put you right by the tiller," he says in a matter-of-fact way as they board the craft.

Plum unties the painter but keeps a firm hold on the rope. Pulls the boat in before leaping over, jumps into the dinghy. "I could wince thinking how I was when we started. When was it, a lifetime ago?"

"Four days ago, yes, seems like a lifetime to me *jou blikseme!*" Comes Wauters' rejoinder. How gratifying to get your teeth into a good old curse. If the *mompie* only knew what was going on here.

Plum is oblivious to the arsenal he's standing too close to. Knows not that he is the naked flame. "We'll go out this once, for old time's sake," says Plum.

"We'll be drawing a line under the last few weeks," Wauters responds. It's just patter, keep it light. *Sien jou gat*, biding my time. "You get a totally different feeling in a large sailing ship, a barque, a brigantine," he says. "A hand has only his tasks and there's always something to do. It's good being directed and not having to think." His jacket collar flaps and traces of spray speckle his port side. Heads down as Plum tacks the craft. "Smoother, *Rooinek!*" Wauters pulls in the sail instinctively, taking the task out of Plums hands. "At the end of watch, you're grateful for your rest. Many is the time I've collapsed into my sleep wet through, too tired to contemplate even stripping down. Soon your body can be all boils from the salt water and the clamped-on clothing. They stuff the hawser pipe but water still gets into the fo'c'sle. A slush lamp goes over and you get a bit of a blaze and a rush for the door; it's all part and parcel. You take it as it is. I found exhaustion good, acts like chloroform. You have to throw yourself into everything, keep going. I did; no time for *scrimshaw* or *rope work* and I wouldn't wish for any man to try and involve me in such things. That's what idlers do and I have no space for such." Plum tacks the boat again, jerkily. "Haul it closer, man!" Not addressing Plum, he starts to talk as an aside: "What is it to be today, skipper? The working suit, the storm suit? How many sails? We set the square sails on the deck and then haul them up. The Master experiments, likes to mess with his sails, all up. Some experimenting is good; you can suggest stuff, he listens, that's a new one. *Ladies pocket handkerchiefs*, *moon sails, studding sails, skysails*. You snigger at first mentioning shrouds, them sound like something at a funeral. One rule about sailing emerges, the bigger name the sail has the more useless it is. Take the *mizzenskysail*, better leaving the poles bear." He looks directly at Plum. Wauters holds a vertical palm to the left. "Mizzen…" Shifts is hand to a middle point and then to the right. "Main, fore. That's a proper ship" He suddenly looks up as if awoken from a deep sleep. He is now out of the reverie and speaking directly at Plum who is tense, planning the next manoeuvre. Coiling loose ends on the planking. Listening to the music of the runnels under his feet, water coursing this way and that. The splish and splosh, the onomatopoeic brilliance of wet words. "The whole kit and caboodle? I counted it once, ropes, reef points, sails, bright work, some 250 bits and pieces all with a life of their own, not to mention the blocks and tackle. What hope would *you* have, '*Goccha*'? Knots, bends and hitches; you not knowing a *Carrick Bend* from a *Main topgallant-staysail* or a *Turks Head* from your backside?" He has got that stare again as though he's transported and not in a good way, fancifully you would say that there is murder there. He could do for Plum out here and feed him to the tide, right now, it's anger served by loss. His face speckled with spray and an intent stare, implacable. "Working your life around heeling, rolling and pitching, the attitudes of the vessel, the state of the tide; the niff of white pine and white oak; shifting ballast, the chains, to get over a bar." He goes off like chewing a length of spaghetti, you can't stop till it's all in. "Russian hemp for the *standing rigging*, Manila for *running rig*. The whiff of men short of a few weeks bathing. The smell of the sea and tar so…right, perfect. Some of the Sea Dogs could tell within a few minutes of the compass where they were by the smell the sea was giving off, or that was their story." Wauters falls solemnly silent and stares blankly, exhausted suddenly, deflated.

Plum has been half-listening through the exactions of that Wauters has insisted upon. "The lover, the soldier, the justice and the pantaloon. That's like us…" Oh, dear. Fearful of a moment's silence Plum felt the need to say something and the only match that he has for Wauters list of things is blurted-out. Wauters gives a look of disdain. Oh dear, did I say the wrong thing? It's better when Wauters is talking so Plum invites the grouser to speak. "What you thinking?" he tenders.

The big man snaps back. "What's it to you! Can't you stow your daft talk. You're like jeweller's rouge, you wear on a body." He maintains his changed demeanour seeming agitated for a moment. In his mind, he is wondering how far Plum could irritate him before he provoked a deadly reaction. Wauters, although thoughtful and contemplative, has a flash point.

"OK," says Plum, in retreat from the danger signals. Plum recognises the change. Thinks for a minute and tries a lame attempt at humour that always went down well in the family circle. He could remember first hearing it and how he caught on to the joke. "Like us here, now, 'It was a dark wet windy night and two men sat in a cave. One man says to the other, shall I tell you a story? The other says, yeah. Well, it was a dark wet windy night and two men sat in a cave…' you get the idea."

Wauters is non-plussed. His companion is, is. What's the use? "Always jabber-blabber, like the screech of chains when the anchors dropping, the ratchet on an engine." He looks at Plum intensely. Plum is not offended. Losing his childhood, in the way he had, he was always wondering, no matter what age he reached, what do adults talk about? He could never, seemingly, strike the right tone that invited an encouraging or detailed response and was inclined instead to force in one of his dad's sayings. "I'm just trying to cheer you up, you're so…Anyway, I bet sailing was not half as romantic as you paint it." Oh dear. Put a rag in your mouth, Plum. The moment is lost.

Wauters' anger is subsiding though. Whatever caused it initially has dissipated, the fetid smell of the jungle and the sparse, woven hut melt back into oblivion. "You can't help yourself, can you?" says Wauters looking to starboard and shaking his head. He almost grins, out of sheer frustration. The pitter-patter of Plum's conversation has weakened him and he cannot even summon his ready rage. Instead, he just throws out a line. "Just shut your goddam trap," he regurgitates gruffly, his eyes fixed, the white prominent. He tries to recover from that which he should not have shown. An outburst like that in Port Elizabeth and…they would be on you. Control, planning, cunning. "Perhaps you had to be there, *jou blikseme!* Look to the tiller, here! Wauters releases the bar into Plum's hands and the little man is in total control, well, notionally."

They sail along in silence. Wauters is deep in the utter exhaustion of his little tirade like the now subsided passion, that indescribable thrill, the one he had once lived in, been consumed by. They sail away. Plum has taken to his command stiffly. His body is so taught with the anxiety of his task and those evil eyes bearing into him. It is like riding a bike. It's all about balance he concludes in his own mind, not willing or daring to share his little thought. Eventually, the silence, like an itch in the groin, gets too much without some sort of attention. Plum opens up. "You see photos of people hanging onto masts up aloft and everybody looking thoroughly miserable."

Silence ensues. Eventually, Wauters turns to Plum. He suddenly brightens up again. A distraction. That never happened. Back under cover. "I've decided," he says. "This jaunt will cost you a dinner. It's time you spent from all that pay what you is hording since. Never trust a man that doesn't drink, eh? Lessons don't come cheap. You can take me to a restaurant tonight. We can go up-town after we hove to and tell them to expect us. A sort of reward for my efforts?"

Plum wants to forget the nasty moments. "That sits well. In fact, that would be just the best."

They sail off with Plum on the tiller, 46 and a bit degrees off the point of the wind.

Chapter 8

They got a place at the restaurant for that evening. Although it didn't really matter, Plum could not restrain himself from looking at the prices being charged. You can't be mean when the other has put himself to so much trouble for you, being frugal was his habit. The restaurant must have been a private house once. Two rooms front and back. Everything painted white. A coal fire in the grate with a mottled tiles surround in the room that they will be sitting in. An absence of that stale brown smell of the mess hall. The tables are laid already, even in early afternoon. Oil-clothed tables, gas lights. A counter in one corner. The booking-in is really easy. Even though the two are in working clothes. As long as you can pay, what's the difference.

Wauters and Plum have changed their clothes. Plum has put Rowland's Macassar oil on his hair, his ritual, his dad's choice was brilliantine. They sit at the table sharing the room with a few other diners. It's still cold outside and despite the fire, regularly tended, chivvied, topped-up, you wouldn't sit to the table without your warm clothes on. Plum speaks in hushed tones. They have a plated meal before them. Wauters has a shot glass with some spirit in it. Plum has a glass of water. Plum speaks confidentially while he eats a potato which he has skewered on his knife.

"Eh, it's not too dear, here. I expected it costing a lot more." He scrapes some gravy up with his knife and runs it across his tongue. "I've never been to a restaurant before. A café, sure, but a restaurant."

Laughter erupts from the back room, the rest of the restaurant is sepulchral. Someone has been having a good time since before they sat down it appears. Wauters half turns towards the noise. He waves his fork in Plum's general direction. "Not been to a restaurant before? It shows. If you insist on eating off your knife like that, you will only end up slitting your throat…and, do us all a favour. Use your fork man." They eat in silence for a moment. The sound of laughing from the back room. "Sounds like somebody's having fun," Wauters states wistfully.

On Wauters' plate is a fish with the head on, Plum has tried to avoid the sight. He chooses to distract himself. "I swear I know them voices…what's your grub like? Sea Bass, right? I don't think I would fancy having my dinner looking up at me like that. Little pleading face like. Mouth agape. Well, they die of suffocation, don't they? A lingering death. Couldn't you ask them to take its head off? That's what it looks like, caught in the moment of its end."

"A bit late now. Put your napkin over your head." Wauters instruction is drowned out. More laughter from the back room followed by louder muffled voice. "So, are you interested in the death of your food, like its welfare? Not a topic that suggests a hearty meal quietly enjoyed." More laughter. "What is going on in there. I think I'll join them. Sounds like more fun, than sitting here, eh? Here we talk of animal suffering and there they couldn't care less". Wauters knocks back his tot and calls up another. Well, he's not paying.

Oh Plum, guaranteed to say the wrong thing. What a stupid thing to have said. "This is great pastry, I'm glad I picked it. Lots of beef chunks and, mushroom, yeah, mushroom. They're doing better here than back home. You wouldn't believe it." At last, a topic, something vaguely interesting to impart. "They can't serve men from the services after ten o'clock in restaurants now! Back home they have all this rationing. They're into everything, saying what's-what. Talk about regulations. Like one of my dad's goodies, I can't do the accent but, then you'll get the picture; it's a cartoon" Careful now, you'll only get that look, more of that smouldering. "A railway station is depicted." Depicted! That doesn't sound like you, Plum. Wauters hardly looks up, fully expecting trivia. "Right? A stationmaster is talking to a confused child who is holding-up a cardboard sort of box, a box." He demonstrates the dimensions in the air. "The man, the stationmaster, is saying to the child, 'Dogs is dogs and cats is dogs. But that there tortoise is h'an insect and h'insects go free'. Eh? It was in a Punch magazine, I think. Punch, eh? Could be a boxing paper, eh?" No reaction from the other. "The governments, rules, rules and more…" More prolonged laughter from the other room. "Nowadays, they have to tell people that fish is not meat, for the purposes of the ration, you see. They go on about a ration of two and a half pounds of meat, either that you eat at home or at a restaurant. Who were they talking about? Do our lot go to restaurants? No. How many could afford to buy two and a half pounds of meat per person? Like me? Us lot? Nobody could afford a restaurant. If you had the cash, even a little bit, you could still live nicely though."

The waiter comes to their table. He sidles up cautiously. "You'll be excusing me. Is your tea all right?" The two men hold up their cutlery as a sign of appreciation. The waiter steps closer. "Pardon me for butting-in. There's these two fellers in the back room, English, you're English, right?" He flits a glance between the two of them, "They're not painting themselves in any glorious colours back there. If they don't shut their gobs-up, they could find themselves in a whole lot of trouble. They're being rather rude about…everybody. There's two local lads in there, for a start, getting, what you might call, agitated. I'll leave it with you. I just don't want me room wrecked." The waiter hovers for a moment in expectation but the two men sit quietly looking at him. The waiter goes.

"Well? What's that to us?" Wauters carries on with his meal. Empties his shot glass again but refrains from re-ordering.

"I don't think so. *Earth receptive; Mountain immovable; water dangerous; wind gentle; thunder arousing; fire clinging; lake joyful; Heaven active,*" says Plum in a serious sort of way.

Wauters looks up from his eating with a look of disbelief on his face. "What the blazes is that supposed to mean, *rooinek*? Dearie, dearie me, why can't you just sit there and hold your tongue. Let them do the talking, you can't go far wrong then". Wauters reproves him but quietly, insistently.

Sheepishly, Plum owns, "It's one of my dad's. There's no harm in it."

Wauters eases back in his chair. "Explain yourself."

"Like buying time before he'd say what he meant. I find it very calming. At home, we could trade on such stuff, like a routine we went through. Gives you time to think; reminds me of happier times. Where does any of this stuff come from? We grow up with it, these things, don't we? Take 'em in, like. Old sayings, family bloomers. No harm in it. When Dad says these things, we look at him with, like, in reverence. He's our leader and what he says goes."

Wauters sees the point, it's only fair. His life was not like that but he is not so rational-irrational, that he cannot understand. "Your Pops, a poet?"

"You don't know what you've got till you least expect it most, that's one of his," says Plum. Where did that one come from. Well, Wauters did open the door. Suggested that it was allowable.

But Wauters has a rejoinder, unexpectedly. *"Dog het gedog hy plant 'n veer 'n hoender kom op…*thought, thought it would plant a feather and then a chicken would come up! There I have got my own back, something from Holland, a saying, maybe."

Wauters looks at his companion quizzically. They carry on eating. The Sub-lieutenants from the Horton Lodge, their ship, are in the back room. The two young officers, whom the spirit hath moved, are feeling omnipotent in the company of clods. No one to challenge them. Enough money to afford the booze and too careless, young, to understand the dangers of their humour, such as it is, sort of satirical.

"Fourteen miles from Cork and you may as well be on the other side of the moon!" says one.

That is the first audible thing comprehended. Plum dismisses it. "They say the Germans haven't got a sense of humour. Perhaps that's why we'll win, eventually. You can only be gloomy, matter of fact, for so long and it starts to put stress on you." He takes a sip of his water.

Wauters has finished his drink and his fish and feels content, calmed.

"Water good?" He enquires smiling impishly. This is another side of Dutchy.

Plum looks into the glass quizzically, frowns, puts the glass down. Elbows on the table he leans towards his companion. "Anyway, the food situation back home…isn't good. There's some talk that food growers are withholding supplies, forcing prices up. Mind you, Russia's in the same boat after the Tsar…Coal's no better. In February, right, the Thames, the river in London, iced-over; it was that cold. People were scrambling for coal! There was this kafuffle; forty-five tons of coal was sent to museums and such, apparently, when households couldn't get transport to move any supplies from the depots; all the delivery men at 'the front', they said. A Marquis, get this, sent his *valet* in the family limousine, down to the depot, to load up; people, the better off, were going on the same trip in taxis." Laughing can be heard intermittently from the back room. "Then they have a shortage of taxi drivers. Some-bugger proposed the idea of women doing the driving and the male taxi drivers started protesting that in the black-out, women are no good as cabbies, won't be able to drive in the dark. So, they're out as far as taxi driving goes. There's all sorts. Me dad says, Mr Yapp, whoever he is, quote…" Plum's eyes swivel as he strives to remember the quote, "…believes that intemperance, intemperance, drinking like, is a bigger enemy than the Germans', where's he been hiding his head? Makes you wonder. You wouldn't believe what's going on." He leans back in his chair to ease his tension. "I hope they put it back together again, society like, when this is all over; there's no saying they will. Still, Lloyd-George, who is not my father…has got the Navy to start forming Atlantic convoys. From what I hear, it's making a big difference, except," he whispers, "now it's forcing the Germans to seek out single ships, hear tell, like ours. They won't challenge the convoys."

Voice from the back room. "And then, despite everything" – laugh, laugh – "they let him be buried in the *Arbour Cemetery*, eh?"

The two Sub-lieutenants come from the backroom and make to go. Sub-lieutenants Hodge and Senior acting stupidly, obviously unused to drinking unsupervised.

"Thank you, barman," says one.

"That was very, very…middle-in." The two titter together.

"Praise indeed," says the other.

Money is sort of thrown on the waiter's desk and the two men leave. A moment later, two other men from the back room also leave the restaurant. The waiter looks after them, then approaches Plum. "I told you it wouldn't end well."

Plum motions to Wauters. He hurriedly settles-up and makes to follow the others out onto the street. He turns to Wauters, still seated. "Come on. We can't leave them to it. We'd better go keep an eye on them." Wauters doesn't move. "Come on! We'll have to go!" insists Plum.

Wauters grudgingly gets up. Plum thanks the waiter, pays him and they go out onto the street. "Perfect end to a perfect evening, eh?" says Wauters ironically.

Outside, on the otherwise breathless cold night, silent street, lights dim, the distant sound of echoing footsteps, a grim expectation hangs in the air. Wauters and Plum can hear the two Sub-lieutenants laughing at a distance and set-off to find them. They see the two sailors just as the other men from the restaurant, the two local men, emerge from a side street to confront them. The two other diners approach the Sub-lieutenants face-on.

Plum has no hesitation. "Hey, you lot! Hang on there!" All four men in front of them look up. The two Sub-lieutenants are suddenly made aware of their peril. "Let's talk about this. There's no need for trouble." Wauters looks askance at Plum. The two men from the café move closer to the two officers and Plum darts forward and interposes himself between the two parties. "We don't want any trouble, do we? These two, they're a bit drunk, they're not in their right heads. I'm sure they regret anything that may have upset you. They're only lads. Look at them."

The two antagonists walk past Plum and are now within striking distance of the sailors. Plum pats one of the men on the shoulders and the chap swivels round and takes a swing at him. Plum dodges the strike deftly. The other man now rounds on Plum and approaches him menacingly. A melee breaks out with Plum fighting off the two men, deftly using his boxing craft, turning a brawl into a form of ballet. Wauters sneaks away over the harbour wall. The two lieutenants run off. Plum notices none of this. Now he faces two righteous angry men and their cause. The fight proceeds and Plum is all alert and moving, dodging. Before long, the two assailants are visibly tiring; the fistfight develops but there is only one outcome there. After one or two small flurries, the assailants back off. All the time Plum is telling them that there is no need for this. They should talk. The two are increasingly wary, a bit of finger pointing and threats and they make a decision on the hoof and disappear into the night. Plum looks about him. No Wauters! "Wauters! Where are you? Are you alright? Wauters!"

A distant voice replies; it is his shipmate, "I'm down here." A little, and less gruff voice says, "I think I'm all right. Nothing broken, I don't think anyways."

Plum looks over the edge of the wall and just makes out Wauters spreadeagled on the shingle below.

"No, there's nothing amiss. I'm *sharp, chommie*, I think."

Plum jumps off the wall to join him. Plum is all understanding. "You were lucky, that's a long way down. Let's have a look at you. Hm, nothing a dose of broken bottles wouldn't put right. I can't see any damage, well not in this light."

"God verdoem dit! I'm just a bit winded, I think. I should have been behind you. I dodged a 'round arm' and lost me balance. Get me up *Bokkie*." Plum helps him to his feet. "*Eish!* Where are they?" And then, seemingly shocked. "You did them? *Ke sharp, Umlungu*." They climb back onto the quay and head off. "You did well for a titchy. They were the Sub-lieutenants off our ship. They owe you. I'm sorry I wasn't any help." He rubs a pretend hurt on his leg. "I was dodging one of those guys and I seem to have lost my balance, like what I said. Ended up down below. Come on *Meneer*. Good job we're leaving here soon. Best go, eh?"

Chapter 9

The never changing scene in a small town. You get to know the man on the milk cart and the green veg man, his red cart and his thin looking horse with the tatty bridle. Wauters is a minor celebrity. His heavy accented voice causes a stir. He can be trusted; he's not one of *us* not *them*. He walks around the normal haunts but cannot see Carmen anywhere. His attention is drawn to someone fishing off the harbour wall. It's her, it's Carmen. He approaches the woman. "Carmen? Carmen! What are you doing?"

She stands up and looks pointedly at her fishing rod and then him. She is wearing a sort of mac, has a hint of make-up, clean and tidy. Rollo sits-up, scratches himself briefly as if farming a flea from his new girlfriend, then, sheepishly, approaches Wauters. Wauters gives the dog a curtailed stroke, the flea scurries away down the dog's back and Rolls bends back and goes hunting for it.

She strikes a nonchalant pose. "Nothing much, drowning worms. Sh! Don't tell. Well, this is an unexpected pleasure. Perhaps you'll bring me a bit of luck. Nothing doing on this tide. No mullet, no coalfish, a few sanitary rags. Sorry do I shock you, you can't ignore them. Look, I would have been here earlier but being as a girl has to mind how she presents, you know." She smiles coyly. "I had to find some clobber to put on." He stares at her without comment, a small smile strives to be released from his lips. "Well? What?"

He sidles up to her with a serious visage. "I need to tell you. We're off tomorrow, sail. I made a dash down here. I couldn't go without saying *tot ziens*."

She imitates him. "I couldn't go without saying…"

Wauters interjects. "*Tot ziens*, see you later."

It's been coming on for a while now. That overwhelmingly satisfying feeling of being with someone who you are naturally comfortable with. She has feelings for the Dutchman, warm feelings. All right, so he's old. But he's also so attentive. Takes her places. He obviously feels something for her. Today, he is going. Who should he tell but her? Lying in bed, she has almost felt his presence, the memory of conjugal nights seep into her consciousness, clinging to that form to assuage the terrors, having a certainty. She feels as though there is something, a bond between them. He's trying awful hard to get close to me, she reflects. If he were to hold my hand, I wouldn't object. If he were to touch me…She breaks in on her thoughts for her own sake, for her sanity. *"Totscenes*, now that's a funny word. So, where is it you're about to go to? Australia? Somewhere sunny and nice I suppose. And here's me on the harbour with me rod." She puts the rod down and sits on a bollard, legs splayed man style. "I couldn't get the images out of my head. I was hot in me bed thinking about the warm sun and sea salt drying on me skin." Hot in her bed, oh yes. Push the covers away, say a 'Hail Mary'. And I was thinking of you in your cold belly nakedness she reflects inwardly. She holds her hands up to a weak sun and rubs them together as if warming them on that seasonally dead winter star. "You've not got a mint ball or summat have you? I have a hankering for a sweet." Wauters hasn't any. He pulls his pocket lining out to show there is no lie. "What a feckin' useless tool you turned out to be, langer." There that's a good distraction, appearing blousy. "Typical."

He doesn't bat an eyelid. She looks towards the harbour. The whole place devoid of warmth, clinging cold, cold like cotton sheets. The urgency of the sea gulls in this arid landscape combing the beach debris for a morsal, a stinky morsal. Where do seagulls go to die? You never see a dead one anywhere. Perhaps they share with the elephants in their grave yard. A neat sort of understanding. "Strange things fish. They say that fish were in the sea and then some of them decided to come onto land. Now why would they do that do you think? They sniffed-out the cafes? Why come on dry land when you can swim so well, you're so well suited?" Rollo jumps-up to her, stands with his paws on her chest, she wobbles for a second as a result of the press. "There they are, down there Rollo, in the cold depths eating dead…all sorts, dead sailors maybe, most likely. Then we catch 'em and eat 'em? Perish the thought. I don't think I'll eat fish again. I suppose there are more fish than bodies. Maybe the chances are a bit slim, but. This cold wind makes your eyes water." She is, gratefully, leading herself away from her warm thoughts. Rollo sits down looking at her attentively. She looks up at Wauters, half smiling. "I might eat you by mistake one day. You never know." Wauters suggests he would be tough eating, anyway, he doesn't plan to die. She goes on. "All that blubber and your stubbly head, them feelers on your face. Like a cat fish! Catfish Rollo! Catfish!" The dog jumps, looks around excited, expectant. They look at each other, eye to eye. "How long will you be gone?" Oh no, she reflects, that sounds too needful. "Not that I'm interested. Just *craic*, you know. Oh, I know, you don't know. Daft question." She clenches her fists drives her nails into the palm and puts on a face. She thought that she had driven those thoughts out but she makes a brief mention of emotion and she feels like being gathered up in his big protective arms that will ensure that she never feels sorrow, fright or loss again. He is an anchor, a safe harbour for all the good in her that has not been required in the past but which she is sure is a resource just waiting to be tapped by someone worthy. "I'm afraid now. I don't want to cut me mackerel open to find one with some eyes inside." She picks her rod up. "What's to say? It's been nice knowing you, and all that." She could easily collapse now and plead for his love in some way, but that would be daft. Such drama. Either it is offered and accepted or left biding. He does not offer any confirmation of what she feels and love is a mutual thing is it not, it has to be? She looks to the sea. "Will I never be able to eat fish again? Will I ever be able to look to a gurnard without thinking of your ugly mug? That's for sure." She imitates a fish gulping. "You inside a whale or some such." We will be back he tells her. "So, this is what it comes to. Me fishing for mullet and you fishing for compliments, is it? No, I know you're not. The boots on the other foot" She hesitates finding that the only strength she can derive in this moment is to pretend unconcern. Constantly contradicting herself. Anyone listening would be confused but not half as much as how she is now. "Go on then, bugger-yourself-off. I never liked you anyway. Go and do whatever it is you're so secret about. But let me tell you, if you go and get yourself kilt, I'll never speak to you again." It goes without saying. The passion rises to fever pitch within her but there is no way she can manifest it. A little catch in her voice at 'get yourself kilt' is barely perceptible. "Come back maimed and you're on your own. Your enough of a burden now without anything else in the mix. Now, skat, leave me alone. I'm sorry I set eyes on yer." She points to the direction she wants him to leave. He hesitates, thinking initially that he will move towards her if only to console her for her all too apparent thinking in all the wrong ways. She even entertains shaking his hand, but refrains and walks away back to her fishing rod. After a brief while, she turns to see him go. "What an odd *mensch*. To think that you could have any feelings for an old fella like that. I need a stiff gin. Listen to you girl. No use getting all girlie over *that*. He's all lies and intrigue and blubber, a thief! You know that in your heart of hearts…but nature's taking you over, you dirty bugger. Your woman's a dirty bugger Rollo, with unclean thoughts, now I'll never get to heaven." Rollo seems confused. What is being asked of him? He lays his head on one side looking on at her. "I'm going do-lally. Piss-off back where you came, blackguard! Honest to goodness, I don't know what you're after but I'm pretty sure it's not me!"

-oo0oo-

Wauters has come down from the camp with a bunch of others. The gunners have been aboard for a couple of days adding the finishing touches to their guns and their mountings, calibrations, with the dock workers, the superintendent. He is carrying a Donkey Bag his gift from the navy. He feels no attachment. He climbs the gangway, wanders around for a minute. Plum runs up to him.

"There you are. Good, eh?" He casts around, traces an arm in the air describing the whole ship. "Come on, I'll show you your new home; it's not bad really, more space than on some billets, that's for sure."

Wauters follows Plum. On the way they pass Logan, the fireman, who is already coal stained. The evidence is in the trickle of smoke from the funnel that is keeping the dynamos ticking-over. He sniggers gruffly. "Bridal suite, you two? Rum, bum and concertina, eh?"

They nod their recognition and walk on, neither wanting to dwell. Then, down a companionway into a hold. There is not much light but they can make-out the extent of the space. Plum is all smiles and eager, that's a bad sign as far as Wauters is concerned. He's going to be stupidly animated again. "Cots, makes a nice change from hammocks, just as good as a bed; a novelty; lifts a corner of the *Donkey's Breakfast,* a decent mattress. Like the Ritz, eh? That's your kip and I'm over here. Yours is furthest away from the companionway, I thought it would suit you better there. There'll be people coming and going I suppose, *the lover, the soldier and the pantaloon*, eh?" Wauters gives him a withering look.

"What did I just say? Even I don't know where I got that one from, me dad probably. I thought you'd appreciate being a bit out of the way. There's yards of room. This is what they call 'shaking-down'."

"I know what 'shakin'-down' means," comes the rejoinder.

They start settling in. The young man is organised. "We'll be out for a couple of days they say and, if all goes well, bob's your uncle."

"*They* seems to run this show, who are '*they*'?" snaps Wauters. He looks around the space with an enquiring eye. Rule one when you're on the run, familiarise yourself with everything, it may save your hide.

Plum takes the latest jab on the chin, but he rides it and comes on. "It's all right you don't need to thank me for looking after your comforts." Wauters does not respond. "You look around this space and one thing strikes you right-off, it needs a woman's touch. How much nicer it would be if someone had spent a little bit of time putting some curtains up across them portholes and ventilators, some 'net' curtains. Knocked-up a candlewick quilt. They've got an eye for it, silk purses from sow's ears, women, a curiosity." Perhaps Wauters can explain it to him. "Why do women get such a bad press on boats? Perhaps they show us up?"

Wauters is pretty sure about women and boats. "Women are bad for the ship." He asserts.

Not nearly a good enough explanation for Plum. "So how? I know that looking for their…favours could cause trouble, I'm not daft. But as far as I can see there's no other reason for keeping 'em off. I'd soon as have them on board as think they're not up to it."

A dark response. "It's deeper than that, *praatsiek. Eish!* Woman are mysterious, frightening. You know, deep."

The other makes light of the gravity of the remark. "It's all those knitting needles and crochet hooks, yeah. I can see the potential. Always the threat that they can stick you." Plum thrusts his arm forwards as if brandishing a weapon.

"No, don't be d-a-r-f-t. It's not that, it's serious man." Wauters puts the comment aside.

Plum issues a warning to himself: Don't press him. You're heading for dangerous waters. It's a childlike interlude. What's this. What's that. He can't resist. He may be putting his head in a noose. "What then?"

Wauters lays off shaking his Donkey's Breakfast, his mattress. "Listen and learn," he says with gravity. "The natural scent of a woman is herring brine, see. They are obviously creatures that came from the deep. They are the living proof of man coming from out of the oceans. There's no extra rib or any of that. They know more about the cold hidden depths than any man could ever know. That's why women are so different, they are at a different stage of…evolving…evolution, the men came first, maybe. Put *them* on the sea and they could summon up their familiars, all sorts could happen. It's a wonder we share the same languages. They are set apart and tolerate the men, haven't you noticed? As though they appeal to a different authority. You must see that there is something a bit uneasy in women, thinking in a different way? No wonder there were so many tales of mermaids in the old days. Who knows, perhaps the period of change was still under way. Women say we are a plague but a Mermaid, always the temptress. Rocks and smashed timbers. The deluge. When they have a baby, they reproduce their kind, not us, a Mummy's boy but they play on that 'he looks so much like his father', a decoy manoeuvre leading away from their real association, see. It will not show at first until they are ready to take over. See the closeness between a woman and her child. No room for men just the children that they can groom to their own ways."

"That's what you get from drinking salt water Wauters. Bob's your uncle," jokes Plum.

That triggers something in Wauters that would not be plain to most. "Om Paul's my uncle."

"Is he? Whatever." Plum is going through his gear, reacquainting himself with his treasured bits. The map of Cocos sits right at the bottom of his bag, all furtive and hidden, not to be seen by any other. It is almost as though he has to distract himself so as to stop himself from saying its name. He snaps too. "We've got a problem already. Cook, or the Mulatto…"

"Lascar," corrects Wauters.

"…and him, have set fire to the Caboose and it's going to take a bit to put it right." Captain just shrugged when they showed him around. He's a cheerful old duffer and no mistake, that one. Nothing seems to stir him. One glance and…off! So, we're on cold rations. Hope you like corned beef? Plum casts a glance around the space. "Well, no cupboards, but a bit of hanging space. We can rig a line up from the ceiling over our cots and put our kit on it, that will be convenient." They contemplate the move.

"You're a good fighter, Plum. Unarmed, took on two biggies? How? I'm curious," ventures Wauters.

A nonchalant reply. "I was fitter. They put a lot into the first few swings and then started puffing." He enacts some clever footwork and dodging. "It's not scrapping, it's discipline and technique, boxing, like Jimmy Wilde, *'The Mighty Atom',* I'm his love child. You know what I find queer about all this?" He continues to look through the kit in his 'Donkey Bag'. "Nobody having a uniform, no saluting. It's totally against 'King's Regs'. I suppose that's not a system you know much about, but with us, R.N.... Captain Cathcart gave me a dressing down for saluting him and not because he wasn't wearing his cap. Gave me a right what for. There's a rum ration though, you'll be pleased to hear. You can have mine." He sits on his cot. "At last. We're off. I'll miss the sailing, but not much else."

Wauters is still on his latest theme. "No scar tissue around your eyes, I noticed early on. That scar on your temple, but that's not from fights, I bet. Well, all together no more damage than any man could get from a shaky hand and a nick from a safety razor."

Plum carries on with his task at hand. "You have to have a clear mind and set objectives, then fall back on training, rather than falling back on the canvas, eh?"

Wauters takes a book out of his Donkey Bag and lies back on his cot. Other sailors pass them and go deeper down into the hold. "Anyway, stow it. That's enough blabber," cautions Wauters. He riffles through the book he has conjured-up then eases up on one elbow. "I don't know how I came to be stuck with you but let's have some ground rules." He talks from behind the book. "If we are stuck together for a time...I need my space, right? I don't want you chipping in every verse-end with what your 'Dad would have said', *mompie*. Wandering around head in the clouds. Have you any idea how wearing that gets? O.K listen, *Babbelbekkie*! We are not all the same, right. Tortoises don't have feathers and apples aren't pears, right?"

"You're starting to talk like me," insinuates Plum. "I'm excited. I'm up for this. It's an exciting time."

From behind his *cordon sanitaire*, the big man growls. "Contain yourself. That's all right for you but I can assure you it's not everybody's experience, I should not be here. This is not my war. I didn't ask to be here. Given a chance of death here or death somewhere else, but death either way, that's my choice, not theirs. I actually don't expect to get on with you. Do you know that, do you hear me?" His head appears from behind the novel. "A confined space, too much jabber; we could fall-out. Ok, at first a bit of a novelty, but you, you could drive a mate overboard. Find yourself a good book." He waves his book in Plum's face. "All right? *Sharp?*"

-oo0oo-

After 'Swinging' the ship in open water, Captain Cathcart sets a course westward, steer two four zero. Full ahead, the running-up exercise. It was all new to everyone. This once inert lump of steel now a lively hub of activity. People gradually coming to terms with their place. At first, it was thought that the gunners should share the watches but they proved so inept at everything else that they caused more trouble than it was worth. Gunners kept odd hours anyway because they could only train under cover of darkness. At last, the galley was working properly. A badly fitted stove had all sorts of problems and minor fires had been a result. At times, the flue didn't work properly and the occupants would have to beat a hasty, coughing retreat as the space suddenly filled with acrid smoke; the shenanigans providing a moments humorous respite for the rest of the crew from their duties and concerns. But, despite the poor amenity and the cramped space, cook and his Lascar mate worked wonders and a steady supply of hot food was invariably on tap. The ship ran into a force eight to nine at one stage, the west-facing coast of Ireland can change in an instant from flat calm to full gale and driving a golf ball, as many a golfer at Ballybunion would attest, after the graveyard hole, can become nigh-on impossible very quickly.

In this eerily dark and turbulent night, the Caboose stood-out, brightly lit. Inside, the cook and the Lascar are working, functioning in difficult circumstances by virtually climbing over each other in this torrid, hot, steamy cupboard. The cook motions to a bucket which is full of food scraps and gestures that its content should be thrown out (with a thumb jerked over his shoulder). The Lascar picks the bucket up and stands at the doorway looking out as the spray speckles his face, the wind tugs at his bod. Is it that urgent, the need to chuck out the peelings? The boat is moving in the swell at alarming angles despite its false bilge. The Lascar commits to his task. Takes hold of a safety line and gingerly moves towards the ships rail. He is soon drenched. It takes the man a moment to get his balance before he winds up to pitch the bucket's content into the sea. He heaves the bucket as a wave breaks over him. When the deluge is spent, the bucket has gone and he is on his back on the deck. The Lascar looks into his hands then cautiously raises himself, hands firmly gripping the rail, looks over the side into the turbulently agitated waves with a mixture of surprise and resignation. Did he hope that the sea would offer-up the bucket after emptying it for him like an animal spitting out some bones? He staggers back to the galley and mimes his experience. Cook rolls his eyes resignedly but offers no consolation.

The ship battles through the deep weather trough. In the dark, Wauters and Plum meet on the deck. They are hanging on to the superstructure and safety lines. Wauters shouts over the racket of the wind. "He's been broadside on. He's turned. What's afoot?"

Plum, almost without thinking spreads his palms to twelve inches. "About a...?" But doesn't say anything, restrains himself. He almost sends himself down the deck with his doing some body English rather than holding on to the safety line and has to scramble to keep upright. He shouts back at Wauters. "I would have thought you would be one of the first to know."

Wauters uses a hand to strain water from his beard. The rough sea's rivulets and plumes grab the sailors, tug at their feet, pull and push them about the deck as if attempting to unseat them to the tune of the wind singing in the wires and the flapping and whiplash snapping of canvas about them. Always clawing, tugging and busy needling, the waves are implacable. Plum contorts in his efforts to stay upright and secure. "Word has it that they're having trouble with a condenser, whatever that is when it's at home. Apparently, it's not something you can't mess with at sea; needs a proper engineer, we're lucky to have power apparently. We're going back."

Wauters takes a grip on Plum's arms. "You can stitch a sail, splice a rope, rig a rudder, if it's all nature, wood and stuff. A lump of metal goes wrong and all bets are off. That's serious! You look a bit green."

Plum blinks as the spray temporarily blinds him. *"Invincible* didn't bobble around as much as this ship. A proper, stable, gun platform. I'll be all right. Getting my sea legs."

"We're going back to Queenstown," adds Wauters.

"We'll never get on station at this rate," Plum suggests as he walks away. "Saved from the war by bad mechanics. You should be grateful they can't mend it as if it was a sailing ship. It's a life preserver."

Wauters nods to himself. Yeah, you keep it up, I say. That suits me fine *chommie*, just fine.

-ooOoo-

Later that week in the municipal library, it could not have been different. No wind to disturb generations of skin flake dust settled on every horizontal surface, hushed airlessness; a space-like vacuum of quiet, replete with whispers of the cloisters. Plum enters the building and looks around from the threshold almost not daring to move further should he destroy the order he perceives. A lady approaches him and they exchange a few words. She points here and there and then walks off, turning after a few steps to see Plum still hovering; she beckons Plum to follow. They pass forbidding rows of bookshelves weighted with sundry tomes, every title a challenge to comprehension. Eventually, they come to the section marked 'General Studies', next to 'Irish History' and 'Gardening'. The lady questions Plum again, but he signifies that he will be alright. He walks down the row of books so designated. Too many books, too many titles, the confusion of strange surroundings clouded by the rigours of conduct, form. He seeks out the lady again and she takes him to the geography section, takes two books off the shelves that she obviously feels may help and hands them to the confused, off-balance seeker of truth. Plum asks a question that elicits her taking him to a well-lit corner. He sits to a desk looking about furtively then produces the map of Cocos Island. He flicks through each book in turn until he finds something appropriate. There it is, a detailed entry of the status and condition of the island. The first entry he reads, 'Cocos Island, not to be confused with the Cocos-Keeling Islands of the East Indies…' Just his luck, there are two islands of the same name. What are the chances of him fetching-up at the wrong one! While sitting at the desk Carmen walks past him. She looks down at him cursorily, they pay each other scant regard. He has the stub of a pencil with which he laboriously writes scrawled notes on his map annotating features, noting distances. He ponders the work as Carmen walks back passed him. He catches a slight hint of scent that she emits. She has a couple of books, he notes. Must be a regular here. He wishes he had that sort of confidence about him. She takes the volumes and books-them-out at the main desk, exchanging a few undiscernible smiley words with the clerk before giving a cheery wave goodbye. The desk clerk smiles back at her but her animation collapses as soon as Carmen has turned her back. All this, Plum notes. He follows her directly to the booking desk, effusively offering thanks for the assistance he has received.

Chapter 10

By the side of the Lee River, it is a pleasant day. The calls of a few late *Godwits*, now scant on the water, pierce the air. Sometimes a single shriek and then a sound not unlike a fret saw used quickly on aluminium sheeting. Signs of spring on the move, comings and goings. Cirrus clouds after a few torrid days. That's a good sign. Wauters and Carmen, dressed against the still, chill weather, amble along a pathway not far from the water's edge; the one, no doubt, that Vaughan tried to follow on that fateful night. Now passive and pleasant in contrast to that vicious enactment. Rollo runs freely ahead of them peeing as though there is no tomorrow, enlarging his kingdom's boundaries at virtually every other step. Ah! the joy of micturition. Yes, there may be a tomorrow but she hopes, in this moment, that it is delayed, cancelled even and that *now* is allowed to persist. This is a happy, content day. All the elements are in place that frame spring's nascent urgings. She has picked several stems with prominent seedpods on them. They look beautiful in her eyes, complete in their simplicity. The sky is beautiful and the water, the play of the breeze. Is it love that heightens her awareness or was the drudgery the impediment? Yes, tomorrow may never match this, that hateful tomorrow with its dreads, changes and uncertainties. But this picture, whatever is to come, will persist and turn into a feeling experienced for comfort and restfulness that cannot find a specific origin, something that occasionally rises in your depths and then, alas, ebbs. A scent, a texture, something ineffable. Referred to in the future in a frisson of pleasantness. Yes, this is the path Vaughan traversed on his fateful night. Will it ever be sanitised, washed clean of that occurrence? The eternal landscape that sees it all and, thankfully, covers it up in shifting dunes, tall grasses, the wilful weather and the furze of the new season, all awfulness brushed away under new growth and renewal. On that day, it will all be replaced, all the hurt and strife eradicated to reach the mysterious point, the discovery of what the point has actually been. Our last view may well be life as it really is. Not this cosy, selfish, diorama that we prefer. But the memory that upswells unbidden, like the onset of a warm water current passing through a bathing episode in an otherwise cold sea. They stop to lean on a fence surveying the scene, Wauters by her side, reticent. She is dressed tidily and is wearing a necklace, white shirt under a belted Tweed jacket, bought second-hand. She is grateful for the full skirt with this persistent wind so chill and her with no bloomers. She is close to raiding her mother's jewellery box, such as it is. The only thing that restrains her is that some of its contents may be stolen and she will be 'named' by wearing it. "Now, this is more like it. Why can't all days be like this? I've just spent nearly a week on the streets with my skirt trying to wrap itself around my head; what a blow it has been. You couldn't fish, the waves were breaking onto the promenade." Her face becomes more beautiful by the day with care. Not that she gives a toss what others might see, perhaps admire. She is working through her own triumph. "I like it when there is a bit of bite in the breeze, but a breeze is enough." Rollo approaches Carmen excitedly. "He wants a game, look! Throw him a stick, what's-your-name. Go on! Throw him a stone or something, to chase." Wauters pitches a stone but the dog doesn't track it and, instead, wanders off down the dunes to the water's edge, walking in imitation of a vacuum cleaner, nose down. "Why did God have to make all of those horrid wet, stormy days, especially if he loves us so much? Is He saying that we should always be prepared for the worse? Prepare for judgement you heathens; it's going to be a bumpy ride! Is that what He's saying? Don't settle. Don't lower your guard, there's evil about. Nothing so dispiriting as a drenching. Rollo! Rollo! What yer doing, you daft dog! Would you look at him with that drift wood. I've been here a lot, on the river, especially since we lost 'Corny', my late dear departed. Why? I don't understand, I don't honestly know. Why am I drawn here? Is he out there, do you think? Standing-off, contemplating me? When I'm alone here…will he come to me one day out of the river? Is he drawing me here away from common sight? It's a pull. When it comes, I'll have me ashes thrown here abouts, if there's anybody left close enough to me to care." A hint to Wauters. "Nah, he's more likely to want to speak to Ronan about the nags. He'll get a bloody shock if Rollo gets his scent." Wauters looks out across the water, seemingly in his own world, calculating but rested. The thoughtful easy words of his partner so far removed from the stream of idiocy that Plum conjures with the added benefit of not demanding a response. She briefly looks into Wauters' face, then looks down to Rollo, now on his back squirming in the sand. How many things coming together in this once, even down to the dog, her sharing its mindless ecstasy. "I suppose some would think on despair standing here looking at such an empty scene, now specially, at the end of winter." She traces around her chin and mouth with seeded stems. "It all looks so bleak and eerie at times but it satisfies the *Godwits*...What is it trying to tell me? Me a good Catholic girl? You'd think He would send me to the cathedral not the bloody river side, would you not? I go to church you know? I always sit at the back and I keep my eyes lowered. Well, I used to. Not so much now, maybe. What you thinking, standing there like a blessed gargoyle."

Wauters chews on a grass. "Just having a quiet moment listening to the sounds. On board, there is this constant drumming of the engines all through the ship. Yes, you get used to it. But when it stops, first it is unusual, a loss. Then, like now, you recover and start to hear that which the ship's noise blankets out. All the business of them about their business."

"I didn't expect to see you again. Well, not so soon." She turns towards him, suddenly animated. Sort of pleased with herself. She gathers her thoughts. "I've been busy. I went into the library, don't you know? Well, I've been twice now," I asked the girl with the ringlets and the spot on her neck, at the counter, what I should read; I'll talk to any bugger now. "I fancied some poetry, for no particular reason, except that poems are usually short in my recollection and, you know, colourful, like those Limericks that you hear. 'Do you have any poetry,' says I? 'I don't know what I should read.' I felt such a div. But you have to start somewhere and her hardly looking-up. 'Yates,' says she. 'W.B. Yeats, he's as good as any and very popular, Irish.' So, Yeats it was. Off I went and gobbled-up all the Yates. Then it was Mr Hopkins, Irish too, a priest I think, although I wouldn't swear to it." She puts her hand on her heart. "What tender souls men are when left to it?" Hint. "You think they're all sulky and matter of fact, like you, and then they come-over all soft and quiet and concerned, caring, like knowing more about love and tenderness than you could ever know or anticipate and we girls, I bet we all lap it up." Hint, hint. "I have quite a habit in the poetry now. I read some Kipling. I blush to say it, before, on hearing the name without the poetry, I probably thought that Kipling was some sort of fish gutting. I found that he wrote books as well, you know? I may have a'read of a book, although the size of them puts you off and Mammy is quite likely to throw away learning left lying awaiting finishing. She can't read, you know, apart from money numbers, which she's spot on with. Any book without numbers, well, she might as well be blind. Books, erm, they must take up lots of time."

Wauters puts his back to the fence. "I always carry a book with me. One day I might read it. There is nothing so good as a book for keeping people at their distance." He looks at her with the trace of a smile about him. "Some people are afraid of books. Others think you're deep into it and won't disturb you. I can't say I have ever learned anything from a book; it's just me I suppose. I've had books before and thought I'd read them but when it comes to recall of what they said, little or nothing, apart from the odd word or situation. Makes you wonder why you tried them in the first place. And then you meet some bugger else that has read the same volume, not too often in sea mates, and all it comes down to is a game of remembering the details, who knows more names or recites bits lost on you. What's the point? Is that all we do it for, the test? I like the practical. Anything I'm shown I can do. But read the same doings in a book and I'm turned-off, lost. What a daft art when some writer or other invents a time and place and then invents a lot of things that *might* go on there, plays around with romance and shit, with people and names made up. They should be honest and rid all that time and place and people thing, just tell us straight what's bugging them. They could easily bring two hundred pages down to one! There seems to be a good trade in murder novels. Could I resist going to the back page straight away to find out who's done the deed, why? I'm impatient see. I can't abide false tension, especially when it's for nothing, made-up blather. *Eish*! Isn't there enough of that without inventing more? But I keep a book by, just to warn people off."

She smiles at him. "And so, what is your book that you *don't* read so readily?"

Wauters sees the funny side. "I *don't* read '*An Outcast of the Islands*', a bloke called Joe Conrad wrote it. He was a master mariner…and foreign, he was Polish, originally, so what is there not to like in such a man? I thought his writing would be easier to understand, me being a sailor too. He writes about the East Indies a lot, which I know a bit about. So, I thought I could place myself in his story, you know, feel it a bit more. Yes, I might read it, one day. Who knows?" Listening to him, Carmen makes a mental note of how, when he speaks at length, like not studied, Wauters' language changes. Listening to him now you might say he was English or American, one of them. At first, he was so guttural it was like he was talking into his reefer jacket, now his tone is lighter, still a noticeable hint but like us.

"But you *don't* read it," says Carmen pursuing the point. He shakes his head in the negative. "That's a shame. But you won't put me off. I've got a dictionary now. I know some new words. I go through the dictionary like it's a book. There seems to be a word for everything." Wauters urges her to tell him one of the words, but she acts shyly and berates him for trying to put her on the spot. She knows the words when she sees them. They both sink into a reverie. He turns back to look at the sea showing a striking profile. Rollo is down in the water. Carmen nudges her man, "Look at him would you. Don't dogs feel the cold? He'll smell like the merry-helen when he dries out," she shouts. "Messy dog! Come out of there!" The dog looks up momentarily, mouth agape, tongue lolling and then carries on with his game. "One word from me and he does as he likes." She fiddles with her necklace. The silence is long only punctuated by the fluting of the *Godwits* which now seems to come from the field behind them. "You know, a thought came to me, and, you might think me a bit looney for saying this. Standing here the other day, just looking at them birds gadding, did I tell you they are *Godwits*? There's a mouthful for you, *Godwits*. They're late. They are usually disappearing by now with winter gone. Fancy having a nose like that, like them sticks that oriental folk use for eating with, you know about them no doubt, don't you?" He nods. "Seems to me like the problem them musicians have carrying around them great big fiddles. It can't be comfortable having that sort of 'hooter'." She indicates the bird's long bill as if she were a trombonist. Wauters raises his eyebrows. "Now that beak is something you *could* shove into somebody else's business pretty well. I bet, in years to come, they'll learn how to crochet using their snouts, they seem well fitted to the task. They would all have the same surname them birds. 'Nose', I bet you, or 'Snozzle'." She looks at him directly and says earnestly, hesitates a little before launching in: "Where was I. Oh yes. When they were many, we were few. Now we are…more and they are…less." She looks straight ahead thinking over the profundity she has just stated. "Me, being faithful and all, trying to understand the God whose name inhabits so many good things. Why is it designed that way, the world?" She moves away from him then turns back abruptly points her finger like that finger of reason. "Then it struck me. There are only so many souls to go around! It's perfect. When people do vile things, they were obviously born at a time when there was a lack of souls to hand out, they never get one and are forever evil because of it. You know, like when people talk about the soul living on, like me thinking I'll bump into my dear departed? Well, maybe, just maybe, he's been transformed into a *Black-tailed Godwit*, gobshite, out there, and is flying around like a good'n and giving me so much pleasure even in his after life, his continuing life." She looks very bright and cheerful as she works through her idea in her head. Her voice becoming more assertive when not being rebuked or worse, ignored, like it was before. He's listening; he's interested, or appears to be. "So, when a poor a creature like that dies the chances are she won't be a bird next time when she's recreated. There are so many people now and everybody having more kids, they've got more money, the number of animals is bound to become less in time as all the souls are taken-up by people." She contemplates what she has said.

"Eish! What can I say? I've seen people die in bad ways. Religion is difficult for me. You live here in no knowledge of the badness of the world. There is no plan," asserts Wauters.

Carmen is disappointed with him. "Wauters, you silly sod." She makes a fist and mock-punches him in the chest repeatedly. "It's all part of the religious war and there will be casualties. Satin inflicts all manner of sick wounds on people, it's his revenge. Him, so deprived, not knowing beauty and pleasure and put away from the joys of creation. Just plain bloody peevish. Many good people are sacrificed. Well, they will put themselves up-front to be shot at, the *Forlorn Hope*. The sufferings of the martyrs, our best troops taken. And, even as we speak, I know it seems to some that the Lord takes our best, but it's because they are the most committed to goodness, that's the reason. What an affront to evil, to be so full of the Lord. In the front line, as it were. They are the ones that Satin hates and fears the most, every-one a martyr. Them Cavaliers and them at the front of the battle, licking their tongues-out at him, showing him their arses. Do your worst, they shout! You'll never break our spirit! 'You must be so sad, lead such a dispiriting existence,' says them that show the world of goodness in their words and deeds. So, they are naturally going to be numbered amongst those most waiting to be hurt by him. Telling of all that stuff that he wants to be left unspoken. That's why the good die young, the innocents." She looks extremely resolute. She looks about gathering her words from the air, "They have not learned to fight but spend their time learning wisdom. Becoming good people and doing. They can't resist the call." She subsides and looks to the river again. She toys with the stems she picked. "Look at these grasses and their seed heads, are they not lovely? Such amazing detail of everything in the great plan. I've always seen it but not seen it, if you catch my drift. It's them poets telling me to look closer and I do. I get all sorts of thoughts lately. I don't think I'll ever know peace again." She points upwards. "I want to do His will." She becomes confidential, *soto voce*. "There's only you I dare mention my thoughts to because I know you're not telling folks, because you don't know anybody anyway and are too secret in your nature to think of sharing anything. You're a clam." She giggles in the telling. Others would shrink from Wauters but she is deep inside him and won't be scared by his frowning, his posturing, feckin' idjet. What has she to lose? If only he would relax a bit and be at ease with himself instead of play acting like the stern father. "If I was to say any of this to my lot, they'd immediately shove a currycomb in my hands and tell me get about my business, bugger off!" She looks out to sea with such a sweet look on her face, but a sad look too. What if…what if I was born cleverer than I think I am and have been wasting my creation because of my given place in life, the luck of the draw? Being born is such a lottery. I like being born; I was lucky being born. But say I'd been born in Dublin, to a priest's family, or that of a doctor? Surrounded by serious folks that discuss stuff. Have time on their hands, read and go to hear a good tenor singing. "I'm not feckin' stupid you know!" she says, irately. "Perhaps they might have farmed me better and sewed some tree of knowledge in me. Alerted me interest. Made me a more generous, loveable sort. How I would love to have been peaceable, revelled in a good nature and not known swear words or use them to feck people off. Showed me how to play a mandolin and taken delight in me noshing an orange, but nicely, like, delicately." She subsides again. "Sometimes I think such outrageous things that don't paint my mammy or daddy in a good way. Yet really, I suppose, they're not as bad as many; more like victims. Oh dear, the very thought of wasting this opportunity, it is a chance, don't you see?"

Wauters has been attentive, interested. "I think it comes to us in different ways." He spits a grass out that he has been chewing and wipes his mouth. "*Eish!* A lot of the time, we see our truth from the words and actions of others, people we come to admire. But then, it strikes me, what if they are having me on. It's so easy to pretend a point of view, pretend being a person with…values, ideas, like them religious nutters, the zealots. They call it sincerity, but it's a trick you can learn. I learned nothing from books. All I know is from the sea. Harsh, yes, but full of fascinating stuff. Reliable." She looks at him in wonder, that he should start to speak about himself, he's like an onion with so many layers. "You know what to expect back normally, nothing. When they went against the sailing and brought in these coal-fired vessels, we lost contact with a great truth, that great teacher and discipliner. We who were one with nature then, where we saw our inner creature and were just getting the beginnings of a notion of what it was all about. You see the lesson in 'yesterday', it would save many a smash if recalled. One day people will look closer at yesterday, history, rather than just leaping off in some fanciful direction, like on a whim. But yesterday is seen as old. Past, useless. It got us here, didn't it?" They fall to silence again. Rollo has had enough. He has a coat full of brackish water which he has saved so that he can shake it all over the couple. They both laugh, one more heartily than the other. "What you need is some brain food. We are going to the *Munster Arms* and I am going to buy something good to eat."

They start to walk off resolutely but after a little way she stops abruptly.

"They would not like me in there. The café was all right, even that took some…getting over. But that wasn't posh. I could pretend in there. And there's Rollo, and him all wet like he is?" she says regretfully. "I'm not wanted there. I'm a *Pavee*, a *knacker,* they'll not let me in there. You keep on pushing it but it will be my peril, I think. You go on, I'll only be an embarrassment to you. You can tell me what you ate, what the people were like. There's a couple of pints worth in that."

He looks at her intensely and prods her on the shoulder. "You're talking about somebody else, aren't you? Look at you. You're better than some and as good as most. Anyone who can spout all that stuff about spirits and all, well, they'd be thought of as good company. What? Her there? She must have gone to the University of Pretoria, for sure. There was a song I knew, from the Australia days, the best thing it could say in admiration of the woman was that she lived in Caledonia and she made good tea. There's lots of scope. Are you that woman or have you got higher ambitions?"

She is diffident. They walk off together.

-oo0oo-

A little later they are outside the *Munster Hotel*. A large imposing red brick edifice. A bastion of the principals of the free market and the aggregation of personal wealth. A cordon sanitaire warding off the hordes of the indelicate and those lacking discernment. Wauters and Carmen stand before the steps of the large building.

He urges. "Come on then."

Carmen writhes as if in agony. "Why are you putting me through this? You're about to be mortified and me. The only thing you'll get here is a kick up the arse and a dose of how's-yer-father! Can we go to the other place with the Gingham table cloths and the old dear?"

He is adamant; it's what she has needed for a long time. She can be assertive. She is no worse or no less worthy than others. Wauters leans over her like menacingly. "No. That brain of yours" – he taps her head – "must need a powerful lot of fuel. Besides, I like a good table occasionally, but it's difficult turning-up on your own, a bit sad. Eating is meant to be a social thing."

She looks up at the towering, glowering building. "I'll only go on one understanding, we go Dutch."

"What?" He bridles.

She elucidates, "We pay half each towards the cost, that's fair." He looks quizzical. "You don't know the term, going Dutch? I still owe yer for the Finny's swindle."

Wauters weighs it. "So, we go…Dutch?"

They have no trouble getting a table. But the people insist that Rollo is tethered in the back yard. Wauters thought that the string they used as a lead, that Carmen used on Rollo, was a gift to doubters. But, as quick as a flash, he had unbuckled his trouser belt and used that as the tether. She sits down self-consciously in the classically furnished room, sort of middle Victorian. The table is set with EPNS. There are flowers in a small vase at its centre. She places her stems of seeds collected on the walk in the little receptacle along with the flowers; they do not look out of place. The waiter tries to take Carmen's chair to help her to sit but she snatches it from his grasp. He smiles winningly and she gives a restrained smile back. Time passes. There is food on the table.

Wauters: "So, what was wrong with the fish? There were some nice fish dishes."

"Too many drowned sailors in them," comes the reply with a lovely smile. His expression acknowledges what she said earlier. She adjusts her necklace nervously and looks about her, checks the cutlery. She looks about like a fox sniffing the air. "I must say, it is a bit nice in here. I could get used to this."

"Have you ever driven in a car?" Wauters asks abruptly.

She looks at him in a surprised pose. "Where did that come from? Aren't we supposed to be eating? I'll try a bit of your Admiral." She attempts the fish and seems to like it. "They'll want us out of here so they can get somebody else in to use this table. We'd better not dither."

He holds his palm towards her in a soothing, calm down gesture. "There's no rush. We've bought the table."

She fiddles with the items set on the table.

"Have you ever been in a car?" he asks again. She looks up quizzically. "My shipmate goes on about all the modern stuff that we are supposed to need. Aeroplanes, telephones, cars, cinemas. Well?"

A woman on an adjoining table has been looking-up occasionally in Carmen's direction. Carmen leans forward. "Don't look now, but there is a woman just to your left, she keeps looking at me as If she knows who I am. If she does know me, she could have us both kicked-out." He gestures that she should get on with it. "No, I have never driven in a car and certainly not been in an aeroplane, not likely. Telephone, that's a Yankee thing, isn't it? Who could I telephone anyway? None of our people think on such things. What's more, who in the world would want to talk to me? A telephone indeed." She lightens up a confiding smile. "Cinema, yes. I went once to Robert McErn's, 'Bobby's kinema', he's from Belfast, yer know. They had a band playing along, set in front of the stage with the screen on it…to play along with the film and everything. I was totally gobsmacked to see people of the likes of me walking about pretty much as I do in the play, up there on that sheet, and music as well. That's not an everyday sort of thing, is it? I'd only seen still pictures before, all stiff and posed. You know the sort of thing, people looking like they are really concentrating, liked stuffed things and always glum, passing wind I think, some of them." She throws her head back and sucks her cheeks in. "Well, at the kinema, and I don't know if this is what happens all the time…we were at an exciting bit, you know, where the girl, stupid bitch, has swooned in the handsome feller's arms, filthy beggar. The band was thumping away, the piano man banging the notes over and over, da-da-da-daa; the girl was about to have something unmentionable happen to her, I suppose. He was approaching her with his hands out like talons, creeping towards her and she too stupid not to give him a kicking. When, suddenly, 'Bobby', Mr McErn, comes storming down the aisle next to me shouting, 'Stop film! Stop or-chesta! Lights.' I thought there was a fire and was getting ready to run. He jumps onto the stage. 'Bobby' is fit to bust. Everybody is shouting and booing and some were throwing bits of buns at him and stuff, dreadful waste." She puts on a voice. "Somebody has said that there are fleas in my Kinema! Well, you've brought 'em in here and you can tak' 'em home with thee! Lights! Start film. Start or-chesta!" And with that, he leaps off the stage and strides past us mopping his neck and brow with a handkerchief. "Up starts the orchestra, on come the pictures, down go the lights, but although the story went on, I'd lost the thread and any excitement had gone but the girl was safe, saved by some other bugger; but even he had squinty eyes a thin moustache and he was wearing jodhpurs, jodhpurs! I ask you! So much make-up on her fizzog, she didn't need that. She was pretty underneath it all; but the paint around her eyes made her look like she'd been in somebody's coal hole. That was the only time I went. It was exciting, in a way, I suppose, seeing such a spectacle for the first time; but it didn't seem to have anything to say, if you see what I mean. I can get all the bother I can handle on the streets here…It's terrible dark in a cinema. You don't know who you are sitting next to. It could be anybody…I'm surprised they allow it. Who knows what goes on, and I'm no prude…I sat by the aisle, just in case? Any funny business and I was off." She makes a sly glance at the woman she thinks is observing her. "There is so much changing. Cars, for God's sake! You know where you are with a horse, although them cars don't make anywhere near as much shit as nags do. A lot cleaner by comparison, I suppose. You don't have to pick your way across the street to miss the turds with cars, do you?" She cuts off and looks to the side whispering. "Oh no, that woman, she's coming over."

An extremely well-dressed woman with a cultured voice approaches the table and addresses Carmen. "Excuse me." Carmen acts as though she knows what's coming and is thinking about leaving her seat, she makes to ease up, tenses. "But I had to ask. I think I recognise you." Wauters rises from his seat respectfully. Carmen holds her breath. "I'm normally very good with faces. I wasn't in your year at St Angela's but the face is quite singular, memorable. Perhaps you were in another year? Please, take me out of my agony. Please, what is your name?"

There is a momentary silence. Carmen looks at Wauters. "That's really nice of you to come over. But I'm afraid you have me confused with someone else. I was brought up in India." Wauters gulps. "My father" – she points to Wauters – "was in the tea trade out there, on the ships you know, so I got schooling where I could. That explains my complexion, see." She looks at Wauters and then points lightly to somewhere beyond. "This seems a nice sort of place. My father and I are thinking of settling here." She nudges his shins under the table. Wauters eyes are starting out of his head at first and then he manages a little smirk. "After my mother's death, you know." A napkin to her eye. "Daddy is an artist now, he has lots of visions of sea life to relate and I am writing poetry and hoping for a publication, so I can share my thoughts around, only serious publishers you understand. I'm in contact with the *Literary Review*"

The woman is taken aback. "It was obvious just observing you that you had an air. One thing St Angela's does for you is to get you to tune you into exciting people, recognise talent when it's about, the aura. What an interesting couple you make, a writer and a painter." She addresses Wauters, "You must be, I feel, very proud of the way that your daughter has turned out? So dignified and animated, so accomplished. We lack a bit of…poise, *Je ne sais quoi,* around here, you know, polish. Starved of good company; and here you are, such an exotic couple; artists indeed. I'm sure that if you did decide to settle here you would make a great contribution to our society. I intimated to Gerald…" She gestures towards her companion still seated at the other table who acknowledges being mentioned. "That's a lovely face over there, such delicacy, radiating such charm. Tell me, sir, are you a modernist? So many schools emanating from France." Gerald, her companion, gestures that she should return to table. "Another time, sir, modern art is so exciting. Still, I mustn't keep you from your meal. Gerald thinks I've gone on a bit. How rude of me, sorry."

Wauters stands up again, the lady bobs slightly and walks back to her table talking to Gerald and nodding in Wauters and Carmen's direction. Still looking towards the interlopers without any discernible expression on his face, "Where in the world did you dredge that tale from? Absolutely masterful. You'd make a brilliant spy."

That, coming from Wauters. "I'm a born liar, like you… 'Dad'! Well, I was thinking of Kipling. He wrote a lot about India, didn't he? He was an author, you know, when he wasn't gutting herring. So many schools in France, yeah, I bet." She reflects a moment. "St Angela's. I think we used to beat up some of those girls from there when they would call us names. When we was *Dukkerin*…" She holds her palm up towards Wauters. And then smiles thinly at the woman "…is good training for such stuff, lying; you have to learn to think on your pins, to tune into what they want to hear and make your pitch. I've finished with this one." She smiles winningly then gestures to her plate. "There wasn't enough of it, especially for the money. But it tasted well, I'll grant you. That menu thing. It had some sweet stuff on it, cakes and such? Hang the expense. Can you remember what they were?" She half smiles again at the well-dressed woman and is acknowledged in return.

"No, but I'll call the waiter over," says Wauters. "He'll bring the menu." He turns seeking the waiter. "I've been to France," he volunteers. "I went to the capital, Paris. The market for the world's pearls is there. I thought I had a trade. Went all that way only to be told I would have to hand my treasure over to an agent. No way was I about to do that. Let go of them and I'd never see them again."

"Yes, very interesting all that travel, stuff but the sweet things? You call the waiter? Can you do that?" enquires Carmen. "What, just call them to you, like that?" she says in near wonder and the settles into her seat.

"Well, this is very nice…I wonder who does all the ironing around here…not to mention the washing, not him, the waiter, I'll be bound. I don't know if it sits comfy with me thinking of these people running around after us…I would rather wash my own dishes…I'd know they were done properly then. Where do we take our dirties?"

Wauters takes her plate and cutlery to one side. Eventually, the waiter appears with the menu.

"And what's your name?" she asks the waiter boldly. He looks a bit awkward.

"My name's…Stewart, madam," says the waiter a little uneasily.

"Well, Stewart, my name is Brianna. Can you tell me where the bog is?"

"The 'necessary' madam, is through here." He gestures off.

Wauters and Carmen are sitting at a small round table in a lounge area. Coffee is served, they look out onto the street. The table has a coffee pot, cream jug, lumps of brown and white sugar in a bowl, which has a pair of silver tweezers set by it. Each have their own cups. Carmen has got through the personal angst but needs must that she finds something else to fret over. "I do hope Rollo is all right." She drains her cup and then turns it over to read the manufacturer's name which is stamped underneath. "I couldn't live like this all the time. I couldn't afford it for one; but holding yourself in all the time. The china is good, two shillings, perhaps more, for a cup and saucer. The bog was spotless, it was a 'Crapper', a proper flusher." She leans in. "I flushed it a couple of times, it was so clever. It was more comfortable than the plank and hole on our site! This coffee tastes different as well. We have the chicory essence, in a bottle, the one with the soldier on the label. A Scottish *mush* wearing a kilt being served his drink by a rather smart bloke who looks as though he has rushed to serve after washing his hair." She sits back in her chair. "I feel sleepy now. They've got the temperature too high in here. They must have money to burn. You couldn't come in here, eat and then go off to work. You'd need a lie down first." She did have enough to eat actually despite her reference to the brevity of the portion. You have to have something to moan about.

"Women are good company," he says, talking into his cup.

She asks enquiringly, "Have you, have you got a wife or anything?"

He nods affirmatively. "Oh yes, well, I *had* a woman. I *had* a child."

She looks a bit taken-aback. She only asked the question to clear her way only to find the patch cluttered and barred. "Where are they? What happened?"

"They were in South Africa. The Australians carted them off, to a camp that the Brits had set-up. I was away. Them, the Brits and the Australians, got frustrated with the *free state* running rings around them. They took away their families, to stop their men from fighting, you see?"

She wafts her fist in front of her. "The bastards!"

He gives her a knowing look. "All is not fair in love and war. They got their own back on me and so it goes."

"I don't get what you mean," she says.

The waiter approaches. "More coffee, madam?"

"That's really kind of you, Stewart. Have you got any bigger cups? There's hardly a mouthful in one of these things." She brandishes her coffee cup. Stewarts nods assent and adds.

"The kitchen has given your dog some meat and water."

Carmen: "Well, that was decent. Give them my best, will you?" Stewart walks away. "How about that. I hope the dog doesn't start to get ideas above his bloody station." She looks out the window while trying to tame a strand of hair which is tickling her brow. She has a jumble of questions to pose, some positive, some negative. He is thoughtful and attentive but distant. I mean, he's had plenty of opportunity to hold my hand or talk about us, a future perhaps. Is it all to do with that dead bloke and nothing to do with me at all? He seems to be so good with all the trappings but is he too good at it? He speaks of one life but seems to represent another, seems quite contented to look out the window, satisfied after his meal. "Go on then. Tell us your story. What do you mean? What went on?"

He leans over. "Well, Brianna." He stretches the name out for emphasis. She scowls at him. "I know you'll handle this with care," he says. "Who could doubt you after your dealings with that lady? So smart, so quick." The waiter returns with more coffee and mugs. Wauters waits till the man has gone, pours the coffee and offers the sugar to Carmen. She takes it and drops four cubes guiltily into her mug. "I lived in *Port Elizabeth,* in South Africa. Eish, memories! That was the centre for the British war supplies, to equip the invasion. All the provisions were channelled through *Port Elizabeth.* I pretended to work on the docks so I could keep an account of what was coming and going and give the information to the commandos, the Boers."

Carmen recoils. "Is that like being a spy? Y-You were spying on the British? They shoot people for less. Some of the patriots here have been shot."

He continues without reflection. "There are some things greater than life and liberty that you have to stand up for. Having been on the far-eastern run I was well suited to the business of shipping and docks, all that stuff. No one better, perhaps, no, perhaps that's a brag. But, in the course of everything, my family was taken away and I could not come out of the shadows to find them or help." He eases himself back his seat. "It's odd how it all happens. Sailors work really hard for their families but are away a lot as well. They think they are doing good and not being *jukka,* quite the opposite, active, purposeful, like dedicated? *Eish!* You arrive home after time at sea with your loot, your child dead from TB and your woman now living with a farmer somewhere up in Pietermaritzburg, you hear that she blames you! What have I done? So, you go back to *Port Durban,* nothing. On to *Port Elizabeth* and trouble. A flask of water and a chug of *biltong* is best you can hope for. Then they start after you and they are so persistent. You would not believe it."

"But you escaped to fight another day," she says, caught up in the excitement while not comprehending the detail. "You had a horrible time. You had so much ill-luck."

Wauters turns half away. "No, that's not how it went, not within a cable's length. That's not an end to it. They got onto me, so I ran off to South West Africa, around Windhoek, fell in with the Germans. But they were into some cruel stuff with the *Horero* and *Narma* peoples in the Kalahari and I was expected to toe the line, the German way, a big mistake? Germans, Portuguese and Belgians came late to having colonies in Africa and they was sore cruel too. The English tried to organise out east but the rest, they just cannibalised, stole.

No, not for me. I ran off again. Now *they're* after me too, the Germans. I tell you; you wouldn't believe it." He sings a snippet from the song that Plum sings. "*They wouldn't believe me, they wouldn't believe me.*"

"Escaped, but you made good?" she interjects.

"*Eish! Verdomme*! God no. I joined Om Paul and that venture fell through. Then it all came out. What I'd been up to in the past. After the *Maritz Raid,* they picked me up. They sent me on my vacation, to London, to Wormwood Scrubs*,* a prison in London. But records are lost, people die, some are sent abroad, exiled, kicked-out, jettisoned. They knew all right, what I'd done. They hit you where it won't show. But then they had this bright idea. I would be given a sort of freedom if I joined the British Army in France or, joy of joy, went into their navy. South Africa wasn't all good, I know that, it was a slave state way back. Comfortable, good money, lots of cash and me from Holland. A good Braai, plenty of drink at weekends; we pillaged all the lands around for labourers. Orange Free State*,* no chance. The allies had their way. The Vereeniging Treaty and the end of the South Africa Republic; they even restored the Zulu lands, would you believe. Om Paul exiled. Maritz's rebellion stamped on, him gone, escaped." A shrug. "So here I am. But I'm a born liar by trade, like you, I had to be. We have a lot in common." She stiffens for a moment. He puts his mug down on the table. Clears his throat. "I have had more aliases than…so many that even the British must have missed a dozen in their indictment." Stewart returns with more coffee and an even bigger mug for Carmen. She smiles at him winningly. He goes. Wauters continues. "Does anybody know what Wauters' given name is? It could be anything. As far as the British, here, are concerned, the crew, I told them I got arrested by the fisheries protection people in the North Sea, if anyone says anything different, I will deny it, convincingly."

Chapter 11

The boiler room of a ship is probably a venue you would not submit a pit pony to. Coal is being fetched from the bunker by the Trimmers, they also ensure the coal in the bunker flows out freely. When a load is requested, they fetch a barrow load from the bunker and wheel it down to the furnace plate. The Fireman has to then feed the boiler fire. He uses a slicing rod to make sure the coal is spread evenly in the furnace and the fire bars are kept free of clinker, a good even burn. The men are ruled by the dials. The place is warm to hot and when a man sweats the coal dust sticks. Should those so encrusted resort to rubbing the sweat away the effect is not unlike the action of emery cloth on a soft surface. Logan and the other boiler room people are busy at their work when Wauters appears with a grease gun in his hand.

Logan spots him and puts his shovel to one side. "Enemy in sight! Watch it lads we've got a visit from the east. Bloody foreigners!" Logan thinks nothing of using the slicing rod as a mock weapon and occasionally thrusts it in Wauters' direction like an epee. "On a sabotage mission, Fritz? Come to do for the condenser again perhaps? How did you do it last time? Come on, spill it. Was it a handful of sand or summat?" The Scottish drawl is indistinct to Wauters. He ignores the jibe. "Where's the *donkey engine,* mate?" Wauters asks.

"Hey-up boys! He's starting out small this time. He's going to bugger-up the *donkey engine*. Shorty, you must keep a watchful eye on our German friend."

"Dutch, fireman. Dutch." Wauters checks him.

"As we know from the news, spies, you lot, come in all sorts of disguises. Same difference. The give-away, that false beard. Stick on a dress, you could be *Mata Hari*, heh lads? Her at the fair, the bearded lady?" Logan has a support act featuring on wheelbarrow, Shorty.

"He's no Edith Cavell, Logan!" says Shorty.

Wauters gives Logan a stare. "You would have to admit that this voice…a very poor disguise if that was the…" He starts to relate.

Logan is on him like a ton of bricks. "You have all sorts...come in all sizes and guises."

Shorty sort of hides behind Logan and throws out rejoinders. "That's a good line chief. I see what you did there."

Wauters opens his jerkin as if for inspection. "See me, carrying a telegraph to send messages, invisible ink sloshing around in my…"

"Hear that banter? 'Sloshing'. A man of many languages, typical skilled snoop. Very practised. Go on, give us a bit of the old 'Gott in Himmel' bollocks. Go on, 'bollocks to the bulwarks'." Shorty laughs in a giggly child's manner at most of Logan's comments. Logan seems to emphasise his Scottishness as a validation of his not being a continental and therefore not suspect, his voice broader. "We had a lot of your sort, up in Arbroath, before all this. Aye, even in Arbroath; easy distance from Der Farter land, Arbroath, see. We were snide-out with them. Shitty *Bismarck Herring* mob. Waste of a good fish, if you ask me. Sold right down the road from the bloody Smoke House too. Pretend to be Jewish jewellers and clock menders, lapidaries, dainty trades, all that craft stuff. Making exploding cuckoo clocks for the export market, I bet."

Wauters goes the other way and baits him with his foreignness. *"Kleurrijk. Wat een fantasie.* Dutch, see. Yes, do you think I'm being too obvious?"

"Blabber-blabber. I bet he could give it to you in mumbo-jumbo African if he wanted. We speak-er the English, here." These last words he hovers-over for emphasis.

"OK, *Umlungu.* Anything else?" enquires Wauters, off-hand.

The fireman thrusts the slicing rod in Wauters' general direction. "Smart arse. I know you'll end up murdering us all in our beds. Remind me, Shorty." He shouts to his mate. "To tell them up top to watch Hymie here, like a hawk." His mood changes like the other mask being turned on the audience. He faces up to Wauters threateningly. "I've got the inside track on you." He turns to his giggly accomplice and back to Wauters, "By the way, where do you keep your Pickelhaube?" He feigns a giggle but it comes across menacingly, the awful laughing automaton clown at the fun fair. He turns to Shorty looking for acknowledgement for his allusion. Shorty sniggers, as required. Logan has a smirk on his face but because that face is covered in black dust with lighter skin around the eyes, Wauters finds the enactment rather funny no matter what sort of effect Logan is looking for. Minstrels spring to mind, Black and White minstrels. Logan flaps. "I bet your name is Helmut, ha, ha! Helmut, helmet. Get it! Handy Helmut..." Shorty is laughing at least. Logan pretends to put on a hat and struts about. "...for when you get the call."

"Nice one chief!" Shorty is pretending to be just this side of delirium. He can be excused to a degree; it must be murder being in this confined hole with a potential schizophrenic maniac.

"I can place you Hen, just by the company you keep. Talk about birds of a feather. Eh, Shorty, birds of a feather, eh?" It's lost a bit on Shorty but he tries his best to ornament it.

Wauters does not immediately get the drift but comes around to it. "What? Me and...Plum? You've got to be daft." Wauters is weighing Logan up. Doesn't want to poison the water but neither does he want to appear weak. Logan takes him by the shirt roughly.

Wauters holds his ground. Logan pushes him away. "Old *Mompie*? Not a chance. Better that he worked with you. He sticks to me like a limpet. He...infests me. He gives me the fever." Wauters smooths his shirt down it having been pulled about by those dirty Logan hands.

Logan tilts his head back slightly and looks at the foreigner through hooded eyes. "I bet. Sleeping together. Inseparable. A man goes to the country, this country, to enlarge the circle of his friends, that's you, eh? You continentals have some...exotic tastes. I don't buy it, the 'you're no friend of mine pal', bit. Well, all I can say is if you get in the way between me and the...captain's cat, just be prepared."

"Be prepared? For what?" Wauters smiles.

"You'll know, come the time, shug," counters Logan.

Shorty addresses Wauters. His thumb in the direction of Logan. "That little twerp did 'im up...at Rosythe. It was a stitch-up."

Like the bassoons to the piccolos, Logan picks up Shorty's theme. "That little bar-steward was Admiral Beatty's, what do they call it? Beatty kept him like a pet, not so much a cat but as a catamite, more like." It's another one of those hovering over words moments for emphasis. Shorty urges Logan on. "While all of us were slaving, putting ourselves into danger, Plum was in the lap of luxury," says Logan.

"He cheated, that runt." Shorty is losing the plot. He steps to the side of Logan not needing protection any more in his clamour to underline his boss's raging. "Logan here, the chief, had some snot on his glove, right. When he was wiping it off on his shirt, the little twerp 'it 'im. Bloody travesty. That's what happens when you play away. Would have been different in Scapa, he would have had his 'ead knocked off."

Logan almost pushes Shorty to one side as fired up as he is. He states very deliberately and angrily, bellows. "I had to come down from Scapa Flow" – pointing to himself – "…to Rosyth. I had a sandwich with a burnt sausage in it…" Shorty chips in that they thought it could have been a sausage. It was some food they'd tampered with. "…half a cup of cold tea, that's all I had all day. They set me up. Then straight into the bouts. I was all right in the first two bouts, sheer willpower overcoming all the odds. Easy, despite my disadvantages."

Shorty emerges from under Logan's armpit. "Yeah, both of them nancies. You did for them, Logan. You bust that fat AB's nose, like a ripe tomato, splosh! Just like a squashed tomato." Shorty giggles almost hysterically, like a pocket banshee.

"You bet I did. But that was fair, see. It's catchweight, yeah, all right. That AB he was bigger than me, like heavier, but he was my height. Short arse, on the other hand, your lover…" he refers to Wauters, "…he could'a run between me legs without touching the sides. It was like fighting a sodding flea. And then I got distracted. I don't know, he must have, like, jumped up and hit me. Imagine him on stilts, Shorty?"

"I can, chief, him on stilts."

"There was no other way…"

"…no other way…"

"…no other way he could have got me. Short arse…"

"…Like a sodding flea he was."

"Tell your boyfriend." He's really close to Wauters now. Head tilted to one side. "He had better stay off my patch. If I come across him, given the right circumstances." Menace. He throws an imaginary uppercut and then signals a knockout. "Make me a laughing stock would he? I'll strangle the runt. Anyway, tell 'im. Logan's not forgotten. There's a reckoning."

"I'm on your side with that, it's about the only thing that has any chance of shutting the blighter up," adds Wauters. Still smiling despite all, practiced, see. Wauters is joking, isn't he? "He's full of himself. He is an irritating bastard. He could do with somebody nailing him."

"See that…" Logan turns to shorty. "Didn't pass your attention, did it? Did you hear what he called his mate? Nice sort of friend to have. Typical German. You can't trust 'em."

"Come on, Logan, we were put together. I'm not welcome here, I know it. But I am no German. A stinking suicide ship and little parrot up there, I don't deserve it, I did not; it's like the asylum ward. What little regard he has for you…No, perhaps I shouldn't go there."

"Go on," urges Logan, sidling up again. "What's short arse being saying about me?"

Wauters is pretending at his best. "It's not good on a ship to tell tales."

Logan checks the gauges and then comes back to Wauters who hesitates until he recognises their urging mounting. Logan eyes him up and down. "Come on *Hindenburg*, you already announced the headlines you might as well tell us your story. No need to be coy. We're all adults here."

Wauters swaps a glance between the two men. "If, you're sure?"

The other two edge closer, Logan inclines his head again. Wauters heaves a sigh. "All right. He told me that you were 'easy'." Logan and Shorty laugh together. Logan's expression changes slowly to a grimace. He pounds his fist into the palm of the other hand. Wauters has landed a bit short. He needs to go again. "He said that you used what he called the *'Highland Charge'*, came at him like a real amateur."

"What did he say?" Logan urges.

"The Highland Charge; he's charging too much, and then he'd laugh; said he'd had tougher tussles with the *kreefs*, tarts."

A more serious look falls over Logan's face. Shorty pre-empts him. "Well, that won't increase your admiration for him, will it Jock? I always knew he…"

Logan spins around and sticks his face into Shorty's. "How many times do I have to tell you, you don't call me Jock, you flea!" He raises his hand to Shorty, who flinches, shrinks away. "I think it's all gone to his head. He's drunk on it." He peers into an unseen endless distance. "Shut up you lot! I don't want to just to beat that squirt, I want to…get his name and shove it down his throat. He will be a joke in any port. I'll bide my time for him. It's coming." He looks towards Shorty. "He's not about to run away, is he?"

Shorty tries to gain ground so stupidly lost. "No chief."

"His time is to come; I'll clock him all right. *Highland Charge*, he can't afford it, that's no mistake. He'll get no change out of me. Heh! See what I did there?" He pauses momentarily more to admire his own turn of phrase than to illicit admiration this time, "Insulting me and my country, what more encouragement do I need? You, Helmut, you keep me informed, do you hear? I've got this furnace to feed." He points to Shorty. "Hand me that shovel! Rat!"

-oo0oo-

The fag-end of winter. The season has been persistent. There is not that freedom. People are more focused on the facts of life, that is, the necessary rather than the esoteric. Will not hang around the streets in company to set things right. Conversation is mainly about the essential and resolution needs to be smart. Wool shawls, scarves, caps, outer garments collect water readily. That tear you have in your trousers, while no hindrance in the warmer airs, can freeze your groin or chap your knees in winter. Carmen now dodges between her duty and the café, which she now routinely visits. Dressed more smarter than previously. Her hair, tamed. Her presence heralded with that whiff of Cologne. She has the demeanour of a boulevardier, treating being waited on as normal, a compact between the waitress, wanting to look after you and the customer, recognising effort; but not friendship, intimacy. The main beneficiary is Rollo, who is putting on weight noticeably. He is new to the delights of sugared morsels and although not a nuisance towards his new companions, can be a bit…insistent. Carmen, on her beat, suffers disruption. She is more susceptible to the comments of some males, although, it has to be said, they seem to react to her new regalia and gilded appearance with a greater degree of circumspection. She no longer is the subject of coarseness and intimidation but seems to attract a better class, one of respectability. When previously it was a grim enticement to a 'bunk-up', now it might be a suggestion. "You'll be coming for a coffee then."

"You should come and meet my mother."

"I like what you've done with your hair." What is the use of a dog that is supposed to look half-starved to elicit sympathy from the punters when that dog is fatter and even, sometimes, can afford to turn his snout-up at scraps proffered? That dog is becoming a nuisance in some ways. He seems to be taking to the full suggestion behind his name, 'Sea King', with a new degree of self-importance. He now spends days away from home and comes back to the *vardo* absolutely shot to pieces. Bits of flesh bleeding like he's been ten rounds with a Tup. Impossible to rouse from his torpor once settled. Then after a couple of days left to himself, he's off again. They all say he's 'honeymooning', fighting over bitches and probably getting his 'end' away. He craves sympathy at times. He'll get none here.

Carmen sees him in his state and has no sympathy because he reminds her of the other dog, Wauters, wherever he is. She picks through the initial impenetrability of Manley-Hopkins and, unlike her, sees a fusion of words that can bring prickles to her eyes. She reads a bit of that *mush*, Kipling. She can feel a rage mounting in her reading stuff, she should have known, where the lack must have made her seem like a divi. She happened to mention, in an off moment, the poem '*Down in the Sally Garden*', to one of the music tinkers and, without breaking stride the guy broke into song, '*Down in the Sally Gardens*' a traditional air she hadn't known previously. She stood as much of the mellifluous beauty as she could, which was only two verses, before running from the place in floods of tears. 'Feck' that poetry for turning a self-contained and inwardly contented woman into a basket case of instability. 'Feck', that there was such wonder and beauty in the world that, till now, she had ridden rough-shod over. 'Feck' that she had the emotional contrivance already there within her to actually be touched, fashioned and tempted by a well-turned phrase, somebody else's observation. This was that bastard Wauters doing. Bastard! That was the worst day's work ever, meeting Vaughan and hearing of Wauters. For were they both not evil? The devil's own? 'Arse!', so this is what it is to be bewitched. If she could only stop and just be cool and weigh her situation.

She tries. So, one bastard mentions another bastard. The first bastard dies and second one wheedles his way into my…puts his great big self between me and the light. Takes me away from Queenstown and puts me into the jade green waters of *Thursday Island*. Tears off all my wool and linen and has me cavorting in the milky-composed waters of Australia, semi-naked, while he is a little way off stripped to his undies, sometimes surfacing from the depths to offer me a salmon sandwich or a plate of oysters sprinkled with spices. A man you could follow anywhere. But God, the dangers that you lead me to. Everything is imagined and whole image alluring but he doesn't feckin' care. No, that's not true 'cus he sometimes does. Look what he's done to me and for me, weigh it. I now know how to use a napkin and I'm known, and I think, respected about. I'm in a world so different from all that I thought I was due and nothing else, to a place that like a long corridor with shops on either side with each one full of new goods to try. She could walk that walk and life would be so much richer and she could be that man's lover. Make him toast and put some grilled tomatoes on it, extra butter on the *padda*. Her contentment in such thoughts was like settling down into the midst of a soft confectionary. But how would she really fair being taken away from all that she knew without the *phral* taking-her-back. The mother doing the money and father saying he thought a lot of me when he sees me down, just to get me chin up. Little things, but permanent things. Not like being abandoned in Australia at the first hint of trouble. Friendless, and him wandering off with intimate knowledge of you to be talked over with his rough mates. "Do you want the trade, dear. Shall I come back later?" Here she was on the cold, blowy street and that poor little woman in front of her, shawl tight to her neck, kept in place by a bony hand and freezing her tits off. Carmen was suddenly brought to her senses and apologised to the bag of bones looking up at her. Could she still do this? Could she lie, knowing now what she knows?

-ooOoo-

It was late afternoon, white horses on the water. A stiff breeze and spray, the little ship trying its best against insurmountable odds. Grey smoke with hints of other colours in it streaming from the funnel. Sparks emitting sometimes and sailors having to brush them off before they singe the rough materials of their clothes, make holes in the deck canvas. Plum is on deck looking out towards the horizon. Wauters walks up behind him stealthily and claps a rough hand on his shoulder briskly, meant to surprise. Plum jumps involuntarily. "What! Oh, it's you."

Wauters smile is like that of a grizzly, a conger eel, a shark's smile. "*Chommie*, idling, are we?"

Plum sets aside the surprise and the frisson of anger. "Just waiting for the light to go, Wauters. Gun practice…Grubs up."

Wauters puts his hands under Plum's armpits and casually lifts him off his feet. "Two questions, will I be able to recognise what it is, but first, is there some left?" Plum is dropped back on the deck.

"I don't know what cook calls it but it's all right, like curry, I think he said." Plum watches him walk away and a little shiver runs through him. He thrusts his hands deeper into his jacket pockets contemplating a few hours in the semi-darkness farting around with that gun.

Wauters smirks as he walks away. He gets food from the galley. When back in the hold, he sits on his cot and finishes his meal, hm, *dat was lekker*. Plum was right, it looked odd but tasted…right, a bit like a vague imitation of *Laksa*. He is pleasantly surprised; it tastes vaguely like something else too, not a *rendang* but, OK, it'll do. Should be encouraged. He puts his food can to one side. Lies back deep in thought. After a moment he sits bolt upright, moves over to Plum's Donkey Bag and rummages through it until he finds the island map. "What a fool. A lot of iron pyrites, fool's gold, heh? So, this is the secret. *Eish!* What a dolt." He studies the map briefly, puts it back into the bag. Riffles through the rest of the contents, the clothes, his father's letters, crap, some more junk and finds some change, coins. He takes a handful of the money and puts it in his pocket. Looking around about cautiously, he has a second thought and puts some of the money back in the bag.

-oo0oo-

Darkness; the stern of the ship. The sound of the propellor below occasionally breaking surface, not enough ballast maybe, a swell? The chart room, the captain's place; the controls of the ship, looking down on its full length. In the roads, you could clew-up the square sails to aid navigation or post lookouts on the bow to pass on your placement in a channel. It would be all too easy to position a sailing boat to take a following wind. Many a crew had suffered as a consequence of a wind from the stern, being 'pooped', taken down by the stern. It was idle sailing anyway as so few of your 'suit' would be exposed to the wind, one mast's sails covering the next. Errata, the mariner's book of half thoughts. The rise and fall of the ship in a big sea could make the poop deck unpleasant and the introduction of bulbous noses on modern ship's bows did much to flatten-out the ride. The poop, the quarters of the captain and conveniently right over the rudder. So many thoughts each one recalling another. But today Wauters just stands on a nondescript platform under the con and the funnel reaching up before him, a waste of space. He can chafe all he likes, there's no going back just to accommodate a man immersed in yesterday. Never do you feel so alone as when you are alone on the high seas with time to ponder. That great fluid flood, restless seas, senselessly churning; mists that bear in with sudden chill. Forbidding oceans, their strength, so immense, their dark depths as little known as the dark side of the moon. The eerie feelings. Fright delivered when suddenly pondering your distance from habitation, help. How can water that slips away like mercury in its placidity in one mode, hit a vessel like a great lump of rigidity, a wall of solid green gelatine, in another phase. How can that filigree of spray, so delicate and ephemeral, when, if packed together with its fellow feather-fluff, throw a ship onto the rocks and smash it there? How can it be a weighty carapace for all manner of monster and harbour them all and each so alien to the other. All predating in an endless round of gnashing and gnawing, slashing; nibbled to death slowly or swallowed live; fancy being eaten whole and conscious, either suffocating or just submitting slowly to gastric acids. On a black night like this, you have to crane over the rail to see any definition, the wake streaking away like a torpedo's run; bioluminescent sea glowing green when it's disturbed by a wave breaking or a splash in the water at night. Algal bloom makes a sea sparkle. Now that's eerie, more solitary making than the dead night sky and its twinkling, distant bodies. Why does man not intuitively understand the sea? Was it a pact? Did he lose his intimacy with that great abys when he became so urgent about the land, made his choice? Was man offered a choice? Why do women alone have a recall betrayed by the scent? Wauters leans on the Taff Rail, expressionless. He needs these times to explore the signs of the sea and to draw some comparison with his own inner darkness, a thing he himself constantly questions, cannot fathom, his great cavern of grief. The contortions of his plotting and his having given free rein to his unnatural, unemotional self. As if matters have developed their own council. As though he has released a force barely contained all his life that parasitised his being, that now sits at his shoulder normally, impishly; a small horned monster of malevolence. Now, it's out their roaming and creating victims. He's got himself in a real stew. He reflects how the game turned sour, how hatred and it's fostering sometimes plays havoc with caution and rationality, all caused by something he has no control over but must now find excuses for. Wauters had been in enough scrapes, challenging adventures and near-death experiences to be fairly sanguine about the whole business of life. His conclusion, no matter. No reason to fret over it. You will die, why grisle over it. There are those faiths in which the adherents are more than happy to sacrifice themselves in order to find absolution. Them Aztecs, waiting for a white-faced bearded man, the saviour; lame folks they were, without the wheel, gunpowder or any knowledge of sea-faring. Happy to just spend their time trying to seek this deity of their imagining, the fair-haired bearded one. To bring him to their hapless cause and then, having invoked that creature, finding it consuming them, becoming the apparition's food. Somewhere he had pieced together the ancient mantra unknowingly which raised the creature and now his beast roamed fiercely, hungrily. A life is worth nothing. We think ourselves precious, yet he knew enough about life, history, to know that hundreds of thousands, millions of sensitive, learned, loving, thoughtful, idealistic people can be wiped-out at a stroke, on somebody's whim, by nature even, back, from where we came. People just wanting to have it put before them and having no regard for what they sacrifice in exchange for their 'free will'. No energy of their own to create something of and for themselves. Quite happy with their procreation and small pleasures and their small fame within closed circles. For this they are resigned to be subservient, burnt and racked. What about that Impaler guy, said to have sought revenge for being buggered at the Ottoman court. Getting his revenge by lowering people onto sharpened wooden spikes through their anuses, slowly, until the device erupted from their mouths. Poor, weak, commanded innocence; timidity to feed a lust. An endless supply. What about it? Does age offer any solution to the problem of why do we exist when we can become so ill that our relatives, who can no longer afford to feed us, can deny us because we are no longer pulling our weight? Could take us out into the wild and leave us to wither. So many finding such a lore acceptable. Why? So that in their turn they suffer the same anxiety, same odd sort of treatment and can call it a legacy; that seems fair? 'Hush little baby, don't you cry. You know your mother was born to die', how frightening is that? And still they make babies all too easily. Wild birds even. What are they thinking, having chicks that will steal the supplies in turn and make a comfortable life hard. By their action sew the seed of the next conflict, such is heredity, succession. There the naïve girl and the silly lad. His purposefulness, but independence is lost to the two of them. They are happy giving up their only precious belonging for illusory reward. How did that happen? She is all right. Surprising at times. What of beauty? Who cares? Fancy being trapped in Queenstown for the rest of your life. You can see yourself, years hence, mooching about that dismal quay. Looking to the horizon with envy, wanting away. The lad, I could screw his scrawny neck. All that jabber, *eish!* Fancy having that as a constant companion. What can you think of somebody that can't see through being gulled by a scrap of paper with a drawing on it that a child could scratch from its imagination? He spits into the largely unseen tide below. Grant you there's something there to be admired. I honestly thought that the two locals would do for him, save me a lot of trouble. But no, he does both of them; a man with that power, and then looks to me. Jumble, jumble.

Someone approaches. It's Logan. Wauters can hate Logan even for interrupting his reverie. Just when he was coming face to face with his own beast the creature, he has been summoning slips away like the cowering wraith it is.

Logan, hot and bothered. "What's the drift?" He wipes his hand and neck with a dirty rag. "Next time I'm born, I'm going to be a rich man. Taste that fresh air. What's up? Why the call, 'Bill'?"

"*Ag, dom, daar is jy.* You've got it wrong Logan. Plum, means nothing to me. We have no history, him and me. I feel a bit hard done to, you going on like you do about him, *Babbelbekkie, jabber-jabber*. He makes my head hurt. Chinese torture, drip, drip, drip all the blasted time. *Eish!* I can't shut the bastard-up. I heard your story about the…short arse…*Praatsiek* and I've been thinking on it. I could relate to it. I know where you're coming from." Logan stands-off from Wauters, wary. His head half turned towards the other, that pose that people sometimes adopt when trying to figure the other out or contemplate a quick departure from the scene. "It's hard to be the butt of people's jokes, enough do it to me. I'm the foreigner, tell me about it," bleats Wauters. He moves towards Logan and the stoker instinctively moves a step back. An animal's instinctive calculation of having enough space there to see a pounce coming, a swords length perhaps? "I have a way we can both get satisfaction. I need my moment too; I have my reasons. We could be maties. We share stuff, right?"

Logan does not look at him. Wauters sees the glow of a cigarette in his adversary's mouth but not the man's expression so much. Logan speaks through the soot dark miasma of the night. A breeze riffles through Wauters hair, raises a collar sightly, which then ebbs, flaccid; falls back. "Do we? Do we really? Me, I don't see it. You two are as thick as thieves, period." Logan's cigarette glows brighter with the exhalation of speech.

Smoke from the funnel, like an imagined apparition about the graveyard, engulfs them both momentarily, Kadar, the dark one, free in the world. Logan coughs and the extended ash from his cigarette, that small bogart stuck between his lips, falls down on his overall, unnoticed. He coughs lightly. "So much for fresh air." Aside. "He's not cleaned the bloody fire bars; I'll kick his arse when I get back. I should get back. I'll have the captain on my neck." Thumbs at the funnel then peels the sodden fag from between his lips, where it has almost become stuck. He spits exaggeratedly over the ship's side. Logan touches Wauters on the chest with an extended forefinger as the man leans past him to hawk over the gunwales. "I'll get him. On my terms and in my way."

Wauters tries to catch the man's attention, get him to look at his face. Fix a man's eyes and that denotes sincerity, don't it? When they look to the left a lie? Summat of that. "Why put yourself in the way of trouble when there is another way? You'll only bring more trouble on yourself, *varkkop*."

Logan reacts. "What's that you said?"

"What?" Wauters opens his arms wide so as to indicate incomprehension.

"I heard the word 'kop' in there, that's head isn't it in your tongue? What are you calling me?" He moves closer to Wauters. "I would hate to think that as well as being a spy you were taking the rip out of me, smart arse. *Kop*, that's head ain't it? What's that you calling me? Shit-head or something else like that?" He moves quickly into Wauters, Wauters is not moved.

"Not even close. Logan, evil him that only thinks evil they say. It's a saying we have in Holland. Like your 'big head' only referring to a man's smarts, like big brain." Wauters points to his own head. "I was just remarking how smart you are like when you don't seem to know it yourself; but it needs coaxing out. It's all in the head. You really ought to be more trusting my friend, if we are to be in an enterprise together."

The fireman frowns. "I don't recall any mention of an…enterprise, you say? I'm here on sufferance. Say what you've got, if you have anything, there's a fire to see to. I seem to have come-up here, on your asking, for nothing. As to trust. This is not the place, the world or the ship to talk of trust." Logan whips the dirty rag from an overall pocket and wipes his forehead. "Do you know who you are rubbing shoulders with here?" He offers a broad sweeping gesture seen even in this half-light. "None but the desperate and the 'impressed' would sign-on to this shit hole? What a posting. Yes, they're all here, trawler men, merchant men. Weekend sailors, aye and spies and criminals, he points to Wauters…full strength bona fido cons. I think they emptied the pubs to crew this tub. Take yourself, for instance. You're shady. More than most."

"I'm impressed too," pleads Wauters. "That's an end to it."

Logan lights another cigarette, having to turn his back to the wind to protect his face so that the light won't get blown out by the pulsing sea breeze. He has put himself in a dangerous position. His back to a would-be assailant, it occurs to Wauters too. Logan exhales from his nostrils and then his mouth. He could be on fire. He turns back to Wauters.

"Let's have no more measuring in tenths let's get to the yards," demands Wauters.

"Nah!" says Logan. "I'm not interested in you and I've wasted enough time. Well, this has been very pleasant, he lied easily, but I have a job to see to." Logan points to the smoke stack. He makes to move away. Wauters calls after him.

"Go now and you stand to make yourself a whole host of problems. You've over-thought things. That big brain of yours, you've been angry for too long. Your thinking's gone rusty; you're springing rivets. I've been at sea most of my adult life. I know bluff talk when I hear it. I see it in you, that there is no strategy, no cunning; no subtlety." Logan stops, turns his head towards the speaker. "You are bound to get yourself more and more worked-up over this bone you're gnawing on. One day, you'll explode and regret it the rest of your life. Listen to me. I can spare you that and serve your purpose. I can help you before you risk a tooth."

Logan turns back a step. Checks his cigarette. "And where did you do all this sailing? Go on, feed me more of your line."

"I was on a *coper*, a grog boat, on the North Sea. We got taken by the fisheries protection. They let my Pops go. He told them that he was *my* slave, you know, *forced* onto the boat. That's another story, anyway. For a man like me who has been dealt lots of lies in the past, that was new, inventive and unexpected. How many are ever ratted-out by their own?"

Logan is dismissive. "So what? All too glib. Too practised. Shows you as the victim and gives you a past that would be hard to disprove, eh. What's your home town then?"

"Delft, where the *'Oranges'* are buried," Wauters offers.

"Oh yeah, where did they lay the grapefruits, then!" Logan guffaws, takes a couple of steps closer, nudges Wauters. Wauters does not share the joke.

"Aye, that was a good joke, nicely conceived," Logan says grandly. "The Dutch royals, as helped my relatives over in Northern Ireland. That could have been a clincher, except I don't trust you at all, so, a bit…wasted. We have Dutch Purse Seine-netters up north and I don't know what it is, but they're not like you somehow. They bring mackerel and herring to sell to the 'smokers'. They are…not quite like you. What is it? Accent? Hm, I don't know This is getting us nowhere. You're clever. I have a feeling about you."

This Logan could be more difficulty than just being a nuisance. What does he know? Wauters thinks that he might just know more about Holland than *he* does. Logan is about to walk off again. The funnel smoke wafts by. "You'll regret it," Wauters says with a shout trailing away in the smoky gusts. "You'll make him the hero. You've got disaster written all over you. Perhaps I was too hasty calling you *varkkop*?" One thing at a time. Logan is so nutty as to do Plum serious damage, get him off the ship, over the side. He's thought about it himself in a sort of off-hand way. He is to be encouraged, kept sweet for now. Tied up in a silken thread and consumed in my own good time. He can just slip away from Carmen. That's what sailors do.

Logan turns back to his would be confederate. "O.K., I'll give you a minute. I'll listen, but no doubt I'll regret it. Go on then." Logan is hooked. Wauters is transcendent. Appealed to the man's conceit and won him. Another example of the great game and his mastery of it. In the background a hymn is being vented, *'The day Thou gavest Lord is ended'*, being sung by some of the crew, perhaps by some of the more scared crew, mislead crew, Plum? "There we go again, the other-worldly putting their faith into mysticism. Listen." He pauses. "It's so nice to have such a close relationship." A statement larded with sarcasm.

"Are you sure you're not just coating me in your own ways? How trusted are you?" Logan flicks his cigarette over the side. Wauters contrives a thought that Logan can take away with him.

"Plum made an ass of you, so the story goes, and you have been angry on it ever since. You thought that you would never have another opportunity to set things straight." He opens his arms sideways with his palms raised. "Well, here is that opportunity. What more do you want? It's war. People die, get transferred, run off. So here you are, the luckiest man in the world. You have the means to satisfy that which had been let slip, never to be recovered. They will hear about it in Scapa, like we had a jungle telegraph. Wish that I should be so lucky." Wauters looks down both side of the superstructure. Then sidles up to Logan warily looking all around him as he speaks. "He's still training, you know. He runs and goes to the gym, the little bugger. Never trust a man what don't drink. He took-on two locals the other night. You wouldn't believe it. They were not the friendly sort, twice his size, well not quite. Believe me. I thought he would be killed. He laid them both out, well, *twatted* them both. Big men. Angry men. The circumstances are irrelevant. But I was there. I ran off, hid. Well, I would, wouldn't I?" Wauters looks down both sides of the superstructure again, are there any interlopers? Another element of a conspiracy, draws you together. "I stood out of it. I hid while *Piet Pompies* did them both. I thought, I had hoped, that they would give him a doing over." He gets into Logan's face. "*Eish!* He's small buts he's tough. He's certainly ready for you; you look a bit lardy around the 'love handles', liver trouble? Too much drinking? He's more than enough for you."

Logan spits extravagantly as he wants to. The fireman wriggles like a fish on a trident.

"But he's a trained boxer. You can see…that straight jab. A good mover. A full range of shots," continues Wauters. "What you got, eh?" Logan moves to interject, knuckles up as though the bell has sounded. "Never mind. Here's the trick. It's beautiful, even though I say it myself." More cautious glances just to raise the idea of secrecy and the trusting solidarity, the hint of his betrayal, what he is putting in the kitty. "I can arrange for *Loskop* to want to give an exhibition bout, he's stupidly self-confident enough to go for it and I have a…little…pull, with the officers, for the arrangements, the bout. "See". Wauters smiles and gestures with his head, a little nodding movement. "It's beautiful. Nobody can mention revenge or hatred or getting even. No chance of come-back. And you, it will be known you were game enough, man enough, to put your name forward to provide a little *entertainment* for the crew." Logan rubs his chin. Wauters has another look down the deck. The funnel smoke gets thicker, blacker, as one with the night, seen only when it curls and writhes around a deck lantern. The hymn has finished and the ships usual sounds take over, the old urging rhythm of things mechanical. The exhausting tirelessness of machines versus man and its omnipotence over him. What have we created? "A few well-chosen punches, you could turn him into a vegetable. I even know where all this could happen even. When we make port again, we use one of the workshops, a boathouse or something for the 'exhibition', yeah, an 'exhibition' bout. We can get the dockworkers in to watch. That's even better. Thank them for their 'hard work', Plum's daft enough to think he's doing good. He's the sort that can't resist such jabber. We can run a 'book', gamble, have some betting on the outcome. There are all sorts of possibilities. You have an even bigger audience to mark your revenge."

Logan has been taking in every word. His face changes from profound scepticism to recognition of his own sort of genius and invincibility. He flicks the cigarette he's been chewing-on into the wind. The butt flies away, hits the deck further off and sparkles briefly like a dud. "What a rat you are Hymie. What a stinking callous, rat foreigner you are." He lolls-about, ponderously. "What hurt has he done you? Yet, here you are, setting him up? That's slimy, if you like." Logan smiles all through his little oration. "All this time you been like 'this' with the little winkle" – he crosses his fingers – "you get right up to him cosy like and then you shop him? Like bayonet work. You look 'em right in the face and shove it in and twist, just for the added pleasure. My goodness, and I thought I was hard." Logan giggles. "What you suggest…hm. Yes, it sounds great, if you can deliver what you say. The officers, the time and place. You're a clever bastard." Logan has bought into it. "But I am not at all sure that the 'brass' will fall for it. Fighting amongst the crew, not good for morale? Getting civvies in on it? Finding a location? And after?"

"What do you care? What do you care? He might ship out or not care anymore. Win, win." Wauters grins.

"Just sort of by the way, what are you getting out of this 'Bill'? Someone as slippery as you…you don't waste your time…for nothing." He leans on the Taff Rail. Spits over the side and spits again. "This feels like doing a pact with the devil." He walks around in a small circle kicking at the Taff Rail posts. He lights a cigarette. "You get the brass on-side and…yes. I'll do it. Good chance I'll feel better about it when it's all over. It's like being ill, having this roaming around insides you. Do it."

He taps the side of his nose, walks off. Wauters shows no emotion stares blankly. Leans on the rail like someone exhausted from excessive exercise. He looks into the dark the ship is leaving behind in its wake as if mesmerised. Looks into his hands. Goes to his quarters.

Chapter 12

There is a supreme lack of drama. No sightings, no alerts. The most adventurous moments are all centred around food, which is…variable; what will be the sensation derived today? Sickness or being sated? A big sea is running; it's invariably a big heaving thing. What has so upset Neptune that he is constantly raging? Perhaps the ship will get sunk by nature before the submarines intervene, as they must. It is dark; spume that speeds out of the darkness only to be illuminated by the ship's lights just before it coats you, flies everywhere a locust sea; waves crash against the ship's side and sometimes the sound of these meetings reverberate like a great drum beating for the oars, is followed by the accompanying spray, the chorus of triangles and cymbals skittering along the plating. Waterfalls of water fall off the superstructure. In turn, the tide pulls and pushes. The ship tussles with the waves, hogging and sagging. Now held in the fingertips of the great surge by its bow and stern, the next, balanced on its fulcrum, teetering on the waist. One minute up, the next down by the head. Sometimes up or down and tilting side to side, within the helpful limitations of the bilge keel. There are a variety of postures and all completely random. The rivets creak, sometimes some may sheer. A panel is stove in, steel plating dented by the blocks of solid water heaved-up from the depths and thrown against them maliciously. The engine races and then calms. They try and keep the screw in the water as otherwise the racing of the engine, when the water pressure is off, might cause over-heating, might take the revs over some limit. The bulbous bow makes the ship less ready to plunge, more buoyancy.

The caboose, which is bathed in a weak golden light, gives a false impression of cosiness. The Lascar and the cook are inside. They wriggle and squirm to afford enough room to pass each other, like some new intimate dance, a culinary tango. The cook is singing, '*Pack up your troubles…*' and the Lascar is beating a percussive rhythm on the kitchen utensils. The cook chops some vegetables inexpertly. Looks down, the slop bucket is full. He motions to the Lascar to empty it. There is some objection to the instruction as the Lascar points to the weather. Why is it that the bucket is always full in the worst weather on the worst nights? The chef insists, he's chopping, isn't he? Where can he put the bits if the bloody bucket is full, eh? The Lascar takes the slop bucket and in the poor shelter of the superstructure ties a rope to it while being wetted by the copious cold spume that whips him, envelopes him, his breath taken away from him momentarily in each drenching. He feels the balance against the rocking deck and while at a standstill can adjust his stance against the canting deck plates. He pulls the knot on the bucket handle to check its security. Losing one bucket was unlucky, to lose two; it doesn't take much to set the cook off at the best of times. Approaching the ships rail, he is all too aware of the clawing fingers of the sea grasping blindly for anything it can get hold of on deck, something to pull into the sea's gaping maw, before falling back into the general agitation like a ravenous sea monster, a massive cephalopod. The tide swells up and over and under the rails; wraps around his ankles, seeking. He feels the grasp. Begrudgingly, it's letting go, as it seeps away. Sometimes it barely licks at his shoes but then another more savage tide emerges from the dark beyond and grasps eagerly at his leg. Somehow, the Lascar contrives, in the act of throwing the slops out over the water, to throw himself over the rail too! He is propelled over the side by the force of his throw and one of those random geometrical changes in the ship's attitude and a horde of savage waves wanting him to accompany them back below. The horror of the situation is immediate. Clinging desperately to the bucket's rope with one hand, he is engulfed repeatedly in these great oozing's of ice cold, sinewy waves, made by the already dead wanting, urging Doomah Sen to join them; submerging him at times beneath the onrushing flood, while he, in a debilitating and frenzied panic, strives for a second purchase and to catch a breath winded from him by the intense penetrating cold. The salt smarts in his nose and throat. The wind is knocked out of him by the icy cold banging him against the ship's side viciously, rivets catching his trousers a tearing the fabric. Thirty-five cubic feet of the ravaging floodwater equal to one ton. But his hands are slimy wet and cold and holding the life line is a supreme act commanding every last scintilla of his powers. His face has a look of abject terror; it would be so easy to let go. Had he only spent more time contriving the knot. That is all that stands between him and eternity at this moment, he cannot even scream his parlousness. What do people think of in such circumstances? As if, when awash with water and all those chemicals that the body produces when challenged, that you can think of anything? Like being prepared for the moment of extinguishment, the body is less alive with concepts, flushed of plans, thoughts of losing life and leaving loved ones. He alone hears his tiny screams, so unnatural and animal like, primal, diminished by nature's howling. He swings to and fro as he is submerged in the next mounting tide and banged once more against the ship's hull which is another, a more callous, bruising means of taking away his breath. Doom laden, as if he needed any further encouragement to let go, it bruises the wrist of his free hand as he attempts to soften the blow by anticipating the contact and holding out his arm as a buffer. This too leaves him gasping, heaving, choking. He yells in his terror and struggles to maintain a grip, all restraint to the winds. Can he afford to change hands? His mouth fills with water, its stings his throat, he splutters as if the sea is trying to make it impossible for breath, for rescue, by every single one of its wiles. The whole orchestra of hell bears away any sound that he might make and what little perception he can muster makes him understand that there is no help, will not be any help. The seas, momentarily, drop away and he swings up with his other hand to grasp at the smeary wet vision that his eyes perceive of the rope above him. The shrieking banshee wind takes away his voice and deposits it somewhere in Saint George's Channel, leagues off. All he does by shouting is wind himself. Even though the throbbing bruised wrist curtails that hand's usefulness, he attempts both hands on the line, then the hand starts to hurt awfully and then only one hand maintains him. Fearsome dread, that his study of physics could help him now? Was the great man, Einstein, ever in a situation that pondered this extinction and would it help him now, theory? Did Euler's Constant apply to life and death here? No, too lofty, too arid an intelligence to actually feel. Just one coalesced thought from his immense number of propositions or the outcomes of Sir Davey or Dalton? After an epic struggle, he gets his foot on the bucket. He has swung his leg up with the help of surging spume and he has his calf lodged across the top of the bucket which makes him feel more secure. He can understand and think now and he can see the ships rail which, one minute, he is well below, the next, level and sometimes even above, looking down at it. Near exhausted, the sea gives him a lift and he is tossed over the rail. He drops heavily and painfully onto the deck numbing his upper arm. He is like a landed fish, his mouth moving as if gasping air, he squirms in the runnels for a purchase, pulled inexorably to the ships side again and perdition; heavy limbed and partially blinded by the salt he wriggles stupidly. He virtually squirms, rather than crawls his way to the galley, holding the bucket for whatever reason, the soppy string trailing out behind. He pauses before the caboose, panting more exhausted than he has ever been before, his lameness added to by his clothes being heavy saturated. Eventually, he rises shakily to his feet. Entering the caboose, the cook hardly pays him any attention, the man absentmindedly passes the wide-eyed Lascar a peeling knife and motions that he should set to work on the potatoes. The Lascar, saturated, hair plastered to his forehead, leans, chest heaving, hangs against the work surface trembling. Cookie pays no attention to him, *"It's a long way to Tipperary..."* taken-up completely with something he has done to the gravy which has made for a consistency he has never achieved before, which he thinks wonderful; leaving him pondering how it was done. Gradually recovering from his near-death experience and fighting the urge to weep, the Lascar finds that screaming in his head which latterly dogged him, is subsiding. He takes a couple of deep breaths, thanks the stars for his preservation, looks to the heavens before commencing the peeling once more with shaky hands, his holding hand wrist smarting, the legacy of his crises. The potatoes now take on a new preciousness which had escaped him previously. How beautifully formed they are. How clever is the skin? Now he does cry but tries to keep it to himself, he is so taken by the vegetable that fate might have contrived that they should never meet. The potatoes are placed reverently into their tub having been observed and undressed.

-oo0oo-

The ship is progressing on a calm sea at last and the brightly lit but insipid sunlight should make the whole world less insufferable. But people are tense and cowering. The Cook and the Lascar wait expectantly. A lookout had informed, a sighting in the offing. The captain scans the horizon. Everyone is sweaty despite the cold. Brought to quarters what, forty minutes ago? The captain looks at his watch and the binnacle. The Quartermaster beside him wipes the beaded sweat from his glistening brow with a forearm. They search the sea for signs. Everybody searches the sea. The pot in the galley boils over and when hastily taken off the heat scalds. Everything in the world is pain. Who has not banged their head on the hatch frames moving between compartments, or tripped on a raised deck plate, out of the blue, previously negotiated without hindrance, spiteful? All are intent, watching. The gunners try and move undetected to their posts. The chronometer on the bridge ticks on. A spanner is dropped and the sound is unnaturally loud, people jump and angered faces pivot to locate the miscreant that dropped the tool. In the waist, an on-looker crosses himself but for some reason feels self-conscious of his action, has the need to give a sheepish smile to those about him. This is the tomorrow from hell, forming out of an altogether more placid vision of the coming day imagined; take us back. Yesterday was a good day, take us back. Tomorrow is all wrong not somewhere you should be exploring. Given a name and yet, until entered into, it is nothing but falsehoods and fantasy. Just how we were plus that pinch of the unexpected. A roll of the dice, a hopeful guess. All or nothing on an errant, ill-considered surmise. We won't look back, hopefully, and say, tomorrow was scary. The dead aren't expected, enjoined, to grieve for tomorrow. So, many suggest that they are better off out of it, away from the coming day with all its twists and turns, its being informed; it's becoming, aware, its lessons and fears, its lost bet and its refused, curtailed, love. This is why suicide was invented, to save us from the looming tomorrow which has always disturbed us. Better to stay in today forever and when the clock says that this one has past, then celebrate today, like as in 'The King is dead. Long live the King'. Today is tangible, has a time-line, a beginning and end. Tomorrow is a fiction. Put a date to it and the mood changes, some future date is not 'tomorrow' it's 'then'. Gain a label and it all gathers credence. But not this day. There may be no more tomorrows after this one is spent.

The captain rings for half ahead slow. The tension continues. The deck crew feel the ship's change of pulse. Someone's asleep, is roused; it's an act of cowardice not to share the general panic and trepidation. Nudge the bastard awake! How cruel to acquaint the man so abruptly with such fears? Then, warm and cosseted in the filing system of a mind, which is said to set about cataloguing what all our waking hours brought to us. Now swamped, washed away by the prodding to sensibility. A man with shaving soap on his face is frozen, expectant. The white in his eyes overwhelming the white of his shaving soap, his safety razor hovering. A moment ago, he searched in the little mirror that had lost a lot of its silvering, trying to find his best profile and recalls his girlfriend telling him that his one eye was bigger than the other. He fingers a measles scar and thinks how the body, generally, is marked by life. How lovely it was at birth and now disfigured, besmirched now. He had chipped at the hair with his razor. Sometimes it glides through the foliage, other times is stutters, digs-in. The hot water for the soap is too hot and makes the skin tender and he will have to get a sliver of paper to staunch a nick in the skin on his cheek that he occasioned earlier. But the blood has its own course. First it swells and then it seeps off into the wet soapiness, like a river delta. Diffuses, thins in texture. Another matelot sits fearfully on the toilet. To die with your trousers around your ankles and to share the deep with your own filth, intimately, horrifyingly. He has never been able to look at his droppings. Some swear by it. They analyse what comes out and it becomes the bible of their diet or the scourge of their drinking. There is nothing quite so assuring as your own smell, which he is wreathed in. He has dropped his cleansing paper, fearing he may not need it. He could finish, go out the door, but actually, he knows in his heart of hearts he does not want to see 'it' coming. More eyes are recruited to peer into the vast seascape, like imposing a sense of order on things will assuage the feelings of rage, fright, anxiousness, wonder and helplessness. False starts and mind games in the observing. The man that was writing the letter, he loses the thread of his thoughts and is all too aware that his cursive script, normally pretty child-like, has deteriorated further into a spidery scrawl. A sort of darkness seeps over his intention and erases his narrative. What will be the dimensions of the interloper? How many have ever even seen a submarine? What *is* the size of the thing they are seeking? How big will a U-Boat look against the panorama of the open ocean? Where will it appear? Most eyes are cast to the port side but what if the sneaky bastard has dived under, playing a tortuous game of now you see me. What sort of sadist would do that? Plum is with his gun crew, fortunate that he has thoughts to occupy himself with. Not like so many, those that rely on others. Fancy, trusting your life to someone else. They who know him can only hope he serves them today against the odds of his record. The initial report said big. How big is big? You can't size such a thing by the width of a fisherman's outstretched arms. How slow, is slow. What is quality? What is fast for one is common place, unremarkable to another. A cyclist outpaces a pedestrian, a dog cart outpaces the milkman's dray, a train beats them all. Then you have cars which are getting faster all the time and the drivers more daring and more reckless. We've all seen those mindless, Tweed attired, goggle wearing idiots tearing about with their fixed eyes staring over bounding bonnets, seemingly getting pleasure from frightening the horses. Step aside animals, your days are past. Why should so many be so tense. How many beans make five? 'A bean, two beans, a bean, a bean and a half and half a bean'. Just put something in your mind that isn't to do with the 'd' word…the end. What if something as nonsensical as that was your last thought on earth? How trivial is that? You might have thought that knowing their mission would illicit some sort of excitement, anticipation, thoughts of resolution, the uncovering of the bloody big surprise prepared for Gerry. But they have all come to know that 'your German' is surprised at nothing and a master of the unexpected himself. He lives for war and to die for the cause, lives to die. He worked towards conflict, you tried to ignore it. Where he thrives, you are reduced. You would rather be in your trawler or waiting counter in the greengrocers owned by the Cobham family. Or be with your woman inspecting the landscape of each other's bodies. You could be wondering how many flowers the rhododendron will have this year's and how the raspberry plant will fair. You actually yearned for the unexamined life although those with intellect think such an existence would be trivial, unworthy. But you never spent time in keen company tossing over all aspects of life, dissecting art, bandying about critiques and knowing what the government should do; your life is far more elemental than that. You have never had such leisure, never known lotus eating, you want potatoes. You have no cause, well not in Fritz's sense of it. There is no trace of the manic in the British, no rousing them to fanaticism. Your cause is to live, yes, to live, to be, I want to live, please, please! Let me alone. Let me be. I don't know why I signed-on, although the money was handy; it got me away from Shona, I didn't have to face up to my dad's anger, the bookie can't get to me here. I just wanted to be left alone! I wanted to go my own way. Make a bit of money. Go to the States. Walk up to Kinder Scout. But whatever has been said previously was probably bravado, lies, your inner idleness triumphing feeding you half-baked conceptions. Those stories you heard of allied triumphs were only consolation for the tragedies we knew and the ones that were vague stories seen on the street corners with their huddles of amputees. Captain Cathcart suddenly feels tired, horribly, leaden tired. His shoulders sag and his mouth dries. He's been robbed and unable to address the thief. He wants to sit. He takes the handkerchief from his jacket breast pocket, dabs his face. There is a little cologne on the material that Mrs Captain sprinkled on there before he left to serve. He sighs heavily. The quartermaster looks up, eyes to heaven. The captain has not anticipated this, yet it is the reason he is here. His lack of foresight means that he may go to his death without that valuable letter to Mrs Captain in the mails. Look, she sewed my initials into the cloth, she put the scent on it, she did her stout stuff, knowing full well what it was he was going to and she never once mentioned anything about not coming back. That would have been self-serving.

If your partner were dying, the fact that both of you are conspicuously conscious of, the outcome, would you not start in about, 'I have always loved you. I hope I have a place in your heart.' You wouldn't do it to them, it's admitting to the end. Satisfying your intemperate self for their dread and hopelessness, giving-up. She said that she would monogram his new nightshirt for when he gets back and she was going to make his favourite Moules Mariniere. In the summer, we'll go down to Winchester to that…Oh stop it, it's never going to be the same! The rising inclination to cry. Put it to one side! Stop torturing yourself. But it goes on and his every indiscretion his every temptation, the loss of the watch she had monogrammed for him, none of it can be denied now. The horrible truth that death is the ultimate failure of your existence. Then there is stuff like the Will and the rental agreement with the Estate. Details about burial arrangements, favourite hymns, with not a thought for the prospect that he may never be found. All the crew, if they were honest, have a regret at this moment, some are more direct about such things than others. Some think about wives and family but there is one who wonders what will happen to his fishing ketch and whether or not his thuggish son will do the right thing by his mother and take to the trade rather than dodging the column and escaping into drink. To think that he had tried so hard to build the business-up. Suffered all manner of deprivation for his lad and what does he do? He says that he's got a plan to start a business tiling roofs! Fishing is a good living, an honest living. We never know how we will face that defining moment. There are those here that have never known love. Some who would have had their fortune assured when this was all over or had a scheme in-hand. It was enough for some that they would never know what it was like to drive an automobile, each to his own. Would never know the new popular-songs coming from America. Some fancied living in America. They had heard it was a land of opportunity, not like the place they scraped-by-in, back home. Once upon a time, not so long ago, that place was lovely, no now. Built-up, coal waste tips, pools drained trees hacked down (those leviathans butchered). It's said that it's time to go when so much around you has changed and your left with nothing to relate too. No shared memory in a landscape you once fitted. Wasters, truants, hopefuls and charlatans, this was the moment that would determine it all for every deviant, every saint and every criminal liar, every self-deceptive, every paranoid, every positively schizophrenic. There is a silence. The slow thump, thump of the screw sounds like the quiet version of that trireme drummer goading the slaves. 'Butty', a sometime acquaintance of Plum, had been the life and soul.

In the mix only an hour or so ago. They first started to notice him shaking, then he developed this glazed look in his eyes and urine started to emit from his trousers bottoms about his ankles. He seemed totally oblivious. You can only stare for so long and then you get stare fatigue. Eyes have their job and they just get on with it. All right, if you have a bit of trouble reading in later life, you might screw your eye up, that can cause an ache, less of a problem if you can't read anyway. Just looking out at that blank canvass of wave upon wave with little or nothing to define depth, dimension, the mind starts to form imaginary patterns trying to make sense of it all. Cleverly, the brain goes to work on your surroundings and soon you are hallucinating, not in a drunken way, but seeing things which are not there, but conjured, projected. Behind the funnel in a place not overlooked, secret, a bloke has taken his under shirt off and is writing on it. He's writing a letter for when his corpse is found. All bollocks of course. About how he loves everybody at number one hundred and two and pledging his few possessions at home. Just short of writing, say goodbye to the dog for me. An epistle that gives offence to learning, no punctuation. There is a bet doing to the rounds, a Bradbury for the first to spot it, Lieutenant Hodge's idea, how cheery to think you will live long enough to spend such money. Naturally, you are looking for something small; can they manoeuvre without their periscope showing? That's how big the give-away will be, a periscope. When it eventually happens, you could hear a pin drop. Perhaps we will never see it. The first we'll know is the imagined furore as a torpedo slams into the immovable object. Silence, expectation, eyes becoming weary from staring. A palpable evocation of doom, hopelessness; unready, unpractised, drained. The waves lapping on all sides. Only the slowed beat of the ship's engines encroaching into the wash-tinged noise of the thumping hearts. A whale breeches! What! The lookouts one by one point towards it, shout the sighting, as if they needed to; everyone turns to where the first man haling points to, he's earned a quid. A humpback whale, bastard! The cry echoes around the ship. People hug and braggadocio is the order of the day. Wauters has seen whales a-plenty. Normally they are tied-up alongside filled with pumped air by the whalers before being hoisted flayed. Great sheets of stomach flesh hanging from cranes looking like crimped hair, a fleshy candlewick, the stokers getting the ovens-up to the mark for the boiling process. The big Dutchman is now clad in a dress bestowed on him by the captain, 'You can wear it on calm days, excused duties. Just walk about the deck. The ship will seem more natural, homely'. A merchantman with a woman on board, the captain's wife, quite a common occurrence once. Captains who not only brought their wives aboard but their daughters too, numbskulls. The contrast between 'Bully Mates' and their scandalous driving of their men and their disregard for life and limb. Men who had sold themselves to the devil. 'Oh, and you should do something about your chin. The beard ought to come off, here's a mob cap.' Wauters has seen humpbacks before, he's seen them harpooned. He has smelled them being boiled up. Whales are wonders to some, a new acquaintanceship, elicit great whoops and cheers from the compliment. He lets it pass, is more focused on his hem line. The order is given to stand-down. A man crosses himself, his confidence now soaring as it was obvious that his hesitant genuflection was the difference between outcomes. The soapy-faced man sits down shakily, collects himself and goes back to his shaving. He should have waited. His muscles are still twitching and the first thing he does is to take a nick out of his face on the philtrum, 'oh shit'! A man tries to light a cigarette only to drop his lighter and look stupidly after it as it bounces over the deck plating. Looks at his hands as though they impishly threw the thing to the floor, beyond his control. His mate picks it up for him; snaps the mechanism and the fire appears. Still the lighter's owner cannot seem to connect the dots and the helping hand takes the roll-up out of his friend's mouth, lights it for him and hands it back without a morsel, an atom, of reaction. The man on the toilet goes back to reading his comic, is encouraged to pick up the cleansing paper. The captain puts his head into his hands momentarily, the sweaty features are sufficient for a wash. 'Thank you, Aida', Mrs Captain, to whom he refers. 'Thank you for being with me, thank you.' The quartermaster looks blank, spent. Without turning his head, the captain calls, "Full ahead, Mr." The telegraph rings. The ship's crew in their groups are passing it off as having been nothing, while being reminded by their mates about how they reacted during the anxious time, 'you should have seen your face'. Plum comes across Wauters as a group of sailors stand about the now fashionable tar, laughing and pointing at his dress, making ribald comments. But none would venture to touch him in a risqué gesture. Wauters is at his hottest. He fumes like a pressure cooker giving off little intimation of what is going on within. Outwardly calm, inwardly alight. Plum isn't going to mock or try to be flippant. 'Is there something in the old tale, women and ships?' The seething man tolerates that. He looks at Plum straight, calm. "The...er...Captain, in his wisdom, wanted to make the ship look more homely. A woman walking around the deck looks natural...he thinks. It's just another bout of 'mock the alien'. On a calm day, anyone surveying the ship sees more detail. So, to witness normality… like domestic? *Eish! Verdomd, Sien jou gout*, eh? *Sharp*? If they could only see me on the Boland now. *Shaka* was killed by his own family, they said he was mad. I, me, I will die of shame no doubt.' He turns to the bridge and allows a small amount of steam to escape his lid as he points his jutting middle finger at the wheelhouse. *Jou blikseme*! Perhaps I'll put some washing out on a line," he scoffs.

"Well, the whales seem to approve," Plum ventures, pointing to the offing. "Yon chap needed a second look. You look like a 'bosted sofa'. Any…any proposals yet? I thought I caught the electrician looking a bit lustfully at you. You've shaved! Really getting into the way of things…proper theatre"

Plum gets a cautionary look. "Come *'First Dog Watch'* and I'll be back to normal. In the meantime, I'm excused duties and flashing my arse at the enemy."

Plum looks out to sea reflectively and takes a serious tone. "What a reminder, eh, if ever one was needed. The balloon going up like that. The change that came over us. I don't mind admitting I was scared. What sort of whale was that? I've seen dolphins, seals and things but nothing like that. Good job it came up again, like it did. We'd 'ave been at action stations…"

Wauters passes it off. "*Calashee Watches*, good practice. It will serve us good next time, you'll see. I have to do my make-up." Wauters pushes through the gathering and walks off down the deck.

-oo0oo-

The sleeping quarters are in the forward hold. It is a cavernous space. The light is that of a misty night glimpsed under streetlights, murky. There is a bit of a row going on further down the cave, misplaced money intermingled with the sounds of confidential hum and sporadic laughing. All human life is here, its sounds bouncing off the steel walls tinnily.

Wauters is in his work gear. Plum is lying back on his cot and chances to look up. Man-lady has a glass preserves jar in his hand which he is studying closely. Plum's interest is aroused. "What you got there then?"

"This?" says Wauters casually. "It's my zoo." He holds the jar up towards Plum.

"Your what? Let's have a gander." He sidles up to Wauters. The jar has a collection of insects in it. "What's that about? They're insects. What do you want with them?"

Wauters scrutinises the collection. *"Ju bliksem,* these bastards. Them's *skollie,* criminals. What bright spark decided, thought it was a good idea, to put all this timber under us?"

Plum says the obvious. "I suppose it's to add buoyancy, if we were breached and we obviously needed ballast."

"Yes." Agitated, Wauters tetchily responds. "The idiots. They used fresh timber, straight from the forest, dolts. Yes. Eish, man! it's a wonder the hold isn't full of Vervets! That was real bad, stupid nonsense, them bought all this lot on board." He holds the jar up.

Plum turns away from the collection a look of distaste on his face. "They make me shiver."

Wauters looks quizzically into the jar. "I got pissed-off with them walking over me in my cot. Revenge is sweet. They are in captivity now. This is my own *Wormwood Scrubs. Wormwood,* bad lands, filled with snakes, a good place for low life. I makes them a good dungeon, this." He holds up the jar.

"What you going to do with them?" asks the young man, his skin beginning to itch.

Wauters shoves the jar towards Plum's face, he recoils. "Bush tucker!" He says in a growly voice. He looks at them intently. "They will die, but not before the strongest has eaten the rest. That's how it works, you know. The strong and the weak. A basic law of nature. The elephant and the tick. When the Oxpeckers come and harvest the ticks, the hawk takes the Oxpecker; on and on. It's perfection, a great system. Perfectly rounded."

"But that's not like revenge, is it? You're just taking it out on them." Plum cannot bring himself to look and has addressed the steel plates, the ventilators, the bulkhead, the superstructure and the portholes.

Wauters settles back with his jar. "Is that how you see it, *umlungu? Die mens kom eerste,* men come first. Man would never have got a foothold in this world had he not stated his importance, ate what was on-hand. Animals are his food. There is a great distinction between lion and ox. You would never eat lion, or would you? You're daft enough to try. Whoever made us had their head screwed-on. Until we came there was no one to keep the herds in order to make catching them easy. All them beef travelling in nice blocks of food, herds. So, they made the lion. The ox's made like convoys, herds, stuck together. A packed lunch. They deserve to be eaten; it is a design. Now we are here the lion is not needed. They are in their own glass jar somewhere else. No, these little fellers, whatever reason they were made for, it was in the past. They're just nuisances now, pests. I'm in charge now. No more footpath over Wauters."

"What happens now?" Plum ventures.

"That's just a sample. I bet there are millions down in the wood somewhere, maybe eggs, maybe grubs. These little sods can communicate. They can tell their bad friends what's going on. Them antennae twitching." Wauters peers into the tank. "See, sending out SOS, like that the Germans invented, SOS, *Notzeichen*. I'll keep them like this, like a warning!" He looks into the jar. "Wauters has convicted you. It's the dungeon for you. Stay away. An example of justice. You transgress you get punished."

Plum is saddened by the plight of the little things. He knows instinctively that Wauters is inflicting suffering. He seems to like paining things. His own head is still humming from the boom clouting him and Wauters' apparent amusement at the Charlie Chaplain sort of occurrence. "But they've got no brain. They don't know about all of that. They just react." Suddenly, Plum is conscious of overstepping the mark with his matey and decides best back pedal.

The lion, the carnivore in Wauters, makes him leap. "Is that what you think *Piet*? Do you see a termite hill without knowing that every termite is a brain cell and all together they make a brain? Those that kill, have they not got the same brains, bodies as us? No, they react don't they, just…react. I've seen it. Some is easy with killing while others take sick. I know that there is no life without responsibility, me more than most. I have been told often enough that we are all responsible for our actions and ignorance is no…let-out, like with that judge. These little fellers, they bug me. They are chilling because they have no reason. They can lay an egg in your ear and fly off. Next thing you know, you have a grub in your brain! Die you bastards!" The jar is put down on the floor and Plum tries to avoid it with his eyes. But he can now imagine it. Someone mentions a flea and everyone itches.

-ooOoo-

The captain is in his cabin. Daylight percolates through the windows. As the ship gently rolls, the sunlight travels up and down the cabin walls. The captain is huddled over his desk, which is strewn with magazines about country life and field sports. A pencil on a nearby shelf rolls with ship, back and forth, held between two books. He heaves a sigh. Goes back to his reading. Will he ever cast a dry fly again? Is all this reading any use? How much time he has spent, wasted in his life he can only sum now when he can muster the thoughts of a number of matters he should have addressed and either put off or let slip. Some say that being a Master Mariner was sufficient achievement for one life. But he could have applied the same brain power to some other, more profitable, venture and been successful in a pecuniary sense. Not have an estate house, he thinks slightly regretfully, although, just to add, it is rather beautiful and is free of rent, thanks to arrangements made with the estate. But is Mrs Captain secure? Will she be allowed to live out her days there should he die? He is not his own captain on land and for all the responsibility and command he has here it is an ephemeral existence for the same worry in another place. He could be retired now and not lumbered with the business of the 'reserve' and war. Safe in a placid landscape and his only plan, his only obligation, the only demand made of him, the scheme to catch 'Gentleman Jim', that giant brown trout that lurks in the deep slack water in the pool just beyond the bridge. He only had so many magazines and has been through them all meticulously before. But 'Jim's' secret must be conquered, it's 'Jim' and me. But what then if 'Jim' is taken by some other hand while I'm away, what then? What if another takes him while I'm here? A king amongst fish but trapped in the confines of the stream. But, then again, he doesn't have to go to war and, unless some nefarious hand tickles him out, he'll be there for lots of future encounters. Much thinking-on amidst the quiet delight of tying a new dry fly and the vague smell of wild garlic in his head.

Chapter 13

Brianna loves every minute of now while neglecting so much. She can sit in the library sampling all sorts of reading but, of course, the library is not a place for dogs and Rollo is left behind. At first, she would get someone to hold him while she set out, but he would invariably catch up with her and assume it was the same old way, which it wasn't. So, she took to tying him up, tethering him. Now and then one of her relatives would release him because of the continual barking that the hound's solitariness would induce. This meant that Rollo would be seen wandering the town by himself, nosing into shops and eating places and not always receiving a friendly reception. The dog could not rationalise his new situation and became increasingly sullen. Brianna hardly saw the change, but then again, she was not looking. If a 'flier' appeared on the street, she was on to it. One of them advertised a lunchtime concert in Cork; the idea of travelling outside Queenstown had hardly occurred to her. Taking the train up-country was not a journey it was an odyssey. She negotiated the ticket buying, arrived nearly an hour before the train was to depart. Boarding the train, she walked the carriages until she found one with a mixed group of folks in it, she was hardly likely to want to sit with the men. She hardly addressed her fellow travellers apart from with body English. She sat glued to the scenery. There was nothing that she saw that had not its own fascination. The excitement of travel. All too quickly, she was in Cork and totally lost as to directions. Armed with her 'flier', she might as well have been from another country in the way she approached people to timidly illicit directions to the concert. She sat in the street outside the concert room. As Brianna, she felt equal to it all, although she would have to improve on her time-keeping and self-confidence. The concert was one o'clock and there she was at twenty-past nine. She sat for so long and then moved to acquaint herself with the venue, making sure first it was the right place on the right day, at the right price, for the right duration. Once assured, she then went off and found a tearoom where she had a pot of tea and some toast and jam. This was how it would be, she told herself. She loved her anonymity. Not standing a chance of bumping into family or customers she had known, meant that she could be whoever she wanted to be. She was somehow livelier in this temporary environment. Walked differently, ate delicately, sipped decorously, tapped her lips after a sup with her napkin, as some of the others did and which she latched onto as being descriptive of manners. How odd to be in a different place, an alien. Her assurance at concert-going was improving even though there was inevitably a little bit of the old her there in feeling a bit exposed at times. When men tipped their hats or gave her a courtesy, like opening a door for her. She decided against coyness and developed a system of head bobbing that conveyed her thanks for the small social duty proffered, but modestly.

She was absolutely taken aback by the concert being given by a group of a few stringed instruments alone. As the musicians sat to their scores her mind raced as to what sort of noise such a small ensemble would make. Had she come all that way and spent not an inconsiderable amount of money on a side show? But even at the bowing of the first note, the 'A' she was struck by the force, the loudness of the ensemble. The next hour and a half were fully taken up with the melodious outpourings. The powerful concentration of the players and the funny faces that some of them pulled in the action of sound reproduction. At times, it seemed that the instruments they were playing were being lazy, had to be bullied into letting go their sounds, as the players ripped into their art with mighty force, like wrestling or producing a baby. Brianna felt a special affinity for the lady cellist who sat legs akimbo around that large violin and was so active in the playing that for all the world it looked as though she was riding with the hunt. How did that woman come to be here and doing that? But the occasion soon emptied her mind and after a while she gave herself to the music, was moved, not only by the melodies but the physicality. Moved by the percussive effect of some of the passages as the bass notes sent a tingle through her whole being with wave upon wave of lumps of sound butting into her. She felt both uplifted but also rather superior at the end of the presentation. It was one of those pieces that has a false ending and some members of the audience started to clap too soon, but she didn't. She waited until the instrumentalists lowered their bows and stood to receive their adulation and then she let rip with her clapping, impressive with its gusto. She smiled in turn at each player. Some of the men in the audience stamped their feet as well as clapping, like one-man bands, clapping and stamping all at once. It seemed a bit…excessive. Then, would you believe, the players sat to their instruments again and did what the crowd was calling an encore. Encore, like so much of what she was coming across in her new existence, was not a tune she had heard before. But short and sweet. Encore, who wrote that? More clapping, more stamping and then everyone was out in the street. On the train back to Queenstown, reborn like Gloriana, Brianna, transcendent, found herself remembering snippets of music, tapping her fingers on her thigh as she looked to a vanishing point with no perception of surroundings. But then the sometimes screwed-up and intense faces of those playing would flood in and she was tipped into smiling, much to the curiosity of her fellow travellers. Back in town, she was fizzing. But her joy was somewhat taken from her because she found that despite the personal satisfaction of what she had achieved, going to Cork, buying the tickets, getting tea, sitting in an auditorium, the thousand and one achievements of but a single day, the whole thing was somewhat taken from her because there was no one of vim, joy and curiosity she could share it all with to contrast and compare. She could set up a stall on the quay and give lectures about the great achievements of mankind, the wonders that proliferated about us and all to be acknowledged in a single day. The whole business of man and the world could stop here, now, with the determined thought that today was brilliant and all that there was, and would ever be. This day was to be sampled to the full before it dribbled away, was lost. Rollo did not seek her out. Late in the day, he found his way back to the camp.

-oo0oo-

The ship is entering Weymouth Bay. A misty grey, windless scene. Weymouth, that place favoured for its sea bathing by the Georgians, the place that Napoleon saw from the deck of the *'Billy Ruffian'* on his way to oblivion. Wauters is in his dress and all seems right with the world. All morning he has been doing exactly as he was told. He cannot help himself. When the wind blows, his impulse is to push the skirt down, while not in any danger of revealing anything, him having his rolled-up trousers on underneath. Moving towards the last days of March, equinoctial gales were expected but had not arisen, it was all 'lamb' and no sign of 'lion'. You have to be thankful for small mercies. Unlike so many places, this bay must have given the casual onlooker, unusually, a view of a sailing ship in something approaching full sail manoeuvring in the roads. In a tight anchorage, one might only see small sails set, especially when only just casting off. A ship which would have been head-up into the stream at an anchorage, that is the wrong way around for sailing, had to be manoeuvred into a suitable position to catch the wind from towards the stern, to get under way. The observer would see no square sails set normally as this would impede the master's view in steering. If you were a lucky ship, you could get a tug, especially in Australia. But some masters made it a point, like of honour, to make their own way. When there were no tugs, and a confined reach, then you could solicit help from other ships in the anchorage who would offer rowing boats to act in concert to tow a craft into position, until viable. This would always illicit a chorus or two of *'Rolling home'* or *'Goodbye, fair thee well'*, carolled from the decks of those not involved in the action. Nothing was more likely to set your eyes moist, the 'impediment' that set them streaming, particularly rife when near to land and a waving-off; it must have been the dust. In the days of fixed sails, it must have been really odd, especially for those waving matelots away, as the ship, so bound by the wind, might not be out of sight for a while, depending on the blow. You might have to camp-out to see them departing from view. Your arms would tire from waving long before they vanished from sight. Thank goodness for the business of tacking. Sub-lieutenant Senior is about the daily routine of a junior officer, nothing much to flex or tax a well-schooled brain. He was greatly entertained by the captain's exercise book of mathematical puzzles and proofs. Later that day he was to pick-up on the chess game he was playing with Hodge, his fellow junior officer, the positions they left each other between their splits in duty. Senior found it hard to have any authority here, just about as difficult as the men found it when they accidently tried to treat him as an equal, one of them. Wauters pondered, now that Logan was on-side the deal was almost sealed. The 'coup de grace' was about to be delivered. 'Talk' it out with Senior and then Plum, it would be a walk-over. The two officers may have laid aside their dealings after the restaurant fracas but not Wauters. Those actions were currency and could be called in like a debt as one of the best influencers or trades you can imagine. He had never had any bother with officers before. In a sailing ship, your life is in their hands. He could imagine the doings that might have led to the mystery of the *'Marie Celeste'*, found in mid ocean abandoned and without any sign of violence. No clues as to what and how. Men that go on the rampage, perhaps standing up to a Bully Mate, were on a loser. Some of the mates wore knuckle dusters on both hands like jewellery. While there was him who could kick a Belaying Pin up and out of the rack, catch it mid-air and lay out any assailant with it before they knew what had happened. Some would still 'duck you from the yards'. He had had no trouble here on board for there were plenty of distractions. Why make life totally intolerable. Wauters kept on moving about and would take one more turn to coincide with the course of Senior, to lay alongside him comfortably. Wauters watches him intently. Finally, his tactics nailed down, he approaches the Lieutenant. "Weymouth, eh? I thought this place was supposed to be a good anchorage? It looks just as dingy as the worst in this weather. Mustn't hang about, I have to change my dress. Don't want to frighten the natives." Senior has hardly regarded him. Wauters could have been talking to someone else. A curtailed glance only. He makes to move away and then turns back to Senior. "I would like a word with you, if you have a moment."

Senior looks him down. "Is there a 'sir' in there somewhere sailor? Aren't you supposed to be about your work now? I think the captain only meant his little ruse to apply when in open water."

In a matter-of-fact sort of way, Wauters comes to the point. "Yes, sir, but that's not my preoccupation today, sir. No, not today. Not this day. I have to speak my mind today; sir, I have no respect for a coward, you."

Senior is wrenched from his reverie. "What!"

"There's no point dressing it up." Wauters tilts his head to one side and knits his brow in a gesture suggesting questioning, contradiction. "You are a coward, that's what you are, right? I've seen it first-hand; I am right. Respect, you, no. Respect only when it's deserved."

Senior turns to the interloper in that way that rank can, a little bit of hauteur, a little bit of threat. "Go about your duties or, or else…I'll put you on a charge. Mad! You're out of order, quite mad."

Wauters holds up his hand softly, undramatically, calling him to halt, mindful of keeping his voice down. "No, no. no, I'm in complete control. You are the one, *you* are the one, the person that needs examining. I was there, see. The night that you brought disrespect to your service? Shocking viewing. I felt…reduced. Aren't you supposed to have breeding in the wardroom? Posh talk over the port. King and country. Good families?" Senior turns away but Wauters turns with him so that he is always commanding the other's attention. "Brought your ship into disrepute? It casts a bad light on a captain when one of his subordinates, no, not one, but two of his officers, you and Sub-lieutenant Hodge, misbehaves. Like you two did. Tie two dogs to the same lead and they will move in the same direction, eh."

Senior grimaces nervously. "What!" Suddenly, he is aware that his voice is loud, he tones it down. "What on earth are you talking about, you awful person. We were told to be wary of you…"

"No, no, no. There you go again." Senior is forced to meet Wauters' eyes. "It's not me under the microscope, it's you. I'm the soul of discretion, you, you've got no self-respect."

The Lieutenant flicks out the back of his hand in a go away, don't bother me, go to your room, motion. No uniforms also means no hiding place. "Go away, go on, I'll deal with you later. Can't you see I'm busy."

Such a dismissive gesture should irk Wauters at the best of times, but here, now? But he is such a practised operator he is the epitome of Zen control with just a pinch of *Kali*, death and destruction, toxicity. Nothing shows, no 'face' to lose. Senior starts to walk off; Wauters adds in a resigned way. "Go, go on then. I'll just have to tell the captain myself how you went on in that restaurant in Queenstown. Yes, I know that's pretty low of me. Perhaps, now you are beginning to see how I got my reputation, half-brother to *Kadar*. I could say that you put me in fear of my life, with the locals. He would listen. Even I was ashamed of what you did, and I, as you know, I'm an evil, unscrupulous foreigner. I was ashamed. *Eish!* Your actions put me into peril too and my shipmate even before we caught sight of the open sea. Who knows, the whole ship; no matter what the locals must have thought about the privilege of the colonialists. I said to my mate, they're daft to make trouble with the locals. There's too much cause here as it is. You was so much in your cups to notice, maybe? You and your little friend? But we were there. My shipmate and me." Wauters has been walking along-side the Sub-lieutenant. Now he has stopped in his tracks, talks to the officer from behind his back. "Yes sir, I would say so. We witnessed your man and you getting drunk and speaking-out sore bad about the Irish, Ireland. Imagine, you would have to be bloody mad or drunk to shoot your mouth off like that in a place which already has…reservations about you, us." Wauters has an aside, it reasserts his self-confidence that he doesn't need to make a scene. "Napoleon came here once, I hear tell, like I said. Weymouth, yes, my *chommie* told me. The bloke must have been desolated. On his way to oblivion, I bet oblivion was nicer. See I know something else, I'm not a one trick pony." He faces Senior, fixes him. "What would it take for the Germans message to the Irish to get through to Queenstown, especially if they were propelled that way? *'Shake off your colonial yoke and join us,'* they would ask the Irish. They've put the proposition to India already? It didn't end there though. You went out into the night and were too far gone to notice that some of the people that you had slagged-off went out after you. Yes, you were probably so intent, so pleased with yourself, that you didn't notice, arrogant snob. Didn't care, it takes a special sort of monster to do that, disrespect others in that way. But you were not far down the road when them angry men were coming up to you with a head of steam, with all sorts of mischief in mind. Recall it now, do you?" The officer tries turning away to hide his chagrin. "Why it seems like only yesterday. Had you been…more…aware, when you spotted them, you would have seen me and my shipmate coming up on your assassins, them *'Thuggee'*. My goodness, you looked scared. God, you were trembling. Not the stuff of heroes. A bit drunk and a sudden threat? Worst sort of threat; no preparation. Heart pounding, was it? Stomach wrenched? Legs shaking? A hint of stirring in the humbles?" He points to Senior's stomach. He has the officer tamed completely now, the chap just has to stand there and take it. A little push with his little finger would see him keeled-over. "Not a situation that you would forget easy, put to the back of your mind, eh? *Verdomt*! I bet you still sweat at night just going over it. The sort of thing that could wake you up from the deepest sleep, get you gripping the edge of your bed, eh. Fact is, we stepped-in. We saved your miserable skin. What did you do? You ran off, like a good'en, you just can't do right, can you? Not something that other little man, Lord Nelson, would have done, run off, I think. Hundreds of years of history down the shitter. We got them off your backs. One thing being arrogant and gormless another entirely being a coward. *Jou blikseme*! You had not your right head on that day. Away with the fairies. It wouldn't do to make such things known. How would you be in a crisis? What sort of respect would you command? No chance of you being given a position of leadership…your careers in the 'heads' and on the windward side too."

The Sub looks at Wauters. He asks what the ransom is, fearing the worst. "What's your purpose? Why now?"

"I'm an easy going" – Wauters puts a hand on the young man's shoulder and squeezes hard – "live and let live sort, even though I am foreign and obviously suspicious, mistrusted." He pauses. Turns away as if making to leave and in transition seems to have a thought come to him. "Oh, yes. There is a little thing you can do, come to think about it."

The Sub interjects, "I've got no money, if that's what you're after."

"There you go you're off again. Such bad, base thoughts, is that how your mind turns? Tut-tut. You are so mean spirited, aren't you? What does my mate call such sorts, oh yes, a downy bird, a downy bird, that's how he sums it. I hadn't got you down for a slob, I thought you'd be right on the mark. I've seen you and your friend playing chess, very deep, very…intellectual, studied, like. I thought men of your sort of station would have some class. You don't seem to have much going for you at all. Bit cheap I would say, *baas*." There's nothing like stirring the pot while you've got complete obedience. Senior just stood there as Wauters left his original script and started to pour it on; he knew when his opponent could see the end game looming-up, it was a bloodbath. This was another occasion when all the officer could think of was running. He could not believe that tomorrow had a dose of this in it. Don't you just hate tomorrow? "I should get my compass seen to if I were you, matey. We Swung the ship and now we need to swing you as you'll end-up right off course and no mistake. You've made a good start at it. You don't seem to have any…backbone. What a terrible leap. Money indeed! How really, really insulting. Is that something you would settle for? Is money everything with your lot? Can everything be snuffed-out with money, do you think? There's a problem with your heading, you shot for the stars and nearly shot your foot off, *verdomt*! You're way off course. No, I was thinking…" He moves around in front of the Sub, straightens the man's lapels and pushes the hair off Senior's temples. Almost enough fun had. Wauters takes a look around the deck. "…take it on the chin man. Have a bit of pride. It's like this. Nothing difficult. Costs you nothing. Bygones will be bygones, on my honour, although I honestly don't think it's the punishment you are due. We, some of the crew, have a mind to give a boxing exhibition match." The Sub looks at him questioningly, quietly astounded, caught off-balance. "Yes, a boxing exhibition. The chap that saved your life, back there, boxed for Beatty's Battle Cruisers out of Rosyth. He was their champion. Big mate of Admiral Beatty, does that shock you? What are the chances of you rising to such heights? Oh no, you're not up to it, nearly forgot. Anyway, he's a keep-fit fanatic and wants to demonstrate his abilities and, wouldn't you know it, there is a fireman that is willing to be his adversary, opponent, for the good of community relations, sort of thing; alien country to you, perhaps. The stoker wants to box against him, a man from the Grand Fleet, nice bit of interplay, heh? Last time the Cruisers won, next time, Dreadnaughts? You couldn't make it up. What are the chances?"

Senior can't quite see the connection or he is so flummoxed that he has lost his powers of reason. The Sub-lieutenant shoots a look of incomprehension. "I don't see…"

"All we want to do, it's not a mutiny, all *we* want *you* to do, is to put the idea into the captain's head. You're a clever bloke, underneath it all. I know I may be flattering you, but it's worth a chance, this once." Wauters looks away and continues talking. "You know what words would appeal. You could talk him around. It's like this, we want a dock building, a repair shop or something. Somewhere with a bit of space for a crowd, next time we're in Queenstown…to stage the fight. No, not fight, bout, use the word 'bout', less…confrontational. Perhaps we could invite the dock workers in, as a thank you for all their *tireless* work, what they've done here." He looks about the ship, while stroking his dress down. "Just an idea. A bit of leverage. I know you can do it. You get the permission and we'll organise the event and nothing else will be said, God's honour. On my mother's grave, wherever that is. You had an off-night. Yeah? You two weren't yourselves." Wauters' gestures about with his arms but then gets right into Senior's face. "Do something right in your life, get this on. You go from villain to saint in one easy move. I'll see you right. Make it known how helpful you were." Wauters stays close. "The men will appreciate it. I'm sure."

-ooOoo-

A breezy day, a welcome relief from successive days of doing jobs one-handed while hanging on to any bit of bulkhead or fixture that would prevent you from be catapulted hither and thither. So much canvas has split on the seams. Stuff is carried away. '*Jou blikseme*!' rolls off his tongue continually and a lot of the kit is proving to be '*Fong-Kong*', second rate and flimsy. There's been some crafty work here abouts on costings, usual Government contract stuff. Things break with a half decent wave. The *Crab*, a portable winch, almost took him in half, came away from its tether, '*jou blikseme*', junk! Spume flies across the deck. It's still blowing while not heaving. Everything glistens, even the sailors in their oilskins, coated in fine spray look like performing seals, shiny svelte black. We are well into the year but the air temperature is still not comfortable. Plum is running an inventory of ordinance. Wauters approaches him. He is an avuncular frame of mind, despite all; smiles a lot. He sniffs around the area in which Plum is labouring, his 'animal' more obvious than normal in his movement. A slip. A break from cover. An overt example of his night time manifestation, his inner werewolf. "Plummy, you little purple fruit, how's your stone coming along?" His humour is strained and obvious. If he thinks that Plum hasn't heard that one before…he sticks his sensitive snout into the occasion and his all-seeing eye pierces every tiny nuance and cranny. He continues with his faux bonne-amie and only manages to arouse suspicion. "What are you doing? You look very…efficient…official today. Have they given you a stripe?"

Plum half turns. "I might get a stripe, across my back, that is: *I am his majesty's dog at Kew. Pray, tell me, whose dog, are you?*"

Another daft aphorism takes Wauters outside his territory, culturally and temperamentally. "I'm my own dog and little time for games, certainly not pool or billiards, English shit. I play my own game."

Plum muses, everything that Wauters says is either defensive or threatening. Why is this man always so testy? Such a juxtaposition, his attitude and his smile. He can be good company. Keeping him on-side is an art and a chore but Plum needs to keep things light. He will ask Wauters for his participation in his plan, his expedition; if there was only some other way around it: it's a matter of choosing the right moment. For the time being, he must defend himself and not be offended, at all costs, not be offended! But Plum is not the most diplomatic. Years of abrasive jokey banter have set him in a mould of reactive back chat. But, either by accident or design, his foot is not far from being in 'it'. "Nearly right. Kew is a Royal Palace not a stick! I can see the problem you must have, it's with you being foreign. How many times has someone said something to you here and you've taken the wrong end of the stick? It could be dangerous or a loss, friendships, mate-ship. Somebody might take you the wrong way. Do you see what I did there? Kew, palace; cue, stick; queue, a line of folks, like at the kinema waiting to go in. Cue, like being reminded what you have to say. See we invented the language; I think we made it hard deliberately, to keep you lot out. We do all sorts with it but you can be satisfied with one meaning. Like have you been to a horse race? Yes? Have you been to a dog race? Yes? Have you been to a millrace? They're a grind." With this Plum has gone through his entire vocabulary of witticisms, just ask him to spell any of that.

Wauters virtually ignores all the above, it might interfere, distract from his purpose. So, they are both waltzing around one another. Neither being able to be straight, to show their actual intention. "And there was me thinking talking was just a way of passing information."

"It can be Wauters, it can be. English can paint pictures, can't it?"

Wauters face is gleaming wet and, face into the wind, his eyes smart from the effects of salt water. "Cut the daft banter," Wauters says curtly. "Says he, changing the subject: Nice and shiny, them." Wauters points at the shells that Plum has cleaned.

"They are beauties. I'm looking after them all. It's a bit like turning eggs." Says Plum, giving the shell nearest him an extra rub with the rag.

The interloper has a tray of sharp rejoinders at his disposal but not now, not now. "You can say that again." Says Wauters scrutinising the shells.

"Yeah, it's just like turning eggs!" Silly Plum, he's not laughing with you. That's not a smile, that is slavering gape. Wauters watches as Plum turns and counts the shells. "HE is very funny stuff, AP not so funny. You have to keep on top of it, except when it's going off, that is. You can laugh if you want to. No need to keep it bottled up." He goes off on something that he half remembers from his days training. "What is done now pays dividends later. Mass production of ordnance is rushed, you see. Numbers, not quality. No wonder we get a lot of 'stumers', duds. Oh well," he says resignedly. "It's a chance to write a message on the shell. You can use your imagination like this, 'Fritz, here's one I prepared earlier', that would be a good one." He wipes his hands on the rag. "All Sir Garnet now." Written in chalk on a shell, 'This is for the Somme'! Plum makes some marks on the wetted bespeckled paper. Without looking at Wauters, Plum asks casually, "Where do you go to in Queenstown? I hardly see you when we're in port?" Then he bites his lip.

Wauters actually feels like saying mind your own *godverdomme* business you bloody gnome but… "You're the one that goes missing. I'm always around. You, you're always out running or down the gymnasium. I'm here. What are you trying to prove? No matter what you do you're always going to be *bietjie klei,* a bit small, a bit thin and little, *paw-paw*." Wauters is letting things get away from himself and is in as much danger of spoiling the plot with his tetchiness. See there, a little thorny jibe. Plum is a bit wounded but would Wauters notice such a thing? Not on your life. Emotion, he's seen too much to think in terms of sentiment. Empathy is just a four-letter word followed by three more.

The lad puts on a brave front. "So what? Didn't stop my idol, the 'Mighty Atom', Jimmy Wilde. Five foot two inches, but a battleship." Plum is a bit emotional, but only on the inside. "He could knock down anybody you put before him, knock 'em seam-rent, as my dad would say, any day of the week. Only the

World Champion, that's all. No Dutch boxers that I can recall made it. Too busy growing flowers and boxing 'em-up."

"Are you a bit touchy about your height? Is that why you took up boxing. Stop the big blokes picking on you?" Wauters pretends to spar but it looks clumsy and Plum derides the attempt, waves it aside. This is not going well for either of them. You get on the wrong foot from the get-go and it's hard to turn things around. He could quite easily blurt something out that his passions are cooking-up but must use restraint.

"You wouldn't stand up with me as big as you are, that's for sure. Know what I'm at, speed, agility, control." He delivers a pretend haymaker. "Bang, you're dead. Wallop. Go on, put up your *'dukes'*. Come on, see if you can lay one on me. Come on, let's do this now." He bobs and weaves. All the time thinking he's made a mistake, challenging Wauters' manhood now, are we? What if it did come to blows, that would be the end of it all. Sublimate your pride, Plum, play it down. Plum backs off, regards the ammunition closely. "No? I don't blame you. You're a bit paunchy. Perhaps you should come for a run. Get in shape." Plum does not know when to stop.

"Run! I would rather eat my own foot," says Wauters, his steely eye boring into Plum. "You're odd, *creepy-kruip*. I see them out running, a good thing if you intend to run away from your enemy. Not all war is that sort of fight. There are other, more important subtleties." Wauters is working on turning his ship around. He went to the brink and now coming over all complimentary and confidential he thinks that it will make a big impression. "Yes, I know you're a good boxer, for what that's worth. I bet you could show this lot a thing or two. It's a pity we're not with the fleet and all the contests they put on, so you could show-off. But you never know." Is there a way in here? He should broach the subject, come to mention it. "You should keep yourself up to the mark. Me, I'm lying down, me and my zoo; smaller zoo now. Just thinking of that useless waste of energy, it all tires me out. I suddenly feel sleepy." A few compliments don't go amiss. Plum turns away back to his work and Wauters slaps him vigorously around the back of the head. Plum shrinks from the blow. Then Wauters gives Plum a knowing look as the other man turns around towards him a touch angry, reactive. "I never was one for rules. You have to keep your guard up," Wauters says snidely.

-oo0oo-

Brianna, as she calls herself these days, has not been idle. Her work was once essential and she was responsible with it. On the streets in all weathers and doing a full day on her pitch. Now, well, she is sort of conflicted. Just going to the river occasionally to confer with the dead departed was once sufficient reward for her efforts. One thing that had changed was that. What, was it, spring? Now Rollo was less eager to spend a day in the town. He started to go missing for a few hours, a day sometimes, seemed unsettled. Going to the river by yourself was not so much fun, in fact you felt exposed in that small wilderness by yourself, alone with the ghosts. She went to the performance of an oratorio, 'Messiah', by a chap called Handel. It was marvellous. All the words were taken from the Bible and set to such beautiful music. Where she had almost blarted at the mellifluous tones of the 'Sally Garden' song, well this was of a totally different order. A choir and orchestra down from Dublin, her second musical venture, only this time on the grand scale. She was totally unprepared for the sweetness that both men and women in the band could wrestle from their instruments. And them women, so upright and focused and just as good as the men at the fiddling, better. And the choir, sublime, passionate. It was a long evening and sitting on stiff wooden chairs made her bum itch and her back ache in turn and she could not help fidgeting the whole evening. The whole crowd, and there were a lot of them, seemed so nice, if just a touch self-congratulatory. There was a wait before the concert; they wouldn't let you into the hall till minutes before the whole thing was to start up. I suppose it was to give you a moment to consider whether or not you really wanted to stay; are you sure this is to your taste? The other breaks came during the performance. At the first interlude, had the man not said that there will be a short break of ten minutes, she may well have thought that the thing was all over and gone home. She would have had so much to think about had she left then. But to stay on and hear so much more. In the second break, she had followed the audience out to the back of the hall. They all trailed off to a bar. So that's where they all went. A man came up to her as she was standing there, introduced himself and asked if she wanted a drink. Well, she had no money to buy him one back so she said that she wouldn't and then it occurred to her that he might be saying that he would buy her one just for the sake of it, to chat maybe. But why would he? She didn't know him from Soft Mick. When it was all over, she pondered on hallelujah and Aaaaamen, which almost got her to her feet shouting it was so rousing. The streets, at the end of it all, were so quiet and no one was going her way, going to the rude streets. They were probably off to them great big Victorian piles out east. But once the drumming of the music and the mimicking of the facial contortions of the lady singers had all been done and dusted, they really did fight with their voices and their instruments, it all looked very tiring, music, she was tired watching. She got into Wauters' case. That feckin' langer. The number of times I put myself his way and he passed me up. You know, on reflection, she could not believe a blind word he had said to her. What was he waiting for? I'm as good as a virgin. That first night, Corny, he was so drunk that he spilled himself on my leg and after that was the ritual; they would be in bed and he would say, in a sort of half-hearted way, 'Do you want a baby', and she would say 'no'. That was enough for him. He would tamely roll over and go to sleep. Some of the woman complained about not being left alone, their men always urging messing, and some said that they actually enjoyed it and encouraged it. It was all very odd. Carmen thought it something of nothing in those circumstances, but wondered in her own mind how Wauters might approach it. She was so full of herself. Since she had loosened the strings of the family and its obligations, she found that there was nothing she would not try. She could remember whole poems now, not that it was any great trick, remembering a poem. Why remember the feckers when you had the book at home. And now she was determined to read the *'Jungle Book'* or *'Just So'* stories, it seemed like a natural progression from some of the Kipling poetry to read his books. None of the Irish poets seemed to have written a book, not that she knew of anyway. Now she could sit, last thing, by the light of an oil lamp at the mirror and look deep into her face. She would have been the first to admit it was not a beautiful face; it would have been too vain to admit to such anyway, even if it was. If you take your eyes by their corners and pull the skin back, it makes a positive difference. She could spend hours, and an extraordinary amount of lamp oil, doing her hair this way and that. Putting this coloured glass against her skin and then another. She had come to the decision that diamonds would do nothing for her looks, but emeralds! That necklace of her grannies, with its green glass, set her off a treat. And then, sod it, Daddy would come over from his *vardo* and rap on the window and tell me to get the lamp turned off, they weren't made of money. She was tired of horses. They had caused her too much grief and they were too much hard work; she had made her mind up to sell the piebald mare and the bay with the foal. No doubt that would get hackles up. But she had real use for money now. Books to be bought and if any more concerts came to town, well she knew the form now and would never be out of place again. There was so much to learn. But Wauters was like a big boulder in her road. It could be that he likes me in his way, she pondered. He is so, different, he's so deep. He's so manly even for an old one. What would I say to him if he said 'do you want a child'? I would think of how robust the baby would be and what a good chance it would have in life. How he would teach it about swimming and such, tell it tales of the sea and it would grow up to be a ship's captain. I would think what passion would go to its making. Oh, how I wish I could swim and fly and drive a car. I will have a telephone and a feckin radio. I deserve it all. What if he doesn't like me? What will I do then? Sure, we're getting along fine. I think he likes my company. But he's canny. Perhaps he's too canny for me. Does it all fall back on the tin of peaches and Vaughan. Vaughan, oh dear, what a pity, a waste. When people don't know, they give themselves away too cheap. He, may be, would have been charming if he had been born into love. But he wasn't and there's an end to it. Three people brought together by chance and me and my *dukkerin'* didn't see it coming. What sort of fraud lying bastard does that make me? But in these conflicting thoughts she looked towards an organ concert at the Cathedral, Widor's, 'Romane' organ concerto. Was that short for 'romantic'? What an adventure?

Chapter 14

Another round-trip over. A sigh of relief. A growing feeling of inviolability. Evening and April in Queenstown. Soft light, the screeching of sea birds. Was that a hint of warmth in the air? In the hinterland, high in the town, there is a wash of green as some of the street trees start budding-up. There are town birds on the quay pulling threads out of rope ends for nesting material. Noticeably, the dock workers are less heavily attired and in the odd burst of intense sun they divest down to jumpers. The light is cheering after the heavy-lidded skies of winter. Costermongers are putting their carts right, displaying produce, although foodstuffs, particularly, are in short supply. Wauters searches the streets eagerly around the quay, nothing. Finally, he ends up at the brown café, the rough bar that the travellers frequent, where he finds Carmen. As he enters the bar, Rollo gets up and walks towards him, his tail wagging. But she deliberately avoids his searching look. She has got herself in such a state. What has she to do to win him? Her body says sacrifice, pleads for the warmth of another human to demonstrate, if nothing else, that we are not alone in this world, the necessity for companionship. Her mind takes her elsewhere. Such is her burgeoning life adventure on her own terms that she sees a way, on her own terms. But each time she establishes her renewed courage and defines her path, her body grabs her by the hair and yanks her back. A man offered to buy me a drink at the concert and although I was too stupid to see his intention, at least it proved I'm neither a dunce nor unattractive, just…cautious. But she is wedded to Wauters. Just because he's away she can't take up with anyone, especially because he leaves her lonely. But that is sacrifice isn't it, ignoring other possibilities? Yes, she is sold on Wauters and ready to offer-up her selfishness and privacy to him, that's all done and dusted. But there is just a hint that this man of the world, this fearless Jack Harkaway, has other priorities. The lack of warmth. The avoidance of intimacy. The fact that the feckin' langer won't even take the trouble to argue with her. He's like the side of the moon that we don't see while the other…What if he just pisses-off and leaves me all rampant and settled in my future as I have discussed with myself on many a street corner? Selling *'Fluke'* and her foal. Now I'm done with the oats and the Piebald, which was such a steel. Screaming inside to tell someone of my conundrum, only trying to elicit approval of my course. I'm going to test the fecker. I'll put him on a spot and find my proof. Best I know now, isn't it? The man at the concert bar, he could have been good company for all I know. But I'm drowned in loyalty without knowing that it is not a wasted sacrifice. Carmen has been there for a little while neglecting her trade. She is in such perturbation that she can't reason any longer, it seems. If only the bastard would hold her hand. Be suggesting something of their future. Make a play for me, 'I might not resist'. In the poems, love is always a certainty such a well-defined and universal thing. But love is also nothing, zero, isn't it. So, what should you expect? We know by the tone whether it's going to end well or not. We should heed the signs. There seems to be one lot telling us of tragedy and another lot selling romance with these poets. There is no doubt they understand both intimately. Must be nice to have had the time to think on it so minutely. I mean, when did I ever get to talk to anybody about romance, it was not a currency we dealt in. The poet representing himself in his best light sends a message to his reader, 'Yes, you could be the one. You could share my bower', although he dresses it all up as them and their and I'm just the messenger, the tell-tale snitch. I have spent so much time telling people how happy and successful things are going to be I've come to believe that is the narrow band in which all life exists. Yet there is me, the saddest, most troubled and friendless person in the world. Come on girl, you have to see that not all romance is for sure. Every time you wish it so it gets up and bites you in the arse. Just to put you in your place, perhaps? Always when you are settled in your thoughts. When life seems to be running on wheels and you know the next day, the day after that and some warm infused future of your invention. The trouble with poetry is that it makes you question yourself and sometimes for the wrong reasons. I have no idea what sort of life Yeats came from, any of them for that matter. But you can only imagine them as being in soft and encouraging societies. Nah! I bet he used to shout at his people and they all crept around for fear of intruding into his deep thoughts, although if that was his sort of sacrificing his life, it was worth it. Life is cheap and short. What view of life is bred by always being soft and encouraging except a false sense of hopefulness. There is no telling that their experience can suit anywhere or anyone else. Life is cruel, I'm a testament to that, I'm a *knacker*.

Isn't that why we read them though? Not to be taken over by what they say but just to compare, to run the rule over them to see what they have to say about our insoluble human condition, give us guidance? What have I to compare with, *'My boy Jack'*, Kipling's son, his being lamented back in 1915? Fancy him being stuck in words that can only induce greater sadness and more visceral hurt. It's not all a bed of roses being so romantic, but then again, they have the words to explain exactly how they feel, exactly, terribly, visually, painfully, masochistically. But no matter what, even if it hurts full to bosting, they still have to tell you about it, you have to know. Then we are not alone, as long as they have not just put some bugger else's story to their musing, like some newspaper writer who must treat any confidence lightly if it gives them something to fill a few columns with. Is that honesty or are they passed the point of being capable of restraining themselves and they have to tell their readers everything down to the hairs on their bums. We goad them into thinking too much of themselves. You recognise traits in your lover and there is that kissing stuff which is a fuse to the dangerously intimate, then you're lost for good glandular fever would put paid to that, *the kissing disease*. But you can't look into the other person's mind to find their idea of what they think is going on. What's the use of you feeling warm and affectionate if the object of what you see as love doesn't like give anything back? Gathers another impression entirely. At the moment, in my black moods, I have love, zero that is. I'm grateful that he takes me around and he's certainly given me a look into another world that my old existence would never have considered. I needed shaking up because I'd let myself go, I was depressed, I admit. To think I could be that girl in the library with the false smile putting the stamp on the books for the return date. Only, my smile would not be false. I would be so happy and content. So glad I didn't have to be out in all weathers dragging my poor owd dog with me. He doesn't love me, that's plain. But love is about overcoming such things, right. What if he doesn't know he loves me? it hasn't quite dawned on him, out of his non-experience of warmth and regard? It may just be like the buckle of a harness, things suddenly coming together and then become inseparable. You can hardly say he is using you girl. He could have had you and you would have been abandoned, silly about it. Silly wench! It's all that feckin' Vaughan business. He just wants to shut me up and me silent in his doings, just as guilty. Yes, he shut me up for sure. As soon as he feels safe, he'll fob me off. Could I be an accessory, due for prison?

He comes into the awful bar with its dingy light and stained walls and ceilings and that shifty Flynney looking him up and down. He gives a cheery hello to the dog despite himself. "Hello, Rollo." The dog had slumped after the first sighting of Wauters now extracts itself from what seems, by the animal's movement, to be a syrupy sticky floor. Then he addresses Brianna. "There you are. I've searched high and low for you and here you are in the Brown Café again. Bit early for you? Somebody palm you off? You look a bit glum. Drink?"

She rises from her seat. "No, I'll get them." She goes to the bar looking sullen. She addresses the barman. They are the only customers. Wauters sits down and Rollo stops briefly to lick a paw then gives his head over to Wauters to be adored. Carmen proffers his glass without any of her usual gleam and spark. "The usual, Flynney. Where does that phantom ship of yours go to?" she asks airily. "You're never away for long and then you pop-up unannounced. Where do you go too that is such a short way and so regular? What did you say your boat was?"

"*Horton Lodge*," he says, matter-of-factly.

"Never even heard it mentioned. I don't recall it tying-up here. *Horton Lodge*? She turns to the barman. "No, never. You heard of that, Flynney? A boat called *Horton Lodge*?" Flynney shakes his head. He hasn't. "Sounds like a name some might put on their house, like '*Beyont'*."

Wauters strokes the dog, which leans against him and nuzzles his snout into Wauters' horny hand. He does not look up, focused on the hound. "Because we are on a navy contract, we sail out of *Haulbowline*. I get the Jolly Boat in and out. They're a bit funny about us telling people where and when we go. In the wrong hands, you know. They say you never know who's listening."

She settles in her seat, sort of squirms to face the man currently so absorbed in the well-being of the dog, now that's an insult for a start. "I want you to give me your hand." He proffers his hand. She looks at it hard and long. The feeling of his hand, all experience and strength. It's all she can do to stop herself from lifting it and brushing it against her face. "Oh yes, I see it all. It's as I thought."

"What?" he asks.

"I don't know if I should say." She goes through her routine, trying to make it all look scientific. Moving the hand through different casts of light, separating the fingers. Tracing her own finger down some line or other creased into the palm.

"I'm not going to die, eh? Is that it? Is that what you're divining?"

She doesn't answer immediately. There is a pregnant pause. She carries on looking; when looking up, she announces, "Now there's a funny thing. It says that you're dead already. This is a strange reading." She takes a big gulp of her drink. "You're here but your hand says you are not. Why could that be do you think?"

He laughs thinking that this is a game of sorts. Pays it no mind. "You can't expect much from a free reading now, can you. *Eish!* A bit of mumbo-jumbo?"

She screws-up her mouth and looks into something distant familiar only to her. "Erm, this is odd. A body not lived-in." The distant spectral miasma seems to have answered her and sets her on a new line of questioning. "You are real, aren't you?" She pinches him lightly. "Well, you seem to be here. You are odd. You see, I began to wonder why you are in my life? I'm not in your palm, hm, yet I'm here, Rollo too, but you? Hello! Who am I addressing? Is there a spirit in the body? You're not just a case are you for something else growing inside yers? Cus that would explain a lot. One day after a long wait a person emerged from the dried-out carcase. The envelope was then blown away in a light breeze leaving the creature behind to flex and squirm like so many new born." Her little self-indulgence at an end she tore into Wauters. "It's that thing with Vaughan, isn't it? You didn't want anything from me. Now tell me, that was an excuse, wasn't it?" She sips her drink. Wauters is attentive not expecting what is to come. "That little man told me that you were, 'helping' him, you got the fruit; you were his guide, like. Well, look where it got him. You could have advised him not to die. That would have been good advice. But I get the feeling that you couldn't really give a shit about him and not for me either, for anybody, come to that." She is now looking at him fixedly, eyes like organ stops and nostrils working. "I was taken in by your tales, your adventure bollocks. But then I thought, perhaps he's just a story teller. Secrets and lies, you know, a Pied Piper, sort of kit. We are so similar, you and me. I understand some of yers but what's this about?" She looks about the room. "I'm having second thoughts about what I'm doing being with you, a stranger. You aren't though, are you?"

He lamely interjects. "*Eish! Godverdomme!* Can I speak?"

She looks back at him searchingly. "No, no, no more tales, although I would like to know what's been going on." No response. "So, what has been going on? We've been walking out, pleasant, I'm sure. Now, just to make it plain, I wouldn't have liked you to take my hand, but you didn't anyway. Quite the opposite. When we're together, you show you're not interested in me at all, really. Like there's a distance between us, a chasm more like. Why am I here? That one about your woman and all? It had me going for a bit…No, I could be anybody, isn't that right? I don't think you thought it through." She switches between all the little things that might add up to one big thing and attributes them to his having to show some interest in her just to sound her out. Very perceptive. Fancy getting tarted up, fancy spilling your guts about all your cherished thoughts and conceptions. She may as well have talked to the wall! And another thing… "You came to see me 'cus you wanted to know how you stood-in with your Vaughan story, see that I was neutral in it all. While me, I'm thinking, I'm to blame, I put him up to it and allowed Wauters in on my call. And another thing…And then you found it hard to find a way out, or you kept on wanting more reassurance, who knows, and we did all that meeting and stuff, dancing around each other. But you were already on your next wheeze, I think. On the one hand, I seemed to pay you a compliment, flattered you. That it was *you* that had awoken something in *me*! That gave you power over me. Me a simpleton, an un-taught *knacker*, just waiting for your spark to light me up and you tricky enough to get me lost in your lies." She lies, "I was reading long before meeting you. I played you, same as the money in here? I might as well have said that I had taken-up Gaelic football, you weren't listening, your mind was on sizing me up and yet you had made such a bodge of getting entangled in the first place you didn't know how to leave go." She stands up. Sits down hastily. Takes a long drink. "And another thing…Then you have these grand ideas, that I relied on you or summat, when all the time I'm watching you from the cheap seats as you, the great actor, goes about his trade. I think you're a feckin' cold fish, Wauters, or whatever your name is, langer! I think you are a masterful liar." She is getting more and more agitated. And another thing… "I'm confident about my readings, can pull-off the ruse…We are both in the same trade. But you, you surpass me…hands-down. I'm just an amateur dealing in women's complaints and roaming husbands, the O'Grady horse at Leopardstown. You played a masterclass. The only thing that gave you away was your absolute…coldness, your silence, indifference and the air about you, turbulent and nasty, always the impending storm. There's a heat coming off you like you are the devil from *that* place. I'm half surprised when you turn up that you haven't got bats circling around your noggin." She puts her fists on her hip and emphasises her words with thrusts of her head. Rollo is now sitting close to her looking intently at her face. Is his partner in trouble, is she in danger? The dog whines in short bursts.

Tell me friend, what do I do? Is it now that I bark? He barks anyway, just a short staccato yap. Tell me. "And another thing…Why do you enjoy being, being so, nasty? I'm surprised you didn't try and murder the witness, like. I bet you're capable of it. Oh yes, you're capable. I'm going to neck this drink and I'm off. I haven't the time to spend on somebody who doesn't give a fig. And they say we don't have snakes in Ireland naturally, but we seem to import them."

Wauters sits aghast. "Where has all that come from?" He is allowed to say, he is dead to rights and her heated indictment cut to the nub of his plans.

She looks at him briefly and leaves without further utterance and no command to Rollo to 'heel'. Rollo seems more confused, his muzzle casts about. She does not answer the barman when he says goodbye. Flynney leans over his bar casually as she exits the door. "Women: can't live with them. Can't live without them."

Wauters finishes his drink, his eyes follow the line of her exit. He may even been touched, a bit. He is on his way out at the door when the barman shouts over. Rollo is at the door whimpering wanting out after his mistress. Wauters opens the door and the dog scampers out, just as he is about to follow when Flynney shouts over again, "That'll be three shillings and ninepence. She's been in here for a while."

Turning and turning in the widening gyre
The falcon cannot hear the falconer;
Things fall apart; the centre cannot hold;
Mere anarchy is loosed upon the world,
The blood-dimmed tide is loosed, and everywhere
The ceremony of innocence is drowned;
The best lack all conviction, while the worst
Are full of passionate intensity.

Wauters does not pay the tab, instead, he decides to stay in the bar. The more he imbibes the more he discloses, and the more he found that old Flynney was a good listener. No one else in the bar, Wauters could give full vent to his fury from the loss of the old ways to the hopelessness, lack of faith in tomorrow. For him, tomorrow had come and all the portents fulfilled. How he laughed, not to his face obviously, at the shaman in Jakarta, part of a drunken bet, as the man had enunciated his fate, he cracked up about it and chose to cast off all the waypoints and conclusions that the funny little joker had proposed in that little smoky den with the heavy scent of narcotics in the air and an unseen, but felt, woman behind the curtain, watching-on attentively. Ready with a knife, perhaps, who knows, the east is the east. 'Buddha's Gong', the opium 'snake' and all. But Wauters was not laughing now. The future was said to be all violence and instability, penury and scrapes. So had that future unfolded. He had become a man who practiced what, some sort of *'Lydford Law'*, another way of saying get yours in first. When Vaughan learned a little too much, to the extent of thinking he had the upper hand; that casual conclusion was going to have repercussions. Did he pull a knife? The recollection is dim, perhaps he was going for his wallet, who knows, but I just tapped him one anyway, better safe? We could share the *kreef*. What, that filthy urchin? I have my standards. Then it *was* his wallet and he put the bribe in. I was bought. Plum was just too easy to get on top of. He was a sort of practice ground for asides and intimidation. With what he thought, he knew he had put himself into danger. If that blabbermouth to blurt out some tale of what he saw going on that night in the dark? Carmen, her case was harder. In between swigs, he wipes his mouth with the back of his hand. If he forgets to top up Flynney helps him out. And they say that life in the sea is hard, full of snapping jaws and unexpected poisons, things tearing flesh from other things. I heard a tale that, sometime ago, in those religious times, when if you didn't abide by the Pope and the word, you know, it spelled danger. This man did something little, harmless. Had an opinion maybe. A good man. A holy man. They sentenced him to burn. Heh, but we're humane, aren't we? They had a rethink about his punishment and his goodness in the past taken into account and, instead, commuted the sentence to being buried alive. He drains his glass with a pained expression on his face. Flynney tops the glass up. He had known so many hard-bitten women that were all about money and little else that meeting this small eruption, this bemused creature with all her hang-ups for a 'reading' took you aback. Well, what was to be done? He couldn't take her, but that would be like a night out in Bangkok and not knowing how old or, sometimes, what sex they were. It would be too much like an assault on an innocent. Yet, Carmen was a problem too and even more so now, especially now that she was in a strop. Nothing like a woman scorned, eh? He would keep her laying-off until well clear of the shallows and then just sail out of her life. He emerged from his thoughts to share with the barman, 'Know what I mean Flynney', this goes no farther is drawled and vaguely finger pointed. The barman is confused only having witnessed silence and a hard stare hitherto. Would that work, or would he have to have it out with her? He had bought the whole bottle which had now surpassed that thing about spirits lifting and happiness inducing; it had morphed into a challenge. The gleaming glass became a thermometer of his mournful temperature. For every level of self-loathing, venomous incantation and vengeful bit of sermonising that passed, the level in his thermometer dropped. He would beat the genie in this lamp. Taunt me, would you? Don't think I'm man enough heh? Flynney looked-on being treated to disparate, disconnected words and phrases, the back ends of thoughts and imprecation. Eventually, he thought he had beaten the bottle. But, even empty, it reigned triumphant over him, as it always did; look what I've done to you little man, it proclaimed. Flynney had seen many a thug and base sort cave in when they took on the bottle in as many rounds as it takes. For a born coward and opportunist, Flynney took much comfort from seeing the braggard and the confrontational fall down at his feet, poleaxed.

He waited until Wauters was totally slumped and then came from behind the bar. Wauters was insensible. "Come on me beauty." He struggled to lift the big, well-muscled man. "Come on, in the chair with you." Wauters made rumbling noises somewhat like a leviathan in the depths 'sounding'. Flynney got his drift. "Come on up for air, breathe deeply." When he was satisfied that Wauters was as near too insensible as made any difference, Flynney, naturally, went through the man's pockets. Little did he know that he was stealing stolen money; it was no more than a shilling or two but would be better as Flynney's shilling or two rather than the daft sailors. The man would be in the way when the drinkers came in. As soon as he had enough helping-hands in the bar, they all got together and literally threw Wauters onto the pavement outside.

At the ship, noting Wauters' absence, they sent out the Jolly Boat, increasingly fearing the worst for him. He was fairly predictable in his ways and had never missed the return boat. No one knew where he'd gone. Perhaps he'd skipped? In the town, the shore party searched and eventually one of the outriders came upon him. The first reaction was that he was dead. But heh, this is not Barbary, this is Ireland, Queenstown; they have a bit of rough house occasionally in the bars but in Cork and its surrounds it's mainly family feuding and the odd cracked head. They approached him gingerly. He was stone cold drunk. They tried to estimate how much drink, by the sniff of it, Poteen, it would take to fell such an ox and were lost in a process of calculation that was beyond them, unimaginable. Later, they tipped him into his cot. The crossing, shore to ship, had not been without its humour or fright. When Wauters started to come too, he made noises like a baby and then, suddenly, would leap-up as if branded and try to clamber over the dinghy's gunwales, knocking the oars out of the rower's hands and rocking the craft precipitously. Putting everyone in jeopardy of a soaking. He took some restraining but it was, in its way, quite good humoured really, his silly antics. They smuggled him aboard. They had no love for Wauters but were willing to make some tale up to suggest that he had been on board all along and as the Watch had actually accompanied the individual, who was to say otherwise? He's crew after all. They got him down into the hold where Plum lay asleep. As soon as the man's head had hit the pillow, he was gone, childlike in the arms of Morpheus.

-oo0oo-

Another day, another thirty cents, as the old saw should say. A dollar would be nice, but it's a dream. The day-to-day normality of being at war is a truly boring experience. You are so practised at what you do that you cannot have any enthusiasm for the constant drills. There's only so much to learn and unlike proper learning you do not 'pass' here until you have deployed your art and either died or won-over jeopardy. Plum managed to jumble up the routine by attending Cathcart's occasional religious services. Even though the congregation seemed to know all the words to only the one hymn, *'The Day Thou Gavest'*, it made little difference. The effect the calm words had over them all, of Cathcart's sermons, could make the day. Little allegories parcelled around river fishing, raising pheasants and shipbuilding at *'Buckler's Hard'*. The understanding and sentiment were right. Plum knew more about dry fly fishing now than had ever occurred to him before. He had formed the opinion that if he was going after Cathcart's big trout the best general lure would have to be, this year, this weather, an *'Iron Blue Dun'*, that's what Cathcart said. The reverence of which the captain spoke of his old adversary, *'Gentleman Jim'*, was touching but his reasoning, to throw such a weighty supper back, six and bit pounds, should he have the privilege of taking it, unfathomable. It is difficult to associate this ship with the ship that they first signed on to. That original ship was almost pristine. This one is rusted in places and would qualify for the term 'tramp steamer' in all respects. But everything is running as it should and the work of maintenance does not cease; but nature will have its way in the end. Plum leaves-off his work to talk to the Lascar who is cleaning cooking utensils in an enamelled bowl on deck. Plum sidles up to the man, not even knowing if the guy will be able to understand him. "Nice day for it." He is surprised when the man replies.

The Lascar has a strong East End of London accent. "I am really grateful to be able to get out of the stuffy kitchen, it makes such a change."

Plum reflects on the accent, not being able to place it and finding it evidently has cultured undertones; it is difficult to match that with what he sees. "Where are you from, then?"

"The *Isle of Dogs*, London. We have a thriving community there. We are Lascars, sailors."

Plum shakes-off his disbelief. "Er, my names Plum, like the fruit." He offers his hand to be shaken. The Lascar indicates his wet hands and declines to shake. "What brings *you* here?"

"My name is Doomah Sen. How do you do." He offers an elbow to replace shaking hands. Plum doesn't see the purpose at first and then catches on and taps elbows, a bit of a novelty. This guy's funny, not like a foreigner at all. Doomah Sen picks up the thread of conversation as the other man seems a bit diffident. "I'm sorry that there is no way of shortening it, the name, it is a bit of a mouthful…I think that the weather is calming down as the year progresses. Perhaps things will calm down. What we suffer eh, doing our bit, you know, King and country."

"Look at you. This is hardly your fight," Plum insists.

"Not that I wish to contradict you in any sort of way, but it *is* my fight too. I have lots of people in India, lots of friends and family. If England falls, they will have no protection. Germany will sweep through the rest of the world of the innocence like a dose of salts, like Beacham's Pills, heh? Europe is India's front line. Imagine all the slavery, the death that will be caused if *they* win. I read the papers about them killing children, the *Belgium Incident*? They have made a mess of Russia and brought the Tzar down; now those poor people are short of food and have an unstable government, terrible. We can only wish them the best. There all sorts of governments there now vying for control. I have no doubt in my own mind that the cruellest variant of those proposed philosophies will take over. Very destabilising, very cruel."

Plum is taken aback. The man is right smack bang up to date and has obviously thought about the various situations deeply. Talk about preconceptions. "You seem well informed."

Doomah Sen is a bit embarrassed. "If you have the gift of sight and can read, you are in a good place. When this is all finished, I hope to go to college, get a degree, perhaps; it is my duty."

"A degree, wow! Are all your people like you?" marvels Plum.

Doomah Sen looks about him, as if scanning a crowd. "I'm afraid I do not know them all."

The thought that universities are for rich people, comes into his mind, probably something of his dad's opinion. "That's posh, university. How could you afford that?"

Doomah Sen carries on with his chore nonchalantly. "My dad is in import and export, to India and the Union of South Africa, and has been saving money for me. I am not to have the life he has had; you see. I am to do my best for England because they have given him a chance in the world. We are all in the same boat." He looks around him in that way again, gives a sly smile and then a laugh. "Very much in the same boat."

Plum, like a dog with a rabbit. "But if you are clever enough to go to college, why are you a cook's assistant? Why not an officer or some such?"

"It is a long process to become an officer and I am not all that interested in a life, a career at sea. In fact, I think I would have to prove I am English and English for several generations for them to even consider me. Even our captain would have had to comply with that test. Just doing my bit, as they say." He places both hands on the rim of the washing-up bowls and turns to Plum. "I like physics you see. We are all so fired-up about Einstein and, and Rutherford, two very great men. I want to work in science, I want to stand on their shoulders, as did Newton with his predecessors. The captain here is a very good mathematician. We have studied a few theorems together, when he has the time. I am studying science here, now, this minute. I think that being cooky's mate I am able to set my mind free and think of other things, the job is not that demanding. I have been having a very exciting time." Even Doomah Sen is slightly unsure of that reflection considering if near death is exciting then yes, it has had its moments.

"Have you?" Plum recoils in disbelief. "I must be missing something. I'm bored stupid."

Doomah Sen reflects on his terror but seeks a means of sublimating his experience. He looks up from the bowl and points a soapy hand towards Queenstown "I have seen you running and exercising and I have been doing the same sort of thing with my head. I have been going through the scientific method and learning the discipline of hypothesis and proof, very important. What do you do, apart from running a lot?"

Plum points at his gun which at that moment has its cover off. "They've turned me into a gunner, although I didn't go to *HMS Excellent*. Still, you don't know what you've got until you least expect it most, as my dad used to say. I told my mate that you were a Mulatto, any relation?"

"Sorry, Mulatto? I don't know that term. I am not as clever as I would have people believe I am. Just to go back, you said 'You don't know what you have got...and then I lost the drift of your assertion. I think it was to do with not knowing the future, is that right?"

Plum had never really stopped to question it. "It's just something we say, like a big version of a polite cough, a space filler. My dad had a lot of them. *'Dukes and Darlings'*, like when you flip a coin, heads or tails. *Six and two threes*, like a different answer for the same thing. That sounds a bit like science now, saying it over. *Gig lamps*, thick glasses. *Buggins' Turn*, somebody getting a job because they know someone in the know; 'the bike', that's a woman that puts it about, ridden by everybody. That's what they called the Countess of Warwick, our king's mistress. 'The bike', everybody rides her."

Doomah Sen clouds over for a brief moment. "That seems rather cruel. I think that jealousy often provokes such sentiments, not to say that *you* are jealous...A trader used to refer to my dad as 'the barber', because my dad was always undercutting him, shaving his profits. Rather funny really, although my father did not see it that way. My dad is a very hard worker. His hands are always yellow from handling turmeric and such. He gets a lot of colds from working at the docks at Tilbury, in that draughty warehouse."

"What's a turmeric when it's at home?" Plum tries to get his head around it.

Doomah Sen sounds it out. "T-u r-m-e-r-i-c, is a spice, like ginger and stuff, a rhizome I think; it is used in a lot of cooking. Very good for your health, for skin. Very yellow."

"But it doesn't stop your dad from getting colds, does it?" The Lascar gestures as if to say, 'true'. Plum is encouraged and trots out one of the little idiosyncrasies of the language that tickle him. Doomah Sen is not the only one to be faced by it. "Here's one for you. Have you heard of a horse race?" Doomah Sen nods in the affirmative. "Then you would have heard of a dog race?" Again, the Lascar is acquainted with the term, nods. "So, what do you feel about a millrace?" Plum looks at the man with a look of quiet self-satisfaction. Doomah Sen does not know whether to laugh or attempt some sort of answer. Plum cuts across him. "We think that there's nothing like a good thick stew with lots of root vegetables and meat, onions in it for seeing colds off, along with being sown into a good thick vest for the winter, that is. A nice hot cup of Bovril goes well on a cold day, rub goose fat on your chest. I even spread it, Bovril, on buttered toast, at home. We know all about a cold climate see, know what to expect. We are on top of illness. It's expensive getting medical treatment, so, rule one, we have all our teeth taken out, at great expense, as a very special gift, like. When you're twenty-one, to stop illness in its tracks. It's common knowledge that the mouth, teeth, are the place where most illnesses come from. Have your teeth out, like when you get the key to the door, taking 'em out, is the best, most considerate gift of all and you are saved all sorts of doctor's bills. Doctors, hospitals are dead expensive dear."

"What a very alien sort of thing to do, how barbaric sounding. Having all your teeth out when an alternative through good cuisine and dental care sounds far more civilised. Not to say anything though. What do they say, keep your own counsel?" There's a pause in the conversation. The Lascar goes back to his washing.

Plum looks about him and sees the Sub-Lieutenant Senior who, when he catches Plum's gaze, looks away exaggeratedly. "That's odd," Plum reflects. *Silly sod,* he thinks.

"What, the spices?" the Lascar enquires.

"No, I mean, yes. No, it's nothing. I'd better get back to the gun. Daft sort of navy where no one wears a uniform. You don't know where you stand anymore." Plum starts to move away.

"You just don't know. Take care now."

The Lascar looks into his bowl of soapsuds. *"Buggins' Turn,* I will remember that one, *Buggins' Turn."*

-oo0oo-

Back in the hold, the soft interior light is barely sufficient to read by. The continuous thrum of the engine hardly figures anymore, a constant companion. Wauters and Plum are in their sleeping area. Wauters is looking at his book or so you might think.

"I had a shufty at your book, when you were up top." Plum chirps-up, feeling a bit left out of things, bored. He would, by preference, get his map out and try to conjure what it was going to be like, romanticise a little. Like, he supposes, from what he hears, others of the crew say what they'd do when the talk turns to Edna Perveance or Sarah Bernhardt, the divine Sarah, that's their romance, he has his map. "Your story, looks a bit dull. Jungles, natives and a bint. You must be finding it that way too. You don't seem to be getting on very well with it." Wauters looks around his book and then returns to it. Plum pauses momentarily. "You remember, I mentioned how we needed a woman here, a real woman that is. A mum or auntie would do. This place is really lacking a woman's touch. We could do with Auntie Dolly here to run-us-up some curtains. She was a dab-hand at such things." He momentarily looks pensive. "Dead now, and her daughter, my cousin, alcohol. I tell you what. In an idle moment, I often imagine that we've got a big picture window over there at the bulkhead instead of that great bear patch and a tiddly porthole. Yes, a great big picture window. You can imagine all sorts of things having a big window in your head. I can be anywhere in the world, just by pretending I'm looking through my window, there. Tropical seas, exotic islands near at hand. You should share my window; it would cheer you up."

Wauters looks around his book. *"Ke Sharp!"* he says dismissively, after he puts the book away from him momentarily. "Eish! Have you nothing better to do, *gin-en-gaap*?" He stops and reflects. "I tell you, *Praatsiek,* everybody is bored to tears. Here, Swansea, here, Southampton, here Dublin, Falmouth. What a tiresome, dreary life." He spits out bitterly. *'Die dood sou meer betekenis hê'.* Death would have more meaning; I think that's what he said, my Pa.

"What?" Plum looks at the speaker with garnering incomprehension. Another bit of *Hogan-Mogan.* Wauters drops his book, drops his guard.

"Listen, an idea comes to me." He is suddenly animated. "We don't need an imaginary window, *mompie*. We can make real excitement, a way that we could make the whole ship happy, give them something to look forward to."

"All you've got to do is tell them they're going home," says the lad.

Wauters rides over the remark. "In conversation, that fireman, Logan, tells me about your boxing match. He says that he almost beat you, except that he had just come off his watch and was tired from travelling and little food and so on and so on. He thinks he could have taken you."

Plum pretends to yawn. "Where he lives, with the unicorns, perhaps he could."

"See that's the other thing. He reckons it was an uneven fight. He had to travel down from *Scapa Flow* and they put him to work straight away while you; well, it was on your doorstep. I hear all about it. Rosyth sounds like a holiday place. No place to exercise a warship, fire guns. Not on that river. You must have had a lot of spare time? Even your admiral had a bit on the side shacked-up in an Edinburgh hotel to relieve the boredom there, heh? That's according to the scuttlebutt. He was looking after you as well. An admiral who was a bit flash. Well, he wanted to win all the time, eh? Everything, eh, and you were part of it."

Plum laughs. "He's plum-crazy, yeah, Plum crazy. I…"

But Wauters is in full flow. "No, you're Plum and crazy. You know he will haunt you for the rest of your life unless you put an end to it, to his daft chatter. He's deadly serious about it all no matter how you play it off." Wauters is warming to his topic, the trap is sprung. "Yes, he is a silly man, but silly people are often the most dangerous, no? *Eish!* This would be the match of all time, well in navy terms. We could call it, what…a decider, yes, a decider. How's that sound? After this there would be no question and he, well he would shake hands and be put in his place proper. A *'roarer',* a broken nag, winded, against the cock-horse, you. I've seen you in action. He speaks about you in such an off-hand way. You're just a light-weight that got lucky. Fortunate on the day." Wauters feigns ecstasy with uplifting gestures. Don't you see what a huge day it would be?" He makes to write in the air. *"Die botsing van die titan.* The *Grand Fleet* versus your people, the battle cruisers, in memory of *HMS Invincible.* What say you?" It had been a while and Afrikaans phrases take some thinking about, he reflects.

"I don't know that I'd want to." Plum thought that all that had been put to bed and is a bit irked by its resurrection. It was no big thing, just another bout. Plum demurs. "He's got no skill. It would give the wrong impression about boxing, entirely. Just a slugger, scrapper, him. He could get hurt. I wouldn't like that, even though he's a big bruiser."

A quick response from the other cot. "You've got no choice, don't you see. Yes, you have no choice." Where did he get that phrase from, decider? Now to substantiate it. Wauters is thinking deeply, quick in his thoughts, passing through many avenues of attack in an instant, as you would expect from a man used to tight spots. "There are only two outcomes, you see, *paw-paw*; either you fight, and you are a hero and this man who, at the moment, really dislikes you, hates you with that smouldering hatred, is put in his place. Or, you don't fight. What are you then, a coward? Word gets about, as you know, not always the truth, maybe. You have such a reputation I hear, why risk it? Not only that, but the thing you could have settled turns into that thing where you are constantly on your guard about, in case he goes berserk one day with his loathing gnawing at him, and he lashes-out. Could happen any time. Takes things too far, goes AWOL and does you real damage and not necessarily with the boxing. Nothing like somebody assured in their own lies and misconceptions. Hits you with his shovel or some such thing when you're not watching. What for boxing then, eh? But a decider. That's once and for all. You know you would run rings round him"

That man's language has changed. When Plum first met him first his talk was lumpy and gruff, now he talks freely with just the odd foreign bit thrown in. Plum swings his legs outside the cot. "You seem very excited by the whole thing *Hogen-Mogen*. Like its *Fred Kano's Army*, a circus act." He subsides again, lying back, looking at the ceiling. "All he needs is a dose of broken bottles, that would put him right. Boxing isn't personal. Besides, you know how odd the officers are on this ship, they're from a different world, their talk is almost…is it English, you think; it's a wonder that they make themselves understood at all sometimes. I can't see them agreeing to such a stumer." No, a war is excitement enough."

"You're coming across as stupid, you know that?" says Wauters, recoiling. "You hold all the cards. You're fit, he's a bit lardy. Your wind is good, his, blown, like an old carriage horse; you're the *'cock horse'*, so much stronger, he's the old nag, winded…"

Plum runs it around in his head. Tries to imagine the faint possibility. "Only it would be catchweight he weighs, well, almost twice as much as me. As to fitness, you don't get to stand shovelling in front of a furnace all day and not get fit. I don't know."

Wauters sits up and shows a sign of despair: "Look, I've tried my best. I have to go below and listen to all his spitting venom. He's going to get you one way or another by fair means or not. You know as well as me how hatred festers, *ja*?"

"This is a sad affair; I don't have any bad feelings for him." Plum is beginning to feel cornered. Wauters monitors him closely, feeling that he is making progress. "But if what you say *is* true. Anyway, the chances of it being agreed to are nil, zero."

"So, I mention it and they say no, that's it, the end. But if it gets the thumbs up, what then?" says Wauters. "There's no backing-out then. People are funny. You offer them something and then just as they are about to bite, they can almost taste it, who'd, take it away? If it was approved it would be all around the ship. Hands would start mulling it over, one for this man, another for the other. Bets would be placed; I've seen it done. It would be a brave bloke who backed out then."

Plum is needled. "All right, all right." He pauses trying to get his head around it. "I need to have a word with Logan."

Wauters holds a palm out, stop there. "*Sien jou gat*, bad move before it's settled, you would make a fool of yourself. Talk to him when he doesn't hate you. You would provoke him if you tried to speak. A sure sign of weakness improving his chances. That makes him more keen. Then he puts it about your cowardice. At least in the ring, there are some rules and you understand it, what you're playing at. In life, *loskop*, you have to admit, you're a bit hopeless!"

Plum is bugged. "Stop it, stop it." He waves a finger to indicate to call a halt. There is a silence. Plum thinks the matter through. He wrestles with himself. Wauters is triumphant. He is wasted here. He should be selling yashmaks to the Arabs. "You're setting me up?" Who is playing the pipe that has got this snake to rise out of his basket? He knows, for sure, that Wauters would make sure that the story would be all around the ship if he turned the proposal down and that awful coward word would be spread over everything. "I'll do it on one condition, it has to be an exhibition bout. A set number of rounds and not just a knock out; say, four five-minute rounds and when they're done, an end. There has to be a referee. A points decider, that's for others to think on, points. The fight is stopped if there's any cuts. No betting, well, it would be pointless." And all the time Plum is thinking sailing, compass, tide, his reliance on this agitator.

"Good thinking, *Piet*," says Wauters with a serious, congratulatory false frontage. That disguised snide way he has. "You've made the right decision *paw-*

paw." Wauters acts out a small, noiseless clap. "Leave it to me. I'll see you right."

There is a protracted silence. Plum looks blankly ahead. Wauters goes back to his book. Plum regards Wauters suspiciously as his 'matey' subsides. Plum makes a whispered aside. "Bashaw!"

Wauters looks up from his book. "Sorry, did you say something?"

"Me? No. A sneeze." Plum has a thousand and one vengeful things to shout at Wauters. But then, that would be the end, the end of everything. He breathes deeply for a moment. "We should be getting some rest. There's a big job on tonight, all hands. I don't think you should wear your dress. Tonight, we become another ship, eh? By the morning we could be Dollar Steamship Line, Eagle Oil, Blue Star, anything we want, a different profile."

Behind his book, Wauters makes a small answer. "I've not heard anything. What's on? *Eish!* Will they never leave us be?"

"They've come-up with a scheme," says Plum lying back, resting on one arm. "The captain thinks that the Germans have got used to us plying back and forth, got a bit wary, perhaps. What we need, he thinks, is for us to change the ship's profile, like, to be from another shipping line, for instance. So, we're going to change the deck furniture around, put up another deck house, you know, to change the outline of the ship and we're going to become part of the *White Star Line,* something like that. Star, see, would be easy to paint, stars, not like drawing a lion rampant or unicorn or something. Not like drawing winged Pegasus or summat of that. That requires an artist. Something simple. It should be fun." In a sudden sadness alien to him, he leans back, patting his stomach. "Here we are having all this fun and back home Lord Belford, what's his face, tells the population that it is wrong, evil, to throw stale bread away! They tell me that there is all sorts of daftness going on, especially around food. Like, the enforced rationing of bread, because, they say, children are the main food wasters. What a palaver. They say that the war effort is undermined by guzzlers. 'Guzzlers', I ask you. That's not a word that you hear a lot, 'guzzler'. It's all going-off at home. Minds are exploding not *mines*. All our most golden thoughts turning to pinchbeck when we don't understand our country too well, as much as we thought and it all seems to be getting away from us." Wauters is only half listening. "Votes for women. It wasn't all that long ago when most men had no rights in the franchise. Yes, 1913 was a turning point in many ways. Every man you had even a grudging respect for *then* is a pompous git *now*. I don't know about Emily Davidson thinking she had to die the way she did, but it seems to some of us that none of us are any further forward. Everybody is expected to go without coal and to eat leftovers? See what happens when we have to submit to government control? The rule makers sitting in offices and not expected to look outside on the real world. What I wouldn't give for a *growler*, a bloody good sausage roll. You foreigners like your sausage, don't you?"

Wauters holds a finger up in contradiction. "Boerewors, proper sausage."

Plum continues, "It does nothing for your moral to think of all them poor buggers, clemmed death. Anyway, rest, eh. It's going to be a whole night job." He lies on his bed in a foetal position.

Wauters lies back, brings the book to his face. He smiles broadly.

-oo0oo-

The activity of repainting the funnel and building the deckhouse goes ahead in inky black darkness, low lying lamps, pointed at the deck, offer meagre light. The captain overlooks the work for a while and then retreats to his cabin. Someone is singing *Roamin' in the gloamin'*. The song is taken-up by some of the crew. There is a bit of horseplay. Someone inadvertently leans against some wet paint, smiles abound as the bloke peals himself away, but all are brought back to focus by Sub-Lieutenant Hodge creeping around, always looking at his watch. The captain is in his cabin is fully focused on the Country Life magazine on his desk, opened at a page of instruction on wet fly fishing; spinners, plugs, how awfully unsporting, trolling is. He takes up a length of thin wood rehearses the casting manoeuvres, especially the 'roll cast' which he will need for his great adversary near the bridge by the hanging willow. The letter has elicited many 'oh, dears' and 'what are we to do's'. The damp patch in the ingle is back and the down spout on the barn is broken, which propels water all over the yard now. The estate forester has dumped a great pile of logs by the kennels and it took the best part of the day for Mrs Captain to drag them under-cover and, ever since, the arthritis in her hand has been playing merry-helen with her, requiring lots of hot water bottles and wearing her big fleece-lined mittens, but to little effect. What is he to do? That's not woman's work and Stephen, the woodsman, always gets a tasty Christmas present from them, every year. You would think he would be more considerate. But that's the big problem with servants. They see all too intimately how you live and whatever the bestowal you make it is invariably looked upon as mean and only breeds resentment in the end; damned if you do. He had a great plan to strip that wall down by the fireplace, back to the brick and plaster it himself, he would enjoy that. But as to the cause of the problem, the flashing around the chimney, that would need the estate manager's assistance and that person is inevitably so 'busy', things have a habit of slipping his mind.

On deck, the finishing touches are put to the star being painted on the funnel; the men seem happy with the finished article. The insignia chosen is that of the White Star Line. A pretend locker has been put together and covered in canvas up at the bow, a nice job by Wauters, neat. Yes, to all intents and purposes, this is a ship that went into the darkness in one form and will emerge changed enough to make an attacker scratch their heads. A new target, where did the other go?

They do as much as they can. In the sleeping quarters with its dim lights, with the perpetual thrumming of the engines aft, some men flake out on their cots still dressed in their overalls, worn out. Stupefied like a drunkard, only left so by a long day and fatigue. Plum and Wauters wearily lie down to catch some sleep after cleaning their hands with white spirit, hardly able to stay awake. A glance around the sleeping quarters reveals other men living other lives. Little personal possessions, keepsakes, that each of them has that mean so much. An attachment to something that isn't scary and that speaks of comfort and acceptance, control even, attractive to those that, here, have none. Something that intervenes in your current obsession. This sleep is so welcome and the men easily capitulate to its oblivion. Wauters passes into sleep almost instantly. The dullness, the engine noise counts the sheep of the hastening oblivion. Suddenly, Wauters is made aware that Plum is heaving, a sound like a cat with a fur ball. He is having trouble breathing by the looks of things. Wauters waits a moment, clears hid head, tries to get his bearings, then goes to Plum's cot. "Heh! *Pawpaw*! You dreaming or summat? Why the row?" He shakes the heaving form who lies there first squirming and then tense, his back arched, pushing the blanket away from him as if it was an assailant, then gripping at his own throat, convulsive. "What's afoot?" Plum is straining to breathe. The more he pushes and kicks at his covers the more difficulty he sustains his breathing. "Tell me, what can I do?" he says, up close, right into the prostrate sailor's ear. Hisses in a loud whisper. "Plum! Plum! What goes on? What's the fix? For God's sake, tell me." Plum is struggling, gasping, clawing at his throat. "You need fresh air, its stale in here. Have you swallowed something? C*hommie*? Tell me! Open your mouth, let me see."

Plum fixes Wauters with his frantic eyes. "Asthma! He rasps. There's...nothing to...be done." He gasps. "It will pass... uh...uh... sometime... I expect."

"There must be something. I'll get help," says Wauters.

But Plum just breathes harder. "No, no!" He lunges out, grasps at Wauters, claws at him. "No...one...should know. They'll...uh, uh..." His body heaves. Contorts, arches, writhes. He arches his back against the mattress, pushes his blanket away frantically. He feels as though there is a ligature tightening around his throat and all his motions are designed to grab the imaginary rope and release its terrifying effect. "...kick me out." He pauses frequently. He is sweating profusely, putting great energy into each fought-for breath.

"You're going on deck. I'll put you on deck. Come on." Wauters uses a fireman's lift technique to raise Plum over his shoulder, but struggles to get the thrashing, agonised body up the companionway onto the deck in a place in the lee of the newly painted funnel, its warm there and the breeze is taking the smell and smoke away from them. He hopes that they won't have been seen, but truth to tell, that's the least of his troubles. Plum seems even smaller now, pallid and thin, taken over by the malady. He agonises to speak. "Uh, uh, nobody...must see, uh uh...me. Please, no one." His frantic eyes search Wauters'.

The huge man has taken on an almost tender air that some would have thought impossible previously. The great ogre has scooped-up the man child and effortlessly, by tortuous ladders, overhangs and narrow passages, taken him up and away from the fug in their rest area. He is all mother hen. He takes his outer jacket off after laying Plum on the deck plates; pulls the garment over the still writhing and whimpering body. Plum rasps something. Wauters lowers his head. "You say what?"

"Nobody...should...know." He grabs Wauters. "Promise me?" His stare speaks of panic, fear. He is at his most pleading. His grasp is a serious clench which suddenly ebbs as he wriggles and tries to urge the breeze into his airways, throwing his head back. He falls back wheezing. All that athletic prowess vanished, gone. Wauters resolves to watch him but the long day takes control of his body. After all the attentiveness he has put into helping, he too is mad tired. His body is placed as close to the recumbent figure as it can be manoeuvred, making sure not to shroud the man's mouth or pressurise his chest Then he slips off into the eager arms of dreams, and he's the man who talks about *Calashee Watches*? All is black. Wauters has small hints as to the predicament even in sleep. A small rain shower at one point, he recalls, stirs him. But he does not open his eyes soon losing the sensation of the sprayed drops on his face. A turn across the current is perceived at one point he notes, but soon loses the will to think about it. But everything is happening in dream time. Time passes until the half-light of dawn. Wauters comes too. He is snuggled up to Plum. He is chilled. Plums body is still. His eyes are open. Is he…dead? The lad smiles weakly. "Sorry about that," Plum offers lamely in a little childlike voice.

Wauters is surprisingly human and has the residue of the evening's alarm hanging about him. "What's to do? Has it passed?" he asks softly, urgently.

How odd to hear Wauters express concern, Plum glories in it. Perhaps it's a new leaf. He smiles at his saviour, manages to raise himself on an elbow. "Give me a minute. I'm better now. Hell, I'm tired." He sits-up with Wauters' assistance. He goes to take the huge jacket off his now relaxed body the one that Wauters wrapped him in, he recalls it all; little Baby Bunting, but Wauters won't have it and makes a straightjacket of the garment around the prone figure. "Asthma. I've not had an attack for years."

"I've seen men with *Grand Mal*, but nothing like that," says the seemingly neutered bear.

"Since a child. I've these attacks, but not since being in the service. I nearly had a 'do' when I was shot into the sea at Jutland; but I was crying and ranting that hard the shakes you know, it revived me, warmed me, probably saved my life, them tears. There's nothing to be done. Just wait it out." He takes Wauters arm. "All I ever wanted was to be was a real lad, you know, and do what they do naturally, without thinking. But this always legged-me-up. I missed my school. I lived inside so much, when I just wanted to run and climb, swim. It didn't seem too much to ask. They said that as I grew up it would affect me less, wear off. A time came when I was all right, seemed to have cracked it and Dad took me to the local gym, put me in for the boxing thing, the breath training would help, he thought. It was either that or buying me a trumpet. But apart from the expense, there were the neighbours. So, we went to the boxing and I could do it. I imagined I'd left the dark days behind; it appears not." He lies back. There are still no stirrings about the ship and neither of them had a watch. But Wauters, while not sensing urgency, knew that before long they would have to get a move on. "That paint, last night, it must have made it kick-in." He takes hold of Wauters shirt tightly. "Nobody must know." He looks askance. "They'll have me for lying on my papers. They'll put me in the 'jug'. I can't be relied on you see. I'm useless when I'm like that. Promise me. Do the right thing." Wauters nods ascent. Each with their own thoughts. He juggles his plans in his head and decides that for this minute it is no matter. "Wauters, I need your help. After this…" He looks around. "I have a plan; it's the only thing that has kept me going through all this…When I'm finished service…I have this adventure planned…I'm going to the *Cocos Islands*, searching for buried treasure." He brightens up. "I'm going looking for buried treasure. What do you think? Isn't it grand?"

Wauters answers without any expression. "I know all about your plans."

"How?"

"I've been through your kit," says Wauters in a matter-of-fact sort of way. Plum frowns. Wauters looks at him directly. "I tell you, it's a mugs game. Them maps, ten a penny. Any port, you find some slob with a hard luck story and a map, that is if they are not selling photographs of their 'sisters'."

There is an urgent rebuttal. "No, no, you've got it wrong, it's real, copper-bottomed. I've heard about them maps, I'm not stupid, whatever you may think. I was down at Pompey, on a training exercise. I met another tar" – he looks away as though trying to form a picture in mind's eye – "he was training in submersibles. I didn't care for him much, but heh, any port in a storm. I didn't know the area and he was a local. We had the odd tour around the town together, he showed me the sights, such as they were; he was all tarts and yarns. He talked a lot about himself and not much else. One day, he said he had to go and see a sick uncle, near deaths door, apparently." Wauters listens intently just to show willing and to keep his charge as relaxed as he could, let him blow himself out. He might sleep again if he does. "We went into the back streets. Without a bag of salt or a long string to mark the way, a stranger would have found it impossible to find his way back out. The old man was awfully sick, poor chap, cancer I would think. Grey, obviously in pain of some sort. This mate of mine was a bit curt with him, a bit short. There came a time when the old fellah asked him if the lad would fetch him a beer, from the 'offy', the pub, down the street. The money was on the mantlepiece. Off my mate went, grudging like. No sooner as he was out the door the old bloke became agitated, asked me to hand down a small wooden box, urgent like. I handed it to him. The old fellah drew me in. Put his finger to his lips. Told me he didn't want the relatives to have what was inside the box. He didn't like my buddy or his family and wasn't about to do them any favours. Anyway, inside this box was stuff, a bulldog clip, an old photo of some woman with a banjo and the map, my map. He quickly laid out the whole story of pirates and stuff that went back to the early 1800s, piracy and the 'Relampago', what was sunk by us. A bloke called 'Mr Thomson of London' had been mixed-up with it all and he had come back here and died but, in the doing, passed on the map. The old fellah had been some sort of worker at this man's hospital, an orderly or some such and shown Thomson some kindness, apparently, and now he wanted to pass the thing onto somebody who would do some good with it, not like the wasters, his lot." He looks up at Wauters. "Am I making sense? I supposed you had seen it because that's what you're like. I know you're into everything but not how much. It's been hard for me Wauters, not being able to stand my ground with you for fear of causing an upset between us and I need you. All those names you call me in foreign because, well, because they would what, be too hurtful in English, right? Almost on our first day, I knew you were the missing bit in my adventure and then the sailing, brilliant. I needed you, the chance of your help. We both had our secrets. All along, I've been thinking that you had the spirit and skill to come in with me to see us through the escapade. When you came along everything seemed to fall into place, it was like divine intervention. There was no way I could have coped, not by myself, and the thought of sitting on this for the rest of my life…Can you imagine? You're a hard man to keep up with. I've been biting my tongue ever since we shipped." Wauters is still looking at him intently but now Plum does not see dread in the man's face. There has been a subtle change. "It's not a 'mugs game', like you say. You have to have a dream else…you have to give it a chance…what's the use? What else is there?"

"Nothing is as it seems," Wauters whispers. "I seem to be in the wrong times and I'm a might confused by it all. You come to me with all these tales of invention, a world I don't fit into, it don't seem to have a place for the likes of me. I'm guarding my patch and if that means trip wires and calliopes, that's fine." Wauters eases himself back feeling the comforting warmth of the wet paint funnel. Plum switches his glance from the stern to Wauters and back again.

"But you've just taken care of me. You didn't have to. It's more in your nature to have put me in a jam-jar and watch me suffer. There is something in you that has taken a knock. I can sense it."

"What do you know, Plum? I've crewed with lots of sorts, the likes of *Paddy Westers*, *Packet Rats*, no hopers, the sweepings from many a mooring. In enterprises that need trust and skill, you form a crust between you and them. When all you've got is scoundrels that got a 'ticket' simply through the exchange of money and walking around a stuffed animal's horned head in a Liverpool pub, ''round the Horn', shite. A load of dangerous desperate *mompies* getting paid just to jump ship in Australia, to bugger-off to Ballarat to seek their fortunes in the gold fields. Even too dumb to know the fields are spent; daft bastards, eish! Meantime, you're supposed to go aloft with them and set the sails? Up in the yards with a force eight at your back and the free board taking on walls of swell straining the safety lines. It makes you hard. It makes you selfish."

"But you must have seen some good too?"

Wauters looks away and then back looking resolute. "If it's a case of you or me, I'll tell you straight, if that's the case, it's going to be me."

"But you told me that sailing was good, the best," added Plum.

"Sailing, great, the best. You sit around a 'slush lamp' in the fo'c'sle pretending to be mates, yet you slept with an eye open. They were like file fish, would eat your liver out as the fancy took them. You tend to put aside those things like when you could work for days in wet kit until, in the end, you were covered in boils, as I said, what I told you, the truth. I had some good years even if I had some unpleasant weeks. The end of the tea trade and, yes, the romance beginning to fade. If you chose to look honestly enough, which I didn't. I didn't like it, I loved it and to have that snatched away from me was like losing my family, for all its tribulations."

Plum gives him a soft dig in his side. "You could have done something else. You're certainly not stupid."

Wauters pulls the jacket, still draped around Plum, a little tighter, mummifies the lad then adjusts his body as close as he dare to the funnel. He half-turns and speaks almost confidentially, "When you're growing-up on your own what do you know? I saw some ships that could raise your spirits. In my mind's eye I saw *'Ariel'* and *'Southern Cross'*, legendary names my Pops, if he was in his drink and sort of mellow, would yarn about them with a tear in his eye. Like *he* was emotional? I wanted to see what he saw, to know that emotion he cried about, to feel that intimacy with nature. Then you knew a ship by her Captain. Whether she had a Bully Mate on board or a Bible bashing master who would whip you bloody with his ceaseless prayer meetings tongue, his damnation rages and manic holiness, throwing printed tracts overboard to passing ships, as if. But the ship. What persistent things of wonder they were." He sort of almost manages a smile. "Always fidgeting with the 'All Standing', how and when they were set. Battling in the trades and sapped by *Calashee Watches*, as some call *'coolashi'*, in the doldrums, waiting, anticipating the blow, with all hands-on watch waiting to be driven into action at little notice; shrivelled, like desiccated, in the doldrums. The shanties; the unexpected beasts and the smells from the whalers or the first sniff of the land…Where do we get that…oneness, today, like being a bit of nature yourself? And you say drive a contraption, an automobile. Look at this ship of ours, what a soulless tub. Who'd want to go to the kinema just to see some actors pretending love and jokers falling about. Yes, I've heard all about 'em and don't want 'em; I can do without the whole issue."

Plum looks at his mate admiringly, encouragingly. Little does he know, what would influence this one. He speaks up out of gratefulness. "I like your sailing thoughts, Wauters," says the recumbent man boy. "I like you're getting stuff off your chest. Wouldn't any child wish they had a dad set them to sleep on bedtime tales like yours where you could sail-off to a land of your own contriving where there's no hurt or pestering? When I saw Wild Bill Hickock's travelling wild west show at Belle Vue, I wanted to be a cowboy or in the U.S. cavalry. It all depends on where you get your influences, doesn't it? Where you get your chance. The things that stay in a child's head. There's no accounting for it. I want the adventure before I settle. Who cares about failure, it's part of living, ain't it? Fancy only having stories of the workshop or insurance office to pass on at bedtime. I need you to be there with me to make it happen."

Wauters can do without such talk. "Rest, eh? I'll help you back. Anything to shut you up."

Chapter 15

Plum looks at himself, his reflection in the wheelhouse windows wearing a helmet. Wauters is in his dress walking the deck as instructed. The captain uses his sextant giving instruction to Sub-lieutenant Hodge and then returns to the bridge to check his charts you suppose. The cook has lots of pans steaming away in the galley; the Lascar is holding an exercise book and evidently trying to explain something to his boss. The cook looks perplexed, makes some comments which elicits a shake of the head from the Lascar; cook shoves the book away and motions that the Lascar should do some work. Below the deck, there is a card game in progress. A man explains his tattoo to another. The electrician and the 2nd Engineer sleep soundly. Just another day to get through, way down upon the Suwannee River. But you can never imagine change. You have to go through a lot of pain to find out about mortality. You can read a thousand books about how deaths occur and read beautiful literature describing all the phases faced by man. Here you are prattling about the confines of your 'beat' and, apart from Osgood's sighting of the whale, this is the safest, the most boring posting in the world. An unbroken view interrupted only by coaling in different ports, the latest rumour. We're safer here then playing around with town gas in an old oven. Within weeks, you have learned, unerringly, how to flip a playing card into a tin helmet and how to hold a handstand as though born to it. Doomah Sen has induced the cook to make a vegetable curry and it goes down well with most of the crew, especially any that have travelled out east in former times, although others say pooh, bah, foreign muck. Coaling is never a pleasure but you stretch your legs and use muscles that more often than not have lain dormant. As the taboos and restraints disappear, the men learn about each other. They know about each other's' wives and sweethearts. There is a pooling of knowledge and the seemingly most cautious confess to daring exploits around the world. One man, a Thames lighterman, confesses to his mate about getting an African girl in trouble and leaving her to cope on her own. He had always reassured himself ever since that it was her fault. Now seeing it was him and that he finds it hard to live with his discovered guilt. Having been at the edge has become a drug for them and this tour was just the ticket. For others, it was an escape from all manner of things while, for some, a death wish. They all come to the conclusion that the enemy is the same stock as them basically. That they feel more affinity with Helmut than they do with, say, Pierre. Before all this kicked off, it was the French that we were most troubled about, they were a possible enemy, nothing changes. Well, they've always been our enemy and the Prussians, well they're Germans, like Bismarck, were always on our side and in their turn had put the Frenchie's in their place in, what was it '70, '71? There is a consolation that 'your German' is from Protestant Christian stock, Frenchie's, they are Roman Catholic, aren't they? It isn't as though they are facing the *Mahdi* despite everything. They don't just come at you careless of death, believing they're dying for more than a cause, like a religious duty, seeking the after-life. Facing an enemy who would gladly give their life away, there is no sanction or threat that can hit home, it's terrifying. Yes, your worst enemy is the one that doesn't mind dying, but that's not your German. They will have the same need for self-preservation as us, won't they? They're not about to just throw themselves onto your guns thinking only of the rewards to come in Heaven. No, they will have sweethearts and a pub that they go to, full of people who know them. Will have a job to go back to, not like some you can name. Your German knows when to give in and, living like he does, you can bet that he sees all of that in us as well and that makes him, well, almost human. Any man that can give up when he knows he's beat, well you can understand them, can't you? It's the others who treat life as being nothing that are the problem; the real terror because they don't share our…feelings. So much goes on when men try to reassure each other or when the war seems to be passing you by. You can be magnanimous and personify 'them' in a pleasant way. If we don't hurt 'them', then they won't hurt us, eh. Easy. I don't hate them, do you? Don't worry. We'll get through.

-oo0oo-

One of the hands runs up the steps to the wheel house and addresses the captain, points urgently away to the starboard side; running seems a bit excessive, almost indecorous, against the usual drift of things. The captain quietly, slowly, like a mantis, draws the binoculars to his eyes and looks to where he has been directed. He does not want to know down in his depths that there is something out there. He scans. In the back of his mind, the incident of the whale plays right next to the fear that this might be it. The chances of any sighting being a U-Boat are, well too slight to be a concern. The captain is not about to raise his sensibilities to panic stations just yet, it would be a fool's errand. Fatalism has seeped in, drowns his passions. He has an acquaintanceship with war now and is more…measured. He quietly issues some instructions to the sailor and the man goes back to the deck slowly as instructed. No need for panic, more like routine. Here, on deck, he collects others calmly and issues them with instructions to look-out on the starboard side and expect a whale anytime, good deflection, a whale, fun, a sighting a natural monster, entertaining. Quite interesting really, but not exciting. Perhaps we'll get a good look this time. Time passes. Tea and sandwiches are brought to the watchers. One by one the men stop looking. The original crewman gets the attention of the captain on the bridge and gives a shrug. As he does this, a submarine comes to the surface behind the chap and the captain points towards it. His, demeanour changes to that of frightened intensity, jabbing a finger in the U-Boat's direction. Soon all are looking at the surfacing vessel as if transfixed. Something appearing out of nothing, well that's magic, isn't it? The captain calls for dead slow on the telegraph. Nothing could have been designed that looks and acts so menacing as a submarine does; black and unnatural, secret and magic, conjured out of nothing. Water streams from its hull like its sweating profusely as, bit by bit, it reveals itself. A puff of diesel smoke emits from it, like a dragon's breath, loath. An unnatural creature of the still unexplored deep, warming to its task. It glistens in the spring light. Sits there having parted the sea and pushed itself through the broken seam. A terrible danger being born. The hatch opens. Men leave the conning tower. So, this is what Germans look like. An odd mixture of all sorts of shapes and sizes, just like us. They are unshaven, almost to a man. They wear odd scruffy clothes, just like us. In this odd moment, the crew some to the rail and satiate their incredulity. There is a smell to the boat, both diesel and the depths. An officer appears, he has insignia, issues instructions; leaning over the edge of the conning tower, pointing at his sailors instructing them hither and thither. Their deck gun is turned in the ship's direction and to the consternation of all aboard a shot is fired. Is this how it will be, no chance of redress? What now for all those cosy chats about the innate humanity of Fritz and his Christian origins? Well, he may not be Christian but he is well drilled. Will it actually be a chilling, clinical finish? The missile sails over the bow, they aren't that good. Perhaps it's just a warning? Cathcart signals for half a stern and the ship judders in response. A second round in rapid succession blows-up in the bow. People not privy to this sighting, below decks and oblivious, are shaken from their torpor; the cards go up in the air. A cigarette drops from a man's mouth and he jumps up to locate it before in burns his cot. People are rushing to the companionways that lead to the deck, muscling each other aside, all courtesy and friendship laid aside. Every man for himself. A sandwich is clamped in a man's teeth so as to leave his hands free for the ascent to the deck. Some crew are in their underclothes, propriety is not of the first order. The captain has to recover from his shock. The quartermaster looks appealingly for instructions. Another shot is fired by the sub'. This one whistles over the bridge. The great noise is unexpected, so extreme in this seascape expanse it should not resonate as it does. Smoke bellows from the area damaged by the bow-shot explosion. A puff from the enemy gun discharge spouts forth as if following the shell home, before getting pulled back by the persistent breeze, swirls confusedly and then breaks-up over open water beyond. The captain wakes from his reverie calls for full astern, the command is telegraphed. He opens a window on the bridge, hails Sub-lieutenants Hodge (who is cowering, looking petrified) to abandon ship, the sign for the *'Panic Party'*. Men assemble, orderly, like the drill. Boats are lowered. Unlike Bruce Ismay and the fate of the Titanic, there are enough lifeboats here, well, enough for the *Panic Party* at least. There is an unexpected calm, good order, all are grim faced. You love it when a plan works and the chances of one of the sub's shells in your lap concentrates the mind wonderfully. Now that you are out of the tomb of below decks you've achieved something and your back thought is that the plan is working. There is a lot to be said for drill that has them well prepared for this unimaginable moment. Some men, who went off to douse the fire caused by the explosion, are recalled. There are a couple of dead bodies. Bloodied wounded, a popular face staggering back to the ship's waist, blood in his eyes, feeling his way, he is eventually helped by a friend. The gunners use the cover of the melee to go to their posts in an orderly and practised manner. The lifeboats are in the water. The ship is quickly losing way. Ting-ting on the telegraph, 'Stop', clear the engine room and boiler rooms. Wauters looks magnificent in his dress, a stalwart image of British woman kind. The U-Boat now has more men on deck with hand guns at the ready. There is no communication from the sub. The boats start to pull away. Wauters tries to act in a dignified manner so as to maintain his woman charade, careful not to show his trousers underneath the frock. Sub-lieutenant Senior has a log book in his grasp, one especially made-up for such occasions, he takes it with him to the boats. Against the expectations of the plan, the lifeboat he is in passes in front of the line of fire from his ship. The gunners wait impatiently for that craft to move away. They may have to fire even if their shot is obstructed. The U-boat's crewmen are gesticulating, jabbering in their guttural language demanding that a lifeboat should pass towards the stern of their craft. "Rechts! Rechts!" Some of the armed men run down the sub's deck gesticulating and covering the men in the lifeboats with their guns. It all plays well for the Horton Lodge. One of the ship's crew has been blown into the water by the percussion of the exploding shell and though stunned he is swimming towards the enemy, his heart full of dread and an awareness that his arm is bleeding but he feels nothing.

The shot is now clear. The captain blows a whistle and at this command a White Ensign is run-up and the ships guns are uncovered. A furore commences. One of the 'Panic' boats is shot at with small arms fire but the shooting stops abruptly as the big guns on the 'Horton Lodge' unleash their fusillade at a good, practiced rate of fire; it is a Turkey Shoot but one delivered with shaking hands and with stinging sweat running into the gunner's eyes. Hearts beating fit to burst. Soon the U-Boat is on fire with bodies strewn about its deck and more than one gaping hole in its superstructure. Some dead or dying are in the water by its hull; it looks and feels unreal. The ship's guns continue firing without let but few if any shells seem to be hitting their adversary. The armour piercing shells have caused immense hurt to the once svelte machine lying off. Some of the men in the boats who jumped into the water when shot at, amongst them Wauters, are hauled back inboard. His dress plastered to his body by the wet, gives Wauters a momentary image of a sealion, or is it a walrus? The ordered chaos subsides as quickly as it sprung. The battle has long since been over but like the wasp on the window in the sights of a frightened householder, hit the bloody thing until it stops twitching. They are real people over there, in the water, dying and the shrieks and the death throws cannot be shrugged off. Striking at your sensibilities, even though a moment's reflection informs, that could have been you. More submariners appear on her deck, confused, hurt. Pointing at their dead and dying in a disbelieving, manic dance about the plating, rattled by the repost and driven half mad by the sight of their friends, shipmates, mangled in the water, insensible. The boat heels over and slowly, sinks, taking with it the licking flames and those too traumatised to leap for safety. The sailors in the various lifeboats wave and create a hullabaloo, the shemozzle is at an end. The men on the ship look quietly amazed. One crosses himself. Two of the gunners smile at each other, one pats the gun. There is a lot of embracing and congratulating. One man sinks to his knees almost passed-out and is helped-up by a comrade. They embrace. Plum looks sad as he observes the space that was once occupied by the U-boat which is now just bits of flotsam amongst the turbulent blood-flecked turbulence risen from the sunken vessel and bursting at the surface; an oil slick with all its wonderful colours catching the light; dead and thrashing bodies, face up, face down and one defiantly waving his fist at his assailants and calling them every dark and splenetic word his tongue can reference. The swimmer with the injured arm hails a lifeboat some thirty yards off and the crew recognise him, haul him in. The arm is not that good. He must have survived on adrenalin. The captain issue orders and the men rush forward to do what they can to quell the blaze at the bow, now quite pronounced, having taken a bit of a hold. If it gets to the ballast in their sleeping quarters, there will be hell to pay and instead of a win it will be a defeat snatched from the jaws of victory. The lifeboats are heading back to the ship. One of them stops to pick up some German survivors. Another of the boat's rows straight past men in the water appealing for help. Some of them getting hit by the oars as the boats pull away, left to their own devices. Soon the whole compliment is aboard and the men that were hurt or killed when the small arms fire was directed at them are laid-out on deck with those that died when the ship was hit, a few of the Germans are amongst the bodies. Wauters musters-up enough canvas to cover all those that have passed. The captain is visibly shaken but has ordered one of the lifeboats to go and look for survivors against their better judgement, they obey. He walks past the crew, congratulating them in turn on the outcome without actually looking at any of them. Wearing a thin smile, he's obviously deeply shaken by events. He returns to his cabin without looking this way or that. Sits at his table puts his head in his hands and sobs.

There were dead bodies on the ship. Captain Cathcart did not know whether or not he had the authority, or the words, to bury them at sea so he decided to take them back to Queenstown. But although covered-up, the dead did not let anyone forget their sacrifice, even if the crew were inclined to do so. Blood seeped from under the sheeting; limbs stuck out from their coverlets. The trickles were quickly washed away to save those traumatised from continual fretting. The ship had to return to port and quickly, anyway. The damage that the ship had incurred may have been structural as well as unsightly. More than one sneaked to the area where the bodies had been laid to look at a German cadaver, only to be disappointed about any illusion they may have had about corporeal difference. The German dead were horrifying, no different from their own dead. Soon to stiffen. Once active, well-nourished bodies, unbelievably torn and jaggedly discomposed. Just young men with fledgling beards fighting for something that they may not have really understood but had been dragged into, socially chloroformed, to do their duty.

The ship, despite its, what was euphemistically referred to as, success, had all the joy of a funeral parlour after the initial 'relief joy' had subsided. The throb from the propeller, a sort of death march tattoo. People believed they could smell the bodies and would imitate the sniffing of a 'pong'. The whole circumstance changed the demeanour of many who in the quiet moments that followed the action dwelt agonisingly on 'there but for fortune', hovered over 'it could have been me'. Some were prompted to write letters of such a loving nature back home that even they could not understand where some of the sentiments came from, they certainly had not issued from their pens and pencils before. What had once been screed about grown-up pleasures and erotic fantasising, small family matters, pets and sport were now taken-up with endearments and sober talk of the perilousness of life that young minds had never contemplated and which would now haunt them all their days and these were all volunteers, reckless men you may have thought but, perhaps, misguided more to the point and sadly delusional about their personal prowess. No one felt like eating. A rum ration was conjured.

-oo0oo-

Queenstown was only just finding out that a ship, unnamed, from location unspecified, was returning there after a success that was unembellished. But everyone knew the minutia of the whole affair as if by a universal creepy psychic ability? Plum and Wauters stood together on the dock getting their first full look at the damage which the ship had sustained. It could have been so much worse if the shot that went over the bridge had struck home. Perhaps they meant to miss? Perhaps they were not after hurting anyone initially and, as sometimes, happens, something inexplicable occurred. Things just got out of hand. The broken and burnt bow of their ship stripped back like it was an opened tin of pilchards with the explosion's scorching resembling the sauce, was a sad sight. Plum believed that after the dramas of this last voyage and the 'lifetime' number of events, that he had come to understand Wauters. Their time together, the illness and the aftermath, showed Wauters to be sensitive, a big man in other ways; reliable, someone you could trust. Some sort of bluff character, the rough edges of which you had to accept and paper-over because there was a good association to be had. He was due his foibles as much as Plum acknowledged that he himself had an abundance of them himself. Plum recognised the inescapable truth, he was odd. Wauters saw through different eyes, so? Whatever he said, no matter what his demeanour, he gave the impression that he could not give a shit. Like acid reflux effects some, the roughly fashioned hatred he harboured was omnipresent, constantly recurring, swelling-up offensively. He did not deal in persiflage. He said what he said and meant it, in a similar manner to Plum's whittering-on with his dad's asides, naturally and uncontrollably. He did not espouse loyalty and certainly did not encompass thoughts of friendliness, mate-ship, chumminess. His hatred was part of his being more than this cause or that. His association with life had only taught him to be a predator. He tended not to question it. Aye, but then, he did not question going to Plum's aid when he'd had the attack. Was not surprised at his own reaction, not questioning of the devotion. Yes, the devotion that he had embodied. The manner of his attention was an aberration, a weakness; it won't happen again. That was the plus column. However, even when making the summation, Plum could not assuage the thought that he was actually making excuses. Was there anything that Wauters could do, any slight, any chicanery that that man could enter into and, because of Plum's circumstances, not be forgiven? Yes, the plus column was long and well accounted for. But the minus column? That was still in the writing. Meanwhile, Plum's obsession allowed the death of his shipmates to go over his head, that was not the Plum of old.

As they stood there, Plum, frightened by what he saw, Wauters just looking, Logan walks past them; he averts his eyes. The Lascar passes them, he has a lot of bandage on his arm. Plum steps aside from his reverie. "You all right mate? That looks a bit evil." pointing to the bandage. "Is that what those stinking Germans did to you? War, eh."

Doomah Sen bridles. Stinking Germans? Where did he get that from? It was a game of word association which no one thought deeply about any more. "I will not be getting a medal for this," insists the Lascar, scientist and good egg. "When the ship was hit, the tremor knocked a pan of boiling cabbage from the stove. This is the result. Natural science, biology with a touch of physics."

Plum looks suitably aghast. "You get that looked at properly, do you hear."

The man nods and then continues to walk on. Perhaps he is conscious of what he sees as a disapproving look from the man standing next to his friend. Perhaps the scalding confers such a pain that it seems to get inside his ears and clouds his perceptions. After all, he does not know the other man nor he this Lascar. But it was there. Perhaps a man that had his roots going back to different relationships with Indians? "I hear. No problems. The medical orderlies are just over there by the dock office, I have been told. I will be all right in a tick." Doomah Sen moves away.

"I like him," Plum announces, absent-mindedly. He watches the man go then turns to his companion. "He's a clever bloke, you know."

Wauters is not so sure. "Coloureds. You never can tell."

"Oh, yes?" Plum queries the response. He is slightly amused by the inconsistent responses that you can count on from Wauters while not really mining it, registering the complaint.

Wauters drops into the cavern of his darker side, just momentarily. He can manage that aspect of him now. "Yes, well, we *were*, use to be, a slave state…Old habits die hard," Wauters tags on.

It rouses a natural curiosity in Plum which he sublimates; slaves, like in the States? Oh well, nothing to do with me, I never had a slave, although his mother sometimes would opine, 'what did your last servant die of', if Plum had demanded too much from her and her always ill, latterly. His map had displaced his mother's travails which normally sprang to the fore when he was, or needed to be, sad, melancholic. Changing the subject, leading himself away: "I was shocked by the recoil, the racket the guns made. What a shemozzle. Why didn't they just finish us off? They had us dead to rights and *Cruiser Rules* gone by the board? That wasn't total war. Perhaps they would have parlayed had we let it go?" A few steps more. "Every bullet has a billet."

"So you have said," Wauters qualifies. "I have had a belly full of it. *Eish!* This is not to my taste." Wauters makes to walk off but turns back briefly. "You, OK now?" He struggles to get the words out. Feigning emotions puts a strain onto a man's calculated sincerity. "No illness, now?" and then, quieter. "Asthma, what a nasty do, *swak*."

Plum runs up to Wauters. "Listen, I'd rather you didn't mention that. They'll kick me out, I told you. Don't get me wrong, I'm grateful to you, but forget it. Best forget it." Plum decides to follow Wauters. They walk on together. Wauters pats him on the head.

The little gesture encourages Plum. "Old wavey navy did all right, the captain. Showed some pluck. Put up a good show. He's odd. I couldn't see him seeing it through, you know," reflects Plum.

Wauters is being tried. He just wants time by himself to brood to unload some of the tension, the baggage he has accumulated. *Eish!* How he hates the intimacy, the matiness of the crew, the desire to be close and have a general understanding. "No problems *paw-paw*. I suppose we have to report to naval intelligence, like they said. Naval intelligence, the two words that don't seem to be a good fit, one to the other."

"What is a *paw-paw*?" asks Plum.

"Sometimes it's tropical fruit. Sometimes it's an idiot," says Wauters nonchalantly.

Plum weighs what has been said. They continue walking off together in the direction of the dock buildings. He has a reproachment with Wauters now. They both know where they stand and yet Wauters care and attention asked more questions than it answered. They both opened-up, which was good. He got the idea over of the *Cocos Islands* and the other didn't say 'stuff it' but neither did he commit. Well, that's something to hold onto, isn't it? Yet there were doubts about Wauters, about moving into his sphere. Was anything straightforward to that man? With the frequency of chat, Plum got the distinct feeling that what he assumed to be Dutch was not as natural to the speaker as one could be led to believe. The stories were plausible but the listener was so mystified by the adventures as not to be led to discuss any detail at length. You can make-up a story but, unless you're really cute. There were doubts. That mysterious man was becoming less mysterious, whether that was a good thing or not. For himself, a man that experienced or had planned little; a person that had a life inflicted on him, the experience of others was invariably bound to be a wonder. But, yes, things were out in the open and the enterprise a little more assured. Now there was just the little matter of getting through the war. Lots to look forward to tomorrow. Yes, tomorrow. You can rely on tomorrow. You have to be realistic about these things. Today and yesterday no good, danger, sadness, tomorrow draws us forward. Hogmanay, a great time, a restart to whatever has gone wrong to date. New hope. New adventure. *Tabula Rasa.*

-oo0oo-

Carmen was dispirited by her run-in with Wauters at the bar. She over-played it; the frustration got the better of her. A thing meant to precipitate a response, a favourable response. A gush, a dredging up of pleasant rejoinders and heartfelt speech, went all the wrong way. It's Wauters' Law, let them go on without interruption, you learn more that way. Ignore the awkward silence; that's just a bit of Poker. Who will give-up the 'tell' first! She felt a bit sheepish, rather foolish now. She could not go looking for him, apologise, that would be a win for him and not further her cause anyway. Going back to the streets was a little bit of comfort in a way, a release. Carmen is being consulted by a man who wants to know something, should he plant cabbage and kale this year? It takes all sorts. Last year his crop was ravaged by caterpillars. Carmen has changed. Is this the real Carmen or was the dishevelled woman the real one? Had she given-in to some generally held conception of womanhood now whereas, before, she had been a truly unique and though smelly, an individual; not aware of or obeying strictures, not conforming? She had changed her hairstyle and looks clean and wholesome. She herself feels that she is too good for the activity she is involved in now. Although restless under it all, she clings to it, her lifeboat. Am I getting out of my depth? I'm a bit cautious in society and have yet come to a complete understanding how it works. So why am I conjuring *this* image of me self? To appeal to what I think society, *they* want or what a certain man wants? Or is *this* me? The pleader is all of a kafuffle about vegetables! Some people, they just can't get real. The man describes the shape, tries to portray extent of the growing area of his plot. "It's only a small piece of land you understand, a 'lazy bed'. You would not be able to mark-out a rugby pitch on it. But it provides a good bit of extras to our eating, you know, well, in a good year it does. But last year, I have to tell you, you know, last year, it was a *divil*. Them Cabbage Whites, goodness gracious, them awful butterflies, they give butterflies a bad name you know; they must have crept into my beds under the cover of darkness, you know. They're not a thing a chap notices straight away when there's a lot else going on, the carrots and all. Butterflies indeed. Next thing you know the leaves are like lacework and the whole issue is buggered. Jesus wept, if it isn't enough to make

Father Dimmock swear, you know and nothing passes his lips without a Hail Mary. What can you tell me? I've tried praying, I think it was *them* that sent me here, like earthly matters, you know."

"It'll cost you a shilling," she says sort of coyly, in a practised sort of way. The poor *divil* finds the issue so fundamental to his existence that perhaps she should have asked for one and threepence, she missed a trick. She's losing her knack. The duffer reaches into his pocket and from amongst his small change he fishes out the shilling and hands it over, places it preciously into her palm.

"If you could help me, I'd consider it money well spent, you know. By the by, don't you have a dog wid yer normally? I seem to remember a dog."

Carmen takes his hand. "Turncoat, he's off honeymoonin' that dog of mine; it must be that time of year. Give us your mit then." She looks inquisitively at his hand. Trying to compose a suitable story with which to regale her client, give him his money's worth. What does she know about lazy beds? Now if it was scrap metal, horses especially, then she would probably know chapter and verse.

The anxious man is agitating. "Well, what do you see?"

She looks even more intently. He lowers his own face towards his hand as if it will suddenly appear written there, the answer to his query. "Is it hopeful what you're reading?"

"Tsk! Hold your water. You don't want to waste your money on a rushed reading, do you? And get out of my face! Who's doing the reading, me or yous," she says tetchily.

"Wisely said. I'm like a cat on hot bricks, you know," he apologises. "I would bloody-well starve as soon as I would give them worms a free meal. The Lord gives, but his creatures take it away, you know. What's that all about? There will never be progress. It was the worst thing that Noah did, letting Cabbage Whites onto his boat. A sore bad thing, you know."

"Shut your gabbing," comes the response. "How is a girl to land on a story that's half plausible with you carrying on? And get your head out the way. You don't want half a reading do you because I can only see half of your mit?"

He stands corrected. "You're right. I'm sorry…well what do you see?"

Carmen, is still looking intently at the grimy hand with its soiled nails; quietly and in a controlled way, she says, "I'm getting chicken shit."

The man is aghast. "What? Nothin'!?" He deflates visibly. His last hope of settlement, seemingly, now, gone.

"Will you listen now," she says. "Chicken shit, put it on your soil with the feckin' plants. The smell will scare off the insects; we know that insects like sweet smelling things, right, scent, like perfume, blossoms." Don't over-elaborate, dear, else you'll have him here all day just for a shilling. "With chicken shit, you get something dirt cheap that scares off your divils and feeds your crop! You get two for the price of one! I'm regretting that I didn't charge you two shillings now," she adds, hint, hint.

"I can't believe I didn't see that with my own eyes, you know," he responds. "It's so obvious, well, it is, now that you've said it. How grateful this town should be to people like you, you know? It's a gift. We are so lucky to have such an oracle, a visionary, you know; that's what you are. It's not everywhere, outside of the Book and the pulpit, that you can get sound advice at such prices. Even the offertory has its hands in your pockets. It's a wonder the priest doesn't hang you up by your ankles as you leave his sermon so as to shake-out any change you may be trying to keep away from them. Right! I'm clearing-out now." He gives her tuppence more, as though he's conceding the world and then leans into Carmen. She turns her ear towards him. "There's much more damage to be done than to cabbages." She leans back perplexed and he gestures her to him again, to come forward so that he can confide. There is a not unpleasant smell of toil about the man. "I have to tell you, well you may have already heard, there's all sorts in the air, apart from Cabbage Whites and that's a fact." He looks away as if expecting a visitation. Then draws close to her again. "You might want to get off the streets, they'll be knocking the small change out of yer. There're grumbles in the town, you know? Yer know, terrible threats of violence due." He gestures in all directions as though the would-be assailants hinted at had circled the town. "They're in the bars, even at this time of day, even as I speak, threatening harm to them English sailors, so they are, them that has just sunk that U-Boat, you know? But I can believe it, rumours, stories, it's a good time for settling scores, just make a story firework and put a lie to it, sort of thing. What's rumour and what is truth, eh? There's violence, I tell you and I don't want to be amongst it. Me so peaceful and who keeps himself to himself. I reach for hope on one day and instead run into the end of the world and the heathens taking over. They're down there at the *'Quay Bar'* this instant. Recruiting fists and such and getting tanked. Not that I'm one to go into bars in the afternoon, you know, no, no, no. My wife would flay me if I did and her up there with the children running riot and them getting shitted-up on the compost heap and playing with me canes. And all het-up and them kids crying after a scrubbing. The dogs barking, the cats in the pantry again and the mice watching and waiting behind some crack. I'm being eaten out of house and home." He makes a gesture of exasperation. "I'll be away. If only you could put chicken shit on violence to make that go away. Young men in hot blood, a bad smell. They're a plague when trotting in the wrong direction. I'm away. There's your money and it was well earned." He taps her hand as if concluding a deal on the nail.

He goes away talking to himself. Carmen ponders for a minute, looks at herself in a shop window, puts a few wisps of hair in place, nudges-up her tits with her fore arm and then sets off for the '*Quay Bar*'.

The *Quay Bar* makes Flynney's Bar look almost quite smart by comparison. The place might look nice to an alcoholic but to anyone else its charms would be…elusive? She could not own to herself what propelled her to go there. No one would believe that there is anything going on, not to the casual observer, like. The whole place is like a morgue. No shoppers, no clatter from that car that the Redmans have bought and use to terrify everybody with, dashing around at a million miles an hour. No carts. No groups of itinerants. No police. But then again, that would be because, if the story is right, all the usual noisy bastards and street idlers are in that bar. There is a man leaning against the wall of the bar, he stands out as singular in this eery quietness, the hush, perhaps, before the wave breaks? He has his head down and is riffling through some coins, passing them one hand to the other and every now and then pocketing one. She approaches him cautiously. "Is this a rough place?" she tentatively enquires.

The man is the worse for drink. "Whose asking?" He looks about him in an unfocused way then smiles a silly smile as if he couldn't see her at first but when alighting on her visage is pleasantly surprised. Now there's a warning. "On a normal day, I would say, no. But you might ask, what is normal? Because I…haven't the faintest idea. Have you? Hey?" He has a finger raised like the sight of a sniper trying to home-in in an elusive target. He stands bolt-upright but quickly subsides. Tries to get a purchase on the wall. He gives her a lascivious smile, spies her in a most indelicate way, so obvious, up and down "I like you…I like all women. 'Shall I compare thee to a summer's day'? A half-light by yonder window with Tudor Bars and a cast metal locking clasp, is in the east. You're not one of them, are you now?"

Carmen looks down and around herself. "Do I look like one of them?"

"No, you don't. But what's the harm in asking? I could have given you a bit of business."

Carmen puts on a very displeased face. "Well, it's very disrespectful to a church-goer like me for someone to make such a lewd suggestion and me in my finery. I should give you a slap for that, you rude beggar!" Carmen says sternly.

"A goer? He-he. Oops! You will immediately notice that I'm not very good about girls, women, the fair…" He looks her up and down again. "…sex. I'm what they call…libidinous. There, sounds a bit like a book from the Bible. They're you go, the Bible's a naughty book. I am reminded of that word again as though my mind is just a tub of molten sinfulness, seething. Which it is not. A bachelor is, by his nature, in the unfortunate position of lacking regular female company. But what makes it worse is that women play on it. If I had a pound for every woman that had said I was unattractive, they would find richly attractive now." He looks her up and down again and the seems to lose his balance. He claws his way up the wall to right himself. "Well, you should know, you're one of them, a woman I mean. What am I to think when a pulchritudinous woman, such as yourself, presents in front of me from nowhere? You reach a certain age and damsels think you incapable and ignore your…propensities, your functionalism. So, they lead you about over it. They know what you're about and the teasing is something rotten. They are all intrigue and innocence while they would be all over a younger fella. Or they being married like the safety of their position, it matters not where you get your appetite as long as you eat at home. A man talks about…*it* and he's a plague, an irritant, one track, flirt, a dirty old man or worse. But a woman has it on her mind all the time, I tell you, despite you being…a woman. I tell you, they think more about…relations, their needs, quietly despise men but use their powers invested to pick and choose. Hand-out little parcels of temptation and in their own time. They use their God-given as a carrot to the donkey, a thing that's nothing to them, that you could make out a shopping list while it's in the doing. Those fateful words to squash any red-blooded male, 'Is it in!' They have their carried image of a real man and, oddly enough, he looks nor acts anything like you. "She rests her fists on her hips, screws up her mouth and taps a foot, in a demonstration of irritation. She can play this inebriate. She's had them worse than this up town. "I'm God-fearing. I have no personal appetite for women, I love them for the necessity of it all, that necessary evil. Damn and blast. Hell's teeth!" He stamps and waves floppy wrists like a man with Tourette's. "Where was I? I haven't been this close to a woman since…" He pauses, his fingers joggling his lips and reflects quizzically before starting in again. He puts a finger out straight, points it at the bar. "This hostelry is a refuge, I tell you, it is part old folks' home, part newspaper and part encyclopaedia. It brings quietude to the mind and reviviv…revevivive, cheers-up the spirits. He turns momentarily to the wall and then seems to panic. Turning back he smiles. "There you are, I thought I had lost you then for a moment. This place and those of its kin should be financed by the state as they do so much good. Give you something tangible for your taxes, best of all, something that has proven worth. Look at me now? Had you seen me not an hour ago. I would have been as miserable as sin. Gloomy, without perspective or prospects. All loss and mournful; no answers and certainly no common sense. Now I am revivi…re…cheered-up completely. I can go back to my lathe a changed man."

She has certainly had enough of this voyeur's blather. "Heh, you, bollock brain! I don't think handling a lathe in your condition is the wisest thing a revivified man could do."

"That was the word I was hinting at!". He gives his two palms a glancing blow. "Revivi, revivi. Smart gal yer are. Yes, no, you're probably right. Now look what you've done. You've highlighted my inadiqua, my inadiqua…"

She gets into his face: "Gob shite!"

"Spot on. I could not have said it better myself. You're right. I was taking advantage, the drink talking." He breaks down in sobs. "What is it you want of me…" He pleads loudly and sadly like a howling wolf. "…at a time when the world has dispensed with me so cruelly. Given me knotty pine instead of the silky mahogany that was once so 'prelevant, prevelant, available'. Now a dog's body, a chiseller. A purveyor of cheap furniture to care-less folks, all out of joint."

She intervenes in his self-pity. "Can a girl get a drink in here?" Aside to herself: the whole bloody world has gone nuts!

He comes around with alacrity. "Can a girl get a drink in here? Has that girl got money?"

"Yes, she, yes I have."

"Then there is no impediment, bar none, which is apt for a bar, just you see what I did there?" He conjures with his hands. "A little jiggery pokery, oops, a small dose of legerdemain. If I was a girl, woman, I would go in that door there." He points shakily at the right-hand door. "Which leads into a small, kind of dilapidated, lounge area, which, I hasten to add, is a might cleaner and more presentable than going through the other door." He points from an unstable platform at that other door. "Someone did a passable job on the bench seat in the 'right' room, good cushions, nice chamfering. But in that door." He points to the left-hand door. "Well, today! Sh!" He sways and minces close to her which causes her to recoil a little. He whispers, "Plotters, sedition, insurgency. Malcontents. Rage and mayhem."

"I thank you for taking the time. Will you be all right?" she asks solicitously.

"Safe as the 'Fort Knox', which is the Federal Reserve of the United States of America, tata-an-tara, as long as I can keep away from thoughts of the opposite gender. Ooh, no, a haunting."

He staggers away and Carmen goes into the pub. She enters cautiously inside the bar lounge. The room is quite dark. Tables and padded chairs, as was trailered outside, unkempt and dusty but with nice chamfering. A small bar area facing her has a large mirror set behind some shelves. A glass jar containing pickled eggs is set on the bar. On the walls are hung some pictures of the Pears Soap variety, *'Bubbles'; Millais, oh Millais, what did you do*? There is a hubbub in an adjacent bar with men taking it in turns to descry the English. Talking about a meeting that the 'Anglish' are having tonight at a local hall to celebrate *their* sinking of *the* U-Boat as an excellent opportunity to *'get'* them. A barman approaches her. "I have to tell you miss this is no place for women, especially on their own. Wrong place, wrong time. Go back to your hubby. There will be some…careless mouthing-off. Just thought I'd best mention it. You go home, dear." He makes to go back to the other bar.

"I've probably heard worse; I might even have said worse me self, thinking about it."

"Please yourself," he says. "As long as you don't come on and say I run an unruly house. What is it you want?"

"I have a mind to have a…sweet sherry."

He leans forward over the bar. "I've got weakened ale or Irish Whiskey, sort of poteen."

She meets his gaze. "No matter. I'll have your poteen, always the patriot."

Someone in the other bar moans about Gary's absence, the barman. "If that's your mind, then you've come to the right place. A whisky it is." He turns away and makes to go to supply the order.

"And a jug of water," she adds.

He stops and turns back, replies sullenly. "A whisky and a jug of water? Will you be wanting a napkin with that?"

The drink arrives and she pays. There are all sorts of threats and imprecations from the room next door. She hears a plot being hatched and talk of getting more people in on it, to 'do-over' the 'Anglish' sailors. The men sound fierce. They take it in turns to raise the rage to the next level, like a fire storm. There are toasts drunk and nationalism starts to predominate. Several have a tale that would, of itself, legitimise what the meeting is moving towards, action, seconded and third-ed. There are voices amongst the most vociferous that she recognises from her own bar. If that was the case then, she assumed, that they would not be amongst the most prominent citizens. She listens long enough then downs her whisky, coughs into her hand as the drink hits the back of her throat, pours a glass of water, downs that, only to notice that in the bottom of the jug there are a number of paper clips and some pins. With that, she's off at a pace. After a while of fast walking, she suddenly realises that she has no one that she can go to for help to tell her story to. Where is she going so purposefully? She has no society and certainly no one sage enough to have a solution. Her lot will want to keep out of it. The less the people know of them the better. As she casts around in perturbation, she looks up the hill and there, almost like a beacon standing above its surrounds, almost beckoning to her, is the Cathedral, St. Colman's. Whether the solution is there or not it seems to be the best place to make a start. There are friends there and there is sense there. If all else fails, perhaps God will inform her, Holy Mother, she signs the cross. She makes her way to St. Colman's Cathedral. This problem needs the attention of wise counsel. In the vast echoing space of the church one or two people are in the stalls, heads bowed. One woman, doing some knitting, sits next to the Confessional. Carmen walks down the aisle towards the altar, her footsteps resounding, drawing unwanted attention to herself; the residual scent of incense with its dry perfume; a feeling of her being a glaring, stand-out presence now in this cavernous aridity, is the product of too many sermons heard from the back row and the anonymity it affords which now exposes her to the enquiry of chance glances, nosiness. 'Oh yes, a young woman by herself'. You can build all sorts of tales about that. Look at her with her hair up and make-up. Tart. I bet she's ruined. Yes, you see it all the time. Run away from home, you can see it, it's written all over her. She's obviously a bit'a no good. Just look at her. You don't dress like that when you're a modest Christian. Yes, pregnant I would say. Just look at her and say 'you wouldn't put it passed her'. Brazen, look at her. This is no place for that. When she arrives at the altar steps, she genuflects. What now? A movement in the pews sets-off a creaking noise much like a pistol crack in this great expanse. The sound speedily tears about the place, ricocheting off the unadorned stone walls, springing off the huge weighty doors, shooting down the tiled aisles, deflecting off the reredos, like a lightning bolt, before disappearing into shreds when met by curtains or waning in a side chapel and there dying a lingering tubercula death amongst the epitaphs with a limp sigh. She casts eager eyes about the place, not really knowing where the priest would be on such a day at such a time, if at all; it's the priest she needs. She has never been so close to the effigy of her Lord, his wounds, the cross and His suffering, set on the wall by the altar just next to the board with the hymn numbers on it. Now such an image has a greater gravity, a special meaning current for her dilemma, pain, agony, blood, innocence. Oh! My dear! My love. That anyone so good should have suffered so much. And now others, so innocent, to be the victims of scorn, ridicule and violence. Eventually, she comes to the sacristy, still adjusting her headscarf which she has fished out from her skip. The priest is sitting at a table smoking a cigarette, he has his back to her. Before him is a boy's adventure magazine. She approaches him holding here skip in front of her like a shield. He folds the comic and starts to turn in his chair. "Oh! The choir…" Believing the interloper to be someone he half expected. When he turns and sees the woman, he has to change his tone. He waves the comic airily. "The choir…it's a hotbed of illicit materials." He turns fully to meet her odd look. "I had to confiscate this one, owned by the arch one that skulks in the stalls. Don't you find it necessary to read that which your adversaries are reading? To prepare yourself for their mindsets and to familiarise yourself with their arguments?"

She is struck by his soft familiarity and softens her look. "I suppose it's only sound…good policy." There is a silence.

He believes that she has something on her mind and his experience they divulge it in their own way, in their own time. "I need your help, Father."

"A confession you mean. Not…" He rises from his seat, spreads his arms in a what can it be pose, as his head goes to one side and not the lying side.

"Problems? Illness? Jesus, no? Nothing like that. Oh, I see what you mean" she looks down to her stomach. "No, you'll be having too much comic, Father," she chides. "No, how can I put it." She intertwines her fingers around the handle of her basket and allows them to have their own wrestling match. "Father, there's some trouble brewing in town and I think there may be violence, bloodshed." She holds out a hand appealing.

"Goodness gracious. And how would one as demure as yourself be knowing about such things?" says the cleric looking to heaven and all the cardinal points.

"Father, I'm no shrinking violet. I'm a bloody *pavee*, there! I attend your church. Have you not seen me, Father?"

"I don't recognise you." He advances, after looking at her a bit squint. "It's a big congregation. Sometimes I can miss recognising a whole generation before catching up with their children again."

"No, you wouldn't recognise me. I'm always at the back, except for Communion and then I feel the necessity to keep me scarf well down when I kneel. I'm a bit of a leper here."

He takes her hand. "I don't see that when I look at you. No, you seem healthy enough to me. Look I can't pull your hand off." He tugs at the hand he's been holding and gives a little giggle. "Heh-ho. Not to say that there is not anything funny in leprosy you'll understand. The Lord was good with lepers." He lets her hand go and puts his hand on her shoulder.

"So, what is this…violence you speak of child?" He lowers his head while maintaining eye contact, he's a tall man.

She starts up. "Father, I had some…intelligence…it compelled me to go to a bar, forgive me, and there I heard some terrible things."

"Don't you find that when we pry, we are liable to be hearing things, stuff, that we might have wished not to hear? Is that not the curse of being nosey?" he says lightly but purposefully.

"By my faith, Father, it's nothing like that. The men in the bar were all very silly and egging each other on. I was horrified. I was in the next room and heard them commit to all manner of horrid things that would ensure their eternal damnation. It's like Leviticus, *'If there is anyone who curses his father or his mother, he shall surely be put to death'*." Perhaps not the right recitation, but like that, people needing deflecting from bad thoughts. Perhaps it's more to do with *"Your blood is on your head, for your mouth has testified against you,* sort of stuff." He is mildly amused by her choice of quotation. She goes on, "Really heavy and unforgivable actions that will destroy lives." She burbles out her story hardly pausing for a breath. "It will be happening in *our* town *this* very evening. An accident based on an incident that will be written-up as being an intentional crime and requiring of a bloody revenge. But mistakenly; people, not a legitimate target for suffering, will get the shit kicked out of them, Father, will be punished in a very un-Christian manner. What are we to do, Father?"

"You have a very…colourful repertoire young woman, he-hem." But he is smiling. "You have me at a disadvantage. Who is about to throw the first stone? Who is prosecuting whom?"

She starts to twist the handle of her *skip* energetically. "There was an unintentional slight spoken in a restaurant, I believe, a little while ago, by a sailor, English of course." He holds his hand up and asks her to take a deep breath and carry on at about a third of the pace. She stops, then picks up her thread more slowly. "Well, Father, two silly young men, locals, they took against it. Which led to a set-to…a fracas, Father, which the injured party, the two Irish boys, now feel must be righted in a totally unreasonable manner, out of all proportion, an excuse really. A lot of the young men of the town are encouraging each other to a totally stubborn sounding, wilful, coming-together and someone has to step-in. There's no telling who will be hurt. The whole thing could spill-over into something that none of the boys can foresee."

Calmly, he enquires, "And all this is to happen in the town?" She nods urgently. "And when?"

"Now, now! This very evening. Come on, Father!" He asks her to calm down. "I don't know if you know, but a ship that uses Haulbowline has sunk a German submarine and tonight the crew are gathering in the Town Hall to have a little get together, a shindig, a bit of *craic,* to celebrate their success, *our* success. So, according to what *I* heard, it's there, the Town Hall." She twists her frame and points, jabbing her finger forwards.

"I do know about it, the submarine, I mean. I fully understand the war and all its ramifications, I follow it closely; how can I not? I see the posters all around the town urging our young to war, asking them to come forward and seek revenge for the sinking of the *Lusitania*; barking propaganda, incitement. I know the boat you allude too, in fact I know its captain, he's an occasional parishioner." Carmen is getting more and more agitated. The priest continues. "A very quiet man, a lovely man, who seeks peace and love, strangely, considering his present calling." He ponders for a moment. She looks to him and then the door and back again. "They are in danger? Tonight, is it?"

She acts as though in imitation of Rollo wanting away. "Yes, Father, yes." She starts to bob up and down in an agitated fashion emphasising the need to be away.

"No, we can't allow it, can we?" he suggests.

"No, Father, no."

"We will have to do something. Let me see…Look here, I have a confession to take shortly…the woman with the knitting with nowhere else to go, perhaps you saw her? You would believe her to be the most sinful person in the world judging by the frequency of her visits. But all she wants is a kind word, someone she can rest her head on, carry her load for her, metaphorically." He motions towards the body of the church. "It's the least we can do. Then, we must, we will act."

Carmen is almost dancing on the spot, she might wet herself with the tension, you know.

"It is surprising when and where the Lord calls on us, eh?" says the priest placing his hand on Brianna's head and saying a few words as if to himself, his eyes closed. "He gives us opportunities to give a good account of ourselves. We don't seem not to have to seek his mission, it comes to us."

The priest conducts the confession while Carmen waits in the cold expanse of the cathedral. At last, the priest comes to her. He pops a biretta on his head that he had taken up to take to the confession with him. He takes her by the hand. They kneel before the altar, there is unspoken, hussy, would you look at her. She's beguiled the priest! He mumbles a prayer before they head off hurriedly. They go to the Gardai barracks in fading light. There, at the barracks, they relate their story. The officer listens to their tale.

Chapter 16

Inside a well-lit, large hall, a small band is playing in front of a crowd largely composed of crewmen from the *'Horton Lodge.* There are a smattering of dignitaries and a small contingent of dock workers. Captain Cathcart sits quiet, detached, this is not his thing. The sailors sit to trestle tables. In front of them is the detritus of a sparse buffet meal and a closely monitored number of bottled beers. One of the men has been asked to sing. On the rostrum, he speaks with the musicians before standing to the front. When he starts to sing, there is a general hubbub but it quickly dies down as his efforts are acknowledged, *'They didn't believe me'*, the Jerome Kern number in the new style, to the rhythm of a foxtrot that is re-writing the concept of popular songs. A song which is so intimate. Which seems to refer to real people and their hearts desires. The men, in turn, give him intense regard; two of them get up dance to the tune in a rather rigid and faulted manner; they have a slight problem in that, at various times, they both try to take the lead part. Along the tables, people now having been forcibly acquainted with their emotions are want to be nostalgic and succumb more easily than was their way. Add to that the tension they have known and emotion is a natural route for escape. One man gets a bit choked-up, opens his wallet and looks at a picture of a plain girl with a jaunty hat, smiling toothily. He kisses the picture. Another man draws a doodle of a woman sparsely dressed on the paper table cloth, which causes those sitting with him to laugh amongst themselves quietly, reservedly. The singer sings the final chorus that many in the crowd have picked-up, and sing along with: *'They'd never believe me, they'd never believe me, that from this great big world you've cho...sen me'.* Rapturous applause follows and the singer picks up on the mood. "Here's one you know." The singer announces, *'You made me love you'*, which they all join in with immediately, while the band struggles to catch up, a cacophony, but who cares? Occasionally, Logan stares across the room intently at Plum with a face like a pickled sow.

Under the noise, Wauters talks to Plum. "I have that Titanic feeling. Shouting your success makes you overlook your weaknesses. This is all too premature. He may find himself having to give out a few 'ducking's from the yards' to get them back to their senses after this. The ruse, worked once; any sensible man would just think himself lucky and try to get out, a posting. We are like them that conjure, once you know the trick their mystery evaporates and you only have that feeling, you've been taken and it won't happen again. It all looks very silly and you kick yourself for having missed the trick in the first place."

"I've got faith in the system," Plum says rather po-facedly. "Besides this seems to be what heroes do, better than just pouring over no man's land to the tune of the whistle in that great tide of…victims. No, forget all this, the minute. I'm thinking past this. I *will* drive a car, *fly* in a plane, listen to Gertie singing at the music hall, *'When the harvest Moon is Shining',* or on *my* phonograph *in my* front parlour. I'm not giving in to fear and you? Well, you of all people shouldn't be thinking depressing thoughts."

"Is that all there is? This world of things? Always tomorrow and always better? It all sounds very trivial," says Wauters with a pursing of his lips. "But then again, I suppose you aren't very clever, are you? A gormless race after mirages, deceptions." Wauters wasn't being deliberately nasty, this is what he thinks and has probably rehearsed the line more than once in his head. Plum can almost laugh-off his abruptness. So, for a brief moment, this assembly can put aside their cares. This euphoria thing is catching and the men are glad to submit to it. They have not a care in the world generally at this moment.

Outside, not that far away, a mob is starting to assemble and to move through the streets. They stumble about, moving from bar to bar, patting each other on the shoulder and swearing at the tops of their voice. Cause consternation amongst the good people and frighten the younger children. A dozen soon becomes twenty, forty and with the hangers-on, they number a crowd big enough to be taken notice of as a force. As they stream through the narrower streets, their numbers swell onto the pavements, forcing them to knock over trestle tables outside shops, with the produce on them trampled underfoot. Precious, scarce, stuffs. The shop keepers know better than to wave a fist or shout after them. Who knows, when they have finished, whatever business, they are on, someone in the crowd may remember a word or gesture offered in haste that was not, at the time, a thing requiring redress. But when the blood is pounding in your ears and you are a limb of a monster, reason seems unnecessary, beyond recall.

In the hall, Plum turns to Wauters. He raises his eyes up to the ceiling. "I'm not saying you are grumpy…sorry, yes, I am! Here's me thinking I could hitch you up with *Vesta Tilley*. Instead, there's you, like a staked-out old goat, waiting to be gobbled up by s-some gruesome monster lurking in a dark place somewhere. Honest, you and she would be good company, a perfect fit. You in your dress and Vesta. 'Tommy in the trench and his girl', a perfect match. You were made for each other. You are so…narrow, you don't understand the possibilities, that's all. You've set your face against…living…the future. Safe in your sailing ships and their hold on you. We've all got to hang on in the hope of… that day that isn't military. Can you remember what it was like?"

The chief engineer, a usually taciturn fellow whose Geordie accent might as well be mumbo-jumbo to some, keeps himself to himself, normally. Hardly ever mixes. Tonight is indeed a rare occasion. He has taken-over on the piano, some are half expecting him to service it, they say. He is asked if he needs an oil can as he adjusts the piano stool. He sits there in an old suit and high collar, white shirt and tie. He composes himself. Cracks his knuckles and starts to play a romantic classical piece with a feeling, totally unexpected; and this a man who seems well at home with a hammer and a bloody big wrench! People are astonished by his dexterity and the feeling he brings to the playing, the emotion. Plum nudges Wauters and smiles, almost willing him to smile. Wauters feigns that he has Beethoven's ear for music.

Streets away even children have joined the swelling crowd and tag on to the back of the press, carnival. The mob is growing and local inhabitants of a less aggressive nature are going in doors. A small element within the mob has a go at singing the 'Black velvet band', but there is not a voice amongst them that can carry it and the singing interrupts the focus on concerted anger.

Plum leans his elbows on the table lost in admiration for the engineers amazing talent. The lovely music goes on. "I saw *Edna Perveance* on the cinema, with Charlie Chaplin, it was," he says, apropos nothing. "What a picture of innocence. What a beauty. You felt as though you were in her company and her so…well, beyond any normal man's dreams, expectations, a bit like my Thalia. Marvellous thing the cinema. Now she's somebody you could walk through hell for. Call me cockeyed."

This was a gift to Wauters. "It goes without saying." He pauses momentarily. "Take my word *Mompie*, if you have any hope of happiness start by forgetting beauty as any sort of recommendation. Beauty is vain and lusted after by others too. Marry a beautiful woman, you're doomed to misery. She'll be tempted away sooner or later, lusted over by some other. She'll think herself too good for you; you mark me." He takes hold of Plum's arm to back-up his proposition. "Beauty is all too often the enemy of passion; they don't like their hair put out of shape you know. There, take the word of a shellback. Always be on your guard in case some other bugger raids your harem. Beauty is not for taking, for stealing. Beauty is in love with itself and can't stand passion, it's too dirty. Are you listening? Go for the woman that opens the door for you and smiles at your wrong steps, does not try to change you, because if she pushes change that means she doesn't actually like what she has and seeks to change it, you!"

By now, the engineer has seamlessly moved on to a hot rag-time number. A real American foot stomper and that grave, aloof man, is belting that piano with real venom. Who would have believed it?

Plum taps the table along with the beat. "This is amazing. We're like two sides of the same person. It's *Jekyll and Hyde* again, me and you. You're like that demon on peoples' shoulders constantly whispering danger, danger. Me, I'm the opposite. Between the two of us we might find the right way." Their conversation is drowned-out as the piano piece comes to an end and the crowd stamp their feet, shout and clap in a most indecorous way that leaves Captain Cathcart wincing.

The evening progresses, briefly. Eventually, beer bottles are held up to the light seeking more content and the last dregs are supped. They prepare to go. The engineer has never been so mobbed, congratulated, the undertaker in him takes a step back. But he finds that he actually likes adulation. The captain was going to say a few words but he felt that this was their night and best leave be. Instead, he spent an inward moment composing a letter to Mrs Captain. Meanwhile, the mob has continued to move forward as every malcontent, with whatever cause, latches on; some having to ask what cause this is.

"It's worth a bit of a 'doings' if, at the end of it, we can all get together for a knees-up. I feel grand now. I'm as right as ninepence. Far better than being black as club ten over the weather and the lack of action. Must have been the paint that did it to me," Plum confides quietly. "Yeah, that's what it was, the paint. I'm sort of refined. I was never intended to be an artisan amongst smells. I got through the business OK though, didn't I? Did you know", they drift towards the door. "Now, I don't want to frighten you but, our gun didn't hit the sub. The others got it. We got two over-shots and a short. Good job there were other guns, eh?

Nothing to do with me I wasn't training it. I felt that I could sleep for a week when it all died down. Back on the old *Horton* tomorrow."

The party has ended. They are piled-out onto the street now outside the hall in good spirits. Hand shaking, the dock workers asking if life was like that all the time in the services. Some replying, yes, of course with a big smile and a laugh, to back it up. The Geordie engineer effusive with a broad grin to match. He liked maths and took to music easily but never more than a hobby. Music had order as well as its ability to stir. Plum and Wauters are still arguing the toss about hope and faithlessness, tomorrow and yesterday, the triumph of evil over good. How easily deceived men are wanting the peaceful life and fall prey to temptation.

"…that's a busted flush," announces Wauters, "I tell you. We can't pull that same trick twice."

Plum holds his line. "I wouldn't be so sure. A lick of paint and…"

The mob starts to move down the street towards them. The crew are suddenly made aware of the red shift of noise approaching them.

"…hello, what's all that about do you think? Has there been a football match? It's not a saint's day, is it?"

"Not good, to my mind," Wauters surmises.

Plum dashes across to the captain who has his back turned to the throng. "Captain! Look!"

All the crew turn to face those tumbling towards them. The chattering stops. The angry gathering halts within hailing distance. The dock workers in the party, to a man, slip away. One of mob, one of the men from the restaurant incident, stands out. The crowd of would-be assailants stop before the town hall in the way that railway carriages come together and then part when getting under way, the chains stretch, then slacken and the coaches clang together repeatedly; it takes a while for the throng to halt. Mulcahy gets spat forward by those behind him when they are a matter of yards from the sailors. He looks back at the followers who are silenced for a minute. When he doesn't speak straight away, there is a rising tide of moaning.

He puts his hand up to silence his people and then after a bit of smiling towards his own and scowling at the crew. "Nice evening for it, wouldn't you say?" A big pregnant pause and a subdued group guffaw from his followers. He starts to articulate in a loud, ponderous voice. "There are them amongst you that's got a reckoning." More murmurs from those behind him. He scans the crowd of sailors. "Yes, I would say that there are certain faces I recognise amongst you that we would like a…chat with, a chat, isn't that right men." He has turned towards his army and they take up his suggestion. When all is settled down again, he takes to striking a pose. He puts his thumbs under his jacket lapels and stands side-on, feet apart. "There seem to be those amongst you that are very disrespectful guests here in our town. There's him." He points vaguely towards Sub-lieutenant Senior. "There's…him." He points in the general direction of Sub-lieutenant Hodge. "And then there's the little one there, him who fancies himself a bit." That would be Plum. "We're not greedy. Them 'ill do. Just the three." Plum looks on warily. This has made him more nervous than the battle experience, the thought of being whisked away by a mob.

Cathcart clears his throat which is drowned by shouts of disapproval from the throng. "Look, you men." He is not heard. "Look, you people." Met by some mimicking his address, muttered rejoinders. "If I might be allowed to say." There is not a trace of a waver in his voice, very matter of fact. "This is a very harmless gathering. These men are celebrating. Doing no harm. The submarine…I'm sure you'll agree, we all agree, its sinking makes everyone safer. We're all one in the same cause."

Dolan who, with Mulcahy, was one of the restaurant assailants, stands by his pal. "Sunk a U-Boat you say?" sneers Dolan. "What makes you so sure that would please us? We may be of a mind that thinks them Germans are on our side against you, you colonialist bastards." A good old line assured of support and which meets with a lot of approval amongst those behind him. Dolan turns so no one is left in any doubt it was him that spoke those daring, revolutionary words and he encourages louder shouts, gesturing with his arms, more, more.

The captain takes a step forward. "I gather." Drowned out. "I gather." Boo hiss. "I gather you have some sort of issue, a grievance?" Furore. "Explain yourselves in a dignified manner, please. Or, perhaps, you could come and see me tomorrow and talk things through. This is not the time or place for intemperate actions."

Mulcahy turns to his people and then back again. "No, there'll be no need for meetings. We just want him, him and the little one, the *Tantoney Pig*, the runt there. The rest of you are free to go. Go on the rest of yous, get along, there's nothing for you here."

"I couldn't do that," says Cathcart bravely, almost foolhardy in the face of the rampant intent. "These men are in my charge. If there is any question of discipline to be sorted here then I am invested with the powers to settle matters. I am responsible for their conduct."

Mulcahy turns to his followers. "And you'll be wanting us all to play cricket and have a jug of tea after, call it quits, eh." He turns back towards the ship's party. "Him, him and him!" he says, his voice now gruff, demanding.

Cathcart: "It's not judicial. I can't allow it. This is, well it's not right." The interlopers laugh grimly. "If we, any of us, have done any harm, then I will see that there is correction served."

"Stuff your…sympathetic court," rages Dolan, drunk on the fact that he appears to be 'someone' suddenly and he hasn't had to fight to state his claim for a change, a Robespierre, Marat in the making. He has an insight how entertainers must feel when they have the crowd with them. "We have our own answer to this. What you will not give to us we will take." The phalanx starts to move forward. A shrill whistle suddenly blows and a Gardai officer with a megaphone intervenes from a side street. He is backed-up by a body of armed officers. Carmen and the priest are to the fore.

Everyone in the contending parties turns as one towards the interloper. The Gardai officer in charge speaks through his loud-haler. "Just be holding your bloody ground there a minute and shut your traps, both lots of you. Load of gobshites. I've heard enough. What *is* this lawless shenanigans here, heh? Dolan, is that you? You've a long way to walk to get home. Perhaps you should make a start back, now? Mulcahy? At it again? Just take a minute. Look at yourself, lad. What a disappointment you are. Look son, if you really want a fight, come along to the barracks of a Friday night, boxing club night, and you can get into the ring and fight to your hearts content. I have enough lads itching for a bit of practice. The rest of yers, I will not condone vigilantism. Stop where you are. Any man that starts anything here tonight will answer in the court tomorrow nursing a sore head, am I understood? We're going to sort this out, here and now. Listen to me. Mark me." He lowers the megaphone and licks his slips before resuming. "I want a spokesman from both sides. One, two, from each side, go on, put your men forward. Crowds only make things more difficult and there is a tendency for might and not right to succeed. Am I right or am I right? In this instance I'm certainly the might. This is what we are going to do. We are going to find out what's wrong and we're going to put it to rights. It's as easy as that." Agitation from both factions. An action that has had the day in its gestation cannot just subside on command. The officer is patient and waits for quiet. He has put his officers between the two groups, facing Mulcahy's army. "So, talk amongst yourselves. Put forward your representatives. OK, I'll take two, three at most, from each side. This is *not* a heathen land, we're a democracy, want to be a democratic republic and it's about time we showed all and sundry that we're capable of shouldering such a burden, making things work…for everybody. We are looking to take care of our business, hear tell. So, we, we should show our intent, our readiness for our futures. But I will not take a crowd from each side, that way madness lies. As if the war is not trouble enough. You people amaze me. Mulcahy, I'm not for embarrassing you amongst your team there but you are determined to be a silly sod, always have been." The policeman has decided that if he can cow the leader, the most belligerent then, if he is reduced, he will hold more sway with the rest. "I cannot imagine what has made you this way. But your way is where madness lies and I'm here to say, as a long-time observer of you in my cells and in the barracks, that anybody that sides with you wants their feckin' head lookin', sorry about being frank." He gives a small cough. "Come on, who's to follow me to speak? Name your people and have them come with me. When that is done, the rest of you, *you* can disperse and I'll leave officers here to see that you do go. Disperse, go back to your bars, if needs be. Just clear the street. And you children at the back, I can see you. One, what are you doin' up so late, and two, mark this night well, this is a lesson that will stand you in good stead. You do anything wrong and it's the *police* you'll answer to, it's not worth it, all right? Dolan if you've no more business here, yer Mammy, poor tired widow that she is, she will be worrying. Me self, I'd kick your sad arse down the road, left to me. You're nothing but a three-time-loser. Get off now or come with me and represent your cause."

The local men put forward their representatives and from the crew the captain selects his quartermaster and the taciturn undertaker of an engineer turned overnight star. They march away with the police. The street is quickly empty. Scraps of litter blow around. The rain starts. The police that put themselves in front of the residual mob, slowly, but purposefully, march them back. Soon they have all disappeared.

Plum pulls his collars up. "What do they say about Ireland, if you can see the mountains it's going to rain, if you can't see the mountains, it's raining?"

"Is that so, *Praatsiek*? You go on. That's enough for me for one night. I'll see you later."

Wauters makes to walk-off briskly and Plum shouts after him. "You're always doing this. What's going on?" And then to himself, "Goodness you're deep."

Wauters is all but gone, he turns momentarily. "See you later. Go to bed."

-oo0oo-

Outside the sailor's barracks huts, the rain is easing. The barracks soldiers in their sand-bagged citadel are larking about in the background. Wauters has arranged another meeting with Logan, he waits patiently. Logan arrives smoking a cigarette, he is hunched-up, the rain is still falling. They come together. Logan gives that smirk on identifying Wauters. "Meetings in the shadows. A bit like a penny dreadful, eh. What d'ye want *Hymie? Is it all fixed?*"

Wauters ushers him to a place where they cannot be overlooked, by the washhouse. "I just got back from a meeting with the police," says Wauters. "I've been and got a message to you. I saw Shorty, told him to pass the message on."

Logan: "The Captain didn't put you forward for the meeting. What business was that with you? You were not invited. I heard it said, you just went, stuck your tuppence worth in. Nosey? Spread a few lies, did you? A bit of disinformation. What's that I can smell on your breath, ugh, garlic sausage, that smell makes me want to heave. Where did you get garlic sausage? Been meeting the U-Boats, have you? Garlic, enough to make you sick."

"I just had to make sure they got the story right, you see. Them men who went for us, our representatives, good men, but what did they know about the ins and outs of what went on. Me, I was there. I was, what, a witness, see," he says in a matter-of-fact sort of way.

Logan uses those tweezer fingers to pull the cigarette stub from between his lips The butt so small it is in danger of burning his lips. He dispenses with the cigarette's remains. "Yes, so? A spy with a story. I reckon we can all sleep safer now. Some hope."

"I told them, at the meeting about how brave Plum was. I put the whole thing in Plum's lap left him to it, well I didn't encourage him he just had the will to help. I hold to the fact he did the right thing. I left him to it, cowardly really. If I had not left Plum, scarpered…," he adds, as close to regretfully as doesn't matter. "I came clean in the meeting, told them the whole piece. Maybe, because I'm foreign, I didn't have any expectation of being listened to and, obviously, capable of anything, lies and all, well you more than most. But they listened and believed me, a different voice; no axe to grind. The police weren't interested. They overlooked what the 'Subs' said, hearsay they called it. We arrived at a decision. No harm done. But it could have been so different, eh? A lot of people learned a lot of lessons, so."

Logan is thinking about going, nothing here for him. "What's that to me?"

Wauters stares unflinchingly at Logan. "If they put forward a man to represent their cause…I said…I would fight him. That would be that. Would settle the honour thing, if that's what's at stake. That seemed to be the main obstacle, 'face', like, when it was all stripped away."

"So?" Logan shrugs his shoulders, draws himself up to his full height.

"They went for it. A little face to face," Wauters goes on. "Don't you see. I've lived up to my billing. I'm an unscrupulous, violent man. Untrustworthy, cunning and, possibly, sadistic to boot. You seem to know all about Germans, what we're like. I fit your bill. As I am not actually German, a neutral, natural thing for me to enter in on, being sort of middling, not on either side. A different way of looking at things, not…*Eich!* Conventional, is that the word?" Logan has lit another cigarette. "We share a lot, you and me. As such, knowing what you're like, it means things have changed around here. The short of it is, that means that…I'm in Plum's camp now. You're too much like hard work." Wauters moves right up to Logan, looks down on him. "Things are, as I say, different now. I have a different opinion now. I've came to say…mark me now. If you go anywhere near Plum, I'll use any device, all my…arts, ill-will, foreignness, you know I have my ways, against you. I could make a mess of you. Things happen around here. Odd things, right out of the blue. You must have heard about Vaughan getting blasted? What have I to lose? Me, a suspect alien? In fact, I might as well get strung-up for finishing you off as for treason, at least I will have had a bit of fun and rid the world of a waster, *dief van die lug*, a 'thief of air'. I think that I may look at you in a certain way anyway in the future, nothing to do with all of this. You've mocked me, said some tasty things, tried to intimidate me. You're just a thug. I could never be trusted how I might react to you at another time. It would be a pity for you to die for a misunderstanding? So best you ship-out, eh, get a transfer. I hate you enough to snuff you out like that!" He snaps his fingers.

"Cowboy," growls Logan. "You change like the weather. What a creep. Come near me and I'll give to you what for, arsehole. I had planned for yer mate, to take him down, but I could take you any time instead; perhaps I can do you both, two for the price of one, eh? Get rid of you now and then him. Like now. Come on, let's sort it. Let's do it now, here, complete the first part of my double. Come on, put 'em up."

A golden light from the wall lights up by the gun emplacement, falls momentarily across Wauters' face. It displays a tight, pursed mouth and narrowed lids. "Fine, I think if they just found you dead it would be no reflection on me. Just dead, another death. We've had a bit of that here already, so what? It's war, lots are dying. What's one more?" There is an increasing menace in Wauters' voice but he's smiling. No, not a grimace but a full-on, beaming smile. "I'm certainly not about to fight like what you'd call fair. I prefer a less subtle method." He sniffs at Logan. "I can smell your fear and your backside, perhaps not as much as your armpits, mind."

"Words, words, childish words, scum." Logan is preparing himself. "So what? That's it? I might have other ideas. I have a reputation to keep. Well, speaking for myself, I'd say this cuts both ways."

"I don't think you fully understand, Logan. I will kill you if you get to Plum. I *will* kill you. I know no rules, see. I have no…scruples. I'm probably back in prison after this anyway. No, I think you should pack your bag and get out this place while you can with whatever honour you can cobble together. Go, because I'm beginning to take a real dislike to you. I don't think you want to try me. It would be a mistake. I'm giving you a chance, meat head. One that you do not deserve. Go on, pack your bags, terrorise somebody else somewhere else."

Logan stands focused, unflinching, while Wauters stares at him intently. Logan throws the long remains of his next cigarette to the floor, takes a step back. Wauters spits on the floor and then draws the back of his hand across his mouth, pushes his glistening wet hair back from his forehead.

The fight starts with a bit of posturing. Both men fixing the eyes of the other. Both men piercingly, icily focused. A large patch of sweat is forming at Logan's armpits. He draws his fists up into a fighting position and muscles bulge on his upper arms. He looks formidable. But Wauters does not see any of that he is finding his balance and looking for the mistake his opponent is sure to make, they all do. They have no conception of Wauters' malevolence, his history, could never estimate it by normal standards, his abiding disregard for human life. What has he to live for? What are his motivations? They circle each other in the semi-dark. A quick punch in this light would be hard to detect. Logan dashes forward and Wauters steps to one side as Logan sails past. The second time as Logan rushes past, Wauters sticks out a foot, trips the man over. Logan gets up. His shirt is sullied. He almost landed on his face.

"Cheap trick," says Logan wiping at the dirtied clothing. "Is that it? That's what kids do. Come on. Fight like a man, Bosch pig!" Logan throws a punch, a glancing blow to Wauters' head, the other man does not flinch. "I've got the measure of you, I've tasted blood." There is a smear of Wauters' blood on Logan's fist. He shows the fist to Wauters. "There's no running away here. I'm going to ruin you. You'll wish yourself back in Bremerhaven." Logan throws more punches which Wauters takes on his forearms. "Wauters is deriving an odd enjoyment from this. He's toying with the other man, wanting to string it out to get the full satisfaction of the moment while his initially smarting temple subsides in the production of testosterone. "It's only a matter of time. What's it to be? Broken nose, jaw? A dose of concussion?" A good kicking with a few stove ribs? Wauters says nothing, drops his arms to his side, looks about him. "Escape? No, not this time." Logan snarls. "You've made your bed."

Logan rushes in and Wauters applies martial arts techniques. Gets the man off balance and then hits him in the Adam's Apple with an elbow swiftly drawn backwards, stunning his opponent, then doubling him up with a straight finger thrust to the man's abdomen, before deftly throwing the man against the door of the boiler room. The door smashes like matchwood, Logan's weight and the force that Wauters has generated to propel him those yards from where they had been standing seemed like sleight of hand. Where was the trick? The door is knocked off its hinges under the impact. Logan drags himself from the heap of firewood and removes a sizable splinter of wood that has embedded itself in his leg. Pulls it out without flinching and discards it. He reaches inside his overalls and produces a wrench. Logan laughs menacingly, taps the wrench in the palm of his hand as he circles his opponent before charging at Wauters who, again, moves deftly. He wrests the wrench from Logans grasp causing the stoker immense pain in his wrist. Now in Wauters possession he looks at the weapon, laughs almost indecently before tossing it to one side; it clatters away into the darkness. Logan's facial expression changes from rage to fear as Wauters uses an avalanche of moves, not boxing but unconventional assaults; uses the side of his hand not his fist, before, in one effortless manoeuvre, he pulls on the opponent's arm in an artful way and dislocates his adversary's shoulder, first turning the arm against the elbow joint then lifting him bodily and wrenching the arm simultaneously. While that pain is still burrowing its way to the centre of Logan's consciousness, he then elbows his adversary in the face, right on the point of the nose, which fells the man to sounds of great pain and anguish, coats his lower face in thick black blood. Wauters stands over the prostrated man fully composed. He smacks his hands together, a sort of exaggerated washing action. "A little something I picked up in the East," says Wauters laconically. "Too dangerous to use normally, but this was a special case. I should get that arm seen to if I was you, or I can yank it back 'in' for you now? It is dislocated." Logan, even amongst the searing pain, still glowers and grizzles as he leans heavily against the wall his nose in the darkness all blood but looking like a black hole in the face viewed in the shadows. "No, OK, have it your own way. Listen to me you wreck of inhumanity. Go anywhere near to Plum and, well, I don't think I need to dwell, *reg*?"

Logan tries to find a way to administer to the two pains afflicting him, his disjointed arm and the nose streaming red, as he painfully raises himself to his feet. "You were lucky. You've not done for me," he bravely suggests. "there'll be a reckoning."

"You seem to have an unlucky sort of life. First Plum is lucky and now I'm lucky." With that, Wauters kicks Logan's legs from under him. The man falls heavily on the injured shoulder, the sudden collapse is followed by a kick to the dislocated joint, so violent Logan yelps and falls back, blacked-out. He comes too slowly, moaning.

Wauters offers to pick him up by his useless appendage, but Logan, fear on his face etched deep, fends Wauters off meekly. "Oh, you're back!" Wauters crouches by the human heap and in a quiet measured voice encourages the stoker. "No. If I was you, I would ship-out? Yes, go. There's been a change in the order of things here, we've moved on. You must see a pressing need for a posting. While you're in the sick bay, if I was you, I would put my time to good use, get your papers sorted." Wauters walks away leaving this sodden mass of flesh in a greasy puddle on the floor.

Chapter 17

The ship is in dock, an expensive sort of victory. The dead have been buried and a thousand and one stories embroidered, embellished to enhance the reputations of some of the lesser protagonists. Plum and Wauters are walking through the town, it was Wauters call. Plum has no idea what the outing is for. After all, Wauters goes off by himself so regularly, why not with a matey this time. To Plum this is a mildly comforting excursion. Does it contradict the impression that he had formulated? Is Wauters pretty stout really, it seems to lean that way. Plum thinks that the jury is out. His will be a watching brief.

"What a shemozzle. I'll miss it when we have to leave here. I haven't seen this much action since our tom beat up that tortoiseshell of the Simpkins's, two doors down." Plum prattles on. "Come on, let on. What's happening? Isn't it dangerous just walking about after what's happened? Funny times, very odd times." There is a pause. Plum is trying to invent a tetchiness meter to prevent Wauters from blowing-up about too much prattle. They walk a bit further and Plum's intuition (which has failed him enormously up to now) gives the green light. *"According to cocker*, old Logan's going to ship-out. Who'd have thought it? He fell off the companion way, broke his arm, it's said; gone to 3*rd* *Western General, in Cardiff*, Wales, for treatment. Anyway, they say he's fed-up lumping coal and he's moving on to oil. He'll make light work of that. There's a joke in there somewhere. You can't blame him, can you? What are we doing here?"

Wauters has resolved not to get nettled by his *Praatsiek* mate. "You'll see."

They eventually come to the cathedral and sit down on a bench outside the great building. It's a pleasant day. The south of Ireland on a spring day takes some beating. The seat is dry, mopped up by a high-pressure system hanging about over Killarney or somewhere like that. People use to the winter chill are testing the air and maybe a liberty bodice is off here or a waistcoat there.

"Lots to say, all around. It grieves me to say it, but for a start. I owe you. I'm not Dutch you know."

Plum is ready to believe anything. "You don't say."

"I'm South African, a Boer, a soldier."

"You do say."

"I was imprisoned by the British because I've been a thoroughly bad piece of work. *Lafhartig en nare*, yellow, nasty. Are you shocked?"

"Well, it makes my little game look a bit pale by comparison." Plum divulges limply. "Sucking-up to you and all. We're as bad as each other, I reckon. Two sides of the same coin. Who could blame you after a life with a father like yours? Given-up like that."

Boosheid hy wat boos dink? Evil him that evil thinks? London is the nearest I've been to the North Sea; it was a story, all a story. Truth and reconciliation. My father, he's buried outside Port Natal. Dead these…fifteen years, less. I hardly knew him. "So…" This takes some taking in.

"The business of the North Sea was…" asks Plum. Everything is up in the air.

Wauters has turned to Plum and before the thought has passed his lips he adds, "All unicorn droppings. I have a lively, particular, sort of mind. Could you trust yourself with a man that can lie with a straight face, can remember his lies? Am I lying now. You know, sometimes I lose sight of the truth completely. What if I robbed your treasure? I've been through your kit as you know, I've told you that. I've set you up for a fight with Logan hoping he would take your head off while pretending to be your friend, yes, I did. That fight on the quay? I ran off. Left you to it. With friends like me who needs enemies?" They sit quietly for a moment.

There is an awful lot to forgive in Wauters' antics. How much could you take before it became impossible? Everybody seems to be using everybody else. Everything that Plum had conjured is now made even more obscure. There's no resolution here. Any man that can romance such an intricate story can weave other tales. "It's about what you do next now, isn't it? I mean, the fact that you have said something is…right." Plum tries to put a spin on matters for his own good. He lies to himself to maintain his own dream as Carmen, likewise, does not want to believe because of her attachment. He wants to believe Wauters, he has to believe Wauters. His whole enterprise hangs on Wauters, too much; the hope is that there are no albatross' in the picture. "You see so many people, especially nowadays, that have lost limbs are making a different sort of life for themselves. If you've lost your lying limb, you have a chance of something different, better." Was Plum convinced by his little oration? They both sit quietly in thought. Plum is pulverised by the lengths of Wauters' deceptions; winded and gasping. What other revelations are there. "Then again, I would say that, wouldn't I? It's to my benefit not to question too deeply, the sailing lessons and all; and so it goes round. Does anybody tell the truth? I bet if you were to press me...or even the most honest looking man, I bet there are things in all our lives that we can't bring ourselves to give up, no matter, be made known even in a situation of absolute trust. Stuff that is too personal or revealing, our, 'very-ness'. Our core. The key to everything that we do, too precious and revealing to show. "The more you find out about people...talk about no man being a hero to his valet. What is truth? I mean, I'm a fairly stupid sort..."

"That is beyond question," Wauters concurs.

Plum has to explore this little flaw, it's in his nature. Autodidacts are sentenced to be perpetually learning. Whereas, he assumes, most minds are crystal clear, focused, his is a central core of decency surrounded by a cosmos of suns, asteroids, minor planets, always in perpetual motion, unrooted. No wonder people thought him erratic, he was always in flux. "...perhaps my worries would not be a burden to someone with a proper mind. You know, you meet people...take our captain, for instance, Cathcart, Captain Cat. I bet you he hates being here. He's smart, does all that course plotting and maths and stuff without thinking and yet, to talk to him, his life seems about this wide." Plum brings the tips of his thumb and first finger together. "Me, I can never just focus on one thing. I start here and get half way along when another thought sparks something else in my head and I wander off into some other idea. Just like a cat shown a lure. Some people are in straight lines and others seems to be like...spraying all over the shop. Going to *Cocos* is the only thing that I can think of that has stayed with me for any time and I trust that as it has stayed with me then it's part of my true purpose. That's the only reason I can think of, that I've stayed with it; It's got to be real, important, like. It draws me on."

"You're a funny little thing, *paw-paw*. Perhaps you don't think straight because you've got too much going on at once, there's truth in that? You obviously don't give yourself time," counsels the big man. "And your brain isn't very big. You should write stuff down more often, a list you can come to and strike stuff off when you've done with them?".

Coming from him that was almost considerate, mulls Plum. Wauters is a bit unsettled. He keeps on looking around the place. "Is Wauters your real name?

Who are you? Your life is not real and your real purpose, anybody's guess. But what is your name? Just so I know who I'm talking to."

"Who am I? I am who I want to be; it's my trade and, at the moment, I'm Wauters. While at one end of the scale there is the Kaiser looking to a new world order, I look to order in my own world where *I* reign. I'm a snoop. Keep your head down and just watch. Double back. Hop-off the train before the destination; never make waves. I am what they call a 'whited sepulchre'." Plum shows that he does not understand. "Look it up. It's not flattering."

"Is it religious, with you?"

"No, *God verbied*! I work for the other side."

What is going on with Wauters. One minute, he is the laughing assassin, the next a concerned and caring kind. Having no origin and surrounded by mystery he's all set-up for surprises. Is it all deliberate, to keep his opponents on the wrong foot, and his friends, come to that. The epiphany, if that's what it is, was totally unexpected. What is more he has said nothing of the incident to a soul. And what is happening about the proposed bout between Plum and Logan that Wauters virtually demanded? That had Plum over a barrel? With Logan suddenly becoming ill and shipping-out that's out the window now. Why is Plum with him today and looking to be in-line for sharing Wauters' secret society. Why? Why today? Wauters had been touched by Plum's plight. What use is power in such a situation when there is no resistance? He'd seen people have fits, probably stuck a bit of something between their teeth till the thing subsided. But that was in another world and was a thing of some curiosity. This was Plum. Yes, he was jeopardising the fight but it was something else and not a moment of weakness. Going soft. Mix with the softies for too long and it weakens you like marriage would, he believes. No, nothing like that. Perhaps it was because it was unpremeditated, that swung it. He didn't have time to form a story, adopt a posture; lost control. Perhaps it revealed something really deep about him long suppressed. God forbid, underneath it all he may have been in denial and a shock was needed to make him face himself. But it didn't save Logan, did it? Logan limited Wauters room for manoeuvre. If he was always to be around with his loathing of Plum, it closed down the wriggle-room, cut off options. Logan was a power and perhaps it was only time before they had a reckoning to see who was *baas* anyway, nothing to do with Plum. But a hurt Plum, a Plum that had a pretty good understanding of Wauters, might just have been weak enough, damaged, to spill his Vaughan story just for the sake of something to say. You know what he's like. Then, on the other side, men have to be top stag. You have to be in control and the right moment is your moment, not his. As to the coming fight, that's something else. His association with Plum would be in the minds of the angry. He was on their side in many ways against the British. The strategy meant pain, but not so much that he could not stand it, he could control that. Get in the ring with their man and take a beating. Such a victory for the town against the interlopers would play well. If Plum had fought, no matter whom they put up, and Plum not being able, willing, to sacrifice himself, that would look really awkward and unnatural. Plum not being able not to use his talents because he seems not to have any guile. if he tried to throw a bout; well, it wasn't in his nature anyway, forget that. But Wauters could lose and everyone would think nothing but a triumph for local manhood, one in the eye for Johnny foreigner. After that, there would be little reason for any increased antagonism. Make them feel as though they rule the roost, to 'scrappers' that's everything. Yes, he would go down dramatically. The big man, Wauters, against their local guy. Big Great Britain cowed by little Ireland. If the ship won, it would be a running sore. A grievance that could boil up time and time again. Beaten once was hard to bear, knocked-over twice, well, a stain on the manhood. Wauters figured that for the sake of swallowing his own pride he would be known as the saint that took all the arrows to prevent a war. His bet, knowing human nature as he did, was that his currency would be high in both camps, opening up a lot more chances for pilfering, skulduggery. How would anyone suspect him after what he was going to pull?

They are each with their own thoughts with Plum none the wiser. Wauters nudges his matey and points towards the cathedral door. "In a minute, I hope, someone is going to be here. Someone so nice, you could not imagine. *Eish!* Smart, she should have gone to Praetoria University, Stellenbosch University, the old school. Someone that could change your life like one of them Bible people that went around spreading the word, a missionary, apostle or summat? Yeah, like one of them." He is contented with that thought, it just occurred to him.

Plum doesn't understand. "What, a teacher?"

"*Eish!* Shit! No man! Don't be thick!" A great big display of white teeth smile enfolding a curse hissed-out, but not venomously; bar talk, different. "It's a woman who, I think, does not even know her own powers and I'm hoping she's in that church right now praying for people to be spared from evil, she would, same for the birds of the air and every flower. She would, I tell you." Wauters looks eager and excited at first but soon lapses after each excited utterance.

"Is she the one that you have been tripping-off to see?" Plum ventures.

"*Natuurlik*, of course. How can I explain to you what is so interesting, frightening, you will see? Fearless. I have not the words in English? I cannot size for you the power of that woman." Lies, lies.

Plum frowns. "Why am I here? Playing gooseberry? Three's a crowd, isn't it?"

"You are here because you are my *chommie*, my friend. She has gained a poor opinion of me of late and I want to reassure her that things are right and this is one hell of a *Jaaver,* me, someone she can trust. If I was here by myself, she might not speak. Even with you here, she might stay schtum. This is important to me. She believes that I am sly, so I show her my shipmate, like to say, see, Plum knows me and he thinks I'm all right." A bit of truth.

"Is that what I think of you? What, you are serious about her?" Plum sees himself used. How can he back-out of this? Caught in his own trap. A footnote in another bit of Wauters' scheming, without choice. This way I will end-up shaming myself, he mulls.

"*Eish, man!* Serious? What's that about? She's really human, man! Someone who leads. Someone you can talk to. A good friend. What is it with this man woman thing? You can't be with a woman without wanting to take her?" A savage sounding conclusion. No thoughts of love here. "What chance does a woman have in that sort of thinking. Can she be rejected because she is not, what, a conventional beauty or like shapely?" He draws a figure of eight with his two hands, shapely. "Accidents of birth? What about the accident of birth about being clever, intelligent? What about that? I've not treated her honestly. I want to set things straight, be straight." A lie tied up in an intrigue.

You want to get off with her? Marry her?

"No, no, shush man, that's stupid talk in war? Stow it; whatever you do, keep that sort of idea hid, right? Else you and me will have bother." Plum is beginning not to like the corner that has been prepared for him. It is a dark corner with a cupboard in it and he is in the cupboard. Wauters subsides and thinks again, not being sure in his own mind what she is to him and somewhat afraid it might be too much. "I don't think so. Nothing like that; I would poison her in no time flat. Then there would be a chance that she would become like me and that would spoil something absolutely one of a sort, too. Plum, this is serious work…I have to make my peace with her. Patch up all the tears and mistrust I have caused." All the time he talks he is carefully picking his way through his circuitous route. His is a row of spaced dominoes teetering. He stands up excitedly as Carmen emerges from the church. "There she is. Come on."

Plum picks her out. "Her, I've seen her before. The one in a brown coat? Yes, I've seen her before. She was with the police the other night, the mob and everything."

"You sure?" Wauters has turned on Plum sharply, enquiringly. The scales fall heavily on Carmen's side and Wauters is staggering trying to weigh things up. They make haste through the crowd coming from the church and approach Carmen. Wauters looks vaguely at Plum his focus at some distance. "She was there? How did she come to be there? Carmelo, Carmen!"

She turns surprised. She looks about her to see if any of the parishioners are attracted to the shout and curious, not one to draw attention herself and that name! She has never looked so well presented. Made-up, nicely dressed. Not too much make-up and so fragrant but not sickly sweet. A little lip stain and that youthful, powdered face, a hint of eyeshadow. She is so much changed from her earlier manifestation; she is a lovely woman in Wauters eyes. His heart beats and wrestles with his emotions not to be effusive. Not to enter the trap. But they are all in the trap now and reliant on the other for freedom, saving. So, with that estimation, is a woman all to do with artifice? Wauters would have ridiculed the person that would venture such a thought. She looked so statuesque now, a tight waist and yes, her eyes so brown and soft like a doe; she has a bosom. The sort of woman that you would ache to walk out with. There was a tinge of the bewitched in his thinking declaration and reaction to her effect. "I was right. Sunday Church. *Eish!* True to form." She gathers her thoughts, shoots a side long glance at Plum. "I'm sorry, this is my shipmate, his name is Plum, he's my *chommie*, my mate. Plum, this is Carmen."

"*Kushti!*" She looks bemused. Cautiously she waits. Why are they here?

"I want to be friends, Carmen. I suppose I'm asking for forgiveness. I want to show you my good bit. Ask Plum here, *Ek is in Orde, 'n goeie man.* Tell her Plum, she doubts me. Tell her I'm a good. You've changed me Carmen, changed me for the good."

"How the feck could I have done that do you suppose? And by the way, I'm Brianna now," she says looking about her a bit warily. "Carmen was my street name and I would thank you for not using it." Plum bridles at her casual expletive. "You're your own man Wauters, everybody knows that. I don't think today people look for Biblical miracles, that's all been exposed. You're what you are. If there is anyone around that could prove what *that* is, *I* would like to meet them. What do *you* think…er…?" She says to herself, *I will beat you, I will, I will.*

"Plum!" Wauters nudges his mate nodding in Carmen's direction.

"Plum. Does he make sense to you? This is the man that plays with your mind; careful, shrewd. He's a bloody weasel. He's very artful." They start to walk off together. She looks at Wauters while ostensibly talking to Plum as they walk along. "Is anything he says true? I think he's had a lot of practice at being devious. A lot of practice, heh Wauters? A lot of practice? Would that sum you up?"

Wauters nods. "I deserve that." He stands in front of her to stop her progress. When she moves this way or that, he blocks her. "Look, ask me a straight question Car…Brianna and I'll give you straight answer. No more games. I want to get rid of my snide. I want to, what do they say, come straight?" Even as he says these things, he doesn't mean them, well not at this moment, but things could change. "Plum says you were there, the other night, the rumpus and all. I was rocked. That you could have been part of that with the cops, betrayed something about me." She looks away. Stares at the ground. "Yes, you were seen. I think you had a lot to do with that evening's events, as a help that is. In fact, I *know* what you did, on reflection; it all comes together."

She obviously feels found-out and conflicted. But she is not going to cave. "Who are you Wauters, what's your purpose? Can't you just leave me alone? Why are you pestering me? Go on, Wauters, argue that statement, own up, big up, I feel I have come up on the inside rail and you are spent, own it. And where do you come from? Why do you keep coming back? My reading, romantic side, would like you to be some sort of spirit, like nature. Only you, you're that awful nature that allows you a couple of hot sunny days and then throws cats and dogs at yers just when you'd left your overcoats at home. Yes, a sort of ghost that sparks a morality tale or some such. But no. You're all too real. Isn't this all about that man that was shot and nothing to do with me at all? I don't know why I bother. Aren't you just making sure you're covered? What do you know…Plum? What do you say? I would go to the authorities and tell 'em what I know if I didn't… I'm…conflicted. No, I wouldn't trade him in, you're safe. Why would I? Vaughan was nothing to me. I would be as bad as he is if I used such as that. I don't want to beat him. It's not that sort of thing. It's shadow boxing. A test of wills, I know that."

"*Chommie* here wants to know as well," says Wauters. "He believes me about as much as you do. Life with people is about discovery, ain't it? You don't give away all your treasures straight away. You open up slowly. With a new name, you can have a new life. You will have to bear with me." He puts his hand on his heart. "I have had so many names, Van Heerden, Jaarsveld, Snyman, Hyns; I have been Andre, Jacobus, Gerhardus, Fabunni, take your pick. You can mix and match, as long as you are anonymous. I am South African, not Dutch, for my troubles. I have been a sailor, a diver for pearls and a spy for the Boers, and the Germans, in South West Africa, that is, not here. Some of that is true. I am here because I rejected the German way. When I saw the devastation they caused, in the Kalahari…It's because I was a spy that I ended up in London. They sought me out, down in Upington, of all places, just back from Praetoria. Middle of nowhere. Clever bastards, dragged me back; the Union gave me up to the English. I thought I was for hanging. But I had a pouch full of lies as you would expect. So, they put me in the service instead, here, for another sort of death. A colonial, what they called, a 'volunteer'. My given name…ready…he looks at them both his arms outstretched, his palms up, halt. It might be to build the tension, or it could be he's dreaming the name up on the spot…Arno Jubilano Prinsloo." Plum and Brianna look at each with an element of surprise and disbelief.

"Yes, it does sound a bit grand," she says. "Doesn't really suit the man. Not like Plum here. Shiny on the outside and soft inside, I'd say."

If you can be controlled and aghast at the same time it summed Brianna. "Well, I never, Arno? Bugger that, I've only just got used to Wauters. What's your story Mr Plum? So, who are you? Which tree did he shake you out from?" She looks at Wauters. "He's a fine piglet, eh. Little Snuffles. Do you follow your master everywhere, Snuffles?"

"I saw you there that night? With the police. Weren't you scared?" says Plum, trying to be polite and overlooking her spiteful characterisation, almost sounding like another Wauters; they'd make a fine pair.

"Absolutely shitless." Plum winces again, you don't swear in front of a lady but these are new rules. "The Gardai were very nice to me, you know. It was quite obvious they didn't recognise me else, well, you know. The last time I was at the barracks was when some old faggot had reported me for 'hanging around on the street'. I went, dragged off, to the barracks, and spent the best part of the afternoon doin' a bit of *dukkerin* with them, doing free readings for the *po*-lice. Them cops are as gullible as the rest, offering-up their palms. Tales of love not returned, how long they would live for and why their dads didn't like them. Just the normal things. Only huge bruisers of men with guns on their hips. Big sods with such feeble concerns. 'Hanging around' indeed. I spend the biggest part of my life trying to warn them off, never mind encouraging the beggars."

"What did they think you were up to? Why should they take you in?" asks Plum, lamely.

Carmen looks at him disbelievingly. "Where have you been all your life? Never heard of a *street walker*? Where did you find him, Wauters? Talk about chalk and cheese. She looks at them both in the ensuing silence. That night? It was nothing. I was in the right place at the right time, with an eye to my business, of course, you'll understand. If there had been a rumpus it would have… poisoned the well. People would have kept a distance from the town if they thought it was violent now, wouldn't they?" As she is wading through her tale, she does not confide that she did it for him, for him alone. She is having a skirmish, no rules and in the doing has found her inner denial melting away. "Not to mention silly Mulcahy. He never changes. Always ends up with a blacked eye and his arse kicked, I think he's got a problem; I think there's a word for it."

"I thought we would go to the bar. Let bygones be bygones, the three of us," interjects Wauters.

"Is that what you think, is it?" she addresses Plum. "OK. What do you think pygmy…Snuffles? Should we go with whatever his name is, from who knows where for who knows what? You've got very little to say for yourself. Come on, speak up."

"I don't know what to say. I'm gobsmacked; I've never known such a fine-looking woman to have such a tongue," Plum admits.

"Don't come the soft-soap with me 'piggy'. Go on, spit it out. Speak straight or shut you gob. I've got a few choice names for fellas that come that, you can bet. Bleedin' soft soap merchants." A small smile, no more than a tic, ruffle her manicured mouth.

Wauters persists. "It would be nice to go to your bar. I can't drink much 'cus I've got this scrap coming up."

The two others in chorus. "What scrap is that then? You? What? Heh? What? When?"

"Fight, fisticuffs, boxing. We struck a bargain with the Irish lads. They would put up a man and I would box him. An offering, to answer for the hurt they say they felt, the reason for their gathering. So, we fight and the slate is clean." Wauters looks at both of the others in turn just to see if they both understand.

Plum didn't know that and she grimaces too.

She steps back from him a little. "But you're an old man, a bit lardy too. She pretends to take an inventory of his body. "You'll be pulverised, splattered. You'll get your feckin' block knocked-off. You say yourself that you're a coward, not good credentials for a fighter. There were some big fellas in that lot and they're always scrapping; it's their hobby, that's how they get their fun. Pick one of the big 'uns and your deed, mullered, Old man"

Wauters tuts. "There comes a time. I ran off when Plum fought the Irish lads down by the quay…" – Plum's eyes widen that truth again, this time for her sake, hardly painting a good picture of himself – "…but that's when I wanted him to get hurt, it's a long story. He's been ill since then and it wouldn't be right to put him forward. even though he's far better at fighting than me, than anyone I've known."

Plum is put out. "Yes, you ran off, left me too it? Yeah. I didn't miss you. You would have got in the way."

Carmen: "What? This little squirt?"

Plums is flabbergasted all over again. "He told me…"

Wauters gives a shrug. "I've tried to tell you what you're dealing with Plum, but you insist on trying to think the best of me. I haven't got a best."

Carmen: "Perhaps you should get with me brothers, they have a bare fists thing most Friday nights for a bit of fun, at the bar, I don't see any amusement in it; It saves a lot in dentist's bills mind you. But I prefer the bit of twine and slamming door method me self. Perhaps they could give you a few pointers at least, them being monstrous daft too. You know you're going to get hammered, don't you?"

Plum has been weighing up Wauters cowardly act. "You ran off. That says so much about you?"

Wauters turns on him, guilt and irritation. "Yes, I ran off, drop it. It says nothing about me right, except, I'm shit, hopeless at boxing, but fighting's a different thing; I've not really done any boxing, too tame, too busy to bother. Besides I could leave that to others." He turns to Carmen. "But I'm not old, well, not as old as you make out. Remarks like that, as keen as a punch to the guts, they wind a fellah…Anyway, who cares? What does it matter if I take a beating? What's else is there to be done? A riot? with who knows what as an outcome? More hurt all around?" Wauters feels he elicited a small begrudging smile from Carm…Brianna. They will meet again. They walk a while, the chat is sporadic. Anything Brianna has is not for sharing with Plum. Anything Plum has is secret and not for public consumption. Anything that Wauters has, he probably hasn't made up yet! Still working on it. The situation's fluid. They part on good terms. Well, there are so many more questions now. So much to pick over, for Carmen and Plum. One thing you can say for Wauters, him, he's not a pint of the usual.

--ooOOoo-

The ship is repaired and renamed. Plum and Wauters approach. They are called back to the ship as the dock workers have left it in a state, swarf and off-cuts all over the place again. Litter everywhere. Suffice to say it looks as though the repair men have done half a job.

"*Ek het gedink dat ons die einde van hierdie*, I thought we'd seen the last of this."

They board the ship. "This tub must be well known by now, to the Germans, that is. They have to have a spy in the town. Many Germans settled in England went over to the Germans when the war was declared. They don't need embedding; their back story is their lives. Totally plausible. It would have been better if they have sunk it, perhaps? I get it that you've got all the strategy worked out, but it struck me that if all the lifeboats are out and the Hun manages to sink our ship, how the hell do you get off? I for one would not approach a ship that's going under, the under tow, and all you gunners are at your posts."

Plum has every faith in the system and dismisses such talk as mischief, pure and simple. They have been sleeping on their insurance, the ballast, buoyancy. Wauters stalks around the deck before they both drop into the hold, the sleeping quarters.

"Same old smell. Same old bugs. *Eish!*"

Plum looks at his mate, all hope lost. "Still the same miserable old git! What happened to your Zoo, I've not seen it around."

Watch yourself Plum, even when they are stunned, they can still lash-out and their bite is venomous. He recovers, "It came down to one, the big one. I let him go."

Plum smiles. "That was good of you."

"Yeah," continues Wauters, "I let him go, about a yard, then I put my foot on him." Plum's eyes start out of his head and he gives a despairing gesture. "I feel quite at home here." Wauters whistles tunelessly casting side glances at Plum.

Plum reclines on his cot, unable to comment on the execution. "At a stroke, we are away from all that…complication. There is no need to think, just do. Now, where were we?"

Wauters lies down too. "My bit isn't over yet though *paw-paw*. You forget."

"What's a *paw-paw*?"

Wauters replies, his eyes closed. "Nothing to worry over, a friendly idiot."

Plum shrugs. "Oh well, that's all right then, isn't it?" They both lie there staring at the ceiling. "You're not fretting, are you? It won't be for real. It'll be like ceremonial. Mark my words. The moment's past…peace and quiet." Plum makes to get off his cot but stops and asks craftily, "Eh, Wauters, can you tell me if I've got a pencil in my bag?" Wauters opens his eyes and stares at Plum, hard. Plum retreats from what he thought was rather a pithy joke. "Well, just thought I'd ask." He starts taking stuff out of his bag in his search. "You know what some bugger has said back home? Somebody who should know better. *'While men are fighting, efforts are being undermined by guzzlers.'* That Mr Yapp, I think it was. That's what he said. Did I mention it? *'More fear of intemperance than the foe.'* Who are these people? Where do they come from? Does any bugger look into their own lives and see only purity? Are they squeaky clean?"

Wauters goes as far as he does with an expression that approaches pondering. "You might have told me that before. I'm trying so hard to block out most of what you say that there is always the danger that I might miss something important, perhaps one in a million. But I'm OK, not this time." Plum gives up searching the bag. Sounds like something you would say…and then I say, what!" Muses Wauters.

Plum pauses for a moment. "Are we besties now? Are we good? Can I be honest with you?"

He walks over to Wauters cot and sits on it. "I've played my cards. I've let you in on it, *Cocos*, the treasure."

"You know my opinion of it." Wauters talk to his pillow. "*Sien jou gat*, you're making a fool of yourself. But then, when it comes to fools, who is a bigger one than me? If I say I like your expedition, would you tell me about it? Anything for some peace and quiet," he says as an aside.

"Yeah. I trust you. I can trust you, can't I?" Plum urges.

Wauters doesn't indicate yes or no. He lies sideways over the cot.

"OK, on trust, right?" says Plum.

"*Jah*, go on.", Wauters submits.

Even that doesn't sound totally convincing. "It's like this. Are you listening?" Wauters holds a hand up. "We take a boat, a steamer to *Colon, Panama*, and then, they've got this new canal, takes you over to the west, to *Panama City*, on the Pacific coast. After that, there's a coast road north; from there, north to *Punta Arenas* in *Costa Rica*, they own the island you know, the Costa Rick-ians. We buy a craft, or hire one there, I would think they would be as cheap as chips. Or we could get a charter, perhaps. Anyway, no great shakes. They could drop us off and come back for us later. It's about three hundred miles to *Cocos*, five degrees three minutes south, by eighty-seven degrees two minutes west, I've remembered it, see. We would land at *Chatham Bay* or *Wafer Bay*. Then the adventure really begins."

Wauters thinks it's the small details that are the clinchers. "How do you finance this trek? Where's the money coming from? We take a boat to Colon. How much is that? We somehow get to go down the Panama Canal, costing? Have you bothered to sum all that? What about charts? What do we live on when we get there?"

"I have some dough saved." Plum coughs up. "I don't drink. I've got no expenses. I've been salting away all my pay since I joined the mob."

"That's mighty good self-control '*Piet Pompies*'. And you'd share that with me? Me with no contribution to make…Have you considered; I mean *really* thought this through?" He goes and sits at the end of Plum's cot and speaks to him in hushed tones. "Having some feeling for what I am, so you think you want to jeopardise your scheme on a, what, knee-jerk offering?"

Plum sits-up. "You're a super-moaner, but you will come through. You're a bloke used to going short, wouldn't mind a bit of hardship. Even if the worst comes along, we have stuff we can do. We can set our hands to stuff. We could get jobs out there. I mean, this is all part and parcel of earning a *Bradbury*. You can do mechanic stuff…I'd eat *Bush Oysters* if it came to it. I'm not fussy. There's a mighty ocean there, we could fish, you've fished, oh no, you haven't. Never mind." Plum taps Wauters on the arm then taps himself on his own temple, indicates he has some nous, he's not stupid. Besides, he reflects once we're there, I'm good. Whatever Wauters does once they get there is up to Wauters. Plum gets up and starts to walk around. He turns to Wauters with an after-thought. It's supposed to be the clincher:

"Oh, and on the island, they say there are domestic pigs, gone wild, that other expeditions left, and goats even. I bet there's tropical fruit just waiting to be picked, grapes and grapefruit and the kind. We will be living like lords." *Plum, you're such a dunce,* thinks his companion.

"And then, if you find this treasure, what then? You take it back to *Costa Rica* and they take it off you? Say its national treasure or some such. What do you do then?" asks Wauters.

"They wouldn't do that," says Plum indignantly. "The Costa 'Rick-ians' are probably really decent folks. We could like, pay a tax or something. I know you can get an exploration licence for sure, like them others have done that went before, where you promise to pay a percent of your find to the government. We'd be home free. All legal and straight. You just pay them a percent, an agreed part. There's been loads of expeditions to the island and no mention of theft, robbery…There's a tale that one man, his wife and their servant, lived on the island for some years while searching, the Costa Rick-ians made him, like, governor. If three could survive then, well, I'm no good at maths, but if three can then two can have extras, there's bound to be stuff over. This war has made people think in set way. After all this fighting they have lost their spirit, see. Some may never recover. But me, I'm in with tomorrow. This is not sapping me, taking away my urge, I'm like a jack-in-a-box, once the Germans are beaten my lid's going to come off in a big way."

Wauters feels like reaching for his book. "Tomorrow! *Eish!* Don't you think I had my tomorrow? You cannot rely on something so vague as tomorrow. Tomorrow seems like a way out of today but for some it ends-up like a drug. Today's tomorrow is one thing but the way we are when that one lets you down then you put more into thinking on the next tomorrow. Like taking opium. Soon you can't live in today at all because tomorrow and tomorrow and on and on. Yeah, it's all right you sitting there puffing out your cheeks, but, *mompie*, what do you know, the Mulatto was a Lascar, that's you, 'Captain of the Heads'. I don't care much for being relied on like you say. I'm not at my best being leant on." He did not like admitting to such things but the confines of the two of them, it seemed to demand giving things up. He knew from his own experience that let the man talk but don't become a victim of him, of his strategy, though. There was a silence as he checked himself and Plum dwelt momentarily on what sounded like a slight being landed amidst a pile of jabber. "It sounds like an adventure out of a funny paper," continued Wauters. "Them as get out of scrapes and never get shot or carved up with an assegai. You're not going to be a burden, are you? There's a lot in that thing about every man for himself. I'm not about being a shield for you. You've got to show some grit, *Shaka*!" He halts momentarily and peers into an unseeable distance. "But, as you say, what would life be without an adventure, not knowing tomorrow helps no end. That you can do something today, or name a day, is good, but just wandering through time hoping that fate will help you out when the odds are all even and unpredictable. Yeah, it has its attractions being away."

Plum claps his hands together. "I know. Great, isn't it? My dad used to read me from a book by Conan Doyle, *'The Lost World'*; Mount Roraima, that was South America. Fantastic happenings in faraway South America, deep in the unexplored jungle filled with exotic and unimagined beasts. Not that far from where we're going…We don't know anything, been nowhere, done nothing, well speaking for myself, that is, and nothing there that would phase you. If they heard you was going that would put the fear of God in them, them creatures! Even when I'm rich I'm not going to sit at home counting it, as some might. Me and my girl, Thalia, yes, I'll have one of them as well, a Thalia. We'll be off down the 'Oring-noco' and such, lickety-split."

Wauters points at the bulkhead. "Your window? Is this what that odd mind of yours conjures with all the time? Some might say that's obsession if not delusion, paw-paw!"

There's nothing wrong with obsession, comes the response. "You've been obsessed, in your own way," Plum offers bravely.

"Yes, well, I'm on a learning program. I'm new to this…optimism thing. I put optimism in the 'shit for brains category' tied up with tomorrow, they are part and parcel. Come on then. So, *Khak*i, what do you see through the window today? That I should ever believe that a lump of rusting steel could be anything but scrap. I must be going deranged like you put a spell on me? *Loskop*. Go on then, tell me about it. I need cheering-up." Wauters lies back propped by one arm.

Plum looks towards the bulkhead and a revelatory look comes over his face, his arms spread wide, like some evangelist. "You've picked a good day." He commences, walking towards his imaginary window. "Straight away, the first thing you notice is that island over there. Do you see it? Green, like vivid green, like a gem, an emerald. There's lots of brightly coloured birds flying above it, yeah like a gem with the coloured birds around the outside, a tiara, calling as they do." He points them out, as if they're obvious, real. "From here, you can see the quiet entrance to *Chatham Bay* where Graham Bennett, *Benito*, as he was called, brought his treasure. Torn from the hands of the Peruvians' churches and traders, in daring acts of piracy, before their shabby boat, the '*Relampago*' was sunk by the navy, the '*Mary Dier*', sunk her. The place where *William Thomson*, his mate, who knew *Mr Johnson of London*, left for the last time, all the while thinking that he would come back for the riches." Plum stares fixedly at his conception, as real to him as a picture window, you could swear that his face was lit by that pure Pacific light. "Look at that sea, Wauters. Look at the colour of that water! How that sun stings your eyes as it reflects off the white sand. Even from here, you can see fish of a reasonable size, unused to the presence of men, innocently going about the shallows. Good eating, you have to imagine, them, the pigs and the goats. The fish would practically jump into any net." Wauters is becoming transfixed, starting to 'see' the place described and unable or unwilling, seemingly, to break the reverie, like it was the snake oil man bringing his precious salve to you. Plum has an excited tone to his voice. "You can imagine lowering yourself into that really, quite unexpectedly warm water, as cosy as you would imagine the womb. Then the white sand beyond, the smell of decaying vegetation in the heavy air, heat carried on a light zephyr. You can strip down to your fundamentals. For the first time in so long, you cannot stop yourself from smiling." He momentarily turns to Wauters. "I think we should start by building a shack of some sort. Yes, it rains, but most of the time you wake up to the sun. There's no big insects, well they never mentioned any in any of the books in the library, so you can only believe that they were not worth mentioning. I'm no fan of spiders, eh, but you get on with insects, sort of. *You* seem to have an understanding. Then we set about it. There is no point is rushing in with pick and shovel, slowly-slowly catchy monkey. Survey the place and find out the most likely haunts. We'll have to start thinking like the pirates thought. There's no point in just piling in." He comes from his revery slowly and looks to Wauters who comes-too abruptly. "Well, you can see it now, can't you? It can change a man, can't it? Hope, excitement. When I get like this, I can think myself capable of anything. Me, once described as erratic. Me that learns little normally but when it comes to the big issues. When it comes to getting ahead, I'm unshakeable."

"I see what they mean by talking to the wall, it fits here. I need to open my eyes wide. I've missed a lot, apparently. But I'm adjusting. I can see some of it now, that you describe." Odd, it wasn't there before…Wauters reflects. "So, keep on trying to sell it. At least I'm in the shop, I suppose that's a start for you. But I could easily decide I need a wheelbarrow instead of a pair of trousers at any time. I could change my mind, just like that."

Chapter 18

It's after dark. The large workshop smells of industry, chemicals, oil, the sickly-sweet aftermath smell of burning and brazing; traces of noxious elements and solder on a scent base of heavy oil. This is the pervading smell now over-laden with pipe and cigarette smoke. Men are gathering and filling the space. There is a general hubbub. The captain and the priest enter together talking about some seemingly involving matter whose nuances shroud their awareness of place and time. Someone organises the crowd to form an empty space in its midst in the shape of a boxing ring. The shed's lights have been brought to bear on the square formed but struggle to make their effect profound, a 'TOC H' lamp at best. Some faces are recognisable. The gypsy boys are there. They stand in a small group out of the way. Conspiratorial verging on awkward. Fighting is a savage art that attracts people to the thrill of violence viewed dispassionately and involving protagonists for whom we have no feelings. If it was called a cock-fight, they would ban it. But man's basic thrill, garnered from innate savagery, ensures that the spectacle survives. We think on bravery, being indomitable are frightened and thrilled by heads being jerked back savagely, wondering at the survival after a stomach busting punch. Our boxing heroes too often are just marionettes put back in the box after they have served their purpose. To think, this was all brought about by a malign old shellback that had malice and bile in store a plenty who no longer exists in immediacy. His legacy, born out of the grim ravages of revenge, serves another, unexpected, cause. But here we are now, in changed circumstances. If anything had been unintended, unforeseen, it was this. That provision for the evening's bout had been ordained for a wholly different purpose is quite remarkable. Nothing seems to go to waste in nature. Things fall into place and that which was redundant finds a new purpose; nature always lies in wait for opportunities. Where, instead of hoping for the young man's come-uppance, the cruel pleasure at the contemplation of his being demolished, now the altered reality of the *mompie* not getting a smacking; what a win it would have been had he been injured, crushed, yeah, fancy that; it would not have been the only injury in obeyance. Hate has been surmounted by cunning and cunning has lost its cause. Everything is blowing itself out, tides receding. Moon and sun, in concert, hold the steady state and ignore the aberrations of human folly; they are the inscrutable persistence, we their slaves. This promotion has been given a frisson of something different. The 'demonstration' bout transformed into a fight between the nations, the Irish and the English, a settling of the history of grievance and done in a day. They should have tried this ruse before a Tournai and our favourites. Name your champion and let them have at it. The crowd have formed the ring; who says you can't circle a square!

The atmosphere is theatre. A dingy hall with a pool of light at its centre. The cheery expectation of a spectacle in a benighted, crude, place. A man appears in the light space formed. He is bear chested and has a long coat draped about his shoulders. Erin, the waiter, cook and chief bottle washer from the cafe is talking to him, straining his neck up to account for the foot difference in height between the two. The ship's captain seated back from the ring on top of a workbench, turns to the priest who is taking a nip from a flask. "I have no time for this sort of thing, Father. I hate it, hate it."

The priest is quite looking forward to the stramash. He proffers the flask to the captain. "Want a nip? The spirits move us. No, I concur, it's not the stuff of the seminary. But it makes a change. You'll have to grin and bear it, you're partly responsible for this evening yourself. Just think on how much worse it would have been had that mob…well, you know…" They both reflect. "Actually, I have done a bit of the old… pugilism; have you? It was thought that boxing was a necessary adjunct to the teaching of young men at church school and youth clubs. See here…" He points to a barely perceptible scar in the tissue on his forehead. "See that, a trophy; it was the result of a head butt I received from one of my more…recalcitrant flock. I knocked him down for his trouble, the imp. He precipitated an action and received a reaction. I prayed really hard afterwards, for I had lost my temper and shouldn't have. I lost control, the inner animal. He was chastened though. Became an altar boy and served well. Never had a peep out of him ever after. He had a good line in smutty photos which he used to sell in the choir stalls. I could have stopped him, but him barely sixteen and so much about life to learn…and so enterprising."

The captain closes with the priest and lowers his voice to the confidential level. "This chap boxing for our ship, I can't say I ever took to him, from abroad, you know." Cathcart has a quick look about him for security's sake. "The report that accompanied him was a rather lurid tale with treasonable inferences. I still can't work out why they didn't hang him. To leave your post, tut-tut. Who can tolerate such behaviour? Why were we blessed with him? What if he had worked some mischief on our ship? Then where would we be?"

"Hanging is it!" Chimes the priest. "So, not much violence there then, hanging and all. Well, if it's anything like our situation, it's totally counter-productive; it only creates martyrs and copycats. It's about as much use as using torture to gather sound testament. Where is your man? Yon feller looks ready to start without him. My he's in fine shape. Must be the potatoes"

"I believe he is undergoing some last-minute instruction from another of my crew, he used to box for the Royal Navy, was a fleet champion…Oh dear, I'm not going to enjoy this, my stomach is queasy; it will be all I can do to not step-in. We should be fighting the Germans not each other. They would be laughing up their sleeves if they knew what we were up to here."

"No, you won't step in or anything of the sort," the priest says reassuringly. "They're young men and most likely use a bit of fisticuffs to let off steam themselves occasionally anyway. They have their own way. A bit of recklessness is a great teacher. Best they expend their energies here than on the street, don't you think?"

The noise level has gradually risen. In murkier depths of this dingy place, money is changing hands, bets laid. The Lascar, Doomah Sen steps into the ring space having pushed his way through the tight packed throng.

"Here we go." The priest takes another nip unselfconsciously from his flask. "Ah, both yer men have turned-up. I was beginning to think it was going to be a no-show, then there would have been ructions."

Doomah Sen is not exactly an authoritarian figure and his pleas for silence are lost in the swell of the crowd. He wanders around the ring speaking noiselessly, to all intents ignored by the press of expectation and rising excitement. Eventually, having given-up trying to gain some semblance of control, he introduces himself to the Irish protagonist. Being a friendly sort, he soon gets into a conversation with the chap, who still has the coat draped over his shoulders. The bout seems to be of secondary importance for a moment. They get on well together. The crowd is starting to become outspokenly vulgar, boisterous; want to see action and the threat is that there are enough people in the place, who plainly don't get on, to make a fight of it without the bother of hanging around for the scheduled contest!

"Who's the exotic fella? I don't recall seeing him before," says the priest.

"Him? Oh, he's an Indian, works in my galley, aboard ship. He has the voice of a gentleman and conducts a polite sort of conversation. Like you and I, he has an interest in mathematics, oddly. They thought that, as he wasn't strictly one of us, that he would be impeccably neutral. So, they have made him umpire." Wauters and Plum exchange a few words. Wauters is stripped to the waist. "I know I shall hide my face if it gets rough."

The Lascar calls for silence and, with a little help from those who were being rowdy themselves, gradually quietens the crowd down. "Gentlemen; no ladies? No, no ladies. Please, gentlemen. Tonight's boxing match is between, in the green corner" – he points towards the Irishman with the jacket around his shoulders – "boxing for Ireland tonight, is Mr Tadhg Heneghan." Some noise of appreciation from the crowd. A few ribald comments. "And in the pink corner, representing the rest of the world…" Some booing and derogatory remarks, "Engineer, is that right, engineer? Engineer Wauters. There will be five rounds of five minutes and I will count to ten if a man is knocked to the floor and if he seems incapable of protecting himself, down there, or is clearly unconscious…" His voice is being gradually obscured by the restlessness of the audience urging an end to the blather and a start to the proceedings. "Yes, ten, before stopping the fight." He motions for the two men to come to the centre of the ring and the general noise starts to rise again. The Lascar gives scant instructions but the two protagonists ignore him. Some people are striking last minute bets. One has taken a mouthful of beer and squirts it at Wauters, causing hilarity.

"Round one will begin now."

A man in the circle looks at his *Hunter*, keeping an eye on the length of the rounds, a makeshift timekeeper who will, at various points, call time on the round, and time on a 'count' if one is deemed necessary. The two men circle each other. Heneghan snakes-out a couple of straight blows to Wauters' head which Wauters takes partially on his gloves. The round is progressing. Wauters has tried to cover himself with warding-off blows but has made no offensive moves himself, just faints. Heneghan speaks to him. "Come on then, yous. Give me something to hate you for. This is supposed to be an international event. Come on, try and land one, get me going. This here is my chin." He gestures towards his craggy face. "It won't feel right if I just knock your block-off for nothing. If you're going to make a match of it put your guard up."

Wauters puts his guard up and Heneghan punches him in the stomach, hard, stinging and vicious. Heneghan smiles and holds his arm aloft, which the crowd appreciate and applaud. Time passes. The two men are in a clinch and the Lascar moves in to try and separate them but only succeeds in taking a blow himself which makes him reel temporarily. Heneghan is virtually chasing his opponent around the ring and has unintentionally landed more than one rabbit punch. His opponent stands like a boxer and can slip punches, sometimes. Like a boxer, but he's not fighting. Does he think that Heneghan will tire from sprinting after him?

"Come on, you devil, hit me, if you dare. What sort of fight is this? Keep your guard up." Wauters does not move his guard this time and Heneghan hits him hard to the head producing a small cut. "You know something, I'm beginning to think you like being hit. I bet there's a word for people who go for that sort of thing, inviting pain. Is that the case or is it suicide you had thought on? Suits me, I get the same rate if I hurt you or if I kill you." Heneghan does some more chasing, punching, resetting without response. "I'm getting fed-up with this. The crowd's is getting on my back. They've came here to see a bit of action."

With that, he delivers an uppercut which rocks Wauters head back. His opponent staggers only to be supported by the front row of men standing at the ring. He is bleeding now and has a number of marks on his face, a mouse under his closing left eye. A punch on a cut, stings awfully but Wauters tries to expunge any such feelings by thinking in terms of enduring. He can fill his mind with gaskets, shrouds, spinnakers and lashings, the depth of a fathom, freeboard, needle and palm; focus on miles away, not here. The more regular and withering punches that Heneghan delivers send sprays of blood flying from Wauters head, spattering the first few rows of on-lookers, some of whom now hold newspapers over their heads for protection. It is a meat market. The rounds progress. Wauters mouth lends a gruesome image, oozing blood from the gums. He has a shirt of blood covering his formerly bare chest.

The captain is looking away and then sneaking a peak. "I think I'm going to be sick. Why doesn't the man defend himself? Even if he can't box you would think that he would at least try and run away. Prevent himself from being disfigured in that way. Yes!" he shouts. "Run away, live to fight another day." He bawls at the priest. "He could run off or feign being knocked out. There is nothing to be proven by just standing there and being clobbered in that way. How barbaric." He shouts again, "STAND-UP TO HIM, WAUTERS!" Then he sits down again looking embarrassed.

"Perhaps your man has a tactic," confides the priest. "Like I said, he'll wait until the man, Heneghan, has punched himself out and then come back at him with cat-like ferocity. Either that or he's after the sympathy vote." Wauters picks himself off the floor again. He has blurred vision and feels as though his kidneys have been ruptured. That being said, he has fallen from a topsail yard and lived to tell the tale, what's the difference? Split second imaginings that occur. What do people live through in their minds when falling from a height? He could drop to the floor, whose to know? Just lie there, it would be so easy to forego a further bashing. But this is all part of the epiphany, if only Wauters could muster such a word; payback, regret, scourging, sorrowfulness. A demand to suffer not because of a masochistic tendency but a time when, from a life of feeling little he has a requirement to feel a lot, to make up for his missed experiences. "But I could be wrong. It will be very difficult to fight a rear-guard action if he has not any head left."

The fight goes on and near the end Heneghan is holding Wauters up and hitting him. Plum throws Wauters' jacket into the ring. He shouts frantically at the Lascar. "Doomah Sen! Stop the bloody fight! Honour's been served. Wauters can't defend himself. Stop it!" The Lascar seems unsure what to do. Heneghan lets Wauters go from a clinch and his…adversary slumps to the floor, battered and bleeding.

The priest takes out his flask for another nip. "Heh, Euclid, you can look now. It was no contest but it was a marvellous martyrdom. To think, we reflect on being burned on a fire as an evil punishment? I think that contrivance has been topped, here. Come on. I'll take you for a pint of truth serum, a beer?"

Cathcart lifts his head and insists. "I shall have to go and see how he is first. I will have to see that he's all right." He makes his way through the cheering and obviously satisfied crowd, in a semi-dazed condition himself. Bumping into people, staggering. He is vaguely aware of some who seem to be suggesting that they have been cheated. What did they want? The man's head? Many seem confirmed that it was an example of the better, the superior quality of Irish menfolk. The numbers have thinned and there are insufficient numbers to define the boxing ring anymore. He stumbles to where Wauters is lying. Wauters is turned-over on his back. There is no concern in the captain's mind about the tricky foreigner, the devious interloper, the malign 'other'. His only instinct is one of humanity mixed with humility. The extent of the wounds are all too graphic; the captain is sick. The priest has followed his friend to the ring site and is party to the captain's convulsions. He takes charge of the man. Pulls out his freshly laundered handkerchief and wipes the vomit and spital from the captain's lips and jacket. That done, a few calming words and a demand to come away. "Let his friends see to him. Come," he urges, "some serum. Let's talk about it."

-ooOoo-

Everyone is bemused by the non-contest. Wauters might just as well have thrown himself under the fire cart if all he wanted was to be wounded like that. Plum looks from his cot at Wauters who after a week of convalescence is looking a little bit better. But the man's face is a mass of cuts and both eyes are partially closed set-in purple-blue sockets. Plum chivvies him.

"You haven't touched your tea, it'll be cold." Plum sits on Wauters' cot facing his shipmate. "How do you feel? People are mighty proud of you. I think I would have had trouble with Heneghan," he lies easily. Heneghan was just a solid platform for delivering big blows. A fighter, a proper fighter could have exploited his awkwardness. "A professional I should think…Doomah Sen, 'in the green corner', thing? Outsiders just don't know the score, do they? He could have got himself in a lot of trouble there. Funny, clever, but what a risk. He could have made your effort a side-show."

Wauters stirs. "Plum," he asks through big lips and puffed-up features.

Plum looks up. "Yes."

Wauters, resignedly, "*Babbelbekkie*, shut up. You are giving me a headache. Look to yourself."

"But I'm so proud of you. You're our champion. You're a hero." Plum folds his own hands together and raises them above his head, imitating a triumphal moment, acknowledging the crowd.

Wauters points to his face. "Is that so? So, if I'd got killed, they'd raise a monument to me? I'll be a super hero? What about losing a leg or something? *Wat 'n mal man. Wat 'n mal mense*…I need my rest now, Pygmy." The name coined by Carm…Brianna has stuck. "Go and play with your gun cotton or whatever it is gets your spirits up."

-oo0oo-

The healing process is a bit slow and Plum's wanting to daub iodine on Wauters' face isn't exactly welcome. But, soon enough, Wauters is almost completely mended. Plum has been able to do some good, as a messenger. He is sent to arrange the bar meeting with Carmen and to appraise her of the circumstances.

Rollo, back from his honeymoon outing, is also healed-up from his various love match bouts. He slinks around, sits, rises. Does some perfunctory hair nibbling and sees to his personal sanitation. Slumps, rises. Without the routine of the streets to fall back on he seems purposeless. His mistress hardly notices his antics. Yes, they go for walks but she hardly comments on his company, despite the dog nuzzling her trying to elicit some sort of response, trying to intrude on her preoccupation, he is her Wauters. Then it was Mr Handel and his oratorio; she has taught herself the 'Sally Garden' song. A local group of amateurs put on a rendition of 'Patience', a Gilbert and Sullivan operetta, which seems to have a lot of the elements of her own situation. Although she exposes herself to a lot of talk of love, she is no closer to the essence of the feeling, the state, its understanding. She is *Patience* and Wauters is *Bunthorne*. She with an ignorance of romance and Wauters the all too fleshy poet. It's all too difficult to sort out the business of attraction that writers, musicians seem to find endless lines of material for plots and sub-plots. She had, unusually, started a conversation with a lady she met in a quayside shelter and that led to reading a book by a new author called Mary Webb. But not all her attempts at improvement worked well. *'Middlemarch'* was a complete disaster and was abandoned early. But what could you expect when the writer pretends to be a fella, what do they know about men? How do they form their understanding? How can it be authentic when women are deaf to reality, their mermaids' ears filled with the sound of the sea. No, she refutes that. Women are all new perspective, it's the men that lack comprehension; take Wauters. He can be overcome. So it was that everything was up in the air. Men-women, the joy of happy songs in joyous plots with tunes you could sing along with. Not only that, but she found that her inbred doubts and self-perceptions, generally, were like shifting sand, like the constant rearrangement of shingle, more like. Her beach was on the move. It was not that thing of endless sameness that had dogged her, but an imp within her that was seeking out stuff with a hungry ambition, ravenously, seemingly to confound her and her fighting back at it, trying to get a grip. Wheat and chaff. None of the poets, writers and composers knew her. The best they could hope for was a scattergun that might wing her, a lucky ricochet, perhaps. The thing that had changed beyond recognition was her spirit, her self-confidence, her willingness to try, to sample. All right, so *Middlemarch* had been a mistake, but it left no injury. No one would try and put their hand on her arse now because she would not be in those places where such tricks are pulled. Her appearance alone, so mature and ordered, would cow them, her Hecate. She was off limits. Now there was no framing her as being of a sort, a type; therefore, all manner of generalisations that just did not figure with her anymore and her new self. She was updated and reshaped with some of the corners knocked-off. Yes, she would go to the bar but it would be as a person who felt out of place there now. Flynney had been so good, so he had, sort of liberal in letting the '*knackers*' go to his bar. Sure, it put a lot of people off wanting to go there, it being shady, crummy. But her people had tried their best to keep their end of his bargain; never fighting, well not in the bar. Not cadging drinks or pinching the ashtrays. When she entered the place now, she would check the condition of the chair, might even have a flick around the tabletop with a handkerchief and she always paid up.

The bar is not quite heaving but there are lots of people ghosting through the smoke-filled air. People are taking turns in singing songs for the crowd. Wauters, still scarred, Plum and Carmen, sit in the midst of the crowd exchanging bits of chat. Plum describes a punch and points to one of Wauters scars. She takes a close look, then pretends to punch him and Wauters puts his hands up as though defending himself. Rollo looks absolutely exhausted and lies on his back under their table with his legs in the air, twitching occasionally. That a dog would have to take up reading to enable it to get on with its mistress! Rollo's vague understanding of life. 'I'm down here!', his mind roared. He would have to have his name changed to Virginia *Woof* to attract Brianna! Yet it was spring and the mutt was leading a dissolute existence around the local farms. He would either find some bitch who would fall for his poor dog act or he would get shot by a sportsman making accusations of sheep worrying.

"How come you can dodge a punch now and yet, here tell," she says, "you were hopeless on the night? You wouldn't see a *pikey* go down like that; yer wench." She smiles broadly.

Plum enquires of Carmen. "Do you know that guy who did this to him? I would put Heneghan down as a booth fighter, something of that. No novice, that's for sure. He was fit and knew a bit."

"Heneghan, mm, he's done a bit. Comes from a family of bruisers out Fermoy way. Used to be a farm hand but some bugger put him up for boxing. He's done quite well out of it. He's taken a few purses but I think it's doing something to his brain."

The evening's singsong developed. The word got around and there were more accordions, spoons and banjo's all of a sudden, more than you could shake a stick at. There were a mix of genres, folk songs mainly and a bit of Irish Republicanism, but no anger, just dewy-eyed renditions of passions. Your success was all tied up with how many would sing along with you or offer a descant. You did not necessarily earn points slagging-off the usual suspects. Rollo did the rounds after a while, feeling his mistress's neglect. Everyone seemed to know him, the dog imagined, and he deigned to let them stroke him or offer a palm full of ale for him to lap. Carmen was paying him little attention; it was her new way. She thought she might sing her much rehearsed song but then they might not appreciate her transformation. Also, she found, it was such a delicate air that was so personal to her now and that to drag it out into the public should be avoided, it was hers alone. She had a private self now that she would, might, only divulge to someone who appreciated her and to whom she could bring all her treasures to adorn. Besides that, whatever she was, she was no singer, to tell the truth. Too many pipes of tobacco, too much rough cider. The last singer finishes his song to scant applause and the crowd is asked for volunteers. Wauters puts his hand up. There is a ripple of applause and he moves to the front of the crowd. His 'fame' is abroad and many an enquiry about his face is proposed along with dire warnings about mixing it with the Irish, jokingly.

"This is a little ditty intitled; it only hurts when I laugh." He sings some of *'The Wind that Shakes the Barley'*. Only, when he put himself in front of the crowd, the lyrics sped from his brain like billyo and after pretending for a moment to try and catch the key it was to be sung in, he eventually launched into the fourth verse and took many an observer and would be chorist by surprise:

'While sad I kissed away her tears, my fond arms around her flinging.
The foeman's shot burst on our ears from out the wildwood ringing.
A bullet pierced my true love's side in life's young spring so early.
And on my breast in blood she died, while soft winds shook the barley.'

Looking around, the crowd are feeling the words and sentiment of the song, the 'sentiment' ably enforced by Flynney's hybrid drinks. When he finishes, he receives universal approval and shouts for more, more and questions about where the other verses went to. He goes to sit down but Carmen pushes him back. Wauters tells the crowd, "I forgot the rest of the words. Do you want another one, or part of one?" The crowd encourages him to go on. "This song is called *Peggy and the Soldier.*" Wauters sings:

Oh it's of an old soldier come from sea,
His musket all over his shoulder.
And it's on pretty Peggy he cast his eye,
And she cast her eye on the soldier.

Oh me gold, me silver, it shall be thine,
I'll give yez all the gold in me plunder,
If you'll leave all your land, leave your husband dear,
And you'll sail all o'er the sea with the soldier.

Plum is mesmerised. The song winds on with its sorry of that awful Jade.

Oh, rock-a-bye, little one, and don't you cry,
Your momma's gone and left you in sorrow.
And if she comes back, well, she can't stay here,
She can go back to sea with the soldier.

And there was more, poor old John, him who did nothing wrong.

He abusèd the man that builded the boat,
Abusèd the captain that sailed her.
He abusèd the wind and the waters clear,
Sent Peggy over sea with the soldier.

The bar is all amazement at the discovery of this tenor who delivered his sorry tale with such conviction and vigour. They were all there with 'John' and his travails and dull would he be of spirit who did not get to their feet when the song concluded, when 'Peggy' well and truly got her desserts.

Plum is staggered: "I wouldn't have thought him capable. He looks as though he's enjoying himself," he says to no one in particular.

Wauters has sung enough and this time when he finishes somebody passes him a glass of whisky which he salutes the crowd with and downs the contents in one and sits down.

"Well, you're the dark horse," says Carmen, sincerely enamoured of his performance. "Where did you come by *the 'Barley'*? A native wouldn't have done it better service. Not another one of your made-up names? Paddy O'Wauters is it?" she suggests. Wauters sits quietly for a moment responding mildly to those who proffered toasts or came over and patted him on the shoulder.

He leans towards Carmen so as to be heard above the raucous noise of the company. "There were lots of Irish in Australia, 'displaced', they seemed to favour being called. They were all right. Whenever they were in their cups it took nothing to get their eyes all moist…Out would come all the laments and the tears. Another excuse for a round of lagers and tales about their abandoned homes. *Bruton Town*, *Sailors Life*, all them songs sung through their tears. I would join in; it earned me some instant mates, as long as they stayed drunk, that is. Have you got any songs er, Brianna? How about you, Plum?"

Plum waves his hand, so as to say go away, not me.

"Me!" she says, in a tone of astonishment. "I could empty the bar with my voice, make the dogs howl and the cats run for cover, wouldn't I, Rollo?" She looks under the table. The dog is motionless, sullen. "The crows would fall from out the sky." The dog hardly looks up and then subsides. "Like the foghorn on *'Poer Head Light'*. We'd have the Gardai in here in a flash if I started-up, thinking that someone was being *mullered*. What a langer you are, you know. You could have a sweet life here with a voice like that, what a voice. Good *craic*, plenty o' company. Whatever yer name is."

Plum says, "My names Plum." She waves him aside. She does not look at him. "Not you, pygmy, him. Whatever." She turns towards Plum. "Isn't it past your bed time? I'll make you up a bottle and you can go to your cot."

"I don't drink," comes Plum's rebuttal.

"You really should," says she, "it might make you interesting. Then again, perhaps not even drink could do that."

"Now children, no squabbling!" Wauters raps the table with his knuckle.

Well, it was what you could term a jolly night. Wauters has found his place if he wants it. They would say ever after that people came into the bar who'd never dared step foot there before, thinking that it was John McCormack himself letting go. Flynney finds himself winking at Wauters, as if they had something to share, an affinity. At least the change he had robbed off Wauters came in handy and he wouldn't have missed it, would he now? The night comes to an end and the three leave the bar.

A few drinks and some banter. The togetherness of a crowd. Throw in a dollop of nostalgia and a soupcon of nationalism. Wauters is now well known and people are beginning to fashion him into a sort of hero. This is a man of unknown depths. Yes, he threw the fight; but the main thing was that everyone won because the nascent insurrection was immensely satisfied by the outcome. Irish manhood prevailed and the feckin' 'Anglash' were shown that, if not for their resources, on a one-to-one basis, our big'ens were just as adept, well, obviously more so, that your big'en. Wauters, bloody and cowed, was only what they themselves, or some, had been thinking of handing out, only on a bigger scale. Fancy sacrificing yourself in such a way. Wauters is a big hunk and not fat and could obviously make a mess of you should he so choose. He's what you might call finely honed and large boned. The years of heavy and athletic toil on sailing ships moulded him into a formidable unit of sinew. Why, and him the most unexpected sacrificial lambs? Of course, some, who had lost money on the bout, would maintain he lost his bottle, but not to his face, not even suggest such an opinion to their friends, so much was Wauters' fame abroad. Shakespeare knew the moment, "gentlemen in England now abed shall think themselves accurs'd they were not here." None knew of what he had done to the stoker. You would have to be very selective with your company to descry the man. For it was self-evident that he was no boxer but all man. Some said 'the fix' was in'. Had they inspected his suffering afterwards they would have a better summation of what he sacrificed. Wauters was of the mind that more than once, prior to the bout starting, the thought flitted through his mind, that his dark leanings and his modest strength could have licked the challenger. But what would have been served by brutalising that man? Since seeing Plum in that asthmatic throttle hold, he had been moved. Wauters had found himself experiencing the suffering too, felt something. How good was that? It was lucky that the Plum, slash Logan thing, had fallen through. The occasion was all set-up, be it for another purpose, almost as though it had been ordained. The thought of taking Plum's place was fleetingly pondered but there was less to that than honour. What a strange word for Wauters, to conjure with the word honour. Such an establishment sort of idea, honour. In his experience, the officers got the salvage dough and the rank and file got the mortuary. The majority of thinking sorts saw how he had done a good thing and a clever thing. Carmen saw it and admired him for it. But that was her secret. She is not about to give that big lump an advantage of any sort. Brianna wanted to beat Wauters at his game, in an area where a different sort of strength was called upon. He must come to her now. She is the catch. She doesn't stare at him but she cannot resist sideways glances. No matter how she had moved-on she was convinced only of the fact that she had moved to a point where they were now equals. Now she would not have to pretend that she came from India and that he was an artist. She was the consummate modern woman. She could see that understanding George Eliot was not that far away while not being the only way. OK, she was found wanting in the first round but she was not about to 'throw' the fight, like Wauters had done. She regarded herself as formidable and with a marvellous opportunity in a society in which, as an unknown, all avenues were open to her, Venus rising from the shell, like it was drawn by that Italian mush, 'Little Bottle'. She had anointed herself with courage. She glanced at him again. If only he would reciprocate. No matter how self-invested she felt and no matter how she talked of her new self and courage, she had this woeful habit of lapsing, going back to him. While displaying an independence of mind and spirit, she had managed to make herself dependent. If he would say something so tender and quintessential, it could still stop her in her tracks. She was a total civilised woman now. To think that she could be so daft, so confused, as to think she could have lived without society. When, as she knew now, she was made for company, for display, for jousting with ideas. She loved conversing with people in a way that she felt there would inevitably be give and take and, at its outcome, both parties could believe they had learnt something worth reflecting on. As a *knacker*, they would have avoided her but in her guise, self, she was one to be sought, to engage with. She was breaking new ground and not subjected to the lore and the elder. She'd bought herself clothing, Open draws, which was timely, as an underwear shop had recently opened in town and she had no compunction about going there, even trying stuff on. Another sly snatched look. If any other woman tries to step in here, I'm not so far from the street that I would think twice about blackin' her feckin' eye. Not looking directly at him but with a mind full of every aspect of his looks. He excited her for some reason and now more than ever. 'What a lovely couple'. So, he's obviously got some decency in him, or he had some ulterior motive that, too late, we will find out about. Even the vagueness, the unpredictability of the 'lump' was sort of exciting. Just when you thought you had nailed him. Does he do anything without it being a scheme, do you think? The sounds of the boisterous crowd leaving Flynney's gradually gives way to a quiet jet black, impenetrable night. Wet pavements illuminated meekly by streetlights seemingly, themselves, shrinking from the unknown perils of the surrounding medieval dark. Everything is going out, damping down. A dense, claustrophobic blanket drawn over the day whose lack of air leads to sleep. The last lamps in private houses along the way doused, with only the last few tended as they cast their insipid light on the griping child, the sated, post-coital pair. Those frightened by the metaphoric end of the day and its animated shadows coming for them to carry them off. Brianna is in a good mood. She has a new form of excitement as well as that thorny legacy that Carmen would never have understood, that *she* found a chore, that *she* wanted to hide from. Except the little fire that she was kindling for him just would not catch light. She felt that she had everything except a 'him' which, for some selfish reason, he could not see. Wauters was somewhat tickled by the reception he had received. So, this is how transparent people live? *Eish!* who would have believed it. Men and women together engaged intimately and not a whorehouse? But what a fear popularity brings. He knew instinctively that he could probably get away with more now than he had previously. But living here? Fancy living in a world where he had to earn money? Away from the ship, and a steady source of income in that which he stole, all gone. There was a requirement for an honest day's work, demanded to be part of a community, to have stolidity conferred upon you, reliability. There would be more scrutiny, more expectation. Yes, there would be latitude but, should his inclination get the better of him, it would be a big fall. In the bar, out of the corner of his eye, he caught sight of Carmen on more than one occasion looking at him. He saw how she made herself part of his glory, her new found affection and fame by association. He had gathered a dependent. He reflected on what she was now, all heliotrope perfume and tailored clothes and her, so immaculately clean and presentable; you could eat your dinner off her, whereas previously, she had been *Jimson Weed*. But fame, yes, such a difficult thing. The unforeseen responsibilities that he already had got a whiff of. It's one thing getting to those heights and by doing something that you will never be called upon again to repeat. But to be in the public eye, continually, an anathema. He thought he could not sustain it in some modes. But being honest, in his real world, he was too callous and determined in his own cause to not trip-up somewhere and get himself landed in the cart. What if Brianna…no, that seemed even more remote now. If he came to a fall through his mania and single-mindedness, if they were closer, he would take her down with him. She did not deserve that. The ramifications of Plum's illness led to confusion. Yes, he deserved everything that life dished in his direction because…he had to throw his weight around; he enjoyed the discovery of danger in criminality, even though it had not actually enriched him, a drug. As easily as he walked, he contrived. He was at his most imaginative dreaming up his own characterisations. Who would he have been today? People were so stupid, look 'em in the eye, stand your ground and they can be made to believe anything. There is always the old schizophrenia gag if called out, get caught in a lie. Own up to having mental problems. Nobody can be chastised for having problems with their heads, you're obviously not responsible; you become a 'poor you' and in need of help. Here he is, he muses, having been canonised, but prepared for the fire anyway, sort of thing. But which way to turn? He could easily have a dose of the Plum's, as he felt inclined to throw his jacket open and to unbutton his shirt at the neck for want of air, the weight of all his concerns bearing down on him, stifling him. Then again, could he actually tolerate the daftness of Plum? The person he was happy to see slaughtered, hopefully, by Logan? Thinking on his feet in a fog of perturbation: She was his for the taking, what then? Any resort of that kind would really seal his fate, becoming known, transparent, responsible. Imagine that! No, he could only ever be a disappointment to her. One day, not far off, he'd do something, conditional to his ways, to hurt her. She could be sunk and anyone else, by association, wrecked too. He had to turn her off; it would be the hardest lie that he was ever called upon to perpetrate but it was good that he was practised in that art.

Plum walked alongside the other two. Stone cold sober, his mind was intent on the surroundings, the feeling of the ample trousers against his legs as he walked, thinking on his run tomorrow. While next to him, seemingly placid and relaxed, Wauters was cracking a tortuous code without anyone having the slightest comprehension of his abacus's furious operation on permutations. Plum had contributed nothing to the evening. He knew one or two modern songs, but standing in front of them and giving vent? How would they have taken the Gertie Gitana offering:

Down the stream gaily paddling his tiny canoe
A lover coming to woo sang her this song
Your voice is ringing like silver bells
Under its spell, I've come to tell you
Of a love I am bringing o'er hill and dell
Happy we'll dwell, my Silver Bell.

No. Plum felt himself to be part of something at last, rather an important part. He too now had a place, an expertise and a hope. He felt that he had an understanding with Wauters. He had been informed, not timidly but not emphatically, that the other man was 'thinking about it', well that was a step forward, no, a giant stride. He had been to the library on a number of occasions now and knew more about tomorrow, *Cocos*, than any other alive today, he though. That's an achievement, very consoling. In a way, it was good that the war stood in the way as it gave him time to get more money together, more information to describe his tomorrow, so that when it came, he would recognise it and act accordingly. Until Wauters had mentioned costs that had not been a problem. Once referred to, it had caused a frisson of concern. But all that remained of the money fright was his natural Spartanism and keeping fit, his needs were few. Yes, he was now acutely aware that he would need lots of funds, so? *Cocos* was, as near as damn it, on the other side of the world. There was an occasional agony experienced, that his great adventure was denied, suspended unnaturally by circumstances beyond his capacity to affect. If it wasn't the war, then it was cash. Life's a bugger! Since the asthma attack, a bit of a cloud has also draped itself over his enterprise. He did not baulk at adversity or find anything to be scared about in the proposition. But what happened if he had another attack? People died from such things. Even though he had an increasing faith in Wauters, who had proven beyond doubt he was up to his own levels of fortitude, he also knew, from bits and pieces, that when you put them all together, Wauters the enigma, was certainly a riddle. He didn't want to give Wauters a pass because he felt that it was in their joint interest He should be on his toes when dealing with him; it was in their joint best interest not to defer to Wauters' dark side. If he gave that man a yard, he would run off with it, he felt. Having come so far from such small potential and meagre imaginings, all was coming together. How easily he seemed to shoulder the weight, especially having always been a follower rather than a leader. All of these transient thoughts as he walked along vaguely hearing Brianna's patter, as if she was in an adjoining room. He mulled the set-to with the submarine. It had been such a fast occurrence; it was all over in a blink. But say that there was another action and, according to the workings of luck, this was their turn? The odds seemed to demand it. Say he was maimed. Maimed was worse than being killed, eh? Fancy having all these plans and being this close only to find yourself crippled, immobilised. Could you live with that? Look what had happened to Matey's uncle. Fancy, after all this time, simply, lamely, that he could end up handing the map on to another? The thought made him shiver. Fancy not being afraid of death but terrified by fate. In such circumstances, would he burn the map like some ancient rite and place that essence into the world to come to be the purpose of his dead self? Apples of Sodom.

Wauters is buoyant. "Great night. Australia over the waters, eh! Good memories." They walk on. "Never a dull moment. What was it you said? Is that a regular sing-song?"

"It's a sort of hit or miss thing," she says. "It takes something, a bit of nothing, to spark things off. Somebody will start-in with playing the spoons or summat…you can never tell." Actually, she is finding it hard to speak about such triviality. She wants to get down to her pitch. She is agitated by this chit-chat.

Wauters asks if they should walk her home. She declines saying she will go back over the fields and unless you know the way you, they would find it tricky getting back; or, is that a concern for her when she can have his company for that much longer. Is that an error, a miss-step? She grabs Plum's arm and shakes it. He has to be got rid of. Her quarry will escape if he stays. She will be unable to speak frankly. "Heh, thingy, Plum, can you go and play with the dolphins for a bit."

What has he done? He'll keep schtum. He virtually pleads to be allowed to stay with them. Brianna is adamant. "No, you can't stay. Go bury your head somewhere, fidget, oink-oink!"

Plum licks his tongue at her. They laugh. Plum goes ahead, looking back occasionally. She gives him the 'v' sign. He walks away briskly. "I'll be at the jetty," he shouts back.

Wauters comes back from his strategic thoughts abruptly, unresolved. He grins. "Now there's an odd character if you like." He looks down the street. "This is nice for a change. What it is to be ordinary and not caring either way. I should have tried it earlier." He has it in his bones, there is a resolution due and the feeling is, now.

Carmen: "This is a right feckin' dull place normally." Even with her claims on a new sort of refinement in other spheres, feeling safe and in familiar company, you scratch the surface and Carmen is there in all her vigour. "You've done your bit to wake it up. You're in danger of becoming like a 'treasure'. Entertainment here is usually summed-up by coming out to see the gas-lighter fire-up the street lamps! He can easily gather a crowd! They treat it almost like its carnival! Only joking. If you squeeze your eyes, it's not such a shit hole." They walk-on in silence for a moment. "I'm curious. Why *did* you take such a beating, *phral?*" So Wauters is elevated to family, closeness, intimacy, a brother. "My lot say you didn't land a punch. Heneghan made you look like a tart."

"I did it on purpose," he states.

"Now there's a thing?" she muses.

Wauters fastens-up his jacket, suddenly feeling a bit of a chill, the claustrophobia now eased. "Me and my background. Would I walk into the enemy camp without a plan? Everybody seems to *know* what *I* am. I had a notion to set thing to rights by doing something that people wouldn't recognise as something I would attempt, a put-on. The other night, it could have been a waste, so easily. Nobody would have backed down. No winner if natural mistrust or the 'flag' had been at issue. *Eish!* If the 'ship' had taken a beating on the streets, the worst events imaginable would have happened? The military would have come in, tried to catch the ringleaders and, naturally, the bad men would have been hidden by their own nationality trumps morals. You can only imagine the bad odour then, what it would breed. If the crew had managed to fight them off, we wouldn't have seen any welcome in Queenstown, no way, ever. A running sore. Sometimes it's necessary to put your hand in the fire, don't you think? Far better to run things on your own terms."

Carmen: "And there was me thinking it's just boys being boys…It all sounds so very serious. Perhaps you think too much, is that possible? Can you think too much? And if you can, how do you know when to call a halt? I mean it could get out of control, if you thought you hadn't thought enough and just…" She puts on a voice. "…I thought too much today and ended-up with a headache. I didn't think enough today, Jesus, anything could have happened!" She looks into Wauters' face. "Me, I can't be arsed. I just want to run and whoop. There isn't enough silliness, it's the greatest gift that freedom gives you, being silly."

She dances around, takes pleasure in flaring her new skirt and pays no mind to doing something daft in front of this 'other'. She feels lovable, exotic, looks appealing, fit enough. Whatever it is that can go between a man and a woman? How does it start asks *Patience*? Is it like this? A moment of unselfconscious gaiety? An opening of the gate falling away from character pretence and 'front'? God, oh no. I'm being obvious. I want him to think that I'm like fancy-free but am I'm over-playing my hand. Wauters adjusts his woollen cap.

"What a difference a night out does to your mood." He watches her not knowing what to make of her frivolity, inclined to clap in-time or something but not doing it, too normal, too expected almost. It's only like a dog walking on its hind legs when all is said and done. Dancing indeed, a way of expending excess energy involving people who are well provided, haven't done a hard day's graft. Ritualistic and without point. A thing that normal people are too spent to take part in, unless mating, drunk or daft. She dances towards him her arms gracefully outstretched as if inviting him to take hold for a reel. Wauters forces a smile, turns to the side, sort of embarrassed. Whatever her ploy was it has fallen flat. Was it for him? to look at her reconstructed figure, get an eyeful to nudge his lust? To see how healthy I am, I can bear children you know. I'm not so done down by this place that I haven't got a dose of amusement in me. "I put it down to you, your fight between good and evil thing. I was with the 'other side', you know, that's when you think it's all up with you unless, unless you rein-in. You heeded the warning shot."

He looks at his wounds reflected in a shop window. Dancing over, she comes up behind him, leans her chest against his back; watches him as he gazes at his likeness. He moves his fingers over his face like a man with a safety razor sourcing bristles. "The hurts not so bad. A nation of one, that was me. I wrote the rules. My own laws and nobody to answer to. Occasionally, you must take the blame for a daft policy."

Rollo jumps up against Wauters, a neglected hound saying I'm here, I'm here.

"You, Brianna, you're another outsider, aren't you?" He turns towards her; she is very close, having ignored the momentary bodily contact that she had devised. "*You* know what it's like to live in your own world. Driven out by the 'steady' mob. A man can come-up with some pretty daft contrivances left to himself. Two against the world, eh?"

Carmen puts her head to one side and looks into his eyes querying his thinking. She points her finger accusingly at him. "You're a dark one, you know that," she says authoritatively. "Left to your own daftness you came up with a really shit way of looking at life. Not much of the philosopher there then; and yet in all your dealings you seem to suggest control and, like, managing things. You need looking after, you know? You've had your joy removed." She makes a face. They walk a little way but in the ensuing silence, she is forced to speak, an example of Wauters' method, keep schtum and let them talk themselves around. If this is to be that cherished moment when it all comes right than best be straight, is that the way that people do it? "You put Vaughan my way, why? I puzzled that one long and hard and couldn't come up with a reason, you bugger. You were always sort of lurking in the background, secretive. You should have stayed out of sight. I could see you, my brother had his eye on you as well, idle bugger that *he* is. But then, I don't think like you, do I? Now we know that there was no reason behind it all. Am I right, Rollo?" The dog looks at her attentively and she bends down and speaks as if to confide. "It was the animal in him. I believe he's part dog and not one of the better bits either." Rollo searches her face and wags his tail, has he got his mistress back? "I've heard tell of some who've killed just to know what it felt like, the experience. How scary is that? You might be one of them. I shudder to think. No connections, no hate or gain, just experiences, the motiveless crime; like you couldn't satisfy your urges in some other way. The perfect crime, no motive but plenty of opportunity. If you are raging that much inside, why not rid yourself of it. Swim the feckin' harbour, run to Cork and back, what's that, sixteen miles? Heck, I don't know. Find a way to free yourself of your tensions. Some of us are in danger of becoming strangers even to ourselves." She takes Wauters' face in her hands and looks into his eyes quizzically. "Who's the crafty one? *I* wangled the fruit, the tins of peaches, out of him; came in handy. I wanted them peaches but *I* wasn't about to pay for them, was I? Obsessed with peaches, so I was. Sounds daft now but, heh, that's little lives for you. It was one sorry tale of someone trapped in a tiny, hopeless world. You set him up. I don't know why. You, the crafty one, could probably read my being simple, even from afar. A bloke that's been places and met others, been in danger no doubt, had lovers?" She lingers on that question, but no response. "But it all fell-in nicely with me and temptation." She stands back. "Work on a fellers' weaknesses. Just some twisted thought, mountebank. Could you explain it to yourself? It was you got the peaches; I know that. You set him up and, perhaps, *I* finished him off?" He looks to the heavens. "So, it was." She pushes him playfully. "The rest is history. You see what you are up against with me? I'm too smart by half. And you had me for a simpleton. Look at me. I'm coming to know my power and it isn't in the *dukkerin'*, that was just theatre. You know, now I can't dwell on the numbers of lives I could have ruined with my profession and I'm sorry for that. I bet we all do it, unthinking things, restricting *them* to what *we* need, our wants. Quite capable of sending them others on a wild goose chase. Who can you trust? Who in the world has the power of self-control, can be strong enough to be their own council, answer to themselves? We all seem to pretend our strength. Is that nature? Like them butterflies with the big eyes painted on the wings. Them eyes, staring at you can, like, stir an emotion in a dumb creature. Then how misled can we be?"

He lets her go on while wanting to be away because all of this is leading nowhere or to an inevitability. She says 'we are due each other'. That 'being single is living only half a life, seeing half of the possibility'. No, Carmen, being single is being free, not being tied-up to some thundering great bollard, then you have their families and friends, all the attendant tethers. You can live with little money but, quickly, there is a need for things. They call it setting-up home but it's really feeding a debt, you are put in the system. What do they say, when bills come through the door love flies out the window? Carmen, lay off. You're a lovely person, one amongst many I may have wronged, but this is all there is. I'm trapped. If I stay here, I am the captain, a fearless captain that can be expected to follow the right course. Oh yes, how long could I keep that up for? With Plum I'm with a crew. I could cheerfully throttle him at times but I can get away from him. You keep on thinking it will all come right, like in the books. Cathcart came clean, he has my records. When he came to me, days after the bout, he spilled his guts. Daft old romantic, *eish!* If he had kept it to himself, he would have had a degree of respect but he chose to absolve me. Him, how had he come to such powers? I think that he thinks too much of himself. He gave me my freedom, said I was a 'straight arrow', a hero. Changed his opinion, there was hope even for the worst sorts, me I suppose. Let's face it, he wasn't up to keeping a secret.

Just a weak old duffer, the after effects of the influence of command in a weak character. You see how they do it? They can like you if they can take you over and make you in their image. They are so assertive in their own cause. What does he really say, 'I want you to like me and when that's accomplished you can swallow my other nine yards'? But I'm not weak. Daft old man, you let me off all my bad deeds, my dereliction of duty and not a word for my pretence and living a fraud of an existence? Knocking around with a priest does not give you the authority to 'free' anybody, offer absolution, there's too many around doing that. Who says that crime doesn't pay? When you have people who think that they have an eye for goodness and think that they can reform others, have a power to strew-about 'rightness', their way of life no less, there is no hope for any of us. Us 'dodgers' can run rings around them because they so affirmed in their cause' they know nothing of deceit, pretence, never seen malignity. They're not of this world.

She is still talking. "A right smart arse. Well, street smart, as used to be. Now I see what real smart looks like, it's chilling."

But all the time, she's thinking craftily, the opioid that is danger.

"I should never have met you in a normal life now, would I? It's these daft circumstances. People thrown together." She pauses a moment, he is silent. "I don't suppose you would like them, but I went to music concerts, with proper orchestras." She bumps into him intentionally. "No, but seriously, I think on it. Ponder?"

She enfolds his arm as they walk slowly towards the quay down the glistening streets with Rollo sniffing at the bins, scenting other wanderers stopping points and expunging their existence, their powers in territories with his pee. Carmen has a bit of the frantic about her and virtually ignores him. Is there a question here? "This is a shifty one. He comes at me out of the blue, because of silly Vaughan, sorry Vaughan. Pleasant as you like. He's a tester. Takes me about. Tells me tales, but never mentions *us* or any vague connection with, you know, a relationship, God forbid." Why is she winding herself up in this way? It's a desperation that she feels as though she has an inkling of what is to come but won't admit it, because it is too crushing. We've been through *Bolgach* and all sorts to get here, for what? "I'd made my mind up in Flynney's. I was going to walk away that time, I should have." She is a mixture of questions she has asked herself a load of times, going through the list. "You didn't weigh on me for any favours even. You're not like the others. That's a bit of a facer. There're more ways to win than the obvious, eh? Why was that? We know, don't we? Because you didn't even care that much about me because I was…unappealing?" She has shifted tactics and wants to explicit denial, flattery even. An apology might even do by now. "Or did you even look? I thought you were the biggest liar on God's earth. But nonetheless interesting for that. Like it was a lure, forcing me to save you, drawing me on, fecker. Appealing to something in me, another me that even I didn't know or recognise at first. I'm left with thinking, here, who was influencing who. Australia indeed." She tuts. He stops walking, her inner self surges. Nothing. Shut your feckin' gob girl. The lack of response, interjection, is a void to be filled.

But he is urged to say something. Forced into the case for the accused. He does not want to hurt her, take advantage of her, promise anything. He cast her fortune in the way that she would, a load of lies surrounded in a pretence. He had no reason to shrink now, his captain had torn up the indictment. "I have to address that one. 'Unappealing', I like that. You were. I should have approached you with a surgeon's mask on. I could have caught lock-jaw or summat. You didn't want anybody. That was the whole purpose of your little…masquerade, wasn't it? What! You didn't want any attention but if anyone had offered it you would have, what, crumpled? What sought of self-deception is that? Now every word of the rest was the truth, sailing, Australia…diving." He gathers himself. "I liked you, never mind how you looked; you were good company, like you'd been to the university in Praetoria. If I had to be here what better than to be here with you? You've seen my choices." He points after Plum. "Who were you that suddenly you became important in my life because of events? Trust me, I've been out with some odd women and had lots of original experiences. I know what women are like. I know as soon as they open their mouths how I should be with them. You only usually meet one woman perhaps in one body, in one lifetime. But in the time that I've known you, you've been all sorts of characters. Look at you now with your fancy clothes, your beautiful face and your joy."

He walks on again and she walks backwards so as to look into his face. "Well, that's reassuring, isn't it?" She says sarcastically, casts her eyes down. "Am I odd looking enough to be in your good books now, or would a wart or two suit me better? It was my man taking a hoof stopped me taking care, that's what! Agh! what's the use? I have dear Rollo here to understand me, heh Rollo? Once he was enough for me, can you believe that? Putting all your faith in a dog! It's awful having nobody to cherish, to live for, straight. Nobody to think on, to do for. So many women take to marriage without so much understanding of the burden that they will have to carry. Imagine me in the camp, the expected duty and being told by the elder. In these times, you have to be grateful to be dedicated to a dog, a clever dog, Rollo." She pats Rollo. She is now walking by Wauters' side. Rollo wags his tail. "No widows weeds, that's for sure," she concludes.

"Nobody took more disguises than me," says Wauters.

"I bet you did, it's that multi-coloured lizard again. I gave up on hope and just made me self-revolting instead, I wanted no part of it. Not like you. You seem to thrive in the middle of it all. What an odd thing to dream-up, a strange tactic. But, all the same, an easy place to hide; it was just me version of make-up, theatre. It's easy enough to get away from any thought of future when you're sad. Loneliness is such a sad do. Settle back and let it all wash over you and suddenly you are sixty and a burden to every bugger. Wash, indeed, me? You can be outrageous in so many ways. But them men, very persistent, you know; no love in them. I despised them. Even if you smell and look like a drain. But you weren't horrible, obvious. like them. That got me on the wrong foot for a bit. That was annoying for some reason. But it only lasted as long as it took me to place you. Well, here we have it. I didn't understand the game, you were the only one with the rules written out, I'm playing blind. I think I understand now but not then." She throws her head back, alters the neckline of her dress, licks a finger and presses back a strand of hair. "I couldn't believe how ugly I'd become and me, not that blessed in the first place." She puffs her cheeks out and makes herself cross-eyed. "So, I set about myself. Wanted to look all right again, it's a treat. Walking out, I loved it; I fell in love with me, I became drunk on me. I forgot what fun I can be. I did myself down. Then it changed. I couldn't have done it for me but I could for you, it was a gift. Charm the birds from the trees. What a simpleton I am. Not only did I turn away the creeps but I turned away them that has charm too. The nice women I've come across out with you, the one in the shelter with her Mary Webb story. I was a traitor to my sex. If the women can't make it right, we're lost. You can't rely on men, blinded by sex and lies. What provokes us to these things, a special sort of madness? Thinking on all the possibilities of knowing you and, for a minute, tolerating your inner rogue. The mind plays tricks. I must be soft in the head. I'm all over the place because of a bad boy."

She elicits a broad smile from Wauters. "What a bundle *you* are. Like my Ma's sewing tin, lots of bits of things and stray buttons and very little complete.

I confess, I came to you wanting to make sure I was off the hook, for what I did, well not so much what I did, what happened, to Vaughan. Yes, I wished him harm. Well, he was weak. Just cause enough. I made up a story that he had pulled a knife on me and that started things off. No, you see, he knew I was pinching stuff and, as I seemed so good at it, I should get him the peaches so he could seduce you. You would be a walk-over. See how easy it is to turn yourself into a hero if the situation demands? *Eish*, woman, what little I know. And then I thought how easy it would be for you to tell on me about summat I had been pushed into. Keep your friends close but your enemies closer, sort of thing. When I heard his plan, all I could think of was that there was a big fat opportunity for striking a blow, getting free. Why? Why him? I never thought it through to him dying. A bit of mischief, get him imprisoned, perhaps. Thinking on it now, he could have been shot for desertion. I never even considered that, till now, just. Where did that come from? What if you or Plum spoke-up? Plum knew something was afoot. That daft cretin, all it would take was for him to tell about the evidence of his own eyes. But could he, no. He wants me to go on an adventure with him, *'bakgat'*, eh, marvellous. Do I turn him down and him so relying in me? How would he go then? I ruin his life and even though he's such a soft nature. Even the softest, kindest folk can only take so much. He might put me in the stockade, he has the power. What does it take for me to suffer all his jabber, the *Praatsiek*? Me, always seeking revenge, payback, not blind hate. I like to think on it as a craft and can come out daft for a dead cause. *Eish!* I'm too emotional and can stick with hopelessness just not to rock me boat. I had some control over Plum. I felt more assured about him keeping it shut. I didn't think about death though, never saw that, *godverdomme*! That was never on the cards. Plum's my friend now, well as much as any man can be…maybe 'cus he knows too much." He laughs, a shallow insubstantial sort of guttural utterance.

She listens intently. "Nasty things happen to you when you are forced to look at yourself," she says. "The seedy things you find. So predictable. The day, so ordinary and…repetitive. It's sort of a way of getting beat-up like you did. It takes some sort of stomach to settle for little or nothing. But when you've got no example, what's to know? There's a word for it, you know for not knowing, not innocence, not ignorance, something of that. Even I wasn't curious about what happened to Vaughan. That silly young man who had such a small ambition, laying me. If women wore their sex on their faces, we'd never have love, no romance. Best that it's all…covered up. Perhaps, if they weren't so curious, they'd leave us alone. You have to sneer at such thinking, that he thought he could have me for a couple of cans of fruit! Even *I* felt guilty. I was a plotter too. It was me that put him up to it as much as any, me and my careless talk. Played on his lusting. See, I'm no innocent. But innocence wasn't the word; too many words and such a world of difference between them." She holds her arms out with her wrists together. "Take me in sergeant, for I have sinned. Guilty, you've done me up like a kipper!" She makes a flourish in imitation of a hanging with her tongue lolling. She announces dramatically, "The end to a little life." She loops her arm through his again as they continue walking on slowly. "Why did I read that poetry? All them lies you told, diving for pearls indeed: oh no, that was a true bit, you say. But just thinking on it so much came together and made a complete nonsense of everything. To think that others know your thoughts. The poets have seen it all, all our weaknesses, typical of men, focusing in on conquests and knowing their every twist and turn. You only have to read to know that you're not special or original, we're all fools for or with some bugger. But it's all put over sort of…hopefully, you're still precious if only a faulted human being." She looks away, bites her lip in a swell of emotion she says, coyly. "I bet you like me a bit." She could easily break down at this moment and sob her heart out. She looks to him closely, wanting a positive answer. He looks on. There is a pause. He looks to her and in a defining moment…raises an eyebrow. She is disappointed. Lad it all out and…nothing. She takes a deep breath. "There's me blathering on, all serious and knowing and believing that everyone is the same. I bet you think I'm trying to put words in your mouth? Do all girls like nasty lads, stinkers? Where's the gain in it? That word, it comes to me, naïve. That's the bugger."

Without turning to face her, mainly because he can't continue to lie to her face, ashamed of himself in a unique way.

"There I was singing. It all came on me so natural like. You offer no hope for me. I'm old and lardy, you often say. But I've been through the fire, I'm reformed. He does not mention the ultimate hurt he suffered and what sent his spiralling out of control, that is his cross. I think I could even stop pinching money from my shipmates, that's always a good sign. Like you a bit? Yes, a bit, a big bit."

"Liar. Listen to yourself. Perhaps I'm trying to egg-you-on to say something flattering, something that might make you sound as though you have a real interest in me, rather than just making sure I keep me trap shut. A silly girl."

He raises his voice. "I could turn you off and excuse me-self into the bargain. I could tell you I'd had the pox or summat, that I'm married and have to go back. I could dream up something final and what could not be altered, any excuse and make you shrink away. You're swallowing the whole bit and ignoring fine details like I rob stuff and from my mates, how come that's not an issue? But I'm facing up." She stares at him. Wauters shrugs. "So, what are we expecting from each other? What's the ingredient?"

Carmen puts her hand to her heart. "A wise one keeps her cards close." She has said too much already. Not mentioned how his presence makes her melt. How, if he laid a hand on her, she would capitulate willingly and wrestle the living daylights out of him in an effort to get as much of him as she could. Wanting to be part of him, mingle with him, gorge on him. Wanting to be wanted to the extent of being careless of her natural modesty and restraint, uncomprehending naivety; a thing never felt before. She has a scream welling up in the depths of here being: "Me, obviously, trying to provoke you and you all sly and calculating. Me trying to wheedle-out some show of real emotion, commitment and you standing aloof there like a big feckin' lump, making references grandly to your 'plan' as you go along. My life has been ruled by lore, what's expected, family, tradition. As to pinching, I can't wear my Ma's jewellery for fear that some other bugger, who it was pilfered from, should recognise it. Am I shocked? No. Now we are both being so honest and giving so much of ourselves, like dancing around each other; try this step, try that one, perhaps, eventually there's a fit? Come on Wauters. Have you lost all your fire, olden? What do you use your 'little man' for, stirring your tea? Am I not full and womanly?" Oh dear, that's impetuosity.

Wauters sort of pushes it to one side because it sounds like entanglement. He doesn't want to even think he understands. "You're everything Brianna and that is that and there's no point in chiding yourself, that would be a shame, would not get me any closer to your secret or you to mine. You could end up as another with their head done by a horse's hooves. Did I ever have any designs on you? No, listen, I was not entangled in that other woman, the fishing girl with the pipe. I'm striving now not to be in a muddle with this new acquaintance, one who maybe is someone else tomorrow. I had this bloody great scheme, my small terror got in the way." He spreads his arms wide. "My body is…is all punched-out just now and not much of an offering, certainly not a temple…all my expectation bound-up in four thousand tons of steamer out there. At this moment, that's the extent of my expectation. What do I know? What's next? Have I any choice? A *dief van die lug,* a thief of air, me, Carmen? It appears to me that you are lucky. Another man who you could take to might be even more unscrupulous than me. This game of mating is the oddest thing about humans, don't you find? Unsuited to niceties as much as you are, not settled on your new woman; how you fall so easily and, regretfully, taken there by all your rough words, your rasping tongue, the spouting for effect? I know what you are. You are something being formed and it's in your interest not to give in to me or give up now, not at this minute, this time, here. I do not want to think that there is hope beyond the next voyage. I'm no fortune teller, I don't need to be, just factual and honest with myself. Our chances between here and Swansea are not good. But, perhaps, one day."

She wraps her hands in a knot as though by containing them she can stop herself from hammering him. "Oh, yes? Who's the bloody fortune teller here, me or thee?" she shouts and by degree the tone rises.

"I'm thinking on the one hand that despite me being old, as you never stop repeating…" He holds out a Hand, a conciliatory gesture.

She suddenly feels sorry for overplaying the age difference. "It's just my joke. You can take a joke, can't you?" She sounded spiteful, she didn't mean to. "Look, I have it all here." She points to her head. "I've got it all sorted for you and me, I might as well be brazen enough to say it, because you are so bloody cagey and shifty it looks as though you will go so far down my road but always looking for an escape route. I'm your safety Wauters, not your enemy."

"Sure," he says wryly. "But my life might not be that long in the living, as I say. That makes me sad, having wasted so much already. Can't you get it, I'm a thief and a no good. I will spoil you, get it!"

She is fierce. "You and your sodding sob story, is there no chance of reforming you. You can stuff talk like that where the monkey shoves his nuts. That's you talking about your side road, your escape route, your, your, your!" What is a man? He's a feckin' puzzle. He can turn it on and off to suit his mood. Where is all that inner strength, the swagger that you showed at the social. Where is the sacrifice that you showed in full knowledge of the outcome at the fight? Is that all acting?

He adjusts his hat again. "But I would maintain that about me and my faults just to try and get you to let go, wouldn't I? What's the issue here? Wouldn't it not be better for you to have known me than not? I think that's my view of you, that's what I know. Am I only of any value for the uses I can be put to? I might be the best lover you never had and you not having to face the sad truth about my way of loving. Better that you ponder what a complete Lothario I might be than be spoiled by an animal without any sensitivity; what I could be to satisfy your imagining. Why spoil it, your sad investment in me, with the sad reality. I'm rough, no delicacy and no ready wit when a woman deserves something soft and appealing, consideration."

She pokes him in the chest vigorously. "How do you, of all people, know what the feck I want?" She is at a loss for words. "I'll be the judge of that, you heartless bastard! Perhaps I'm some sort of pervert. Perhaps I would like a full beard or a bit of a belly, like yours me'self; perhaps I'm jealous, there's that story, the Beauty and the Beast and I'm the beauty. Perhaps I'm queer and find an attraction in malformation, weirdness. Perhaps I'm like, like that Mary Shelley? You have no idea what's in my head, it just comes to me. That's what makes men and women so odd."

He checks. "Isn't the imagination of romance stuff something all people have got in common? I'm thinking that, as I stand here, all embarrassed and in the wrong, so easy to pick-off; I'm imagining you would take the risk, taking-up with me. Because you're a woman that can fight her own corner and could take from me all that she wanted and not be too concerned about knocking-off rough edges or turning me pious. What if you turned me into something that you found you could have no respect for, trailing after you?" He gives her a lingering look. "For amongst all this talk of emotions and longings and shit, there is reality, a course, matter-of-fact reality. *You* could take what *you* wanted and dump the rest, and what then of me? Role reversal, I would be licking-up to you so that you wouldn't run."

"There you go again," she wails. "Making *your* plan. How do we know how things will be? You *hope*, don't you? If there's at least a root, a reason for people being together that they can sort out the fine details when and where? As long as the basics are right. Otherwise, apart from the depth of your thought and the honest broker thing, you're just talking a load of shite. What's in it for me trying to prod you my way? Is it treats you're after? What's your best offer Brianna?"

"I have my plan, Brianna. I don't want you selling yourself."

She is nearing exhaustion. "Just look at yourself now, all set-up for life. You've obviously got a route of your own planned so what's so wrong about me pondering on one too? There's the road for a fearless wench to take. You don't have to take this blather. I think you're excited with me and disappointed by me at the same time. Besides, what would it take for you to pinch my gold tooth under the guise of a kiss?" She tries to deflect the intensity which is hard to sustain.

"Is that what I'm keen on doing? Imagine," he continues. "Me going through your purse while you're thinking of roses and perfume. You don't need my reassurance, scant as it is. What is romance in time of war? Urgency, always the last shot at, whatever. War sums up romance, doesn't it? Love is…whatever…whoever is at hand at a particular moment in time. If there's no passion there can be no love. Can anyone attach to anyone else at these times knowing full well it's just an excuse for coupling.?"

She shrugs off his assertions. "You can think what you want. Under it all, you men, you're of a type. Your animal takes over. You just want to *slip a girl half a yard of cory* and leave them to mop up the mess." She turns on herself. "No, I don't believe that! That sounds like the old me, right there. I might be interested in you, but heh, this is no livestock auction. I'm not looking at your conformation." She stamps the ground frustrated. "I feckin' give up. I haven't a clue. Me Mammy never mentioned love and yet she got by. Why is everything so complicated and me always so straight. They write about love, its pointers, its, its meaning, its universal look, the signs. Have they all known it? Really? Or is it just something they know will sit well with their readers or cover them in a cloak of sensitivity? Did they ever know love?" Rollo relieves himself against a shop wall. They begin their walk again. Silence ensues.

"Tomorrow we're off, no rumour. What's to say, there's a pretty good chance we don't come back, as are the odds on every voyage? Chances are I won't come back…well for some time, depends on the Germans. You girls you just don't know what goes on. When the guns went off, when we sunk the sub amongst all that blood and shrieking and dying, it felt like all the air had been wrenched from my lungs. Your ears are made deaf to anything less than another explosion. Plum tells me the Germans are changing their tactics and ships like ours are *the* target of choice in the future; single ships with no escort. We were once *that* lucky, like before, when we had no expectations. Now I have them all. It's almost like some sort of awful test, like witchery. If I get killed it was an assignation, if I don't, it was the beer. The idea of an adventure has lots of appeal, there's only me at stake. I can imagine that. But being domestic? That's almost as scary as the Big Man pointing at you. Would it be like putting a halter on a wild nag."

She acts as though stunned. In that last sentence, a book of what ifs. The sudden realisation that their game of conversation is finite. Her head whirls and she looks askance. Meanwhile, he drones on in the background but his talk sounds muffled.

She half heard. "Who knows what will happen? A widow, again. How would that sit? I might rob you of all that good thinking you've put in and only double your loss, treble it. Sentence you to a sadness that you'll never shake off, think yourself doomed. Deflect you from your music and learnin' for good just when you are on top of it. I'm not even sure that I am free of the law yet. One day they may well reel me back in. If you are willing to wait…" This is his only way out; wriggle around permanence, offer hope.

They stand in silence and she quivers slightly. She comes too. He puts a fatherly hand on her shoulder. "I have to go now and you're getting cold."

Her: "So that's it then, is it? What a story and you holding yourself in such high esteem? Well, I'll tell you, you old, lying bastard, hateful lump of shite…" – She fights back her tears – "…me, don't get it wrong. I don't have any affection for *you,* I just wanted a bread earner! Yes, you saw right through me. You're so used to telling stories you've created a liar, liar! With you, it's all Apples of Sodom. Do I not have a voice in this, eh, eh? Fine speech, have you been practicing? You're acting like a castrated hog. You can vaguely remember your purpose, don't know how to go about it? Would that be right? What if I do want to wait for you." She is near shrieking, casting her arms about. "What if I thought that knowing I'm here for you that it might make your survival all that…much more easy for you? You're keen, aren't you? Yes?"

"Sure." He lowers his head.

"Then what else matters? I've wasted a lot of my years up to now, what's a year; some months to me? I'm owed."

He struggles to remain objective, even him. "Everything has concertinaed and all piled-up in these brief moments. I can't run away from my duties, I'd end up like Vaughan; it would be wrong to make plans, state promises and not be here to do the deed. Please, just live your life." He casts his eyes down the road in the direction of the jetty. "I hope they bring the *jolly boat* over looking for us else we'll be spending the night on a park bench. I'll have to catch Plum before he gets me into more fights. Yes, Carm…Brianna, I'm sure there is love between us and with a fair wind I'll be able to claim it. Who knows?"

She turns away and walks off, turns and shouts back. "There you go again you arch deceiver. *Jack Harkaway*. Do you want me to cry as well at your passing? You don't change. Me crying, that is the next best thing to you killing some bugger else, eh? Getting your highs witnessing the hurt you inflict on others. You missed your purpose in life. You should have been an actor." Her voice is getting louder and shriller. She stands animatedly pointing at him, enraged, beside herself. "No, you haven't changed, you've just changed colour, you blend in like them…lizards you hear about. You'll never really change, it's all surface 'wid' you. You're a liar and cheat and, and, a clown and a monkey, a *divvy*, a feckin'… langer. Yeah, and you're probably as mad as a hatter. Sly as a fox, hateful as an unbroken Killarney stallion. I hope I never see you again." She takes a few steps then turns back still shouting pointing jaggedly. "Blackguard! Even with all this blather about your imaginings; you're scheming even now, I can tell. The soft let-down. So, I'm probably not good enough for yous. Is that what you're thinking? You could do better off elsewhere? Ditch her quick. I don't need her. I'm home free. She's as guilty as me. And me, I'm not pretty enough and my tongue is that of a scold in need of a brank."

He motions towards her and tries to take her in his arms but she storms away. He stands quietly with a smile on his face watching her go. Rollo seems conflicted. Who does he follow? She does not look back. He motioned to hold her; did she miss a trick with her passions so aroused? When she is out of sight, she starts to talk to herself. "What a bloody cheek. What an arrogant bastard." She stands still. She takes deep breaths. "If you start that crying again girl, I will never speak to you again…You're obviously better off without…*that*. You couldn't trust a man like that to be let-out on his own. How can you have any hope for a man that has no 'life-line'?" She sits down on the kerb, takes deep breaths, puts her head in her hands. She feels queasy. Rollo eventually pads-up and looks into her face. He's made his choice, for better or for worse. "What would a man do in a situation like this, heh, Rollo? He'd say, 'go on, go, cut your loss'. Plenty more fish in the sea'." She looks upwards to the sky and points. "God, did you send him to test me? Am I now on the front-line fighting them evil-doers? I should be grateful, right? Get a promotion? Well, I think it's a bloody cheap trick." She stutters and cries. "That you didn't warn me, you sent me on a suicide mission. You almost kidded me-up there. And me, especially me, when I'm so straight 'wid' you…I could so easily have fallen for him." She bawls momentarily uncontrollably…and what sort of trouble would that have been? Here's me all hot and steamy and he's all cool and *when, if,* I come back. He beguiled me, like with a potion, witchcraft. None of that happened, just a stupid woman and her dreaming. They put some nutmeg in my drinking water, made me see things that weren't there. Made me dream. No, never. Every time he went out, you'd be shit jealous of what he was up to. What little plan he was contriving, against your friends, *you.* About as straight as a dog's hind leg. No reference to you, Rollo, you're a good dog. She hugs him but he wriggles free, she's been strange with him lately, he's unsure. She stands up. Leans against the wall, looks up at the stars, the crescent moon. "Why are all the things in creation against me? I must be ill-jinxed. All them exotic places he says he's been, he picked something-up and now I'm infected. Why does life offer me a quick glimpse before…snatching it away?" She bends over sobbing. "Why is everything just out of reach, always. I could gladly be a pagan if I thought the sun, the moon and the stars could deliver me that thing that I want, need." She pauses, pushes aside a tear. "I love you Wauters, or whatever your feckin' name is. I love you. You devil." The thought then enters her mind, impishly, that it was the losing that has upset her most. She failed.

-oo0oo-

The swish, the smell of the sea becomes more apparent as he follows in the wake of Plum. That background music to his life, the ebb and flow. A dog approaches him in a servile manner but as soon he attempts to stroke it, the animal yelps and runs off. He walks faster. He is almost at the quay when he sees Plum sitting on a bench. "Oh dear, *paw-paw*, that was horrible."

"How's that?"

Wauters sits heavily on the bench, occasionally looking back from where he came. "A fork in the road."

Plum is on to it instantly. "The catering truck turned-over again? Anybody hurt?"

Wauters looks at him in quiet disbelief. "I have a serious dilemma and all you can do is say these stupid things?" Plum holds his hands up as to say sorry, bites his tongue in an effort to restrain himself, but it's hard.

Wauters intertwines his fingers tautly. "I find that I have nearly developed principles, after all this time, worrying; suddenly I know what a cat with fleas feels like. No rest. Now I feel sorry for cats? Me! Bitten all the time. Plagued by scratching, the original hair shirt? Things coming at you in a bad way, out of nowhere. Worrying, even when in quiet moments. How I long for that peaceful ignorance. Now, fleas, fleas, fleas. I feel an end to that." He looks over his shoulder. "Yes, it would be flattering for me to have that woman on my arm. But I do not find it sits well with me, you know? All that dynasty thing, like giving up your freedoms for the next to have an easy ride, that tomorrow, that is not the me which I am jealous of. Romance is for the young, an energetic, lusting thing; It should be a comfort reflecting on such when we're old. But I am old, but apparently, no wiser. I would be but a *second* in her life, all the satisfaction would be hers. I could not live with it. I am restless in all things, intolerant, a bit of a bully, yes. Even now, I want to leave this mess behind me and move on. I made a bunch of mistakes and it has all backfired. I was someone that should have stayed anonymous, a non-person, not infecting others. Never staying long is a habit that is hard to shake. I need to keep moving less mortality catches me up. I live on lies and once my acquaintances see through them, I am made small." Plum maintains his studied silence while Wauters looks solemnly into his open palms. After a moment, he brightens. He claps Plum on the shoulder. "I'm sold on your mad-cap scheme for my sins. Get me out of here." Plum is switched back on. "How mad does that make me, eh?" adds Wauters, or whatever his name is.

Plum lights-up. "It's on then? You'll go, *Cocos*? grand! I'd convinced myself that you were as good as sold on her. What a day! Yowzers! As the cowboys say. Yippee!" Plum jumps up and tries to hug Wauters but he is shrugged off. Wauters smiles grudgingly. They start to walk off.

They look out to *Haulbowline Island* trying to see if the Jolley Boat is about. Wauters confides. "You know, for a minute back there, she almost got me going. What I find, when it comes to calculating work, women are naturals. You have done the right thing Plum, stayed focused on your fitness, not being led astray. Not polluted by…lusting or such. Discipline, that's something we have in common, it's a good way to be. That woman, she would have had me stay here and go to the bar in the week, get a job. And then there would be children, she don't know it, but she had babies written all over her, she's not a girl, it would be urgent. I did a good job. I didn't say no. I'm all maybe and sure that *could* happen. She thought that she had me in her control, I showed her. So, *Praatsiek*, about this island."

Plum starts up. "Well, it's three hundred miles west of Costa Rica, there are strong currents. We would have to go to Punto…"

Wauters grabs his arm. "Shut up!" He laughs. "I'm going to have to learn what I can say to you without setting you off. Go on, walk ahead. I'm tired. *Jabber-jabber*, you're going to have to learn to be a bit, sorry, a *lot* more private. You see, you *can* think a thought without having to announce it, tell the world. You can be as boring as you want in your own head and nobody'd be any the worse off. If we're goin' to spend a lot of time together…keep schtum. You know they killed *Shaka*, his own family killed him, they did it because they said he was mad. Let that be a lesson."

His voice trails off as they walk off together. Plum is singing, '*When Irish eyes are smiling*'. Plum interrupts a verse just to mention a thought, a reflection, that didn't need saying. "The lover, the soldier and the pantaloon." He looks for the rebuke from his shipmate, there is none. "So, you're South African?"

The song is picked-up again. Wauters easy response sneaks in under his song like the soundless owl flitting through the night sky. "I could be," replies Wauters. Plum floods his brain with *Earth receptive; Mountain immovable; Water dangerous; Wind gentle; Thunder arousing; Fire clinging; Lake joyful; Heaven active*, just so he doesn't have to think.

Chapter 19

The simultaneity of life is incomprehensible. The world and its doings are characterised by Brianna on the quay sitting down fishing, a medium sized fish at her feet. Elsewhere, others are focused on the essentials, the nature of *their* existences, feeding a horse or listening to *'La Boheme'* in concert or questioning their mortality on a steamer trudging through the Celtic Sea. Everything relates to the individual, their observations and reactions delivered to us through the filtering machinations of our ears and brains and the education we gave them and we call it reality. She looks out to sea and sings to herself, *'Peggy and the soldier,'* quietly. Rollo is pretending to be asleep. He is on alert for a flea that he caught from a lover. Brianna has a flea, but it's not an insect. She is trying to recall that song, *'Peggy overseas with the soldier'*, a girl so in love and so daring that she cares not for uncertainty. Woken by a new knowledge, an awakening, she follows after her lover. And her with such a formative lack of understanding about the immensity of the world and the circuitousness of the minds of others. "Rockabye…little one and…don't you cry…Your mother's gone and left you in sorrow…da-da-de-da. She abused the man that build the boat. Abused the captain do-de-do-de-do-de-do." The song echoes and dies.

A bearded man stands over her who she did not see haul-up. He has a creel and a fishing rod. He points at Rollo. "Dog fish!" This catches Carmen's attention. She smiles thinly, believing the man is cracking a joke about Rollo, which, of course, he is. The man leans over and prods the fish lying at her feet. "That's a nice-looking Coalfish you have there. It'll make good eating. I got not so much as a nibble down on Lynch's Quay. But the chap next to me got a dog fish, fishing off the wall, too! The event was so rare and unexpected that I could not but dwell on the thought that I was being singled-out. Having my nose rubbed in it for my ineptness. What bait are you on?"

She pays him little regard. "Luggers. I've not really been concentrating."

This could make the man feel worse. A man and a dog fish and a girl with a fish she doesn't want! And such a fish. Not something you see that often here; that is even more a kick in the teeth. It's a sign, it's a sign! Perhaps now is the time to pack away your rod, the Great Deity trying to tell you that your light lies elsewhere? He could do with the toilet really. "Do you want it, the fish? You know, if I didn't know better, I'd say that was a pollock." The man points at the sleek shiny creature that she has clubbed lying at her feet, a little trace of blood in the corner of its mouth. There is a bit of urgency about him. "The fish?" he repeats, pointing towards the creature just in case she doesn't know what he's referring too.

She doesn't look up. "Yeah. Take it. I can't say I fancy it. It's full of sailors."

The fisherman looks at her doubtfully, unseen by her. He picks up the fish, so floppy. Senses the weight in his hand, glistening like a jewel, slippery, clean and fresh smelling, a twinkling eye. He looks at it closely and it looks back in its dead intensity but looking at the sky, really.

Carmen continues her theme. "They eat the sailors you know, fishes. Is that what they call a food chain? Are we all cannibals by nature? As long as we can't see an actual limb sticking out its gob we don't really care. Especially in these times?"

The man catches her drift. "I am not too taken with such fine points, but I know that in sieges there's been cannibalism, but only after the dogs, cats and rats have all been eaten," he exclaims. "As long as I have a full belly, that's about the limit of my concerns. Assure me, it's at least an admiral in there. Just take the epaulets off and it will fry-up nicely. Who's to know?"

She nods her head, yes. He walks away. Now, alone again, she looks out to sea and tries to rekindle that evocation that she was beavering away at before being interrupted.

-ooOoo-

The *S.S. Ashmore Lane*, the ship's new name emblazoned in fresh white paint. The seamless repair to the hull. The smell of the new paint borne in by the wind occasionally, which puts Plum on his guard. Wauters, clean shaven reacquainted with his dress and a nice mob cap along with new crew not knowing his history and saintliness, pointing at him, ribbing him, repeating the same old tired lines. Fly away from the ship, looking back, and at a thousand feet, already it is appearing to be a speck. How can a speck hold so many spirits, so much divergence, hopes, betrayals, awful intent and tragedy? Love, fear, anger, sex. Gradually, lowering to sea level, there is a periscope interposed between the viewing point and the *'Ashmore'*. A sunny day, a cast-iron routine. A weapon bloodied and a complement not a little self-confident. The crew are singing a new song, only lately doing the rounds. Some know more words than others and, anyway, you can always weave in your lines, a bit of filth, a description of your enemy, not too flattering: *'It's a long way to Tipperary'*.

-oo0oo-

In a parallel universe, Carmen is at a desk. She has made a career move and blagged her way into a job at the library. Her lying ability is of the top drawer. With her coming from India, so she tells them, she has no paper-work to show her scholasticism and apart from that it's only a desk job, she doesn't need to know about categorisation or any of that bollocks; she figures she can look into such things while on the job. She is completely plausible. This new her, is so different, it's like the difference between Queen Elizabeth I and that altered vision, of 'Gloriana'. She is very smartly dressed and has changed her hairstyle. She did well in the horse-trading; well, she wasn't going to be able to look after the nags and stamp the books eight hours a day. She is very smart, can hold a conversation with anyone. Her interview for the job was a triumph and enthralling. She regaled her listeners with everything they wanted to hear and added to that a colourful story that might have come straight from the pages of the *'Jungle Book'* or Aesop. The bit about her travels in the East was especially so vivid, replete with those pearl divers, the file fish and the starfish and the exotic scene. People were entranced that one so slight and dainty could have undertaken such travels without being jumped-on by the natives. As she sits there, she cannot but reflect that this environment suits her demeanour, this is what her calling is. Being unphased by her lies, her precocity, picking things up so easily, she becomes an indispensable gem. She has offers from some of the few men that venture in to loan books, to 'walk out', although she declines them politely, knowing now exactly what sort of companion she is looking for, certainly not a milksop. When she examines her elusive partner in her mind, it is no coincidence that he looks a lot like Wauters. The sadness being, of course, that Wauters does not read and is, therefore, highly unlikely to come her way in this 'fusty' environment. She wears some cosmetics well. Her hair is now cropped, like a pageboy style. In all, she is sort of the acceptable face of a suffragism here where there is so much prejudice. Up and doing, a little hard-nosed. She wants a man who is equal and not that image born out of the rites of her former self, because she has an opinion and should have the latitude to express it. But that man in her mind. Such a deliberately etched image, is no confection. Not subject to whim or occasional fancy. She has met the man and would know him the moment she clapped her eyes on him again, anywhere. She no longer goes to the camp, has taken rooms at the house of a fellow church-goer (who can vouch for her tenant's good qualities and virtues). She buys London periodicals and is happy to assimilate new ideas, becomes acquainted with the war and its doings. Knows about the Western Front and has a mind to help those poor fighters that succumb to shell shock. If she hears of any such sufferer in her midst, she will not hesitate to work to ameliorate their hurt. The lady at the lodgings is teaching her to play whist. Her life is so busy and her expectations of herself so altered, well, it is like being reborn.

A woman approaches her desk with a book which needs to be stamped-out. "Why in the world I picked this one I don't know." The woman flutters. "But he's a modern writer and people speak well of him, I thought I'd give it a snoot. I've been reading George Eliot and do you know, I didn't realise it, George Eliot was a woman!"

Carmen looks at the spine of the proffered book. "You'll be thinking of Mary Anne Evans." She has been down this route already. She comments that there is a lot of that business of the female that dare not speak their name, Jane Austin started that way, did she know? '*A Lady*'. Then she feels a pang and some of her assertion melts momentarily. The book proffered, '*An Outcast of the Islands*'. She bites her lip a momentarily looks to the side, to collect herself. "There we go." She confides, "You can't go far wrong with Conrad and '*An Outcast of the Islands*'; I think you chose well. That's a gripper. One of his best."

Brianna, meaning resolute, strong, stamps the fly sheet, at this moment she needs to live up to her name. The woman smiles and takes the book. The woman flutters again. "I'm such a goose. I wish I'd your experience. I would save myself a lot of trouble. You can't help feeling with some books…" she confides in hushed tones, "…that after the first page you should give up reading. You know, instantly, if you don't sit well with a style or topic." Brianna, nods encouragingly.

"But there are exceptions. I'm glad I stuck with '*Little Dorrit*', say, but that was only due to the writer's reputation."

Brianna makes a mental note of '*Little Dorrit*' for her reading list. The woman goes out from this echoing temple of scholarship and social recognition. She goes, to be remembered here only by the miniscule sloughed-off particle of her skin in the dust, her legacy. Everything is quiet. Brianna smiles after her. As the woman walks away Brianna cannot resist opening the drawer that has a pouch in it that she received anonymously a day or two ago that contains five matching pearls. She can also not wash from her thoughts that those gems had come via Paris where the pearl market was and Wauters' back-side, where he had hidden them from the diving masters who were renowned for searching everywhere. The woman, now outside, cannot wait to start the new volume, opens the book and reads the epigram on one of the introductory pages:

"*Sleep after toil, port after stormy seas, Ease after war, death after life, does greatly please.*"

-ooOoo-